Lying on the bed is Jank. Beside his head lies the squat gray plas of a sensedeck, a deck obviously modified or repaired, held together by macroplas tape.

The sensedeck is running, a chip is loaded.

Every few moments he twitches and murmurs, out-putting the same data endlessly.

The twitching turns convulsive. The murmurs rise into shouts. "Stinking trogs! Weed-eaters! *Take it take it take it! GONNA GET YOU ALL! EAT YOU ALIVE! BURY YOU!*"

Abruptly his eyes snap open and gaze straight up at the ceiling like a man gone blind. He is nearly sitting up with the violence of the convulsions wracking his entire body.

"Machiko-*sama*!"

Machicko turns from where she stands beside the bed to see the headman of *kobun* coming through the room's door. He looks to her with an expression of startled amazement, amazement turning to revulsion, horror, and suddenly it all clicks.

She feels it in her belly.

"*COVERRR!*" she roars, turns and propels herself forward, away from the bed, into the headman of the *kobun*, toward the safety of the corridor.

Then the explosion erupts.

STEEL RAIN

SHADOWRUN

STEEL RAIN

Nyx Smith

A ROC BOOK

ROC
Published by the Penguin Group
Penguin Books USA Inc., 375 Hudson Street,
New York, New York 10014, U.S.A.
Penguin Books Ltd, 27 Wrights Lane,
London W8 5TZ, England
Penguin Books Australia Ltd,
Ringwood, Victoria, Australia
Penguin Books Canada Ltd, 10 Alcorn Avenue,
Toronto, Ontario, Canada M4V 3B2
Penguin Books (N.Z.) Ltd, 182-190 Wairau Road,
Auckland 10, New Zealand

Penguin Books Ltd, Registered Offices:
Harmondsworth, Middlesex, England

First Published by Roc, an imprint of Dutton Signet,
a division of Penguin Books USA Inc.

First Printing, March 1997
10 9 8 7 6 5 4 3 2 1

Series Editor: Donna Ippolito
Cover: Romas

 RoC   REGISTERED TRADEMARK—MARCA REGISTRADA

SHADOWRUN, FASA, and the distinctive SHADOWRUN and FASA logos are
registered trademarks of the FASA Corporation, 1100 W. Cermak, Suite B305,
Chicago, IL 60608.

Printed in the United States of America

1

The sound brushes her ears like a feather, like the haunting whisper of a breeze on a forlorn winter's night. Slipping through the mists of her sleeping mind like a phantom . . . a specter . . .

A single footfall, near-silent.

Very close.

Coming from just beyond the rice-paper walls of her room. So subtle a sound it nearly eludes her notice. Yet, for one who has trained mind and body and spirit to remain alert, though she sleeps, this subtle sound is just clear enough, distinct enough. She realizes what it portends even as she awakens. She has heard sounds like this before. She has spent whole months of her life listening for such sounds, learning their subtle codes and the Way of the people who make them. For even the smallest, most trifling of sounds might reveal the tread of an enemy, an assassin.

And tonight the sound she perceives, this faint, faint touch of a soft-soled shoe to *tatami* flooring, is the sound of one who does not belong.

Coming for her. Coming now.

As she opens her eyes she sees the intruder's seething heat signature through the veil of the rice-paper wall beyond her feet. The radiance shed by his flesh paints him clearly against the shadowed canvas of the night. He seems almost to smolder in a flickering aura of flames, like a demon, a fiery monstrosity of muscle and steel, bulky and broad and heavily cybered, now pausing just a step beyond the rice-paper doors to her room.

She sees the impending assault in his posture. Her duty is clear, and she has only a moment to prepare.

She shifts her right hand across the lacquered *honoki*-wood that sheaths the katana lying on her stomach, the twining serpents of the sword's steel *tsuba,* guard, and the fine-grained *same,* shark skin, wrapping the grip.

Then she breathes.

She settles her spirit.

And the killer comes.

He smashes the doors into fragments, bursting through paper panels, splintering wooden supports. The weapon encasing his right forearm erupts with a deafening roar. Bullets tear at bed sheets and bedding. Mere flesh would be ripped to tatters. But she is no longer there. She is a bed sheet flung into the air, twitching and twisting like a tortured ghost. She is a specter darting from shadow to shadow, tumbling, rolling away.

The killer snarls as if enraged by her deceit. He ducks as a lacquered *honoki*-wood sheath flies at his face like an arrow. He winces and jerks as the disk of a small hand mirror glances off his brow. The thunderous stammering roar of the gun skips a beat, then another, but the murderous barrage erupts anew.

The killer tracks her with computer-assisted precision. Bullets rip at the lacquered floor and pastel-paneled walls so near her feet and back she feels splinters of wood raining against her skin. She is barely an instant ahead of the assassin's onslaught when abruptly she turns, her long, lustrous black hair swirling around her like a cape, the gleaming blade of her katana rising before her face, ready to meet the enemy head-on.

It is no ordinary blade. This blade, this sword comes from four *masume* steel bars, hammered, folded and welded into four million layers, then forged, shaped, ground, and polished to a diamond, dikote-tempered hardness by a master of the ancient Masamune technique. One blade may take months to fabricate, smith and mage working ever in concert. The result is as strong a steel as the hand of metahumanity can forge—strong and hard, yet pliant.

For rigidity is death, a dead hand. Brittle and weak. The living hand must be pliant, like a leaf in springtime.

Poised, prepared, she pauses, motionless, an easy target. The stammering autofire weapon zeroes in at once. A torrent of metal-jacketed shells stamped out by spiritless machines clashes against her steel. The bullets blaze like fire, tracking toward her belly, her breast, her throat. Always the sword is there, guarding, defending, swaying like a willow in a breeze, supple, unhurried, deflecting the ruthless stream like so many burning drops of rain.

Yadome-jutsu, it is called. Arrow-cutting.

The killer roars as if possessed by outrage and disbelief, as if witnessing the impossible.

It is neither possible nor impossible. It goes beyond luck or instinct, beyond talent and skill and rigorous training. Beyond even magic. It is the Way and the Way is the Void. Without thought, without feeling, without intention or design. It is all and it is nothing and it comes to her now as naturally as she breathes. It is, the ancient masters would say, above all a matter of timing.

In everything, there is timing. Even in the Void. And the timing of the enemy is the essential element in all battle.

And now, abruptly, the gun goes silent.

The killer grunts. His movements lay bare his mind. He rushes to reload. No time. He snatches at a second weapon. Too late. For she is already moving, flowing forward like a wraith, breezing through clouds of harsh gun-aroma, rising tall and large of spirit before the killer's face.

The killer lifts one massive armored fist and out snaps a gleaming steel spike, but this is irrelevant. It is useless now. For she sees the Way with perfect crystalline clarity as never before in all her experience. And the Way is death. The resolute acceptance of death. The warrior's death. In this moment she may choose either life or death and so she instantly chooses death, merciless death, reckless and uncompromising.

Death. Inevitable death.

The killer thrusts with his spike, but her katana rises, glaring like the summer moon on a rain-swept night.

The sword is her spirit, the spirit her sword, striking strongly, thrusting inexorably upward, piercing armor, metal, and bone, slicing through sternum and larynx, till finally the tip of the blade slides inside the killer's cranial vault.

The hands of the killer reach toward her—snapping, grasping, clenching—but she is already drifting away, an autumn leaf buoyed on a silken zephyr of wind . . .

With a flick—*chiburi*—she clears the blade of blood and gore. Honoring the blade. Restoring its sheen. A young blade, no older than she who wields it. Bearing a polished pattern like the icy rains of the fall, a shower of silvery teardrops. The swordmaker's silent lament.

And the assassin falls, like a boneless husk.

A gentle, swift end.

2

For a moment more, the night is still and silent. Machiko holds herself motionless, katana poised. She listens for the least sign that the assassin has not come here alone. She watches the body of the corpse. She sees the blood streaming into pools that shimmer with a slowly fading light. She feels the bits of blood and tissue dotting her chest, her hips and legs. She marvels at the crude brutality of the killer's assault, and she wonders why he came, who sent him, for what purpose. Then something detonates.

A dull thump rocks the room. It is enough to startle her, to shake her slightly off-balance, to put her once more fully on her guard. Till she sees the broad sea of blood spreading away from the sunken head of the corpse and the churning cloud of heat rising, swelling, gradually fading from view.

A cortex bomb? No. More likely a dead man's button. A kill rig. Triggered by disabling wounds. With the obvious purpose of precluding even the most casual form of interrogation. Machiko wonders if the killer knew he carried such a device. If he did, that is significant, for it would testify to a degree of fanaticism whole worlds have above the mind of the average street samurai.

She ponders this a moment. She breathes. Then, pandemonium erupts.

From another part of the house, her father shouts, *"MACHIKO!"* Her mother's sudden cry of fear seems very shrill. The household alarm blares loudly, then whoops. Every light comes on. The room around her glares with a stark brilliant white. The discomfort to her eyes is intense, but passes swiftly.

Outside the house, she knows, emergency strobes will be flashing, providing a beacon for the local security force.

She looks from the corpse to the ruined panels of the sliding doors, to the wreckage scattered about the room, and back again to the corpse. The brilliant light makes the corpse of a killer seem less a demon than merely a machine, more a machine than human norm. His body is sheathed in black and guarded by heavy armor. His shoulders and arms bulge with augmentations: dermal plating, weapons, a gyromount, tactical computer, and more. A machine designed for killing. Now devastated. Ruined.

To what end?

A pang of sorrow rises out of her stomach, flowing all through her like a tide. It is always this way with her. It is her flaw, her vein of compassion. With the sword in her hand and an enemy before her, she feels born of the selfsame metal of which her blade was forged. Afterward, she mourns. The fiery blossom of the dawn, spotted with dew, mourning the death of night, her *sensei* once said. But now the quality stirs her to frustrated fury. Should she not feel gladdened? At least satisfied. This is 2058. The Sixth World is full of violence. She rose from sleep to defend herself from this dog of a killer, an attempt at vile murder, and she has prevailed. She has fulfilled duty and honor and avoided the specter of shame that would come with failure. Why is it that she sees nothing in this victory to celebrate? No cause to rejoice. Why does it seem that the taking of this dog's life is nothing but a cruel waste?

Here, in the guest wing of her parent's modest house, it is all futility and pointless destruction, a minute shifting of balance in the ceaseless battle that is metahumanity.

A battle right or wrong but never truly won.

If only she could discern some reason. Some motive for the attack. It would give this death meaning, however minuscule.

It would, in some way, make sense of it.

But the time for such reflections comes abruptly to an end. The norm driver and bodyguard assigned to her parents appears amid the wreckage of the doorway, clad only in shorts, a blocky automag in hand. He is tall for a Japanese, nearly as tall as her. He looks to her as if amazed to see her standing. He bows as if suffering a spasm, sudden and brief.

"Machiko-*san, what*—*!*"

Before he can finish, her parents are there, her father's face crimson with alarm, her mother's full of fear. "We are safe, now," Machiko says. Briefly, she bows. "Forgive me."

The bodyguard and her parents hesitate. Machiko does

not. She must report this incident. She must alert Nagato
Corp security, for an investigation must be begun. She turns
to the telecom on the low, black-lacquered stand beside her
ruined bedding. She kneels and enters a telecom code. The
logo of Nagato Corporation comes instantly to the screen,
replaced suddenly by the harried features of a man in Nagato
Security Service uniform.

"Duty ops officer!" the man blurts.

"Situation Four," Machiko tells him. "Advise your
command."

"We have a prior alert—"

Abruptly, another man fills the screen, a lieutenant of the
Nagato Corp Security Directorate. "We have attacks on two
other GSG within the last several minutes. You are the
senior member reporting. What are your instructions?"

Machiko frowns. "Contact Sukayo—"

"I have just dispatched a trauma team to Sukayo-*san's*
location!" the man tells her. "You are the senior GSG
reporting! What are your instructions?"

Astonishment makes a muddle of Machiko's thoughts.
What is this man telling her? Sukayo injured? The senior-
most member of the Green Serpent Guard in need of a
trauma team? How could that be? The mere concept shakes
her no less rudely than the bomb born by the assassin. It
makes her feel as if being woken violently from a dream.
"The Chairman. What is his status?"

"Situation unchanged. I have no reports."

She awakens to the realization that here is the point, the
granite breakers around which all shock and puzzlement
must swirl unheeded. Honjowara Okido, Chairman of Nagato Combine and its leading corporate enterprise, Nagato
Corporation. The Green Serpent Guard are the Chairman's
elites, his servants, agents, and warriors. First and foremost,
they are sworn to safeguard his life, no matter the cost.
Abruptly, Machiko realizes that the status of the Chairman
now is irrelevant. Until seconds ago, she would have considered the home of her parents to be tranquil and untroubled.
She must stir herself, look ahead, anticipate any other threats
that may be coming this night.

She must wake up!

"What is the Chairman's location?"

The lieutenant replies with the code word for the
Chairman's estate.

"Initiate Rapier Wind."

The lieutenant nods sharply and looks to his console, tapping keys. "Security Defense Force notified. Responding in support."

Machiko breathes, struggles to calm her spirit, to think. The ancient masters have written that even the most vital decisions should be made within the space of seven breaths. The spirit must be resolute. Smash one's boots to the earth and pass through a wall of iron. Machiko considers. She hears her personal commlink beeping. Yes, she has declared an alert. All that can be done will be done. GSG stationed at the Chairman's mansion will mobilize. Every member of the guard not currently on duty will be notified of the alert and will respond at once. Nagato Corp security forces will go on alert and contribute every available officer to aid in defending the Chairman. She can think of nothing else. Nothing she can do from this room in her parent's home. Her duty now is to prepare for combat and to join the balance of the Guard at the Chairman's estate.

She breaks the telecom link and stands. A quick rush of padding footsteps and a soft cry like a sob give her warning. Her mother seizes her arm, snares her waist, clenches and clings. Frantic to see and frantic to hold. To make sure she is unhurt. For she is yet a child, in her mother's gaze. A child raised and loved like the flesh of one's own flesh. That she has grown tall and slim as only a meta may grow, as only elves ever grow, matters not. An elven child, yes, but no child of elves.

Gently, she draws her mother's head to her breast, and softly says, "Mother . . . I must go."

Her mother sobs, sniffs, and nods.

"In Buddha's name, *what is happening?*" This from her father, now standing a few brief steps away. His face is still crimson and his breathing seems harsh, labored. He lifts a hand to his chest as if suffering a twinge of angina. He casts a worried glance at the corpse of the assassin, the ruined bedding, the telecom. "Machiko—"

"Please be calm," she says. "We are safe. Security Service is responding."

"But the Chairman."

"He is well. Be calm."

"You said security—"

Machiko struggles to find the words to explain what

appears to have happened, events she has prepared to meet at least a thousand times, yet now seem somehow impossible. Her mother looks up at her with an expression of pain and awe. "Two other members of the Guard have been attacked," Machiko says quietly. "We must assume that an attack against Chairman Honjowara is imminent. That is procedure."

"Who would dare—!"

"Father, I do not know."

And now her mother makes an obvious attempt at self-control. She brushes at the tears. She says in a small voice, "You are not hurt?"

"Mother, I am untouched."

Her mother nods. She bends and picks up the *honoki*-wood sheath, showing it as great a respect as that due a sword, lining the cradle of her hands with the silk of her own night-gown, offering the sheath with a tiny bow. Machiko bows and accepts it. "Your duty," her mother says softly. "You must go."

"Please forgive me."

"Your fidelity honors us all."

But then a uniformed man steps through the wreckage of the doorway. The uniform marks him as a sergeant of the Nagato Corp subsidiary responsible for all police services within the boundaries of the Nagato Manor Residence Community. The sergeant's gaze jumps immediately to Machiko. His surprise is plain. And he bows. He bows very deeply.

This is not unexpected.

But for the thong girding her hips, Machiko is nude. Yet her station in the hierarchy of Nagato Combine could hardly be more apparent. The jade green grip of the katana she holds is merely a clue. The far bolder statement is made by the stark white kabuki-mask of her face, the pure jet mane of her hair, the twining green serpents circling her arms, legs, and torso, and coiling over both shoulders to her breast. What the sergeant does not see is the twining serpent logo emblazoned across both her palms. What perhaps he does not notice is the tall pointed ears hidden beneath the voluminous black hair, and the strong almond contours of the eyes, veiled by a Japanese landscape.

"Please excuse me," the sergeant blurts. He glances at the corpse of the assassin. "An incident was reported—"

"Yes," Machiko says, forestalling further remarks that are not necessary. "Nagato security is responding to this location. These are my parents, both Nagato executives. See to their welfare. Secure the house and property and await further instructions."

The sergeant casts another look at the dead assassin. "This person lying here—"

"Is not your responsibility."

"Please excuse my ignorance." The sergeant bows abruptly, then turns and curtly orders two other security officers to search and secure the grounds. He directs a pair of medics to attend Machiko's parents.

Machiko turns to the green lacquered chest containing her wardrobe.

She must dress.

3

For the warrior there can be no distinction between battle-field and bedroom. The sword must always be sharp, the arm prepared to wield it, the spirit ready. There is therefore only one uniform for the Green Serpent Guard, used for ceremony as well as combat.

Machiko dons cushioned underwear to guard her breasts, her groin, elbows, and knees, and *tabi* for her feet. Over this, a lightweight reinforced silk *gi*. She straps an Ares monofila-ment dagger to her left calf and a compact Walter PB-120 holdout pistol to her right. She fixes armored vambraces to her forearms and armored guards about her shins. The vam-braces mount snapblades, shuriken in the form of both stars and spikes, and, on the left, a rugged portable commlink.

Over all this she pulls the *montsuki,* a large-sleeved top, and the *hakama,* broad-legged pants, and the *kamishimo,* or over-vest of the Guard. These garments are green with blood-red trim and insulated with ballistic armor. They bear the *mon* of Nagato Corp and, over disks of black, the twining green serpent logo of the Guard.

At the left of her waist, she holsters a Beretta 200ST auto-matic with spare clips of ammunition. At the right, nun-chaku. Over her belly, a *tanto* furnished to match her sword, and, at her back, she slings the katana.

From the depths of her wardrobe chest she draws an SCK M-100 submachine gun. This she slings under her right shoulder.

The guns are of course fully loaded and ready to fire. They are, like the katana, like the other weapons, furnished in the brilliant jade-green of the Guard.

Machiko turns from her wardrobe to find her parents being attended by the medics. Her father lies on the floor on his back with an oxygen mask covering his nose and mouth. The look on his face is reassuringly familiar, a look of annoyed self-restraint, stubbornly resolute. It is on account of what he refers to as the "vile traitor" in his chest. One day soon he will have no choice but to agree to replace it with a cardiac prosthesis. Until then, he tolerates the occasional pain. He will not give himself to the surgeon's blade until he is left with no choice, and so he must tolerate the occasional pain.

Mother kneels beside him holding his hand. She seems well, fragile but in control. The bodyguard stands nearby. The medics appear competent and focused on their work, monitoring her father's condition, communicating via portable telecom with a doctor at the local hospital.

Machiko feels content to leave. Duty demands that she leave, leave at once, but now even her flawed heart is content.

She catches her mother's eye. They exchange brief bows. Her father lifts a hand in acknowledgment. Machiko bows in reply, then turns and moves determinedly to the front of the house.

She is barely through the entryway to the garden surrounding the front walk when she encounters a man in the dark gray blazer of a Nagato Security Service supervisor. She points this man to the room where the assassin lies, then steps toward the driveway and car. Her commlink begins beeping.

She opens the cover on her left vambrace and glances at the small screen there. The face she sees is that of Gongoro, another senior GSG, tonight responsible for security at the Chairman's estate. His face, like hers, is a kabuki-style mask as white as chalk, eyes like black pools, his mouth a burning scarlet wound. He does not talk so much as growl.

"Sukayo, Mitsuharu, and Jiksumi have all been attacked. They are disabled, if not dead."

Machiko feels her pulse accelerate despite her effort to keep her spirit settled. These three whom Gongoro names are the three most senior of the Guard. That any one of them should be attacked and possibly killed is astonishing. That all three should be disabled in the same hour of the same night seems so far beyond comprehension as to require the intervention of gods. Sukayo-*san* studied the Way under *sensei* Kuroda himself. He is as close to becoming the perfect weapon as any mere meta might ever become.

"You are the senior acting member," Gongoro growls.

"What of Ryokai?"

Gongoro's growling rises into a snarl. "Ryokai is junior to both you and I! If you do not feel competent to assume command, say so now!"

So this is the point of his call. Machiko scolds herself for failing to grasp the fact sooner. Of course the chain of command must be made clear. Gongoro is right to snarl. And naturally he would be among the first to demand that the issue be settled. "If I am the acting senior, then command will be mine."

"You *are* the acting senior!"

"Then I command."

"What are your orders?"

"Dispatch details to stand watch over Sukayo and the others. Remain on alert."

"What enemy are we expecting?"

"That is for security to determine."

Gongoro breaks the link. He has never been a man to waste two words when none will suffice. He cultivates martial valor by means of the deliberate attitude that he is inferior to no one and thus can never be defeated in combat. A worthy concept in a warrior. Fanaticism in all its forms may be extremely valuable. But Gongoro goes too far. He is like the man in the ancient parable, forever swinging a naked blade. Such men earn few allies. They may influence others by the fear they inspire, but not by respect.

Machiko moves to her car, a Toyota Tachi Monarch. The gleaming body is tinted the green of the Guard and bears at front and rear the twining serpents of the GSG insignia. It starts with a throaty rumble. A key on the driver's console ignites the blue and amber emergency strobes that rise like louvers out of the front and back hoods.

She is a registered security agent of the Nagato Corporation and is now engaged in urgent corporate business. That is meaningless in regard to New York law. However, in regard to the corps responsible for enforcing the law, it is not without significance.

Machiko steers the Tachi Monarch down the curving driveway to the street, past a phalanx of arriving emergency vehicles, and on through the winding lanes of the Nagato Manor Residence Community. She exerts herself to keep her speed below 90 KPH, to keep her spirit settled, her mind balanced and calm. She keys Ryokai's commlink code into the car's console telecom. He answers in two moments.

Her first glimpse of the man gives her concern. Ryokai appears to also be in a car, driving. He appears to be in some pain. The familiar white mask of his face is set into a grim mold. A black strip of some fabric rings the top of his head. The sable hair above it appears wet and matted. The rear of his left cheek is veined in red.

"You are injured?" Machiko asks.

"Head wounds," he says with a grimace. Yes, head wounds bleed profusely. What is his point? That his wounds look worse than they are? "It's minor." He curses. "Machiko-*san*, what's happening? Gongoro told me about Sukayo-*san* and the others. Were you attacked, too? Are you hurt?"

"Not touched."

Ryokai nods. Machiko glimpses this as she pulls the Tachi Monarch through a curve, tires shrieking. Ryokai's gesture is revealing. Under normal circumstances, Ryokai would express relief to hear that anyone had escaped injury. He must be feeling his wounds, minor though they might be.

"I'm thinking that the Triads are behind this," Ryokai says. "The one who attacked me may have been Chinese. He wore a kill button. It split his skull wide open and ruined his face, but I thought his complexion, and the things he grunted as I took him—"

"He spoke?"

"The inflections seemed Chinese. I'm not sure what he said, but it sounded like Chinese."

Ryokai has many strengths. His skill at languages is not one of them. Machiko herself knows barely enough to make herself understood in Mandarin, and that is just one of a seemingly endless number of Chinese dialects she has encountered around the New York–New Jersey megaplex. "There are many Triad groups in the plex."

"Yes, but how many would risk a war with Nagato Combine?"

"Very few."

"Perhaps we should speak of this to the Chairman, Machiko-*san*."

Machiko shakes her head. She skids the Tachi Monarch sideways through an intersection, turning in front of oncoming traffic. Horns blare, tires scream. The Tachi Monarch immediately seizes the road, straightens, and accelerates. Machiko rides onto an entrance ramp of the Long Island

Expressway. "Our first duty is to defend the Chairman. Let
security examine the bodies of the dead. Then we will see."

Eight lanes open wide before her, leading across the
Nassau boundary to Suffolk County and the eastern districts
of Long Island. She veers to the far left lane and presses the
accelerator to the floor. A cruiser marked for the Lone Star
corporate police briefly falls in behind her, perhaps to provide an escort, but cannot match the Tachi Monarch's pace.
She has no need of an escort, regardless. When traffic fails to
yield to the Tachi Monarch's flashing strobes, she slaloms
onto the center median and continues on with unchallenged
resolve.

"I'm arriving," Ryokai says.

"Two minutes."

The commlink ends. Another kilometer and Machiko
steers the Tachi Monarch down a ramp to a local highway
surrounded by an ocean of trees and all but barren of traffic.
Another minute brings her to the gates of the Chairman's
enclave, a sprawling expanse of hills and woods used not
only for the Chairman's personal residence, but as a park and
recreation facility for Nagato executives and their families,
and as a secure retreat for high-level meetings.

The gateway is divided into entrance and exit lanes by an
armored booth with gun ports and weapons pods. Tonight,
ports and pods are open. Armored security vans occupy both
the entrance and exit lanes. Troopers of the Nagato Security
Defense Force bearing automatic weapons and wearing full
body armor flank the vans. Troopers and vans wait behind
blast shields risen out of the roadway. The blast shields bear
the *mon* of Nagato Corp and the simple directive: STOP!

Machiko dims her driving lights and slows and steers
for the exit lane. A squad of troopers swarm around the sides
of the Tachi Monarch. Machiko lowers her window. She
must prove her identity via voice-rec and retina scan. The
instant this is complete, a trooper orders the blast shield low-
ered, the exit lane cleared.

"Proceed!"

Machiko keys Drive. The console telecom bleeps.
Machiko nearly forgets she is driving when she sees the face
that appears on the small display screen.

"Honjowara-*sama*." Reflexively, Machiko bows. The gesture here is little more than a nod of the head, but she gives it
great reverence.

The Chairman gazes at her sternly. The weight of his responsibilities shows clearly in the deep-etched lines of his face. The force of will that brought together the three main clans comprising the Nagato Combine burns fiercely in his eyes. "Machiko-*san*," he says in a tone both grim and momentous. "I now have the preliminary report of the Nagato Security Directorate. You must know that Mitsuharu-*san* and Jiksumi-*san* did not survive these despicable attacks. Sukayo-*san's* condition is very grave. For the immediate future, you, Machiko-*san,* must be prepared to act as senior member of the Guard."

"Yes, Honjowara-*sama*." Machiko swallows. Breathes. Nearly puts the Tachi Monarch into the trees standing just beyond the exit lane of the SDF checkpoint. "I am prepared."

Again, the Chairman watches her. This, the man who rose to control of the Honjowara-*gumi* by the age of eighteen, who founded Nagato Corporation and extended its holdings throughout North America, into Asia, Europe, the Middle East, who alone condemned anti-metahuman sentiment and brought his New Way to the clans. This man pauses to watch her, evaluating her reaction, perhaps seeing so deeply that he scrutinizes her spirit. Then he says, "Machiko-*san*. I know that Sukayo-*san* would give the Guard willingly into your hands. Do not doubt your ability. You are ready."

"Yes, Honjowara-*sama*. Thank you."

The telecom link ends. Machiko feels her pulse racing, her back and hips are drenched in sweat.

Command of the Guard.

Till this moment, it had not seemed real.

By Buddha's mercy . . . let her be ready.

4

The broad lane leading to the Chairman's estate is lined by the private vehicles of GSG, Nagato security cars, and armored shock vans. The lane ends at a cul-de-sac. A wall of reinforced stone rims the broad circle, rising high to embrace the gateway at the rear of the cul-de-sac. An MVN-17 armored personnel carrier with turret-mounted hard points sits squarely before the gates. More troopers in body armor wait beside the carrier. Lights atop the walls fill the circle with daylight; gun ports in the walls stand open. Armored drones and Yellowjacket light-attack helos buzz and thump, sweeping by overhead.

The manicured parklands flanking the approach lane are full of troopers, some accompanied by paranatural hounds.

Machiko slows the Tachi Monarch to a quick halt just short of the cul-de-sac, pulls the car onto the grass beside the lane, and parks. The sight of the vehicles, the armed and armored personnel, gives her pause. She has played a part in many alerts, both for real and for purposes of training. This time is different. This time the responsibility is uniquely her own. She is the one who declared the alert. Was she right to do that? Would Sukayo-*san* have initiated Rapier Wind? the highest level of alert? The enormity of the forces she has called into action brings her a twinge of anxious uncertainty.

But she remembers one essential fact. That was no gutter-punk who attacked her. An assassin so lavishly augmented as the one who attacked her would not come cheaply. And no unprincipled "samurai" of the streets murdered two GSG and brought a third, the most senior, Sukayo-*san,* near to death. Assassins so highly skilled and so fortunate as to succeed where others have failed could only be purchased by those with serious resources, dire motivations, objectives that must be identified and plans that must be neutralized.

No . . . she must dispense with uncertainty. There is a

threat in the events of this night. A threat that must be answered. A threat that goes beyond the attempted assassinations of the senior five members of the Guard.

A threat against the Chairman, perhaps all Nagato holdings. And therefore against all that she values, all that has ever had meaning, and all that she serves.

What must she do? Is Rapier Wind enough? Or does duty demand she go further? Machiko is unsure. The express purpose of the Guard is to defend the Chairman from harm. However, she is well aware that the Chairman has occasionally called upon various GSG, herself included, to perform special tasks, to act as his personal agent in certain special matters. But will he allow her to take on a task of her own choosing? A mission to lay bare this new threat to Nagato Combine? To see it defeated, by force if necessary?

This she does not know.

Her spirit yearns to seek out this new enemy and send her steel slashing viciously, mercilessly, through any who would threaten the Chairman, but she calms herself, settles herself.

She breathes.

Tonight, her duty is clear.

5

"Another GSG, sir."

Major Hakatoro Saru of the Nagato Corporation Security Defense Force nods once to his executive officer and waits, arms folded and set, feet planted upon the hard black pavement of the cul-de-sac. He has seen the dark green-tinted Tachi Monarch gliding smoothly up the approach lane to the verge of the cul-de-sac. He is familiar with the expensive and flashy vehicles favored by the elves of Nagato Combine's Green Serpent Guard. He considers such vehicles an arrogance, yet another proof of elitist attitudes, and thus another indication of the contempt with which most elves regard the balance of humanity, Japanese or no.

Hakatoro is also familiar with the slim, supple figure now coming into view, standing up beside the flamboyant Tachi.

A rare exception to the rule.

She is known as "Machiko-*san*," but many of the security troopers under his command privately refer to her as "Jade Tiger." She walks with the bold, long-legged stride of the warrior who knows no fear. She can be harsh and arrogant in manner when she perceives a need for discipline to be reinforced. Hakatoro, though, understands the need for discipline. He knows the difference between the necessary arrogance of a commander, or leading member of the Guard, and the brand of arrogance that is no better than puerile vanity.

Machiko-*san* knows this, too. This and more. Hakatoro has heard that other appellation used for her by the younger members of the GSG. "Sword witch," they call her. It is said that in the training hall of the GSG, located here on the estate, Machiko-*san* has never been defeated, not with swords, not even by Sukayo-*san*, who, if mere talk can be believed, once actually defeated the master swordsman who founded the Guard, he who trained the first of the GSG, the one known as Kuroda-*sensei*.

These elves are of course the most arrogant of warriors, and even the lowest warrior will exaggerate. Yet there is something about Machiko-*san* that gives credence to the stories about her. One does not have to look very closely to see the steel in her eyes, or the warrior's compassion in her heart, forever battling to win her spirit. One does not have to listen to much talk to realize that she is a physical adept and that the mana in her is strong. A ferocious combatant. One who rightly approaches the Chairman's estate with the warrior's bold stride.

As she approaches the gateway, Hakatoro advances a few paces ahead of his weapons teams to greet her.

They bow.

"Are your forces arrayed to your satisfaction, Hakatoro-*san*?" Machiko-*san* asks in her throaty voice of authority.

Hakatoro nods. "I have biologicals in the woods, assault teams on the perimeter, lasers on line, assault guns, and a SAM unit on the hill. Any hostiles will be fragged, burned, or blown to bits, Machiko-*san*. Defenses in depth, reinforced by your GSG. We are ready for the devil Fuchi itself."

Machiko-*san* looks at him sharply. "You have information that Fuchi presents a definite threat?"

Hakatoro hesitates. A peculiar question, this. He is a moment recognizing that Machiko-*san* has taken his chance mention of Fuchi as a serious statement. This is odd because they have joked about the notorious giant of Fuchi Industrial Electronics on many occasions in the past. Everyone does. Fuchi is well-known for the villainy of its black operations. "Excuse me, Machiko-*san*," Hakatoro hurries to say. "I have no such information. I meant only to emphasize that the forces under my command are prepared for whatever enemy we may encounter."

Momentarily, Machiko-*san* nods. The throaty voice softens. "You must forgive me, Hakatoro-*san*. We face a very serious threat. Five senior GSG were attacked tonight. Two are dead."

Hakatoro scowls. "Impossible."

"It is so," Machiko-*san* assures him. "Sukayo-*san* himself has been seriously wounded. I have just been informed by the Chairman that I am now acting senior of the Guard."

Hearing this, Hakatoro straightens his already rigid, erect posture. The stature of the Green Serpent Guard is of course very high. They accompany the Chairman everywhere, watch

over him twenty-four hours a day. They are empowered to
use any means to ensure that he is safe. Even the most junior
member may demand immediate access if he or she should
believe that the Chairman's safety is in question. Yet, the
senior member of the Guard is said to stand especially close
to the Chairman, at his right hand, and to have his ear, much
like a *sanro-kai,* or "special consultant." The senior member's stature is especially high. Had Hakatoro known of
Machiko-*san's* recent rise in status he would not have spoken
so informally. He would have addressed her with the degree
of respect accorded the senior-most of the Guard.

"I do not know how long this alert must go on," Machiko-
san continues. "I am hoping that Security Service, or perhaps
the Intelligence Directorate will shortly be able to provide us
some data, such as the identity of the assassins. This should
assist us in evaluating the level of threat we face, and its
immediacy."

Hakatoro nods. "The SDF will be on alert for as long as is
necessary, Machiko-*san.* I will advise my command to make
all necessary arrangements."

Machiko-*san* glances aside.

Hakatoro follows her glance, and finds two other GSG
now coming through ports in the gateway, coming toward
Machiko-*san.* Ryokai and Gongoro, both senior GSG.
Gongoro was tonight the senior GSG on duty at the estate.
Both bow in approaching Machiko-*san.* Gongoro, arrogant
dog, gives a bow that is at best perfunctory, and does not
wait for a bow of acknowledgment.

"You will inspect our deployment?" Gongoro says in a
clipped tone of command.

Hakatoro restrains himself. He has no authority over
members of the Guard. It would be inappropriate for him to
snarl at this dog over his churlish manners and thus cause an
incident. It would be particularly inappropriate in light of the
current alert.

Instead, as Gongoro completes his question, Hakatoro
faces Machiko-*san* and bows. "Does the senior member have
any other requests of the Security Defense Force?"

Machiko-*san* glances back and forth. Her eyes then settle
on Hakatoro, much as he had expected. "Not at this time,"
Machiko-*san* replies. "Thank you, Hakatoro-*san.*"

They bow.

Hakatoro returns to his troops.

6

Gongoro gives no visible response to being interrupted by Major Hakatoro, but Machiko is not deceived. She knows well the measure of Gongoro's anger. She is quite aware that he does not like being interrupted, especially by members of the security forces, especially by norms. For now, he will do nothing, because duty demands his attention, and because, here in the cul-de-sac, he stands under the guns of Hakatoro's men, and those men are Hakatoro's hand-picked best. In time an opportunity will come whereby he may repay Hakatoro his affront, and Gongoro will seize it. That is how he operates.

Ryokai's eyes dart back and forth as if expecting lightning and thunder to erupt at any moment. And that is Ryokai, ever sensitive to the rise of conflict.

"I will inspect the deployment," Machiko says.

And her two brothers of the Guard follow her through one of the ports in the gateway.

Compared to the brilliant light flooding the cul-de-sac, the terrain beyond the gateway is nearly lost in darkness. The low hill that the Chairman's rambling home surmounts is sheltered by massive oaks, some rising thirty meters and higher into the night. Such trees cast heavy shadows. A person with only the benefit of a norm's unaided vision could easily miss her step. To Machiko's eyes, the hillside is dark, but the teams of GSG and SDF stationed about the discreet slope of the curving driveway provide guidance, orientation. They are beacons of warmth amid the darkness. They stand out like lanterns among the trees, the manicured garden plots, and sculptured bends of a water-course.

"I have extended our perimeter," Gongoro remarks.

This is quite obvious.

A team of five GSG, armed with M-22 assault rifles with integral grenade launchers, and supported by an M-107

machine gun, wait barely fifteen meters upslope from the
gateway.

Under ordinary conditions, only a third or half of the Guard
is on duty at any one time, and would stand watch over only
those areas providing the most immediate means of access to
the Chairman's person: the room or garden or hall where the
Chairman happens to be, adjacent rooms and corridors,
household entrances. It is the responsibility of the Security
Defense Force to guard the actual estate, to patrol the property, to seize any intruders and repel all attacks. The SDF is
responsible for this and other Nagato facilities. The Green
Serpent Guard is responsible specifically for the Chairman's
life. Whether the house and grounds of the estate are attacked
and reduced to burning bits of vulcanized ash is of little significance to Machiko, so long as the Chairman himself is not
injured.

However, Machiko can only conclude that Gongoro is
right to extend the Guard's perimeter. The entire GSG membership is on hand. Tonight, they can afford to spread themselves across the landscape. Tonight, duty demands it.

"I have doubled the guard on access passages to the
Chairman's rooms and increased the body detail to eight."

Again, Gongoro has chosen correctly.

The body detail is composed of those GSG assigned to
provide close cover over the Chairman's person. It is the
detail's duty to follow the Chairman from room to room, in
the lavatory, the Chairman's dressing room, even from one
side of a room to another, should that seem warranted.
Should an assassin suddenly appear, it is the detail's responsibility to physically move the Chairman out of danger, or
kill the assassin, or, if necessary, take the bullet themselves.
Bullet or knife or bomb or poisoned dart—whatever weapon
is used. Here at the estate, the body detail ordinarily numbers
only two. Tonight, though, they must be prepared for everything and anything. Prepared even for death.

Especially for death.

Machiko takes a tour of the hillsides. Experienced members are posted with late-comers to the Guard so that every
team of GSG possesses a natural leader. The teams' positions on the hillsides are tactically sound. The few members
Machiko pauses to scrutinize appear prepared for combat:
uniforms, equipment, weapons. All properly outfitted.

At the main entrance to the Chairman's home, Machiko

finds Ujitaro. He sits cross-legged on the broad steps in the
shadows of the curving pagoda-style roof, flanked by more
than a dozen GSG. He looks like any other member of the
Guard, except that he carries only sword and dagger for
weapons. He has little need for physical weapons. His
greatest weapons flow from within. He is a powerful mage,
and all the more powerful for the powers of his snakes, the
naga. Awakened creatures easily ten meters long and as
weighty as an adult metahuman. It is said that the creatures
are not merely sentient, but are also magically active, and
that they serve to guard both Ujitaro and the Chairman from
attacks via the astral plane.

All Machiko knows for certain is that the naga's venom is
no less deadly than a shot from a magnum automatic. She
has seen the creatures take down heavily armed hostiles in
body armor. It is a sight that encourages respect.

Tonight, the naga lie across Ujitaro's shoulders and lap
and across the width of the steps. As always, Ujitaro appears
unaware of the serpents' weight.

Machiko pauses and bows.

"Nothing to report!" Ujitaro says in his harsh whisper.
"Concern yourself with meat bodies and leave mana to me!"

It is nearly a rebuke.

Yet, rather than take insult, Machiko suffers another rise
of uncertainty, a silken wave of dismay. All is in readiness.
Gongoro has deployed the Guard expertly. Ujitaro has command of the astral and requires nothing of anyone. What is
left for her to do? How is she to contribute? What should she
be doing now?

The night offers no immediate answers. She turns to look
down the curving slope of the driveway to the gate. She feels
a subtle yearning. She wishes Sukayo-*san* were here. Sukayo
would know. He would know what to expect and how to
prepare. He would evaluate the few scraps of data that have
been pieced together so far and explain what it all must
mean.

"Younger sister," he has called her, too many times to
count. And that is how she feels now. Young and untested.

Out of her depth.

Always she has seemed possessed of a mind and spirit best
suited to the way of the sword, to martial discipline and individual combat. Till now, she has always been content to
leave all larger matters concerning a world of enemies and a

multitude of threats to her "older brother," and those with the breadth of understanding and the depth of wisdom to grasp such difficult arts as strategy, to determine what is the proper course. And now she feels regret, dismay. "Older brother" is not here now. The Guard is now her responsibility. She is the acting senior member. What will she do? What must she do?

A first step abruptly comes to mind. She turns to Ryokai. "Where were you when attacked?"

"At my condo."

"You were sleeping?"

He nods. "I had just laid down."

"Was the assassin cyber-augmented?"

Ryokai hesitates, frowning. "I am wondering about this myself, Machiko-*san*. He carried much equipment. I'm not sure if this was built in or merely strapped on."

"What weapons did he use?"

"He carried two Ingram smartguns and fired them in unison. He also had an Ares Predator II, which he used when the Ingrams ran out of ammo."

"Did you have any warning of the attack?"

"Not till he came near my bedroom door. The door was ajar. I heard him breathe. Then caught sight of his heat signature."

"How did he make his attack?"

"He opened fire as he came through the door. He pushed it inward with the toe of his boot. I anticipated the moment and managed to tumble from my bedding as he opened up. One shot nicked my scalp. Fortunately, I had my Ceska at hand. I snapped off three rounds and caught the assassin in the head, neck, and shoulder. Then the kill button split his skull."

Machiko considers all this, but the mention of the Ceska briefly distracts her. Ryokai has always favored the Ceska 120 as a backup pistol. Its eccentric design appeals to him. Since their earliest days together at the GSG academy, he has always been intrigued by things that are quirky or unusual. His interest in the *kiseru* is just another example. He has quite an extensive collection of these ancient weapons, which resemble pipes for smoking tobacco, but are generally a meter in length, made of iron or steel, and come equipped with a handguard. They were used as truncheons by feudal-era yakuza, who, being of the common classes, were forbidden the use of swords.

"How did you deal with your assassin, Machiko-*san*?"

Machiko explains in brief what occurred with her, then says, "Consider this, Ryokai-*san*. One assassin crashes into my room like a rhino and unleashes a storm of automatic weapons fire. The other, attacking you, exercises a degree more subtlety, but carries SMGs favored by so-called 'street samurai.' Do these seem like the methods of professional assassins? These killers go about their tasks all wrong."

"Their methods do seem crude."

Machiko nods. "If I were to undertake an assassination, I would choose my ground with care, and utilize timing, to ensure that I could close with my target, and then take my target's head with one clean stroke of my sword. There would be no hail of bullets. No confrontation. No discernible noise. It would be like a formal execution. One clean stroke."

"It might be hours before the bodies were discovered."

"Precisely." Machiko nods agreement.

"And yet both assassins did succeed at two relatively diffi-cult tasks."

"Finding us."

"Yes. And getting to us."

Finding Ryokai at home could have been luck, but finding Machiko at her parent's home, rather than at her own condo, that hints at more than mere luck. It would take planning. Perhaps even the support of a skilled decker. The Nagato Manor Residence Community where Machiko's parents live is Nagato-owned, but operated and secured by a subsidiary, and that subsidiary maintains a complete security establish-ment. A skilled decker with experience at sleazing informa-tion from computers could have breached the Residence Community's computer system and determined that Ma-chiko had been cleared through the Community's main en-trance earlier in the evening.

Further, neither assassin set off any alarms while making their penetrations. This definitely speaks of a decker's sup-port. A sufficiently skilled Matrix operative might seize con-trol of windows and doors and other facility devices, so that an assassin might penetrate a "secured" facility merely by placing one foot ahead of the other.

"Amateurs," Gongoro growls.

Machiko breathes. She turns to face Gongoro, and says, "Amateurs did not kill Mitsuharu-*san* and Jiksumi-*san*."

"What do you know of it?"

"I have seen them fight!"

"You forget. Mitsuharu has been on medication since his oral surgery. Jiksumi indulged too often in wine."

This changes nothing. "Perhaps the killers were not trained as assassins. That does not make them amateurs. No amateur would survive against Sukayo-*san*. And the extensive augmentations of the killer who came for me indicates a highly paid operative. A skilled combatant. To do what they have done takes discipline and organization."

Gongoro sneers. "Like *teppodama*."

The idea gives Machiko pause.

Teppodama are "bullets." The term is used to refer to the occasional need for the lowest-ranked members of a clan, the *kobun*, to perform tasks like those of a warrior. *Kobun* are rarely warriors of a degree comparable to members of the Guard, but they may at times be called upon, like warriors, to demonstrate their loyalty to the clan by placing themselves at risk. They may risk injury or death, or perhaps only the chance of arrest and imprisonment. The point is that they must be prepared to prove themselves in ways that go beyond mere words, not only for the clan but for the oyabun, or the Chairman, as Honjowara-*sama* is properly called.

"You conceive of some similarity between these killers and loyal *kobun*?" Machiko says.

"They are muscle!" Gongoro growls. "Nothing more than muscle. The killers were crude. They relied upon brute force."

"But the killers' augmentations," Ryokai says.

"This proves nothing!" Gongoro exclaims. "I could go into Manhattan's Terminal zone and be outfitted with a mountain of surplus cyberware for nothing more than the price of a Tachi Monarch." To Machiko, Gongoro says, "If this killer had been so highly paid and efficient, you would be dead."

Indeed, Machiko feels compelled to admit, if only to herself, that Gongoro does have a point. The mere presence of extensive cybernetic augmentations does not prove anything. The metal could be junk, so much non-functional dead weight. But there is another point Gongoro misses. "You were not there," Machiko says. "You do not know how close this killer came."

"I know that you live."

Machiko steps near him, to within one arm's length, and says, "I live because I sought death."

And there the discussion pauses.

Gongoro dares not sneer. Machiko makes it this way deliberately. Once her words are spoken, she waits, holding Gongoro's gaze. She feels again the grip of her katana in her hand, though the sword remains slung at her back, and the unyielding spirit that led her to defeat her attacker, her enemy. Gongoro recognizes this. She sees the recognition in his expression, growing wary, and in his eyes, becoming hesitant, uncertain. At length, she sees it in the brief bow of acknowledgment he accords her. Thus he admits that, regardless of the killer's skill, she has gone where few would dare, where fewer still have the spirit to survive. She has gone to death, faced death, embraced it. A failure to honor this would be a very grave affront, demanding an immediate response.

Ryokai bows as well.

"I speak out of loyalty to the Honjowara-*gumi*," Gongoro says, and this once his tone is nearly civil. "I tell you these killers are muscle. They are *kobun*!"

"Of what clan?"

"The Yoshida-*kai*."

This would seem absurd but for the immense gravity of the circumstance. The Nagato Combine is composed of three main clans: the Honjowara-*gumi*, the Toki-*gumi*, and the Yoshida-*kai*. What Gongoro is suggesting is that a staunch ally of the Chairman and his Honjowara-*gumi* has for all intents and purposes committed treason. "That is a remarkable opinion, Gongoro-*san*," Machiko says in her quietist voice. "An opinion that could lead us all onto dangerous ground."

"Do you fear such opinions?"

"What I fear is that you are insane. What *kami* whispers into your ear that you would conceive of such nonsense?"

"You fear what I say because it is true!"

"The Yoshida-*kai*," Machiko says, "has been the leading partner to our clan for nearly two decades, a valued ally since before either of us were born. They are traditionalists, yes. They have reservations about the Chairman's New Way, yes. Their leadership has sometimes objected vehemently to the Chairman's decisions. Yes. This is so. But it does not make them traitors or enemies."

Gongoro's next words emerge like acid. "Yoshida-*kai* is rank with hatred for all metas."

"You exaggerate."

Gongoro snarls. "There are those among the Yoshida-*kai* who would gladly aid in the extermination of all metatypes. They would like nothing better than to begin with we who are most dependent on the Chairman's philosophy. They consider the Green Serpent Guard to be an insult directed specifically at the ancestors of their clan."

"That is absurd."

"It is fact!"

"You are saying that Yoshida has harbored resentment over this affront since Kuroda-*sensei* emerged from the Tir and pledged himself to the Chairman's service. That is more than twenty years ago. There would be no Nagato Combine if that was so. Yoshida-*sama* would never have joined. He would have reviled the Honjowara-*gumi* as a clan of *kawa-ruhito*, untouchables, utterly despicable subhuman refuse. He would have begun a war with the sole purpose of eliminating every last member of the Honjowara-*gumi*!"

Gongoro laughs bitterly, and briefly. "Twenty years ago, Yoshida Gennai was a tired old man desperate for allies. His son has proven to be just as weak. The people I speak of are now in the position whereby they could seize control of the Yoshida-*kai* with very little effort. The attacks against our members could be and probably are the first in a series of attacks by which they will seize control of their clan, perhaps the entire Nagato Combine."

Machiko breathes. "If these people wanted control of Yoshida-*kai*, they would not begin by attacking the Guard. They would kill Yoshida's son and take control. You have put the porter before his luggage."

Gongoro looks at her like she is the one gone mad. "Once they have seized control, it will be too late! We will be expecting their treachery. Now, they have succeeded in taking us unawares. In one night, they have cut down our best and brightest."

"And so they have rendered the GSG impotent? You speak nonsense."

"Do you deny Sukayo's ability as a leader? Do you suggest that we are not poorer for his loss? Then what of you? Sukayo's protégé. How fit are you for command?"

This is infuriating. "We are like bricks in a wall. Never

mind who is killed. We have many more bricks and all are capable of leading the Guard."

"Now you are the one who exaggerates."

"If you truly believe that Yoshida-*kai* is our enemy, it is your duty to relate this to the Chairman."

"It is not my duty. It is yours. You are the senior member."

"And you are senior next to me. The distinction is of no significance if you believe that our clan's foremost ally is in fact an enemy plotting to destroy us."

"No, you are senior member. The responsibility is yours."

Machiko looks to the tree limbs overhead. This will be a long and trying night. Again, she wishes Sukayo-*san* were here. He would know how to answer Gongoro.

How to silence him.

7

Several times, Machiko-*san* seems at pains to lower her voice. Ryokai sees little point.

Despite the pounding in his head, it is clear to him that Machiko-*san's* words and Gongoro's growls carry far against the quiet of the night. The GSG standing watch by the main entrance to the Chairman's house can follow every word. And several times, though his eyes grow blurry with fatigue, he spots the faces of GSG stationed on the hillside turning to gaze uphill. It is troubling. The seniors of the Guard should work out their disagreements in private. This open display of dissension can only lead to further trouble, perhaps trouble enough to involve the entire GSG membership.

"Do not lecture me about duty, Gongoro-*san*," says Machiko. "I know my duty. Do you?"

Gongoro growls an angry reply.

Ryokai closes his eyes and tries to conceive of a means of ending the conflict peacefully. Yet he knows it is probably hopeless. Machiko and Gongoro are like mongoose and snake. It has always been this way between the two of them, ever since their early days at the academy of the Guard. Their mutual animosity first took tangible form during barehanded combat instruction. Grappling techniques. Gongoro twisted too hard, some say accidentally, and snapped Machiko's wrist. Some weeks after that, during sword practice, Machiko swung her *boken* with such force, even with her wrist still in a cast, that she shattered her wooden practice sword, smashed the helmet on Gongoro's head, and struck him stone-cold unconscious.

Later, she apologized, but not before telling Ryokai, privately, of feeling Gongoro's burning resentment. Of his despising her for being female. For being forced to train with her.

"When I lifted my *boken* I felt I possessed all the power of a whirlwind. I had no mind, Ryokai-*san*. I could not help myself."

And often it has seemed just so, whenever she lifts a sword. Like a whirlwind arising. A force, once unleashed, beyond anyone's control. A power as sublime as nature itself.

Gongoro snarls, "You are a witch with that sword in your hand, but your spirit is weak. You will not speak for the GSG. You will not tell the chairman what he must be told. You will kneel like a woman and, like a fool, seek consensus."

Machiko-*san* grunts. "You are intolerable."

"So you would say, because I am right!"

"Because you have the manners of a barbarian!"

Abruptly, Ryokai feels the ground beneath his feet tilting, tipping him backward, off-balance. For a fleeting instant, he expects to hear the roar of an explosion, uprooting the earth, feel the force of a shock wave, bowling him over. This does not occur. Instead, all is quiet, serene. He sees a faint stroke of white, like a blur of the crescent moon, through the dark canopy of the trees. He moves his feet to regain his balance; but strangely, his feet drag the earth. He glimpses a brief expanse of black night sky. He feels his back strike the ground. The pain in his head swells immense . . . and then, through eyes that keep drifting closed, he finds himself lying on the ground. Several people bending over him. Gazing at his face, the side of his head. A man in camo, but with medics' insignia on his chest. Two men. They are using strange words and fumbling with bandages and other items, difficult to make out.

"Ryokai-*san* . . ."

The voice is soft, almost tender, and yet so clear it might be coming from beside his ear. He tries to turn his head to look, but the pain in the side of his head now throbs down his neck into his shoulder. He feels himself wincing.

A gentle hand brushes hair out of his eyes, and then he sees her, leaning near. Her expression seems almost furious with concern. "Why did you not seek treatment?" asks Machiko. She looks toward the side of his head. "This is no scratch. You are still bleeding."

"Something tore the scalp," says the medic.

It is very embarrassing. Shameful. To be lying here so foolish and weak, while she, Machiko, gazes at him so sternly. How could he have allowed this to happen? He strives to sit up, to lift his head from the ground, but suddenly Machiko's hands are at his shoulders, and other hands too, and it is like the whole weight of the earth is pressing him back. His head throbs viciously. For a moment, he can see only blackness.

"Be still," Machiko is saying. "You must be treated. Ryokai, you are drenched in blood!"

It is not important. He had to come here to the estate, first for the Chairman, then for her. He must do his duty for the clan and for Machiko-*san*. He must prove himself an ally against Gongoro's venom. He must be strong, stronger than he feels, perhaps stronger than he has ever been. Perhaps Machiko does not know it, but she needs him. Now more than ever.

She leans so near he can smell the faint scent of sandalwood in her hair. "You are going to hospital," she says. "Do you hear me?"

Ryokai feels his cheeks grow warm. The shame is almost too much. Perhaps this gives him the strength to say, "Beware Gongoro."

Machiko questions him with her eyes.

"He wants control of the Guard. Do not let him bait you."

Faintly, Machiko nods. "Be still."

The words caress his ears like tender down.

8

The night grows very long indeed.

Machiko searches the deep shadows of the hillsides with her eyes. She listens. This is her duty. To keep spirit settled and a broad gaze upon the night. She has known many such nights. The waiting is not difficult if one regards one's own body as already dead. Tonight, though, her thoughts constantly stray.

Within the hour, the leadership of the clan begins arriving. Some could be described as *shatei,* like "younger brothers" to the Chairman. Others would be best considered like *wakashira-hosa,* members of the board of directors. Some represent the clan, the Honjowara-*gumi;* others represent Nagato Corporation. All are part of the Nagato Combine. They are escorted up the slope of the driveway by Major Hakatoro, greeted before the entrance by Machiko, and accorded every degree of respect their status demands. In light of the current emergency, all must be scanned for weapons before being admitted to the Chairman's home, but this is expected. Duty demands this be done and none offer objections. No weapons are found. The leaders of the Honjowara-*gumi* do not generally carry weapons, except on certain occasions, for this would be dishonorable, a serious breach of conduct, and wholly at odds with the Chairman's New Way.

A hundred years ago, at the heart of Tokyo's Ginza District, the Honjowara-*gumi* was controlled by violent gangsters. The clan battled the Ginza Tiger and others for control of gambling, restaurants and bars, narcotics, and a multitude of illegal enterprises, till, at times, the streets ran with blood. Little changed when the clan made its move to North America. The criminal bosses remained in control till the end of the millennium.

Then came Nagato Kurobuchi.

He came to power as the protector of Honjowara Okido, who was then a child, and his mother, recently widowed by the very violence that had haunted the clan since its earliest beginnings. He shamed the gangsters for violating basic tenets of the clan, for doing violence to the wife and child of the oyabun, Honjowara-*sama's* father, and for other crimes, such as revealing secrets to enemies of the clan, and for having personal addictions to narcotics. He added to the gangsters' shame by reminding them of their ancestral ties to the feudal-era *machi-yakko,* who, though commoners, banded together to defend towns and villages, merchants and farmers, women and children, from marauding bands of unemployed samurai warriors.

He forced all to see the dishonorable Way of living they had been leading, full of treachery and treason.

"We must have a New Way," he declared, and through all the tumultuous years of the food riots, the rise of the megacorps, the VITAS plague and the Dawn of the Awakened, and finally the Great Ghost Dance, Nagato Kurobuchi pursued his New Way.

That Way included organizing the clan to function as a corporation, and preparing to meet the Sixth World not as gangsters, but as honorable persons not unlike the former *machi-yakko.* Not as renegades against their heritage, but as true servants of the people.

When Honjowara Okido assumed his role as head of the clan, he expanded this vision to include not merely people, but all peoples, including metahumans: elf, ork, dwarf, troll.

"The samurai's word is harder than steel," he declared. "We must prove our honor and resolve to be even more durable than this. We must move with the tide of the Sixth World or be swallowed by our enemies. We must forge an alliance of clans or face destruction. We must welcome all into our house who would serve us loyally and aid in fulfilling our mission."

Thoughts, feelings, memories—all this intrudes on Machiko's mind and spirit as she passes the clan leadership to the doors of the Chairman's home. It stirs her unworthy heart. Again and again, she looks to the doors of the entrance and yearns to go inside, to learn what the leaders know, to hear what they will tell the Chairman. For she will learn nothing of the threat facing the Nagato Combine standing out here in the dark. She will find no answers in the night. Here, there is only Gongoro's venom and her own uncertainties. Yet here she must remain. She is a warrior of the Green Serpent Guard. She is acting senior member. She must stand the watch. She must command. She must stay where her steel and armament and skill will do the most good. This is her duty.

She resists the thought that her duty to the clan perhaps stands larger than her duty as a warrior. Her duty is to serve as she is best able to serve. As a warrior.

Then, her commlink beeps.

She keys the link on her left vambrace and flips open the small screen. The face of the Chairman's personal aide immediately appears. "The Chairman asks that you join him in the Autumn Garden Room as soon as you are able, Machiko-*san*."

She acknowledges this and looks to Gongoro.

"Speak of Yoshida," he growls lowly.

9

At the end of the corridor is a door paneled to resemble wood the color of honey. Before the door stand six GSG, familiar faces all. To the right is a wooden bench of some dark-hued wood. Beneath the bench, seven pairs of shoes.

As Machiko approaches, she lifts her hands, showing her empty palms and the twining serpents emblazoned there. The senior member of the detail responds with a brief bow in the manner of GSG standing watch. He bows from the shoulders only enough to indicate respect and does not lower his head or his eyes. Machiko bows in the same manner.

"The Chairman is in conference," the senior informs.

Machiko nods. "I am called here."

"Should I announce you?"

"Did you announce the others?"

"The door remained open till the others were inside."

"Then announce me."

The senior turns and kneels, one knee to the floor, and slides the door open only enough for him to peer into the room. It is strange for Machiko, watching this. She has rarely been formally announced. As a senior member of the Guard, in performing her duty, she has walked in and out of rooms where the Chairman was holding conferences more times than she could hope to recall, without anyone appearing to notice. She could walk in and out at will. Now she stands and waits while another GSG looks into the room and waits to say her name. It makes her feel odd, unsettled, as though she pretends to be someone or something she is not.

In a firm, clear voice, the senior says, "Machiko-*san* of the Green Serpent Guard."

And, abruptly it seems, the door is slid fully open and the Autumn Garden room comes into view. A familiar room. A quiet room, suitable for contemplation, for reflection. The style is traditional. Furnishings are minimal. The ceiling is low and gives the space a private, comfortable feel. The floor is wood of a brown like caramel, covered in clear waxy varnish. The walls wrapping around to the left simulate rice paper panels. The long wall on the right, opaque in the night, like rice paper, may be turned transparent during the day to provide a view of one of many gardens, the Autumn Garden, lying just outside.

Opposite the door, on a low dais of varnished wood, sits Chairman Honjowara. In place of his usual suit, he wears a robe bearing the Nagato *mon* and the lotus and reed pattern of the clan. The pale pastel colors of the robe only seem to emphasize, to exaggerate, the stern gravity of his expression.

Machiko bows, and briefly moves her eyes over the GSG body detail. The main group waits, one knee to the floor, three to the Chairman's left, three to his right. The remaining two wait just inside the room, facing Machiko from just beyond the doorway. None give any sign of recognition or acknowledgment. The task of the body detail is to evaluate threats, to hold themselves ready, to act. Polite greetings would distract from their duty. Anything not essential to the performance of this duty is absolutely prohibited.

The leaders of the clan sit before the Chairman. Six males, one female, one ork, one elf. These are the leaders' most obvious distinctions. Their commonalities are far more imposing. They share the Chairman's grim expression. They are all dressed in dark, conservative suits that tonight seem like the uniforms of generals, each lapel adorned with a pin bearing the *mon* of Nagato Combine. They are arranged in two precisely ordered files, four on the left, three on the right. They sit on round cushions that appear to provide only a modest comfort, laid directly on the floor.

Before each of them lies a small black lacquered tray with matching tea service.

"Machiko," says Honjowara-*sama*. He extends a hand to the one remaining unoccupied cushion. This is located at the end of one file of leaders, on the right.

Machiko bows and moves to her appointed place. Here, she puts one knee to the floor; in this case, the cushion. Members of the Guard do not sit while on duty. Neither do they eat or drink. She is therefore served no tea.

"Arinori," says Honjowara-*sama*.

A panel along the wall to the left slides open and the

Chairman's personal aide steps into the room, bows, then **kneels**.

"What is Sukayo-*san's* condition?"

The aide makes brief use of a portable telecom. "Sukayo-*san* is still in surgery, Chairman-*sama*."

Honjowara-*sama* nods; then, with his eye still fixed on the aide, he extends a hand toward the room. To Machiko, it seems as though the Chairman gestures directly at her.

The aide says, "The Chief of Surgery at Mather University Hospital informs that Sukayo-*san* is suffering from multiple trauma injuries, such as would be consistent with the effects of an explosion. Sukayo-*san* is in a most critical condition. It is not yet known whether he will survive. It is expected that the surgery will continue for several more hours."

Since this news seems directed at her, Machiko bows to express her gratitude. The news is hardly reassuring, but she reminds herself of one inescapable truth. Sukayo is not yet dead. And this leads her to a second greater truth. Her "older brother" has immense force of will and a relentless fighting spirit. If fate but allows it, Sukayo will survive, no matter the degree of his injuries.

Again, Honjowara-*sama* nods. The aide withdraws. Honjowara-*sama* then looks to Bessho Chikayo, chief of the Nagato Corp Directorate of Security.

In Machiko's view, Bessho-*san* exemplifies the sort of leader whom the Chairman has described many times in discussing the New Way. He appears the meticulous corporate executive. His suit is pure Dunhall Lane, conservative and refined. His manner is polite and dignified. He manages his directorate with efficiency and dedication and tolerates nothing that would hint of gangster tactics from either the Security Service or the Security Defense Force. His hand-picked deputy, chief of operations, Colonel Satomi, is a veteran of the United Canadian and American States armed forces and a former director with the NYPD, Inc.

Bessho-*san* briefly bows in answer to the Chairman's look, then says, "It will be several hours, Chairman-*san,* and in some cases days, before precise details are uncovered. However, I am now able to provide you with a better summary of what has occurred. I will call on my deputy to describe certain technical matters."

Honjowara-*sama* nods. "Proceed."

"We know now that all five of the attacks on members of

the Guard were initiated at approximately five minutes past the hour of one a.m. All five members were attacked at locations they have frequented regularly. Sukayo-*san,* Mitsuharu *san,* and Ryokai-*san* at their condos, Jiksumi-*san* at the residence of a friend. Machiko-*san* at her parents' home. In each case, the attackers utilized automatic weapons. In the case of Sukayo-*san* and Mitsuharu-*san,* explosives, possibly grenades, were also used."

Zoge-*san* politely coughs. This man, seated nearest the Chairman on the left, is thin enough to seem gaunt and sufficiently tall that he could be an elf. Yet he is not an elf. He is in fact of Korean lineage. He goes by the name Zoge, "ivory," for it is said the Chairman considers him as valuable as ivory. He is a lifelong friend of the Chairman and one of the Chairman's most devoted servants. He is also an authority on matters of finance and corporation law.

Honjowara-*sama* acknowledges him with a glance.

"How did these attackers gain entrance to the various sites where the GSG were attacked?" Zoge-*san* asks.

Bessho-*san* replies, "Moments before the physical assaults began, all five sites were invaded via the Matrix. Physical security systems were thereby neutralized."

"You say these attacks occurred simultaneously."

"That appears to be correct."

Coordinating the efforts of five individual assassins is not a small task. Further coordinating five individual Matrix runs adds yet another layer of complexity. The point does not seem lost on the clan leaders. Several expressions turn particularly grim. Machiko's own regard for the people behind the attacks goes up several notches, and she feels absolutely corroborated on one point of disagreement with Gongoro. Whoever these people are, whatever their strengths and weaknesses, they are anything but amateurs.

"How many of the attackers were taken?" asks Ohana Toyonari, another of the Chairman's close advisors.

"The ones who attacked Sukayo-*san,* Machiko-*san,* and Ryokai-*san* were killed," Bessho-*san* replies. "There is evidence to suggest that the ones who attacked Mitsuharu-*san* and Jiksumi-*san* were perhaps wounded before making their escape."

"How did Sukayo-*san,* who is now near death, manage to kill his attacker?" Ohana-*san* asks.

Bessho-*san* says, "It would be premature to attempt to

describe this in detail. An autopsy is being performed on the killers as we speak, and we have hopes of learning more from Sukayo-*san*, should he regain consciousness. However, it is clear from the damage to Sukayo-*san's* condo that a brief but intense battle occurred. It appears that Sukayo-*san* was able to inflict a number of wounds on his attacker, perhaps using improvised weapons. His attacker was found a short distance from Sukayo-*san's* condo. This attacker was apparently fitted with some form of cranial explosive, like the other two attackers we have recovered. A preliminary examination indicates that the one who attacked Sukayo-*san* would likely have succumbed to blood loss had the cranial device not detonated."

Ohana asks, "What form of cranial device did the attackers carry?"

Bessho-*san* looks to his deputy, Colonel Satomi, who bows and says, "The exact nature of the device has not yet been determined. But it is clear from the extent of injury inflicted, that the devices used were of a type generally known as microbombs. A small quantity of high-energy explosive, often in gel form, combined with a detonator. The detonator itself may be linked to various bioware such as a pain editor or damage compensator, which monitor pain and injury to the body. The microbombs utilized here were sufficiently powerful to fracture the skull and deform the bones of the face, thus complicating the process of identifying the attackers."

Ohana-*san* says, "Surely the attackers may be identified by fingerprints."

"We are pursuing this avenue, of course," says Colonel Satomi. "However, the means of identification presents less a problem than the location of the appropriate database. If the attackers have been arrested or otherwise registered within the UCAS, the Confederate American States, Cal-Free, the Kingdom of Hawaii, or Japan, we will shortly know who they were. If they are from other territories, we may have to negotiate to obtain the desired information."

"Negotiations may cost us valuable time," Honjowara-*sama* says with decision. "What can we determine from the information available to us now?"

For some moments, no one responds. Machiko recalls Gongoro's speculations about anti-metahuman sentiment in the Yoshida-*kai*, but hesitates to say anything here, before the leaders of the clan, before Honjowara-*sama* himself, for it is all just speculation. Guesses. Perhaps nothing but baseless fantasy.

Bessho-*san* bows, and says, "The equipment, weapons, cyberware used by the attackers appear to be of military quality, but this by itself is not sufficient for us to draw an inference as to the attacker's origins or organizers. Cranial bombs, for example, are sometimes used to ensure that couriers with implanted data systems are not subjected to interrogation. Such devices have been used by terrorist organizations worldwide, also to prevent capture and interrogation. They have also been utilized by the covert operations teams of various multinational corporations, by Triads, by NAN groups, and by certain clans of Philippine and Japanese specializing in terror and assassination."

Colonel Satomi bows and says, "I would add that the simplest forms of cranial bombs can be implanted for a price within the reach of almost any individual. Perhaps less than one hundred thousand nuyen. However, I have arranged for these devices to be examined by an explosives expert. The specific mechanisms used will almost certainly provide clues as to the manufacturer of the devices. This may aid in identifying the origins of the attackers."

Honjowara-*sama's* grim expression turns dark with discontent. He looks to Adachi Dosan, chief of the Nagato Corp Directorate of Intelligence.

Adachi-*san* bows, and says, "It is apparent, Chairman-*san*, that the attacks on the GSG were planned and coordinated with considerable skill. Minor troublemakers such as exist throughout the New York megaplex would lack the resources to conduct these attacks. I would therefore speculate that we are facing a substantial threat. However, the motive for the attacks and their desired effects are troublesome issues. At this juncture, there can be no definitive answers to the questions we are all asking."

"You have some conjecture?" the Chairman demands.

Adachi-*san* bows, and says, "In theory, an attack on the Green Serpent Guard may be considered an attack against the Honjowara-*gumi,* or Nagato Corp, its Chairman, or the entire Nagato Combine. The Guard is one of our foremost symbols. Its members are recognized throughout the plex. They are generally considered to be not merely the guardians of the Chairman, but representatives of the Chairman and all he controls."

Honjowara-*sama* nods, seeming slightly less discontent, but by no means satisfied. "You say then that these attacks presage greater offensive actions directed against Nagato Combine and its Chairman?"

Adachi-*san* bows. "Indeed, Chairman-*san*. I strongly suspect that these attacks may be the first tentative steps in a campaign intended to embarrass the Honjowara-*gumi*, to make us seem weak. The Triad organization known as the Large Circle League has for many months been engaged in a campaign of harassment against our great ally, the Toki-*gumi*. We believe the League responsible for the beatings and kidnappings of a number of hospitality girls, the burning of the Bronx *pachinko* parlor, the abuse of patrons of several simsense theaters, and, most seriously, the unexpected sweeps of certain BTL labs by the Winter Systems police service."

The Chairman's features darken again. Machiko understands why. It is not the Triads or the difficulties of the Toki-*gumi*. This is old news. It is Adachi-*san's* mention of BTL. Better Than Life simsense chips are a thorn that strikes personally at the Chairman's ribs. The Honjowara-*gumi* maintains no BTL labs and does no traffic in the chips. Machiko has heard the Chairman declare more than once that the dreamchips turn people into useless slaves of direct brain stimulation. He has forbidden any member or employee of the Nagato Combine to make personal use of BTL. It is his expressed intention to one day persuade all the clans of Nagato Combine to forego any involvement in BTL trafficking or production.

"The Large Circle League," Adachi-*san* continues, "is thus succeeding in making the Toki-*gumi* appear weak to their Bronx competitors. Minor troublemakers have been encouraged to make bold moves. All the more so because the Toki-*gumi* is part of Nagato Combine and Nagato Combine has done nothing to support the Toki-*gumi*."

"Yoshida-*kai* offered to send support," says Ohana-*san*. "The offer was refused. Toki-*san* is determined to cure these problems himself."

Adachi-*san* bows. "This fact is unknown to the Large Circle League. It is unimportant. The leadership of the League knows the Toki-*gumi* appear weak. They know we have done nothing. They are encouraged. Perhaps they begin to suspect that we are also weak. Perhaps they anticipate that if the Toki-*gumi* are threatened with extinction then the other clans of Nagato will have no choice but to step in. Whatever the case, I am led inevitably to the suspicion, Chairman-*san*, that tonight the League has struck the first blow, with the sole intention of proving that they do not fear even our most redoubtable warriors."

Zoge-*san* politely coughs, and says, "How pale will the forces of the Toki-*gumi* appear once it is known that members of the Green Serpent Guard have been murdered in their own beds?"

Adachi-*san* bows. "Indeed. Precisely."

Machiko feels her cheeks begin to burn. She feels shame over what Zoge-*san* has so succinctly put into words. But even more than this, she feels appalled over her own great failure, that until this moment she had not imagined that tonight's attack on the GSG could be directly related to the troubles of the Toki-*gumi*. Now that Adachi-*san* has explained it, now that Zoge-*san* has summed it up, it all seems so simple, so obvious that only a fool could fail to see the truth. How could she be so great a fool? so blind? She has gazed upon the world with too narrow a spirit for too long. She has been a fool to ignore the greater issues affecting the future of Nagato Combine! Hour after hour she has spent in training with Sukayo-*san* and others of the Guard: sword training, weapons training, strength and endurance training. She should have been training her mind, inquiring into Sukayo-*san's* grasp of strategy and all that he knows of Nagato Combine's enemies.

Now it is too late for preparations. The crisis is upon her and the entire Nagato Combine. And she feels ill-prepared to face this new challenge.

Yet, somehow, she must meet it.

That is her duty.

Honjowara-*sama* gazes with a stern eye at Adachi-*san* for many moments, then broadens his gaze to include the entire gathering of leaders. "The Triads have long been our adversaries," he says in a voice almost hoarse with defiant anger. "The Large Circle League is a large and powerful organization, the dominate Triad faction in the megaplex. They are ruthless hoodlums, but their leaders are not to be underestimated. How should we respond to their growing menace?

How should Nagato Combine respond to support the Toki-
gumi? Do we make reprisals for these attacks on the Guard?
Do we go to war? What are your recommendations?"

Adachi-*san* bows, and says, "For the moment, Chairman-
san, I believe that we must gather information. Our top priority must be to confirm that the League is indeed behind
these attacks on the GSG. I propose to convey this need to
my intelligence operatives. Bessho-*san* should be availed of
every resource that will assist in gathering and evaluating
evidence from the scenes of tonight's attacks, particularly in
regard to the corpses of the attackers. Once we are assured of
our enemy's identity we will be able to plan how we may
gain the offensive."

Honjowara-*sama* moves his eyes slowly from one leader
to the next. With a nod, each signals agreement with Adachi-
san's recommendation. Honjowara-*sama* then gives his own
nod. "Very well," he says in a low tone. "Transmit hourly
reports to my aide. We will meet again in twelve hours' time
to review the situation. Until then, our forces will remain on
alert."

The meeting is at an end. Honjowara-*sama's* expression
seems full of ruthless determination. The leaders bow
deeply, showing great respect. They get to their feet and turn
to go.

"Machiko."

She looks to see Honjowara-*sama* briefly extend a hand
toward the cushion beside her feet. She bows and again
lowers herself to one knee. The leaders of the clan file out.

The door to the room slides shut.

The GSG of the body detail are silent and still, seeming
hardly to breathe. Machiko feels as though she shares the
space with the Chairman alone. It gives rise to a pang of
uncertainty. What does the Chairman want of her? Will he remind her of the shame she feels for her brothers of the Guard,
who allowed themselves to be murdered? Will he speak of
her personal shame, her failure to see what others have seen?
Will he command her to kill herself? This would be merciful.

Honjowara-*sama* claps his hands. A servant brings
tea, places the black lacquered tray at Honjowara-*sama's*
side, then fills Honjowara-*sama's* cup. As the servant
leaves, Honjowara-*sama* looks to the senior member of the
body detail, and says, "You and your other members may
withdraw."

The senior of the detail bows. "Please excuse me, Chairman-*sama,* but this is forbidden."

Honjowara-*sama* sternly says, "I am defended by Machiko-*san,* senior member of the Guard. Do not argue."

The senior of the detail bows. The eight withdraw. The door to the room slides closed. Honjowara-*sama* sips his tea. He extends a hand to the cushion located nearest his left and waits until Machiko has moved there, then says, "We have many enemies, Machiko. And there is much we do not know. The modern conflict is fought in small rooms by men and women with many questions and too few answers. We must seek to clarify the situation. Always, we must seek clarity."

Machiko bows. "Yes, Chairman-*sama.*"

Honjowara-*sama* sips again from his tea. "There are many who would say that the members of the Guard are like statues, that they show no emotion. Yet, I have spent many hours with Sukayo-*san* in kendo training. I live my life surrounded by the Guard. I am used to your stark white faces. I have learned to see beyond the impassive masks you maintain. Thus I know that you, Machiko, your spirit is large and full of turmoil. You know what it is to feel the conflict between duty and compassion, between that which must absolutely be done, and that which our finer emotions yearn to see made real."

Machiko bows. Honjowara-*sama's* words only confirm the depths of his insight. "I have often felt this conflict, Chairman-*sama.*"

"And tonight, *neh*? There is something on your mind. Something you have not said."

Machiko bows. "It is true, Chairman-*sama.*"

"Perhaps this involves matters you do not deem worthy of the attention of the leaders of the Nagato Combine."

Again, she bows. "This is so, Chairman-*sama.*"

Honjowara-*sama* gazes at her sternly, then says, "We must seek clarity, Machiko. Clarity as concerns our competition. Such clarity is born of knowledge, and such knowledge cannot be elicited from gods, or by analogy with the past, or by mere calculations. It must be obtained from those who know. When people talk, we must listen. Even the idle gossip of fools may be pertinent."

"It is perhaps a matter of gossip, Chairman-*sama.*"

Honjowara-*sama* gazes at her and waits.

It is embarrassing, the prospect of relating Gongoro's wild

speculations, especially in the wake of Adachi-*san's* explication of what must surely be the truth. She does not wish to seem a fool. Yet, even the talk of fools may have value, Honjowara-*sama* says. Perhaps a value she cannot discern. "I have heard it said, Chairman-*sama,* that Yoshida-*kai* is full of hatred for metahumans, that they regard the elves of the GSG as an affront to their honor. I have heard it said that Yoshida-*kai* are traitors and that they plot to destroy our clan."

"Who speaks thus?"

"An elf."

"A member of the Guard?"

"Yes."

"What do you believe?"

Machiko breathes, settles her spirit. She says, "I believe that the Yoshida-*kai* are our allies, and that the Triads, the Large Circle League in particular, have long been a most dangerous enemy. I believe that Adachi-*san* is correct in his evaluation."

"Should we make war on the League?"

Machiko bows. "I will make war on any enemy that the Chairman should select."

Honjowara-*sama* pauses to take another sip of tea. Machiko feels his unrelenting gaze even though she averts her eyes, looking to the corners of the room, watching for enemies who do not show themselves. "You have heard the leaders of Nagato Combine," Honjowara-*sama* says. "They have long experience dealing with uncertain circumstances such as we now face. But you, Machiko, you are the warrior among us. What do your warrior instincts tell you now? What course of action do you recommend?"

Machiko considers this at length. She feels certain that Chairman will be as much judging the quality of her intellect, her insight, as any course of action she may suggest. She does not want to misplace her step. She has felt such shame already this night, she would rather die than fail to meet the Chairman's expectations, what must surely be expected of the senior member of the GSG.

Deeply, she breathes. She says, "I recall the words of the ancient masters, Chairman-*sama.*"

"Explain."

Machiko bows. "The Chairman has said that we face many enemies. The ancient masters have written that, in such cases, the warrior must draw both sword and companion sword and assume a wide-stretched attitude. The warrior should sweep the eyes around broadly and attack. To wait is bad. Cut to the left and to the right. Drive the enemy together, and when they are piled up like fish on a string, cut them down without giving them room to move."

The Chairman seems to spend several moments considering this. "And how may this strategy be applied?"

"Chairman-*sama*," Machiko says. She bows deeply. "Draw the companion sword. While Nagato Combine's regular forces utilize routine channels of investigation, allow the GSG to utilize other resources."

"You propose to investigate?"

"To seek the truth, Chairman-*sama*. The truth of our enemy's sword."

"Do you propose to make use of gangster tactics?"

Machiko breathes. She breathes twice deeply, and determines to hurl herself upon the sword of the Chairman's question as though she were already dead. "Chairman-*sama*," she says. "I propose that we are already at war. Our enemy makes war on us. We must find and defeat this enemy or face destruction."

"You speak as a warrior."

"I do."

The Chairman gazes at her with an expression like adamantine steel: hard and wholly unyielding.

It is many long moments before he gives his reply.

10

The interior of the building is like a maze, and it's dark. Neona's mirrored Porsche shades turn the black of night into twilight, but that's all. There's no lights, no jazz in the sockets. She finds a bank of public telecoms on one dusty, graffiti-layered wall, but the vidscreens are dead and the datajacks are red and brown with corrosion.

She nearly shrieks when she sees a cockroach almost half the size of her foot crawling onto her sneak. But instead she merely jumps half a meter into the air, trips, falls, then goes scrambling, gasping, fighting the fear, back the way she came.

She's safe here. Safe as it gets. The corridors are strewn with every kind of litter and devil rats rustle everywhere—*but there's no people!* No cutters, no freaks. No jackboys or razorpunks to give her a hassle. No slags trying to shag her and no trogs wanting to tweak her condition a little nearer slab city.

She finds a stairway of steel rising to an elevated gangway. The rusted steel creaks and sings with every step, but the gangway holds. Both sides of the gangway are lined by narrow doors like locker doors, and abruptly she realizes where she is: a coffin hotel. Abandoned, derelict. Left for dead in the devastated wastes of the Zone. The Slag Heap. Somewhere in Long Island's County of Suffolk. It's buff perfect. Absolutely jewel. She pushes and kicks at doors till one slides open. The space beyond is a black pit, probably big enough to lie in and not a millimeter more, but that's all she needs. Exactly what she needs. She pulls the rickety metal door shut to keep the bugs out and feels her way around. There's a small tridscreen, a thin mattress, a couple of blankets, all the comforts of home and all she'd dare ask.

She sits, pulls the blankets up over her knees, and leans back into a corner. She's hungry, but she'll survive. Once she gets to the city she'll figure a way to sleaze some nuyen. The gray nylon carrypack she holds clenched to her stomach contains a macroplast-shielded Fairlight invader, and with tech like that she's sure to find work slurping data or busting code red or some fragging thing. She just needs some sleep. A minute to breathe. Stumbling through the Zone half-crazy with terror and buzzing on adrenaline wears a body out. She feels like she's been running for days. Probably running around in circles. Give her the trons of the local telecommunications grid and she'll find her way home in a flash, like the 'Lectron Angel she is, but throw her meat body into the Zone and she'll freak. She ain't meant for this kinda squat.

She closes her eyes and suddenly she's in a dream, the nightmare that's been looping through her head ever since she met this slag called Gamma. As real as simsense and as chilling as roaches climbing her spine. Someone's got her tied down on a bed of cables writhing like snakes and he's prying open her skull. Microtonic tools clack and clatter and whiz and the air smells of solder and burning skin and she feels the truth turning her stomach and churning through her bowels. He's putting a deck in her head—*a cranial cyber-deck!* Now it opens a plate in her skull every time she needs an upgrade, new memory, more processing power. Now it's risking frying her brain every time she test-drives a new component. No way, *no fragging way!*

She wakes up shrieking.

And abruptly cuts it short.

The gangway outside is rattling. The door to her little cranny crashes open and there bathed in a pale shade of moonlight is one of Gamma's cutters, a big mother-reaming razorpunk like out of a combat biker trid. Neona squeezes back into her corner and looks frantically around, but there's only one way out. She searches the dark, her mind, her pockets for any kind of a weapon, but she already knows she's got nothing.

"Kept me up all effing night," says the cutter. "Let's go, jackhead."

"Don't . . . don't hurt me," Neona whimpers.

"Move it, slitch!"

She's shaking so hard she can't hardly stand up. The cutter reaches through the doorway and catches the back of her neck and jerks her ahead, through the doorway and onto the gangway. She stumbles and gasps and snivels so loud it echoes, and then turns and rams the hard macroplast corner of the Invader's casing into the cutter's groin. Terror makes her strong and quick.

The cutter shouts in pain, and he roars *"Fraggin BIFF!"* but her feet are slapping the gangway to match the pace of her hammering heart and she's down the stairs to ground level before she has time to think about breathing.

She hears other shouts, rattling equipment, pounding boots. Which way? Which *way out*? She runs and runs, tearing down passageways, scrambling around corners, banging through doors, tripping and sprawling over mountains of litter and junk. Moonlight glares into her eyes. She scrambles through a jagged hole in a concrete wall and then tumbles down a pile of debris.

When she wakes, she's lying on her back. Her breath is rasping and her nose feels broken. She can't move. Her head's pounding like it's under a fifty-ton pile driver. The crescent moon fills her eyes, burning like a white phosphorus incendiary charge. She can't see the hands holding her wrists and ankles, but through the burning glare of the moon she can just make out the slim figure towering over her, leaning on his mage's wand like a cane.

"Why did you run?" Gamma asks.

She struggles, tries to break free, tries twisting her head around to catch sight of her Fairlight Invader, but it's no use. The hands are too strong, the moon too bright. Already, she can feel Gamma's fingers walking up her spine like a thousand little roaches, forming into a glove, a glove that gives a little tug and makes her straighten her head, a glove that squeezes down slowly, slowly, slowly, till she's sure her skull's going to split under pressure, and the pressure builds and builds, till it's too much, too much to withstand.

"Angel, why did you run?" Gamma asks.

She nearly blacks out. It's hard to think. Hard to remember. The pressure eases a little, but it hurts. Oh, frag, *it hurts*! She'd do anything to stop that hurting. Anything at all.

"We have an agreement."

She's grunting, trying to answer, to nod.

"Haven't I treated you well?"

"Sorry . . ." She snivels. "I'm sorry . . ."

"After everything I've done for you."

The pressure eases. She's panting, gasping, breathing. She remembers, too. Everything he's done. When she was bone busted and broke, Gamma took her off the hard-core streets of the Bronx, gave her Matrix work. He gave her space in his doss. He's lining her pockets with fifty nuyen an hour. Why did she run from him? Is she crazy? Brain-fried? She's had it worse, a lot worse. Shick, Gamma's treated her jewel.

"You're an ungrateful little wretch."

It's true, but so hard to admit. "Always been . . ."

The glare of the moon subsides. She catches sight of Gamma's head, the buzzcut hair, the impassive Asian features. He smiles softly, faintly, but she can see the subtle sadness in his eyes, the hurt from her betrayal. "I understand," he says in a voice grown tender. "You've had a great deal of hardship. Hard luck. You're so used to running, slot and run, isn't that right? You're afraid to stop running even when you're safe. You're always afraid Mr. Johnson might be just a step behind you."

The mere mention gives her a shiver of nerves. She steals a quick glance around with her eyes. It's been a couple of years already, but she's still running from that job in Miami. How could she have forgotten that? Her Mr. Johnson turned out to be dirty. The Miami job was a setup. She got some wiz tech out of the deal, but her chummers all got dusted. She barely escaped with her life. She made it through Philly, Baltimore, New York City. Now here she is on Long Island, the Zone. Hiding with Gamma. Hiding in the Zone. Her and Gamma and his cutters.

What was she thinking? She's got jack for brains. Run from Gamma? Is she blasted? totally scrambled? Gamma's the only chance she's got. Gamma said so and it's true.

"Sorry," she blurts. "I'm sorry."

"Let's go back to the doss, all right?"

She chokes back a sob. "Jewel."

The cutters help her up. She's a little unsteady. She feels like she's got bruises all over her body and a trickle of blood slips out of her nose. One of the cutters hands her the Fairlight Invader, a little dusty but no worse for wear. Gamma cradles the back of her head and gently presses a kerchief to her nostrils till the trickling blood comes to an end.

"I really care for you a great deal," he says softly.

Neona closes her eyes, and whispers, "I know."

The Leyland-Rover van waits in the street, just on the other side of a pile of rubble. Neona moves through the sliding side door to one of the bench seats behind the bucket up front. Gamma sits beside her, slips an arm around her shoulders. It's a comforting feeling. Reassuring. She's going home, and she's exhausted. All she wants is sleep. One of the cutters takes the wheel. The others take the bench in the rear and the van starts humming, moving out.

It's a long slow ride. Around piles of debris cast down by crumbling buildings. Through streets full of burned-out hulks and stripped-down junk. Past forests of withered lifeless trees and oceans of gnarled twisting vines. Ponds and puddles with a stench so strong it burns the eyes. Whirling dust demons. The cutter at the wheel sends them banging through ruts and potholes and bouncing over sprawling debris, but he does not turn on the headlights. The fog curls and flows everywhere. Never shine headlights into the fog, not this fog. It attracts bad things.

A low brick wall appears on the left. It supports a sign. An old black sign with faded white lettering. Neona's seen it in daylight and knows how it reads: "King P Psy Ctr." She doesn't know what that means. She knows that the buildings lying just beyond, on both sides of the rutted road, look ancient, medieval, big brick castles with bars on the windows and metal gratings over the doors. Maybe a hundred years ago, this was some kind of psychic research center, or maybe a gov lab. It looks like the kind of place where a person could scream and scream and never be heard. A place where razorguys in black synthleather burn holes into people's brains with burning metal brands.

It gives her shivers.

But it's safe. It's home.

They pull around to the rear of a building and park. One of the cutters tugs open a heavy metal door and Neona precedes them all inside, down a flight of stairs to a broad open space: the "commons," they call it. Mostly it's just doss space for the cutters Gamma keeps around: cots, a table for eating, and other accommodations. Neona's telecom and couch are right in the middle of things.

As she enters, Neona spots the only other girl she's seen with the group. Her name is Poppy and she's kind of a cutter, with cybereyes and hand razors. She's also Gamma's girlfriend. Now, though, she's lying on a cot on her back like she's unconscious and her face is a purplish mass of bruises.

"What happened to Poppy?"

"She took a fall," Gamma says. "But don't worry. She'll be more careful in the future."

That's reassuring.

11

The AC Plutocrat spends a brief eternity settling onto the aeropad. Gordon Ito is up and standing by the side hatchway door before the rotorcraft actually touches the pad. A small crowd of people rush to arrange themselves around him. An anxious-looking female steward stands between him and the door.

"Do it," Gordon says, finally.

The chopper's rotors are still pounding the air outside, thumping rapidly, but the steward turns and shoves at the door. One of Gordon's exec protection specialists adds a quick thrust and the door jerks open, admitting a cyclone blast of wind.

Gordon thrusts his hands deep into the pockets of his platinum-hued trench and moves briskly down the steps to the aeropad. People run to move out ahead of him: the chief of his personal security detail, two physical adept protect specs, his confidential assistant. The latter all but shouting into a wristfone to be heard above the gale of wind.

The aeropad sits atop Tower Five of Fuchi Industrial Electronics' monolithic shrine to economic tyranny, soaring two hundred and fifty stories above the Manhattan streets. The wind always rages up here. Gordon knows that better than most. It howls and rushes chill and ruthless over his cheeks. He feels its bite as a matter of routine.

Double transparex doors slide open before him and he strides into the aeropad transit lounge. White-gloved Fuchi hostesses bow and intone the usual insipid greetings. The rhythmic thumping of the Plutocrat's rotors resounds against the lounge's floor-to-ceiling windows, pursuing him as far as the elevator.

By the elevator waits Bucky Freese with an urgent expression and a mouthful of potentially disastrous remarks. Gordon cuts him off with a two-word snarl.

"Not now."

Idiot.

Freese is a freak with a head full of wire, a talent for decking and damn little else. The checked sports jacket he wears over his Stuffer Shack tee and striped cargo jeans provides the only hint that he belongs to one of the most powerful megacorps on the face of the planet. A uniformed security guard starts dressing him down for not displaying his Fuchi badge prominently.

Gordon snaps his fingers, gestures. The guard desists. Freese joins the small crowd on the elevator.

"Uh . . . Mr. Ito?"

Gordon's confidential assistant does the honors, turning to Freese, glaring at him, then saying, simply, "Shut up."

Freese blinks widened eyes, but shuts up.

The elevator doors slip closed. The elevator hums, descending, descending briefly, and slows to a halt. The doors slip open. The uniformed guards posted to the hallway outside straighten their posture as Gordon and his small crowd move out. At the end of the hallway, Gordon turns right and he and the crowd enter his personal preserve.

As he steps through the door to his office suite, his platinum blonde senior exec sec and the protect spec who watches over her are both on their feet.

"Get Donelson," Gordon says.

No one wastes words. The exec sec turns to her telecom. The techs with the security detail start sweeping for invasive electronics. The security mage goes into astral overwatch mode. Gordon snaps his fingers and his confidential assistant provides a Platinum Select cigarette and a flame.

"Mr. Xiao called," his exec sec informs. "I'm to tell you he called for you in Boston—"

Gordon cuts that off with a sharp gesture. He already knows about the call. Just another move in a game that has yet to fully unfold. Gordon had been in Boston early this morning, well over eighteen hours ago, handling a special matter for Xiao, a matter that only makes him wonder why the head of the Fuchi Special Administration had wanted his chief of operations away from the office. Whatever it is, it's sure to be different. Something so far unmentioned, of course. Something Xiao does not want Gordon to know about. At worst, it bears a direct relationship to the reason for Gordon's hasty return to the towers, and that would be very very bad.

Donelson, Gordon's deputy, comes through the door from the east side of the office suite. "I want status on Chrome Horse. Fifteen minutes."

"No problem."

Chrome Horse is a special op against Xiao. A fact-finding op. It pays to keep informed.

Donelson goes out. The chief tech with the security detail steps up. He shows his open palm. Lying on his palm is something about the size of a fleck of dandruff.

"Looks like another IntSec model, sir. They seeded the carpet. We'll be clean in a few moments."

Fuchi Internal Security. They never quit. Gordon's got the tech to neutralize the really sophisticated techniques applied against his office suite, so IntSec keeps trying this primitive shit. Seeding his carpet. They managed to get a bug into his exec sec's clothes a few weeks ago. Gordon's got an op running in response to that, too. Payback is a bloody slitch and he'll see that they pay in quad. IntSec's problem is that they're jealous of his budget, his overt budget, those portions they've managed to find out about. What worries him now is the budget that no one knows about, the shadow budget, for the ops that no one approves, because, regardless of how things go, no one really wants to know.

He takes a drag on his Platinum Select and starts snapping his fingers. The techs rush it. The senior tech sweeps Bucky Freese and Gordon as well, and says, "All clear, sir."

"No calls."

"Understood, sir," replied his senior exec sec.

Another sec has a cup of his brand of Brazilian coffee steaming inside his private office. He motions the sec and the techs and bodyguards out, then motions Bucky Freese inside.

Behind his gleaming onyx desk, the doors sealed, security tech on, Gordon turns in his high-backed synthleather chair to face the broad unpaned window overlooking the Hudson. He sips his coffee and draws on his cigarette. He considers Freese, shifting nervously in front of the desk, never really at ease without a datajack in his head. The key to the man is tech. Computer tech. Hardware or soft, it's all one big toy. The more powerful the toy, the greater his interest. Give him a specialist group with access to some of the most powerful toys in existence and he'll only want more of the same. Give him the freedom to play with his toys and he'll swear his undying loyalty.

"What went wrong?"

Freese coughs, clears his throat. He sounds nervous, saying, "We got sleazed."

"How bad?"

"It was like . . . somebody knew we'd be there. They popped in and blew us away, sucked out all the guano before we got more than a dime."

"How is that possible?"

The silence from the front of the desk gives Gordon warning. He turns in his chair to face Freese and finds the man fidgeting, rubbing at his brow, his nose, his chin. He doesn't seem to have any answers and that's bad because Freese is supposed to have all the answers. In his relatively short tenure with Cyberspace Development Corp, a Fuchi subsidiary, he engineered some major advances for the code in persona chips. He is a brain and now he is Gordon's brain. One of his jobs is to play a little game. He skates into Fuchi financial datastores and moves numbers around. Sometimes he fiddles with interbank accounts. He likes to think of himself as a kind of watchdog. Every time he succeeds in transferring funds from one part of Fuchi, say, the Pan-Europa division, to Gordon's finger accounts, he comes and tells Gordon just how he did it, so that Gordon can order improvements in security.

What Freese is saying now is that someone beat him to it. Gordon doesn't like that. "I asked you a question."

Freese rubs at his jaw. "I never seen anything like it."

"You're the expert. Explain it."

Freese stands almost motionless for going on thirty seconds, staring at the front right corner of Gordon's desk, then rummages through his pockets and pulls out a chip-carrier. "I could show you," he says. "I got it all . . ."

Before he can say anything further, Gordon points at the desktop. Freese puts the carrier down. Gordon reaches over and picks it up. A record of the run that went wrong? Evidence that might conceivably be used to crucify the entire Special Administration? Evidence that will shortly be eradicated beyond any chance of recovery. "This is a record of the run?"

"Yeah. Just the main bits."

"You have records stored elsewhere?"

"Uh, no." Freese shakes his head. "I figured I better be careful. Guano like this could cause trouble."

Faintly, Gordon nods. "Good thinking."

Freese smiles nervously.

Gordon taps an optical key in the touch-sensitive top of his desk and an entire workstation console winks on. A display equipped with multiple displays and a full suite of dataports rises out of the desktop. Gordon taps a few more optical keys and slides the chip from Freese into a port near the display's base. Another tap and the record file from Freese's chip begins executing.

The first scene to appear is direct from the Fuchi private telecommunications grid—the floor of a narrow cavern formed by the cool jet cliffs of a pair of colossal datastores, soaring up infinitely tall into the black electron night. Between the two massive datastores burns the cobalt blue beam of a datastream, looking as hot as the interior of a nuclear furnace.

"ID the stream," Gordon says.

Freese replies, "Funds transactions between Fuchi Union Trust and Fuchi World Bank. An average of ten thousand transactions a second. And they're both on the Fuchi private grid."

Simplifying the task of an intercept.

On Gordon's display, five iconic figures now materialize beside the blazing data stream, Freese and his team of deckers. The sheer volume of the beam make the decker's icons seem puny and frail. Their iconic forms resemble construction workers: hard hats crowned by flashing blue strobes, blue-striped vests. All synchronized to match the blue of the datastream. They set out two lines of glowing blue traffic cones, and, between the two lines of cones, begin construction of a temporary node, a dataline junction that will vanish without a trace once the job is complete.

It's a tactic they've used before. Gordon takes a drag from his Platinum Select and watches the milliseconds tick by on the counter at the top of his display screen. So far nothing unusual.

Just down the datastream hovers a violet globe sizzling with red veins like the markings on a soccer ball. Probably Killer IC of sufficient strength to induce lethal feedback and fry the brain of any decker it attacks. Not a problem for

Freese and his team unless they frag their Fuchi access codes
or set off a system alert.

Freese and his team open neon blue toolboxes. From
the boxes they take jet black panels. They fit the panels together to form a large black box surrounding a section of the
datastream. The box has two circular ports, allowing the
datastream to pass untouched through the center of the box.

Then they step through the walls of the box.

And into a sculptured node.

Freese and his deckers move into position on the verge of
a vast virtual highway a thousand lanes wide and stretching
off to infinity in both directions. Iconic sedans fill every
lane, streaming along at a speed almost beyond comprehension. As each sedan approaches it flashes its value in nuyen.
Freese and his deckers, now resembling police, pick out various sedans with jabbing fingers and wave them down a
newly constructed exit ramp.

Briefly, the exit ramp winks, *Dataline To Secret Caribbean League Accounts*. A counter in the exit ramp's pavement keeps a running tally: ten thousand nuyen, fifty
thousand, a hundred and climbing. Freese's team is selec-
tive. The sedans they finger never total more than five digits
in nuyen, never less than four. Nothing large enough to instigate an immediate alert, and that's all that matters.

Someone somewhere will have to explain what happened
to the missing funds, probably within a matter of hours. Not
Gordon's problem. His problem is the Special Administration and Fuchi Americas' ruthless competition. If a VP in
some banking subsidiary has to be sacrificed to the cause,
it's a necessary expense. An investment to secure the future.

"This is where it happened," Freese says.

The greenish haze infiltrates the scene. A whirling five-
pointed star like the Matrix icon for the entire Fuchi private
grid appears in the electron night just above Freese's iconic
head. An oval portal rimmed in sizzling electric green rises
out of the pavement of the exit ramp. Iconic sedans sent
down the ramp pass through the sizzling oval and vanish into
the black interior of the portal.

Before Freese or his team can react, twenty million nuyen
are gone.

"What's happening?" Freese shouts.

Three of his deckers continue waving sedans down the
ramp. They move like zombies, badly configured semi-

autonomous knowbots, stilted, jerky, puppets on strings. Another ten million vanishes into the portal. Then Freese looks up.

"Slag that fragger!" Freese shouts.

One of his deckers draws a shimmering neon sidearm and opens fire on the whirling star above Freese's head. The bullets wink *Sparky IC.* The star spins into a blur. The bullets abruptly reverse direction and separate into a stream of whirling fragments. The decker screams. As the bullet fragments strike, his iconic body is immersed in a storm of sparking discharges like lightning flashes.

Then he winks out.

"Bucky, he's dead!" another decker shouts. *"Jim's dead!"*

"This is impossible!" Freese shrieks.

Three of the deckers direct an unbroken stream of sedans down the exit ramp and into the portal. Freese yanks an item from his police-style equipment belt. *Trace and Burn!* it winks. He fires a liquid stream at the whirling star and then suddenly he's screaming too and it's all going completely to shit.

Freese slams through the walls of his temporary node and then Gordon's display screen goes blank.

Gordon looks across his desk at Freese.

"What the fuck happened?"

Freese's face is gleaming with sweat. He looks considerably worse than a deckhead who's suffering from dump shock. He looks scared. "I'm not sure what happened."

This is not an answer that Gordon likes. If someone offered to fling Freese out the nearest available window, Gordon would feel tempted. But that's purely an emotional response. He lights a fresh Platinum Select. "What's your theory?"

"It's still evolving."

Gordon leans back in his chair. He sips his coffee. "You tried to trace utility. You got dumped."

Freese nods.

"Your opposition used the Fuchi star for an icon. Internal Security?"

Freese shakes his head. "There's no . . . there's no record of IntSec being involved. I checked."

"Three of your deckers appeared to lose control of their icons."

"We're not clear on exactly what happened with that."

Gordon nods. "I'll tell you what happened. Somebody's got program code and talent as good as our best. What does that suggest?"

Freese spends a while working that over, looking more anxious than before. "I'm not sure," he says finally. "I've been thinking about it. I don't think the hostile used program code that slipped out the back door. Nothing this hot ever slipped out."

"Then what?"

"Something new," Freese says. "The hostile scammed us. My temporary node turned green just before the attack. I think that was a deliberate effect. That's where the attack really started. I think what the hostile did was create a mirage. He superimposed his own code over the temporary node I constructed. A node within a node. Then, when I moved against him, I became in effect a decker intruding on a hostile node. He redirected my trace, and the redirect inserted tapeworm IC into the trace code. And the worm rode my signal right into my workstation CPU. I had to crash my workstation or the worm would've scrambled every pulse of hard memory I had."

"Which tells us what?"

Freese hesitates. "The slag's hot. His code is hot. His system, deck, whatever, is liquid fire. Hoi, I'm not even sure if what I just said is possible."

"Did he come in through the Matrix?"

"I got my team working on that. We're searching the archives for any indications. But if he sleazed the SANs like he scammed us I doubt we'll find anything."

Gordon doubts it, too. Doubts that someone with the talent to breach the Fuchi private telecommunications grid would stumble over the telltales that would record the intrusion. Not if that person had help. Not if, like Freese, that person was up to date on the latest access codes and security protocols. The hostile might have jacked in through the Matrix or even a Fuchi mainframe—no way to know just yet—but it's almost a certainty that whoever scammed Freese had help from the inside. That's how it works.

There's no denying that the walls of the Fuchi grid are tallest where they meet the Matrix, but it's also a fact that Fuchi mainframes maintain defenses in depth. It's just as easy to get burned by Red-12 security somewhere on the inside as at the outer walls. And getting out alive is no less a feat than getting in. The rare few who've managed it, in so far as Gordon is aware, all had help from the inside.

"Who knew you were making the intercept?"

"Just my team."

And maybe a spouse or live-in, or a friend or friends of friends. But never mind that for now. Gordon can see he's got plenty of work ahead without carrying out every calculation to the final decimal point. Obviously, he's going to have to launch a special op merely to find out precisely who had advance knowledge of the intercept and how that knowledge was used. Obviously, whoever sleazed Freese is a threat and that threat must be terminated. Gordon must also decide whether or not to roll up the special operations group under Freese's control before it becomes an embarrassment of cataclysmic proportions.

Deckheads are no less expendable than banking VPs. It's really just a question of whether or not the expenditure is warranted. Fortunately, Freese and his group work off-premises, under the auspices of a Fuchi subsidiary, so Gordon at least has the option of making some plausible denial of responsibility.

"I want you scanning for any indication that the intercept was noticed and traced back to us."

Freese nods. "Okay. Sure."

"Start now."

Freese takes the hint and departs.

12

The building lies on the far side of New York City, beyond the Hudson River, in part of Newark's Sector 6 known as Little Asia. As buildings go it is rather small and unassuming, four stories tall, made of brick, small windows of reinforced transparex, and more than a century old. It is easy to miss, situated between the bright, colorful facades of the Willow Club and the Holy Savior Buddhist Temple, overshadowed by the brilliant neon and sizzling laser displays lighting the rest of the street, turning night into day and directing the eye to the many restaurants and bars and nightclubs and *pachinko* parlors and small casinos and stores and other businesses pervading the district.

This one small, unassuming brick building might be considered wholly unremarkable, unworthy of notice, except for the transparex panes of the revolving door leading into the ground-floor lobby, each marked with the mon of the Honjowara-*gumi*.

It has been the traditional headquarters of the Honjowara-*gumi* for more than four decades, located on Bergen Street.

Machiko arrives at four a.m. when a Hughes Stallion security chopper of the Nagato Security Defense Force alights briefly on the roof. Mere hours have passed since the attacks on the GSG, and Machiko has had no rest. Nagato forces remain on alert. The threat that faces them remains a mystery. New attacks could conceivably arise from any quarter. Despite this, in just a few hours' time, Chairman Honjowara will travel here to the Bergen Street headquarters, to the very heart of the Newark plex, to conduct his monthly "Open House."

The very idea of exposing the Chairman to any unnecessary risks seems like madness, given the situation. Yet Machiko is sworn to obey as well as defend, and the Chairman will not be dissuaded.

"He who enters with a gun in hand reveals his fear," Honjowara-*sama* told her. "Remember this as you review the security preparations. Remember that our enemies will be watching."

Already, forces are in motion, preparations begun. Machiko finds that Major Hakatoro's number two, Captain Oseki, a very reliable and experienced officer of the Security Defense Force, has activated a command center on the second floor of the headquarters' building. Oseki has ordered barricades into place, blocking all vehicular traffic from the street running past the front of the headquarters and from the alleyway located to the rear. No pedestrians may pass the barricades without first proving their identity and submitting to weapons checks. Technical teams are sweeping the block for anything resembling weapons or explosives. Special observation teams that include GSG snipers are even now taking up positions on selected rooftops along the block. Security choppers patrol the sky, alert for any unusual activity both from air traffic and on the ground.

Machiko puts on a headset tuned to the SDF frequencies and takes a brief tour of the block. She finds it difficult to keep a settled spirit, for everywhere she looks she sees a potential avenue of attack: from the surrounding streets, the alleyways, the rooftops. The presence of an advance squad of GSG, standing watch at the barricades, reassures her only a little. No more than the small teams of SDF performing weapons and security checks. She would like the entire block fortified on a scale equal to that of the Chairman's mansion. But that is not possible. The Chairman forbids it, for it is a matter of image and prestige.

The event of the day soon to dawn will be an event of the Honjowara-*gumi*. Nagato forces must therefore step aside. The SDF must maintain only the most minimal presence. Even the GSG must take care not to overshadow the clan's own force of irregulars, for it is the clan's own people who must be seen as having the dominant responsibility for security.

A company of hand-picked *kobun*, all in the signature red and black suit jackets of the clan, suit jackets rather than body armor, all trained in the use of weapons, primarily handguns, line the barricades at both ends of the block. Many are experienced fighters, but they lack the training and discipline of the SDF, and could hardly be considered warriors on the scale of the average member of the Guard.

Still, Machiko takes the time to meet and confer with each of the handful of *wakashu,* or young headmen, responsible for supervising the *kobun.* These headmen are important persons within the districts their particular factions control. They must be shown respect and the acting senior of the GSG must be seen showing them respect.

At four-thirty a.m., a female officer with the rank of deputy chief arrives from Omni Police Services, the corporation currently responsible for law enforcement within the Newark city limits. The deputy chief informs that OPS will be posting additional patrols to the district, and has several emergency teams on standby near the headquarters building. The deputy chief is of course quite content to allow the Honjowara-*gumi* to run its own show. Relations between Nagato Combine, the Honjowara-*gumi* in particular, and OPS may be characterized as generally excellent. That is due to the fact that Nagato Corporation owns a significant bloc of ownership shares in Sapporo Corp, which owns OPS. It is also a fact that the chairman of Sapporo is a distant cousin of Chairman Honjowara and their relations are usually cordial.

At four forty-five a.m., a council of district executives arrives, along with their headmen, coming from districts across the entire megaplex. They and the *kobun* who will soon meet them here on the streets of Little Asia will assist the local headmen in ensuring that peace and order are maintained throughout the entire hood.

Zoge-*san,* the Chairman's counselor and lifelong friend, is on hand to speak with the district executives and their headmen personally. He reminds them that the day of the Chairman's Open House has become a local festival, the festival of the lotus and reed, symbols of the clan. No unseemly incidents can be permitted. Suspicious persons spotted in the district should be detained for questioning. Rowdies and drunks should be apprehended and handed over to the OPS police. The *kobun* may utilize any degree of force necessary to see that the rules are obeyed, but always they must be discreet. On this day of all days, even the oldest of grandparents and the youngest of children must be able to walk the streets without fear of incident.

Of course, the *kobun* should follow all the usual guidelines for patrol of any clan district.

"The majority of our people live within a few blocks of their employment," Zoge-*san* says in a quiet, clear voice. "They do not drive, they walk. If you see people are having difficulty crossing the street, command traffic to halt. If a man drops litter on the sidewalk, call his attention to what he has done and why it is wrong. In all cases, you will be seen as the personal representative of the Chairman, his strong hand, intervening in the ordinary affairs of ordinary persons, like the father who correctly takes a keen interest in the lives of his children. Thus the people will be assured that their father watches over them and guards them. Thus you will earn the people's respect. And thus you will ensure that our clan continues to enjoy the support of the very people we must serve if we are to survive and prosper."

The senior district executive leads the entire group in a robust pledge of loyalty, then several loud and enthusiastic cheers, then gives the headmen their various assignments.

At five a.m., the street vendors begin arriving. They come with carts and portable stalls and an immense variety of wares, many with shirts and hats and other items bearing the mon of the Honjowara-*gumi*. All must prove their identities. All must be checked for weapons. Machiko tours the entire block for a second time, searching for any means by which she might fine-tune the defenses. She hears over her headset the GSG snipers reporting in, all clear. She is barely back to headquarters when she is approached by a district executive, a nervous man from a faction located in Trenton.

"Machiko-*sama*," he says, abruptly bowing. "Please. A matter for your attention."

Machiko opens her mouth to ask what has occurred, then merely follows the man as he turns and leads her to the alleyway at the rear of the headquarters building. Here, she finds two ork males in brown synthleather being restrained by a group of some eleven *kobun*. The headman of the group bows, and says, "These two were told to stay away from this alley. They kept hanging around and finally they attacked two of my men."

At a word from Machiko, the orks are stripped of their possessions, all but their clothes. Machiko examines these items one by one, but sees only a handgun, a few knives, credsticks, other paraphernalia common to lowly criminals. Nothing to suggest the assassin. The orks' jackets and various signs and symbols tattooed onto their hides identify them as members of a gang common to lower Manhattan, the Axemen gang. Street bangers. Such individuals carry weapons as a matter of routine. They probably wandered into the district with nothing more in mind than simple larceny.

But is this truly all the orks had in mind? How can Machiko be sure? She must make sure and she has little time. She could ask questions, but the orks would surely lie if they have sinister intentions. A formal interrogation is out of the question. The Chairman's motorcade is already en route. It will be arriving within the hour. If she is to order the motorcade to turn back, she must have some definite reason.

"You are on the wrong side of the Hudson," Machiko tells them. "Perhaps you are lost. Because you are strangers here, you will be shown leniency. You will not be punished. However, your property is forfeited to the men you attacked."

One ork snarls at her. "Frag that!"

The headman of *kobun* lashes out. The ork's head snaps backward, bleeding from both nose and mouth. He goes on snarling despite the blood, despite the obvious pain of his injuries. His snarls rise into vicious shouts of menace when Machiko orders the pair stripped of their Axemen jackets, and the bloody ork struggles, struggles like a rabid animal.

Machiko examines the jackets. All that she sees and hears amounts to nothing more or less than what she would expect of bangers, ork street bangers with bad tempers and no manners. Gutterpunks. Not a significant threat.

"This district is controlled by the Honjowara-*gumi* of Nagato Combine," Machiko tells the orks. "We have rules and we insist that these rules be obeyed. Gangers are not allowed in this district. Today, you will be escorted away. Do not return. If you return, you will be killed."

The bloodied ork sneers at her, then spits.

Her thoughts appear confirmed.

However, a display of such disrespect as spitting implies is intolerable. Thirteen pairs of eyes widen with shock and outrage, and the *kobun* react without waiting for instructions. Six of them drive the offending ork to the ground and begin administering a vicious beating. The other ork merely watches and so he is not punished. He watches Machiko as she uses her commlink to contact OPS. Machiko makes certain that he sees her doing this.

Within thirty seconds, an OPS cruiser comes roaring up

the alley. The heavily armed and armored officers from the cruiser immediately ask how they may help.

Machiko says, "These persons are trespassing. You will please arrest them."

The orks are placed in handcuffs and driven away.

Justice comes in many forms. In Manhattan, the NYPD, Inc. shares the responsibility for justice with various other organizations. Here, in the district centered around Bergen Street, the Honjowara-*gumi* of Nagato Combine shares the responsibility, just as ultimately all people share the responsibility. The justice of the clan is fair and swift and, above all, founded upon respect. All people and all property must be shown respect. That is the basis of civilized society. Those who have no respect for anything but their own selfish desires, for criminality and mayhem, are dealt with accordingly. Barbarians are brutalized. The Way of such persons demands it. A brutal punishment such as a beating is the barbarian's own unique path to the Buddha nature, and, hence, to true enlightenment.

On any other day, Machiko might have taken some small satisfaction in helping another along the path to enlightenment.

Today, it is an unwelcome distraction.

13

At five minutes before six a.m., the first grayish hints of the coming dawn streak the night sky and the headlights of the cars leading the Chairman's motorcade turn down the alleyway that runs behind the headquarters building.

The entire length of the alleyway is lit by floodlights and lined by *kobun*. Every window that might provide an assassin with a line of sight to the rear of the headquarters building is under observation by a GSG sniper. Every roof and every side alley is being watched by Nagato SDF personnel. Machiko and the balance of her advance team wait at the rear of the headquarters watching, watching everything, the roofs, the alleys, and now the motorcade.

The first three cars are full of Nagato SDF. These rush past the rear of the headquarters to their screening position at the end of the alleyway. Next, two armored security vans. These come to rapid halts just past the headquarters building. An SDF heavy weapons team and a GSG assault squad immediately assume positions flanking the vans. Then come two Toyota Elite limos and the Chairman's Mitsubishi Nigthsky armored limousine. The doors of the limos remain closed until the trailing vehicles of the motorcade, more vans, more cars, have taken up screening positions inside the alley. The limo doors remain closed till more SDF and GSG teams have assumed their positions. They remain closed till Machiko has moved her eyes around one last time, till she breathes and settles her spirit and moves to the Chairman's limo.

The doors of the Toyota limos spring open. More GSG emerge. Machiko raps a knuckle three times against the rear door of the Chairman's limo. The door on the other side of the limo from where she stands immediately swings open. Ryokai climbs out. As he straightens, Machiko opens the door before her and out steps Gongoro. The entire arrival has

been choreographed to keep an assassin guessing, to perhaps
bait a killer into attacking prematurely. It would be a foolish
exercise in futility against some of the more devastating
weapons available in the plex, but such weapons are rarely
used. Mortars and missiles do no one any good. The far more
likely threat comes in the form of a lone assassin, who, with
gun or sword or bomb, is willing to die if death will yield
success.

"Interrogative, report," Machiko says into her headset.

"All stations report clear," Captain Oseki reports from the
command center.

Machiko draws the limo door open fully and out step the
Chairman's secretary and his aide, then Ohana-*san* and other
of the Chairman's close advisors, and then finally the
Chairman himself. Machiko and Gongoro position themselves to screen Honjowara-*sama* from either end of the
alley. He is further protected by the twelve GSG today
assigned to the body detail.

The Chairman glances quickly around, but strides directly
to the rear of the headquarters building and proceeds inside,
closely guarded by Ryokai and the rest of the body detail.

Machiko breathes deeply. The potential for disaster will
haunt her throughout the day to come, of this she is certain,
but at least the first step has been made without incident.
They have gotten the Chairman here alive. Now they must
keep him that way.

Next on the schedule is a meeting in the fourth-floor conference room. The Young Dragons of the Bergen Street
Youth Association, in their black suits and red blouses, serve
a light breakfast. The atmosphere is formal and tense. All the
senior leaders of the clan are in attendance: the *shatei,* or
younger brothers, the *wakashira-hosa,* or directors, the
sanro-kai, or counselors. The bosses and assistant bosses and
special consultants or advisors. Some hold official positions
within Nagato Corporation and some do not, but the point is
of no importance. These are the men and women who make
the decisions. They set policy and issue the orders. And here
for the first time Machiko must stand just to the rear of the
Chairman's right as the acting senior of the Guard. Here, she
must present herself as capable of leading the Guard and
keeping the Chairman safe. It is a provocative experience, a
challenge to her both as a warrior and as a woman, to keep
spirit settled and mind and body focused. Those of the

leaders who were not present at earlier meetings, who are only now learning the fullest details of what has occurred, ask many questions, and several of them direct questions at Machiko herself.

At some length, Honjowara-*sama* declares, "Machiko-*san* was attacked while she slept. Did you not hear that she killed the assassin? Do you see a mark anywhere on her person? What other proof do you require of a warrior's ability?"

The Chairman's tone, his expression and attitude, settle the issue.

The meeting ends; another begins. This time in the smaller meeting room on the third floor. A less formal gathering of underbosses and district executives selected for the rare honor of a personal meeting with the Chairman. In terms of the forces they each command and the financial power each of them wields, they are not without significance. But as the Chairman himself has said, they are the roots from which the tree of Nagato Combine has grown, and so must never be undervalued. Over the years, many district executives have risen to positions of importance both within the Honjowara-*gumi* and Nagato Corporation. Many of their children have received full university scholarships and serve in the clan in many valuable capacities. They are hard-working and very loyal and always on the watch for likely recruits. They are, as well, a crucial source of intelligence concerning not only events in the megaplex, but rumored happenings affecting the globe.

Few questions are raised. The talk centers around specifics. The Chairman impresses the gathering with his command of even the most modest of clan endeavors. His words appear designed to generate enthusiasm. He concludes by presenting various awards.

As he exits, a pair of Nagato security officers enter to conduct routine interviews regarding district activities. Machiko again feels the conflict between duty and emotion. She lingers several moments. She hears talk about the activities of competing interests, including Triads, specifically the Large Circle League, but nothing about assassins, or the likelihood of further attacks against Nagato Combine.

She catches up with the Chairman on the second floor. A meeting with a delegation of business persons, primarily *mizu shobai*, people of the "water business," bars, restaurants, and nightclubs. A few of these persons have shady or questionable reputations, so, in addition to the body detail, Machiko again stations herself almost directly at the Chairman's right and remains there throughout the meeting, focusing on the questionable individuals exclusively. None more than glance at her. More than a glance at her or any of the GSG in these circumstances would be impolite, as well as suggestive of sinister intent.

As the Chairman departs, Machiko approaches the owner of a successful string of nightclubs, a frequent guest at the Chairman's Open House, for he is a man with connections and influence on both sides of the borders of Little Asia.

Her inquiries gain her nothing.

Perhaps she is a fool to waste time asking questions. The warrior's Way is death, not words. She struggles against feelings of frustration. She has little experience in gathering useful intelligence. Perhaps she merely gives exercise to her own arrogance in hoping to discover the truth of the threat facing the clan.

She pursues the Chairman to the ground floor. He will now meet with some of the ordinary working people of the headquarters district. Several have already been admitted to the lobby. They are treated as greatly honored guests. They are admitted one or two at a time to the western-style sitting room near the lobby. They are met at the doorway of the room by the geisha of Madame Fujitomi, proprietor of the Willow Pond Teahouse, the oldest, most distinguished teahouse in Little Asia. Two of these magnificent geisha, in traditional regalia, kneel and then bow their heads to the floor while offering words of greeting. Two others bring gifts, beautiful small bouquets, and small booklets bound in black synthleather. Each of the booklets contains a formal portrait of the Chairman and an inspiring message scripted by a master of traditional calligraphy.

The geisha then usher the guests forward. The Chairman himself invites them to occupy one of the pair of sofas situated to the left and right of his own sofa unit. The geisha serve tea. By then, many of the guests appear rather flustered, unsure what to say or how to proceed. In such cases, Honjowara-*sama* smiles. He smiles paternally and asks quiet questions. Always he inquires about his guests' lives, their living conditions, their jobs, their families. Have they any complaints? any suggestions? Perhaps some member of their family is experiencing difficulties. Perhaps the clan can help.

The Chairman's manner is such that most people quickly
gain confidence and say what is on their minds, though
always with great reverence.

Machiko's concentration is disrupted by a beep from her
headset, then Gongoro's voice, saying, "Machiko, Checkpoint Zero. An old man is causing a disturbance."

Machiko lifts one hand to cover her mouth and the wire-
framed mike beside it, and says softly, "Explain."

"The old man asks for you by name."

This is perplexing, confounding. Why would anyone ask
for her? Before the question can finish forming in her mind,
she has the answer. The old man is named Uekiya and of
course he asks for her. "Stand by," she tells Gongoro.

She strides from the sitting room and down the hallway to
the front lobby. The hallway and lobby are guarded both by
GSG and *kobun,* for here in the lobby some dozens of people
wait to meet with the Chairman. Young Dragons of the
Youth Association supervise the visitors, and more of Madame Fujitomo's geisha keep them entertained. Machiko
moves directly to the revolving doors and through to the
sidewalk outside. Here she now sees the crowd she has heard
so much about on her headset. They fill the whole street.
Many linger near the headquarters.

The sidewalk directly in front of the headquarters, as well
as part of the street, has been roped off. Here, more of the
Young Dragons distribute to passersby free copies of
the latest issue of *Wavefront Honjowara,* a monthly journal
describing major events affecting the clan and plans for the
future, as well as important news related to Nagato Corp and
Nagato Combine as a whole. Here, the crowds gathered outside the velvet ropes watch several large displays now running trideos about the clan, its organization and objectives,
its relations with the clans of Nagato Combine, its continuing efforts to rid its districts of crime and improve people's
lives, and so on. The twenty-odd *kobun* posted here, and
their headman, spend most of their time talking, answering
questions, and making conversation, hoping to enhance the
clan's image. The only true elements of security here are the
four GSG flanking the revolving lobby door, and the four
Nagato SDF officers in the red and black jackets of the clan
who clear visitors to the headquarters through their security
checkpoint.

Also at the checkpoint stands Gongoro and one other, a

skinny old man with thin white hair, dressed in the plain gray linen clothes of an ordinary worker. Uekiya-*san*. He carries a dark canvas bag and a small box wrapped in pastel gift-paper. Even now he asks in a loud voice that wavers with age for Machiko-*sama* to be called. She is nearly to the checkpoint when he sees her.

He smiles and draws a handgun from the canvas bag.

"*Gun!*" Gongoro roars, and in that very instant he is moving, moving forward, hurling himself bodily at the old man, and the SDF officers and *kobun* standing nearby are reacting, too.

It is all so sudden, so completely without warning, that the scene is unfolding before her eyes before Machiko can draw a breath, open her mouth, and shout, "*STOP!*"

Gongoro slams into the old man like a battering ram. Two SDF officers and one of the *kobun* are falling against his back even as he drives the old man to the pavement.

People shout, a woman screams. The crowd nearest the checkpoint surges back and away, and more shouts and cries erupt as people are banged about, some knocked off their feet.

Gongoro, the four SDF officers, and three *kobun* are all piling atop the old man before Machiko can reach them, shouting, "*Get off! Get back!*" She uses her hands like weapons, striking blows, paralyzing arms and legs with pressure-point strikes, even kicking, in her efforts to rescue the old man.

Finally, she is face to face with Gongoro. He gazes at her as if she is insane.

Of course he does. The realization all but overwhelms her with shame and anger. Until today, their seniors—Sukayo, Mitsuharu, and Jiksumi—monitored activities inside the headquarters. Gongoro routinely monitored activity at the barricades or up on the rooftops. Machiko herself kept watch over the front entrance and the security checkpoint. So she knows Uekiya's story. So she knows that he has come to practically every Open House since the first Open House. So she is aware that he has owned the small market just up the block for decades, that he has been robbed many times by gangers, though never on this block, and, as a result, habitually carries a gun, a compact Fichetti 500.

It is more than a gun. Uekiya has come to look upon it as more than a gun. He has never been robbed while carrying the gun, and, for him, it has become a *kami,* a kind of Shinto deity who guards elderly grocers from violent gangers.

And so it was arranged, years ago, that Uekiya-*san* would be permitted to bring this *kami,* his guardian gun, to the Open House, so long as he surrendered it at the checkpoint. He was told by the Chairman himself to give the gun to Machiko, to ask for her by name if she was not present, so there would be no confusion.

She failed to communicate this to anyone now working the checkpoint. The responsibility for this incident is hers alone.

For an instant, she fears the old man is dead. He lies half on his side, half on his back, unmoving. Yet, as she summons medtechs via her headset, Uekiya-*san* breathes and pushes slowly against the pavement, struggling to sit up.

Machiko kneels at his side. "Uekiya-*san,*" she says, gently gripping his shoulders. "Do not exert yourself. I have summoned medtechs. Be careful. Please."

But the old man will not lie back. He sits up. He covers his face with his hands and affects a series of bows. It is as if he feels ashamed for having caused this terrible incident. "Please excuse me. Excuse me. Forgive me, *please*! I did not—"

It is almost too much to bear. "Uekiya-*san,*" Machiko says, "please do not apologize." She herself bows, but the old man still holds his hands over his face. "You are blameless, Uekiya-*san*. The fault is mine, Uekiya-*san*."

Then, two medtechs are there. Machiko holds the old man's shoulders till it becomes clear she is interfering with their work. She draws back onto one knee. She notices the new wall of GSG, SDF officers, and *kobun* standing between her and the headquarters entrance. She hears the onlookers around her asking questions. Some speak of seeing the gun. Others recount to their neighbors how they were pushed and shoved and banged around, and Machiko realizes that this incident must be explained before rumors begin raging and the reputation of the clan is further smeared.

She stands and looks around at the crowd and says in a loud, clear voice, "A terrible error has been made. The guards at the checkpoint were not informed that this honorable gentleman, Uekiya-*san,* has the Chairman's permission to carry a weapon to the checkpoint. The responsibility was mine, and I will answer to the Chairman for this shameful failure, as soon as we are assured that Uekiya-*san* is all right."

People grow quiet. Several of the onlookers bow as if impressed or perhaps embarrassed by her statement. Gongoro glares at her as if disgusted. Machiko can well imagine what his opinion must be of her now, but she does not care. Whether she is fit as the senior of the Guard is irrelevant now. If Uekiya-*san* is found to be all right, she will escort him to the Chairman directly, and in any event she will explain what has happened and ask to be punished. For a failure of this magnitude, here before the headquarters, during the Chairman's Open House, her punishment should be severe.

The medtechs treat Uekiya-*san* for several bruises, cuts, and scrapes, but the old man is lucky. His *kami* guarded him well today. His bones may be old, but they are not brittle. Nothing is broken. He has suffered no serious injuries.

When he is ready, Machiko helps him to stand. He is still bowing and hiding his face and asking forgiveness. Machiko feels the pain of his bruises and shame for what has happened. She bends to pick up Uekiya-*san's* canvas bag and his gift-wrapped present, a gift for the Chairman. Uekiya-*san* accepts them still asking forgiveness, still hiding his face.

"We will go to the Chairman now," Machiko tells him.

He bows and bows, asking forgiveness.

With an arm around his back, her hands at his shoulders, Machiko guides Uekiya-*san* ahead once more to the checkpoint. Only one can pass at a time between the uprights of the weapons sensor, so Machiko moves ahead, taking hold of the old man's arm to lead him through.

The sensor naturally detects all her weapons and begins beeping. The alarm is immediately canceled.

She draws Uekiya-*san* ahead.

The sensor beeps.

Uekiya-*san* hesitates. And suddenly Machiko finds his free hand descending to his side, his eyes broad and round and gazing into hers with a look of awe. "Forgive me," he whispers. "Forgive me." And the hand at his side is dropping the gift box and dipping into the canvas bag slung beneath his shoulder, and the look on the old man's face is changing from awe to fear to terror, and then something beyond it, beyond all emotion, beyond existence.

The Void.

In the fleeting moment that all this occurs, Machiko feels
her own emotions go from wonder to puzzlement, then to a
sudden chilling certainty that something is wrong, something
so far beyond mere wrong that the beeping alarm from the
weapons detector is practically meaningless.

In the periphery of her vision, she sees Gongoro looking to
the sky as if to beg the gods for assistance in dealing with
one very trying old man. And she realizes that Gongoro does
not understand. He does not see what Machiko sees. He does
not perceive the threat.

No one does.

So now she is the one moving as if by instinct, clamping
down on the spindly old man's arm, twisting, pressuring
nerves, forcing Uekiya-*san* to bend. And as he bends she
drives her whole body against his flank and back and thrusts
him face-down toward the pavement. As the two of them
fall, she glimpses Gongoro's look of astonishment. She hears
exclamations of shock and surprise. Then, she sees a boiling
cloud of smoke and dust spreading across the concrete earth,
billowing up around her and Uekiya-*san,* and she feels the
earth shaking, roaring with an explosion that seems to erupt
inside her own head.

In the final moment, she wonders if she is dying.

When she wakes, she is lying on a couch in a small quiet
room. Her eyes seem full of grit. Her ears are ringing and her
head feels as if it has been split open. She lifts a hand to her
brow, her nose, her mouth. Some parts are so tender and full
of anguish she cannot bear to touch them. Gently, she
brushes at her eyes with just a fingertip. Her eyes are bleary
and sore and difficult to focus, but momentarily she finds a
Nagato medtech, a female elf, seated beside her, seated on a
stool, now checking her vitals with some piece of equipment.

"Don't try to get up," the medtech says. "You appear to
have suffered a minor concussion."

Machiko spends some moments trying to speak. Her throat
seems full of phlegm and dirt. "Where . . . Where is . . . ?"
She coughs harshly, till her head seems ready to split. "The
Chairman."

"The Chairman is fine," the medtech says. "He has
ordered that you remain here with me. You are to lie quietly
and rest."

"Uekiya-*san.* The old man."

"I'm sorry," the medtech says. "I don't know who you

mean. Several people were injured in the explosion. That's all I know."

Machiko searches for her headset, but that seems to be missing. She tries to work the commlink on her left vambrace, but it refuses to function. She feels barely conscious, a thousand years old, and very, very tired.

Someone, the female medtech, squeezes her shoulder. "Try to stay awake."

Machiko finds she lacks the energy to ask why.

It is enough to merely try to obey.

14

Exactly how many hours go by she is unsure, but when she wakes Machiko finds it is after 11 p.m. She manages to slide her legs over the front of the sofa and sit up without feeling like she may die. Then she begins coughing.

The medtech brings her a bowl into which she may spit, and then a glass of water so she may rinse out more of the grit that seems to coat the inside of her mouth.

"Thank you very much."

The medtech bows, then steps into an adjoining lavatory to rinse out the bowl.

Machiko spends a moment looking around. Immediately before her is the varnished wood stool the medtech used for a seat. Beside her left ankle is the large orange box of the medtech's emergency medical supply kit. Machiko takes a plain white linen cloth from the kit and lays it open over the wooden seat of the stool. Fine linen would be preferable, but this will do. She lays her left hand on the cloth, presses it firmly against the stool, her fingers tucked under, crab-like, all but the little finger, which is fully extended. From the sheath at her waist, she draws her *tanto* and moves the razor-keen blade to the third knuckle of her little finger.

Here, she will perhaps save Chairman Honjowara the trouble of punishing her. It is the traditional means within the clans of atoning for failure. It is called *yubitsume,* finger-cutting. Certain remarks Honjowara-*sama* has made suggest that he does not consider this practice to be entirely in agreement with the precepts of his New Way, but Machiko is sure he will accept her offering. He is a man of great vision, seeking always to move the clan ahead, but his roots were formed in a different age, before the advent of the Awakened. He understands the classical forms.

As she settles her spirit, preparing with one determined

cut to do what she must, she becomes aware of another, the medtech, lunging at her, seizing her hand, and shrieking.

GSG appear as if out of nowhere, six or seven of them, Ryokai among them. The knife is wrenched from her grip. She is forcibly pinned against the cushions of the sofa.

Have they all lost their minds?

Then the Chairman's counselor Zoge-*san* is there, commanding her to rise, to go with him . . .

Understanding comes slowly. She is not to be permitted to atone for her failure by means of *yubitsume*. The only alternative is plain. She finds her sword on a black lacquered stand at one end of the sofa and gets to her feet.

She needs a moment. Her balance is uncertain. She feels a bit light-headed. Ryokai slips an arm behind her and steadies her shoulders, but his favor is not necessary.

Zoge-*san* turns and leads her out. The others draw back and bow, honoring the Chairman's counselor. Machiko steps into the hallway and abruptly realizes she is on the headquarters' third floor. Just down the hallway is one of the western-style offices Honjowara-*sama* often uses while visiting this part of the plex. Flanking the door and standing opposite it are as many as twenty members of the Guard. Quite understandable, given all that has occurred. The senior of the detail bows to Zoge-*san*.

The door opens and she and Zoge-*san* enter. The office is small and private and quiet. The carpeting is green, the paneling like a burled wood of a neutral brown. Honjowara-*sama* sits behind a desk of polished oak. He gazes at a telecom screen, tapping briefly at the auxiliary keyboard. Machiko advances three steps, then kneels and bows. She puts both knees down and bows till her brow brushes the carpet. The sudden rush of blood to her head threatens her balance, and for an instant the carpet seems tinted in swirls of red, but she recovers. She bows a second time and then extends her arms, lifting her sword, making an offering of it. Drawing against grip and scabbard to expose a small portion of the blade.

And then she waits, bent forward, sword offered, blade exposed. It is difficult to maintain the posture correctly. Her arms subtly waver. Her mind seems vague and prone to wander.

She realizes Honjowara-*sama* is approaching when she catches sight of his feet. After a few moments, the sword is snatched from her hands. She breathes and bows, then turns aside, bends forward and pulls her hair from her shoulders to make a clean target of her neck. She holds this posture for what seems like a very long time. Then she hears the sharp click, like that of a sword being thrust firmly into its scabbard.

This so surprises her that she glances toward her side. Honjowara-*sama*, standing over her, and looking very resolved, thrusts the katana toward her as if to return it to her hands.

Machiko hesitates, confused.

Again, Honjowara-*sama* thrusts the sword at her.

"I am not worthy," she says softly.

Yet again, Honjowara-*sama* thrusts the sword at her.

This baffles her completely, but only for a moment. She nearly lets slip a moan when understanding finally comes. In this, her moment of unbearable shame, Honjowara-*sama* acknowledges the years of service she has rendered. He honors her not for what she has done, or failed to do, but for what she is. That is why he returns her sword. She bows deeply. She turns toward her Chairman and bows again. She accepts the sword and lays it on the floor before her. She removes her overvest, folds it, lays it over the sword's scabbard, then draws the scabbard clear and lays it at her side. She rolls the blade of the sword in the fabric of the overvest, then pauses to prepare, to settle her spirit, to breathe. The warrior's Way has rarely seemed so clear to her. Already she can feel the tip of the sword slicing into her stomach, cutting upward, cutting three times, resolving everything. She does not fear it. She welcomes it.

One last time, she bows to her Chairman.

"Machiko," he says, after a moment. "You will not kill yourself. I forbid it."

Machiko puzzles. How can this be? First, she is denied *yubitsume*. Now this. Can her Chairman despise her so greatly? Surely, he understands how deeply she is ashamed. She nearly led an assassin directly to her Chairman. She allowed an explosive device to be detonated at the front of the headquarters building. Her original error involving Uekiya, failing to warn the checkpoint about him, seems of no significance compared to these two immense instances of failure.

"Sheathe your sword, Machiko-*san*. You do not understand." In a powerful voice, a voice of command, he adds, "You are injured and not thinking clearly. Do you hear me?"

She hears. And she recognizes that what Honjowara-*sama* says is so. She does not feel quite herself. Doubtless, she is still suffering the effects of the blast. Yet, she does not feel as though she is suffering unduly. Her confusion is not the result of mere mental trauma. Her shame is not an illusion.

"Sheath your sword, Machiko," Honjowara-*sama* says quietly. "We will explain."

Naturally, she obeys. Her life is not her own. It is neither her privilege nor her responsibility to decide when her life will end. She will end it when her Chairman wills, once he has explained. She draws her katana free of the folded overvest and slips it into its scabbard. She lays the sheathed sword over the folded overvest and settles herself, preparing to listen.

"Zoge," says Honjowara-*sama*.

Zoge-*san* coughs and clears his throat. "Machiko-*san*," he says, "do not be in such a hurry to die. Perhaps you believe that you have failed in your oath to the Chairman. You are wrong. You should feel no shame. I tell you that you have performed well. Very well indeed.

"This afternoon, shortly after you were called to the checkpoint, there was a brief disturbance in the lobby. A man shouted as in alarm. This was one of the medtechs you summoned for the old grocer Uekiya-*san*. The Chairman heard this shout and inquired and learned of the initial incident with Uekiya-*san* and his gun. The Chairman became very concerned, as Uekiya-*san* has been coming to the Open House for many years. The Chairman decided to investigate the situation personally. He was passing through the lobby on his way to the checkpoint when the explosion occurred.

"Our experts believe that the old man carried a shaped charge in his bag. By knocking him down, you directed the blast against the ground, the street pavement. Perhaps the only direction that would not have resulted in many deaths. The grocer's body absorbed much of the back-blast. You yourself were partially shielded by his body."

Machiko looks to Honjowara-*sama* and finds him gazing at her steadily, sternly. Not the least sign of doubt appears on his features. A brief nod of the head answers all questions. It confirms what Zoge-*san* says. Machiko realizes that, despite the enormity of her failures, she apparently has had the inadvertent effect of preventing the Chairman from being harmed by the blast.

For this she is very grateful.

She reaches to her sword, exposes part of the blade, and bows deeply and waits. It is a good moment in which to die. How bitter death would seem if she came to it knowing that she had not only failed, but had failed to protect the Chairman as well.

"Machiko-*san*," Zoge-*san* says. "Do you not understand? You saved the Chairman's life. You made no error."

Machiko bows. She understands perfectly. If Zoge-*san* were a warrior, he would also understand. "Please forgive my rudeness," she says, quietly. "But certain facts must be mentioned. I did not warn the checkpoint about Uekiya-*san's* gun. I allowed an explosive device to be detonated at the entrance to the headquarters during the Chairman's Open House. If not for the weapons detector, I would have led an assassin directly to my Chairman. These are the reasons I am shamed, so greatly I cannot bear it."

For some brief while, the room is silent. Machiko waits, gazing at the exposed portion of her sword. She recalls a poem in which an ancient samurai warrior, in contemplating the end, regarded death as a lover, his sword as death's sweet kiss.

"You speak of warning the checkpoint," says Honjowara-*sama*. "This is not relevant. You are not the director of a corporate unit, or a headman of *kobun*. You are the acting senior of the Green Serpent Guard. The personnel of the Guard were chosen and educated by the masters of the Guard. It is assumed that they who come to us in the uniform of the Guard know how to wield the sword they bear. It is not your obligation to delineate to every member every small event that might possibly occur. It should not have been necessary to warn anyone concerning Uekiya and his gun. Have you forgotten why there are no ranks within the Guard? Every member of the Guard is individually responsible for fulfilling the duty of the Guard. We speak of members being senior or junior to other members, but this is merely an indication of relative experience. As the acting senior, you are responsible for organization, for monitoring discipline and training. You are to see that posts are properly manned. That responsibility is shared by the other senior members, but that is where your responsibility for others ends.

"We have interviewed every witness to what occurred. We have reviewed the record of security cams. The facts are clear. The gun was not drawn in a threatening manner. Gongoro overreacted. The personnel at the checkpoint overreacted. That is not your error. Do you understand?"

"Yes, Honjowara-*sama*," Machiko says, though she does not understand, not really. The error is hers. She knows this. If the Chairman wishes to declare otherwise, that is his right, and she will agree that he is right. Given the time, she will make herself accept what he says, believe what he says. But now, in this moment, it is very hard.

"Nagato security was responsible for keeping weapons away from the headquarters. Doubtless, the explosive device was brought to Uekiya's store before the perimeter was established. You could not prevent this. You went to the grocer's aid as duty demanded. You were not responsible for detecting the explosive, yet you did detect it. You could not prevent the explosive from being detonated, yet you prevented grave loss of life. You hurled yourself at death, Machiko-*san*. There is no shame in this."

Machiko struggles with her growing confusion, her pain. She gazes at the exposed length of her sword. Yearns to feel the lasting comfort of its kiss.

"The warrior's course is one of fanaticism and desperation. This I know. But you must learn to heed your own advice, Machiko-*san*. You gaze at the world very narrowly. Your vision is a keenly edged sword. But when the fire and thunder has passed, you must step back, broaden your gaze. In this way, you will see correctly what has occurred."

Tears rise into her eyes. She fights them. "Chairman-*sama*," she says through a throat grown tight. "You wish me to live? To continue to serve?"

"I command it."

The issue is therefore settled. Her heart and mind still rage with a tumult of conflicting feelings and thoughts, but this she will survive. It is her duty, *neh*?

She bows deeply and takes up her sword.

15

Sleep does not come easily, and when it comes it is fitful and full of trouble. Her dreams are unsettling and confused. At one point, she wakes to the conviction that the Chairman has been killed, assassinated. Yet, the conviction unravels like a poorly tied knot, fading into streaming tendrils of fantasy, before she can free herself of the tangled snarl of bed sheets wrapping her hips and legs.

Later, she imagines that she herself has died, impaled on a thousand shiny blades that run with the rivers of her own blood.

A thought comes to her through the mists: assassins sometimes have backup. She feels a compulsion to rouse herself, rise to the Chairman's defense before another bomber appears. But now the climb to consciousness is long and tiring and saps her of her strength. Before she can open her eyes, she begins slipping, slipping back . . .

Then, bright sunlight fills the room. Her body aches. The bed sheets are damp with sweat. She pushes a sea of hair back from her face, stretches and yawns, and then discovers the stark white features of another GSG in the open doorway, peering in from the hallway outside.

She breathes, and asks, "What is the Chairman's status?"

The member steps fully into the doorway and bows. And now a second white face looks in from the hallway. "Honjowara-*sama* has moved on to Nagato Tower. Ryokai-*san* invites the acting senior to devote the morning to contemplation."

The idea seems typical of Ryokai, something he would suggest. He is sometimes too much the diplomat. What she really needs is time to recover from yesterday's injuries, and to settle the tumult of her spirit. Time to accommodate herself with the prospect of living. Perhaps she holds herself to too high a standard, demands more of herself than any mere

metahuman could ever hope to achieve. She sees this as
nothing less than her duty. For her duty is to protect a man
absolutely in a world where no degree of protection can ever
be absolute.

She looks to the GSG members at the door, and says,
"Why are you not with the Chairman? Are we not still on
alert?"

"Ryokai-*san* directed us to remain here in case the acting
senior should require assistance."

Assistance? Again, that seems like Ryokai talking. It is the
custom of the Guard to stand watch over members disabled
by injuries, and she has already been the subject of at least
one deliberate attempt at assassination, but these facts seem
like mere excuses. More likely, Ryokai-*san* feared that she
might repeat her abortive attempt at *yubitsume*. Or perhaps
he knows of what transpired in the Chairman's office and
posted a watch to ensure that she does not attempt suicide. A
foolish concern. Even if the shame she felt last night were to
return with all its power, the moment for death has passed,
and the Chairman has spoken.

Life is but a fleeting sorrow, a tear shed and wiped away
in the blink of an eye.

She looks to the two GSG at the door. "Report to the
senior in charge at Nagato Tower. I will be along shortly."

The two GSG bow, turn, and go.

Machiko gets to her feet. Every muscle aches. Her eyes
and throat feel as if rubbed raw by sand. But this is meaningless, as meaningless as yesterday's shame. The Chairman's word will be her law. She must heal herself and return
to duty.

Nagato Security has delivered her duty bag. From it she
takes a spare *gi* and *tabi*. She leaves yesterday's clothes with
a headquarters' matron to be laundered and takes the stairs
to the lobby. There is none of yesterday's hustle and bustle.
The lobby is staffed by only a pair of attractive hostesses,
one elf, one norm, and one kobun, an ork. The atmosphere is
one of tranquil quiet.

The street outside is noisy, congested with traffic, the
sidewalks full of people moving to and fro. But there is an
order to the noise and to the movements, every part moving
in harmony. Several passersby offer Machiko polite bows
without missing a step. The pair of kobun standing watch on
the headquarters entrance bow and asks how they may be of

assistance the moment she steps onto the sidewalk. No one gawks or stares. Few people seem even to notice her. She is a part of the clamor and ceaseless activity of the district. She belongs. Her chalk-white face and sable hair and elven traits mark her as an indelible component of everything that gives this district life. She is shown respect when noticed, when it is polite to notice; otherwise, she is just another aspect of the scenic background.

She turns and forces her legs to an easy jogging run. She runs up the block, turns the corner, then another, then sprints down the alleyway passing the rear of the headquarters. She completes a full circuit of the block and starts another. The crowded sidewalks are no problem. A path always opens before her, and she saves her sprints for the alleyway. She goes on for an hour, then two, then climbs the stairs to the headquarters roof and, sword in hand, begins the dance of death, the *kata* of One Thousand Enemies. The ritualized movements are agonizingly slow and demand more of her than any amount of mere running. The sweat is soon pouring off her in rivers, every muscle crying in a chorus of torment, but the song is one of power, the power of flesh, spirit, and mind blending in perfect harmony, like the steel of a Masamune sword, forged to near-perfection.

She goes on till her katana seems made of lead, her arms and legs as weak as butter, her body a puddle of gelatin, and then she breathes and goes through it all again.

And when at last she puts one knee to the cool slate roof and rests, she feels beyond mere physical fatigue, beyond exhaustion. She feels as if an inexhaustible river of energy pours into her flesh, as if all the resources of the plane of mana have become an eager servant to her will.

She feels reborn.

She showers and dresses in her spare uniform, assumes all her weapons, and descends to the ground-floor kitchen. The chef on duty there flutters around her like a butterfly, trying to be helpful. She needs no help. She makes her own meal—fish and rice and fruit—Buddhist parents would certainly approve. Then she calls the Nagato Corp operations center to request a chopper ride.

The ride lasts only minutes. Nagato Tower comes plainly into view as the chopper passes over the Hudson. To Machiko's eyes, the tower is itself a metaphor for Nagato Combine. It is a shining, mirror-finished monument to the

Chairman's New Way and the strong bonds between the clans of the Nagato Combine. It stands like a warrior, determined and strong, tall, yet close in spirit to the earth, rooted in the bedrock underlying Manhattan isle. It is located in Downtown, between the river to the east and to the west, the soaring skyrakers ringing Central Park and, to the south, the immense monoliths of Fuchi-Town. It is proximate to the crude glamour of Times Square and the decadent beauty of Neon City, as well as the abject squalor and violence of the Lower East Side. The consortium of interests that built it exert influence across a vast territory, and weld considerable financial power, but has yet to approach the dominating force of the great megacorps.

The *mon* of Nagato Combine marks all four faces, some forty stories above the street.

The chopper descends briefly to the aeropad on the roof, and goes thumping away into the brownish haze of a Manhattan morning as Machiko crosses to the armored security port adjacent to the pad. She pauses to prove her identity, then takes the elevator down to the second-floor command center for Nagato Security. She is informed that the regular Security Service force on site is on full alert, supported by tactical teams of the SDF. She rides the elevator to the thirty-eighth floor and finds Ryokai and Gongoro both standing the watch with the GSG detail before the entrance to the Chairman's suite of offices.

Ryokai and Gongoro follow her through the entrance to the GSG duty office, a command center in miniature. She barely has time to sweep her gaze across the bank of monitors lining one wall before Gongoro says, harshly, "The Yoshida-*kai* sent the bomber."

Machiko does not look at Gongoro. She knows well what she will see, features twisted by hatred. She looks instead to Ryokai. He glances back and forth, saying nothing.

"A fool could see it!" Gongoro growls. "Only another clan could find someone like Uekiya. He was ideally suited."

"Ideally suited for what?" Machiko asks.

Gongoro looks at her like she is a fool. "To cause an incident and disrupt the Open House," he says gruffly. "To cause further embarrassment to the Honjowara-*gumi* and Nagato Combine. To make us seem weak and ineffectual. To show that even the people at the heart of our districts desire to see us destroyed."

"You do not believe this was an attempt at assassinating the Chairman?"

Gongoro snarls. "Only a fool would hope to walk a bomb past the weapons' detectors at the checkpoint! Yoshida knows we are not careless enough to pass people through merely because they may be well known. Even members of the Guard must prove their identity at checkpoints. And Yoshida knows this well. The attack could have no other purpose than to kill GSG and our clansmen!"

"Then why was the bomb not detonated as Uekiya-*san* approached the checkpoint? Why did he wait until the weapons' sensor gave its alarm?"

"Obviously he wished to be at point-blank range in order to achieve maximum effectiveness."

Gongoro's argument is tempting, but Machiko mistrusts it. This is Gongoro's narrow view again—the Yoshida-*kai* again. It serves only to remind Machiko of the Chairman's warning about the necessary fanaticism of the warrior perspective and the danger of taking too narrow a view on the world. Gongoro's viewpoint seems doubly narrow, excessively fanatical. Perhaps even paranoiac.

Machiko breathes, settles herself. "There is something deeper here than what you say. Uekiya-*san* was a loyal supporter of the clan. He was a friend of the Chairman. He brought the Chairman presents. They often discussed botany. I do not believe that he willingly carried this bomb."

Gongoro sneers, looking disgusted.

"You should speak to Ujitaro," Ryokai says.

"He knows something of this?"

"I cannot say, Machiko-*san*. I only know that he appeared at the checkpoint shortly after the bombing. He appeared excited. Later, I found him in conference with Honjowara-*sama*."

"He said nothing to you?"

Ryokai shakes his head no, and shrugs.

This is too familiar. Machiko feels a sudden rise of frustrated anger. Ujitaro wears the uniform of the Guard and yet he often behaves as if an entity unto himself. He chooses his own deployment in every situation. He speaks only to those whom he considers worthy of his attention. Machiko has rarely heard him exchange more than a handful of words with anyone but her "older brother" Sukayo-*san*, and that cannot continue. Sukayo-*san* is not here and may not be available for duty for many weeks to come.

Machiko turns to the door at the rear of the duty office. Beside that door is a palm scanner and intercom. She lays her hand to the scanner, and says, "Ujitaro-*san*. It is Machiko. Please open the door. We must speak."

A long silence passes.

"Uji—"

The intercom beeps.

The door slides open.

The space beyond is black. The light from the duty office carries across the threshold, but only as far as the armored screen that rises from floor to ceiling, shielding the rest of the room from view. Before the screen wait three of the naga, their serpentine heads nearly on a level with Machiko's chest. She bows to them respectfully. The beasts lower their heads a bit, but follow closely as Machiko advances through the doorway and steps around the armored screen. The door whispers shut behind her.

The cool of the room becomes immediately apparent. A sound arises like a distant murmur of many voices, carried on a spectral wind. She finds Ujitaro, his heat signature plain, seated cross-legged on a cushion at the center of the room. He holds his arms crossed over his chest, his fingers arranged in mystical signs, his head bent back as if to include all the heavens within his gaze. The naga flow around him, over the floor, his folded legs, his shoulders, even his head, like rivers of smoldering heat.

His voice, when he speaks, seems inhumanly deep, as if rising from a vast abyss. "Power ebbs low. The lattice frays. Sources grow weary. Why do you come?"

Machiko bows. "Duty demands that we speak, Ujitaro-*san*. Until such time as Sukayo-*san* returns, you and I must communicate. We must exchange information so as to better defend the Chairman. Do you agree?"

A long pause ensues. "What do you know?"

Relating this takes some time. There is little that Machiko knows for certain, but under the current circumstances even mere speculation has some value. "And now I would ask what you can tell me of yesterday's bombing."

Moments pass, seemingly without end, until finally Ujitaro says, "The old man with the bomb. Another sent him."

"Who sent him? Do you know?"

"A tendril of power. A slender limb of the cosmic whole. A discreet coalescence of particles bound in mathematical harmony."

Machiko has rarely heard such talk, but ventures a guess. "You mean that Uekiya-*san* was controlled? controlled by a mage?"

"It is plain."

"Do you know this mage?"

"I know him by his work."

"Do you know his name? where he can be found?"

"Where among the planes would you discover the higher mysteries? Where would you lay bare the secrets of power, the key to the cosmos, the one formula to unify all existence?"

Machiko ponders this. Ujitaro seems to be describing a mage of great power, who seeks great truths. Clearly, this mage poses a great danger. "I speak of the mundane world, Ujitaro-*san*. You say this mage sent Uekiya-*san*, the old grocer with the bomb. Then this mage is our enemy. We must find him. Where may we find his meat body?"

Another long pause ensues, then Ujitaro says, "Speak to me of mana. Speak to meat of meat."

It is all Ujitaro has to offer.

Yet, his few words have provided important intelligence, or so it seems to Machiko. A mage sent Uekiya-*san* with a bomb, doubtless under some form of compulsion. This means that the forces of their enemies include a formidable mage, and this means that Nagato forces must be prepared. Machiko takes the stairs one floor down and strides to the offices of Bessho Chikayo, chief of Nagato security, to relay news of this new threat.

"Thank you, Machiko-*san*," Bessho-*san* says once she is done. "This news confirms recent speculations. Investigative officers of the Security Service have just completed a series of interviews with the friends and relations of Uekiya-*san*. It appears that the old grocer closed his store early on the night before the Open House, many hours before the barricades went up on Bergen Street. He had several visitors just before closing the store and remained inside the store all night. Neither his wife nor his two sons nor their wives could account for this break with his usual habits. Neither could they persuade him to leave the store. He claimed to be taking an inventory."

"These 'visitors,'" Machiko says.

Bessho-*san* lifts a hand before she can finish. "They were seen only by the wife and she is unable to provide a description, or to state with certainty how many visitors arrived, or whether they came separately or together. She believes they were all males, but is unsure even of this."

Machiko frowns. "Was she under some form of enchantment?"

"Apparently a spell of some type. This was the speculation of my officers. You have just confirmed it for me."

Machiko bows and leaves Bessho-*san* to take appropriate measures, such as the redeployment of Nagato assets to better prepare for assault or intrusion attempts by arcane means.

She is barely as far as the stairs, heading for the GSG duty office, when her commlink beeps. She flips open the small vidscreen on her left vambrace. The face of the Chairman's personal aide gazes at her. "The Chairman asks that you join him in his office as soon as you are able, Machiko-*san*."

"I will come at once."

Yet, when she arrives, Machiko finds the Chairman, not in his expansive office, with a panoramic view of lower Manhattan, but rather secluded in a small chamber immediately adjacent. The GSG of the body detail stand watch at the door to his chamber, rather than from within the chamber itself.

"So the Chairman insisted," the senior of the detail explains. "He meets with the Lady of the Tir."

Machiko refrains from showing her surprise. "When did the Lady arrive?"

"Ten hundred."

Almost two hours ago.

Machiko touches the intercom beside the door, announces herself. Honjowara-*sama* replies, "You may enter, Machiko-*san*."

The room is quite small, furnished in tatami fashion. At the center of the floor is a small rectangular garden of stone and white sand, perhaps half a meter long. Beyond this a plain black lacquered table where Honjowara-*sama* sits cross-legged, facing the door, in a tailored black suit. At the left of the table, kneeling, is the woman known only as Sashi, Lady of the Tir.

Precisely who she is, or from whence she comes, is as much a mystery as her relationship to Honjowara-*sama*. A

mystery of considerable duration. She is called the Lady of
the Tir simply because she is obviously an elf and so much
about her is hidden. Machiko herself knows only the most
superficial of details. The Chairman calls her "Sashi." She is
always elegant in appearance, her hair coiled into elaborate
coiffures, her slender figure sheathed in sumptuous robes.
She looks to be of Japanese lineage, despite her lustrous
golden hair. She arrives in executive limos, accompanied by
bodyguards, but the guards always remain with the car. She
always comes and goes via back entrances and restricted corridors. She speaks to no one but the Chairman, and has no
need to, for the Guard is always notified moments before she
arrives and is expected to provide an escort.

Some say she is Honjowara-*sama's* mistress. If so, she is a
type which Machiko has never encountered. She is as likely
to appear in the middle of the night as in the middle of the
day, and is as likely to stay through the night and the day that
follows as for only an hour, or the span of a mere few minutes. She has appeared as frequently at the Chairman's estate
as here at Nagato Tower, and various of the other locations
where Honjowara-*sama* spends his time. Machiko has seen
her gaze upon the Chairman with pleasure and even affection, but never in a manner that might be deemed indiscreet,
even by a jealous wife.

To Machiko, she seems more a special friend or confi-
dante, an associate of many years.

Honjowara-*sama* gestures casually toward the cushion at
the right end of the table. Machiko moves there and descends
to one knee and bows. Honjowara-*sama* gives brief acknowledgment. Sashi then politely offers a bow of her own.
Machiko answers this very briefly, with just a faint movement of her head. She would give no response at all but for
the informal circumstances and the stature of the Lady
kneeling opposite her.

"You seem well, Machiko," says Honjowara-*sama*. "You
are fully recovered?"

Machiko bows. "Yes, Chairman-*sama*. Thank you for
your concern. I am healed."

Honjowara-*sama* nods approvingly. "In these times every
member of Nagato Combine must keep fit and strong. This is
doubly true for those of executive levels, Machiko. Those of
us who are viewed as leaders. The rank and file of Nagato
Combine look to the example set by their leaders. If we are

filled with a spirit of bold self-confidence, our people will be inspired."

"I understand, Chairman-*sama*."

Honjowara-*sama* briefly looks to her with a stern eye. "Twice now you have thwarted the attacks of assassins. In this latest incident, you were seen in the best possible light, full of compassion for an old man's bruises, then, alone, acting boldly, selflessly in the face of destruction. This has not passed unnoticed, Machiko. Word has traveled throughout Nagato Combine. This morning, there are many who take a new pride in belonging to an organization defended by the bold warriors of the Guard."

Machiko bows. "I seek only to serve, Chairman-*sama*."

Then, it is Sashi-*san* who speaks. Her voice is like sunlight dipped in liquid gold, resonant and soft, very soft. "You are perceived as large and bold of spirit, Machiko-*san*." She pauses to smile, then adds, "Your honor is great."

Machiko bows politely in acknowledgment. Yet the Lady's comments puzzle her. Why would the Lady of the Tir say such things? Obviously, she would know anything the Chairman might have chosen to tell her, but why does she now speak of such things to Machiko? What is her role in this informal meeting?

Perhaps the Chairman merely wishes to echo and enhance his own remarks, and thus emphasize what he has said.

But why should emphasis be considered necessary?

"Arinori," says Honjowara-*sama*.

A paneled door along the wall to Machiko's rear slides open. The Chairman's personal aide enters. He moves to Honjowara-*sama's* side, bows and kneels; then, at a brief gesture from the Chairman, turns toward Machiko.

"I found this artifact on a visit to Kyoto, some years ago," says Honjowara-*sama*. "Give me the benefit of your opinion."

The hands of the Chairman's aide are draped with fine linen, upon which lies a wakizashi. Machiko examines the short sword, its intricate grip, its scabbard, with her eyes. The sword itself appears to be of a customary length, about 46 centimeters. Its grip, wrapped in *same,* shark skin, appears carved out of ivory. The *tsuba,* or guard, appears fashioned out of steel, ornamented in gold, and formed into a design like billowing clouds. The lacquered green scabbard is decorated with an inlaid pattern like a forest of reeds,

chaped or capped at the end by a golden *kojiri* in the form of
a coiling dragon. The scabbard is also fitted with both
kozuka and *kogai,* the customary small knife and "headpin,"
their handles inscribed with the images of a tiger and a
waterfall.

"Give me your warrior's keen view," says Honjowara-
sama.

This can only have one meaning.

The warrior's view regards only the quality of the weapon
as a weapon. Machiko bows. Reverently, she draws the short
sword from its scabbard. She rises and draws back, away
from Honjowara-*sama* and his Lady; then, with katana in
one hand, wakizashi in the other, she begins the *kata* of Two
Waves Crashing.

The short sword's quality immediately becomes apparent.
Its grip seems almost to meld with her fingers and hand. It
moves like an extension of her spirit and will. It is of a
quality like that of her katana, produced by a master. She
returns it reverently to its scabbard. She bows and kneels.

"A most excellent weapon, Chairman-*sama*."

Honjowara-*sama* nods. "Its *tang* is not signed."

This remark, so casually offered, only heightens her
opinion of the sword. Some of the greatest masters of
Japanese sword history left their blades unsigned. They
believed that anyone worthy of their work should be able to
identify the maker without reference to a signature, and that
persons incapable of doing so were not worthy of knowing
how truly valuable a sword they held.

Machiko runs her eyes once more over the weapon, lying
over the linen-draped hands of the Chairman's aide. With
the Chairman's permission, she bares the blade and examines it closely. The thought that springs abruptly to mind is
irresistible.

"This is an Osafune blade."

Honjowara-*sama* nods. "Sukayo-*san* has expressed this
same opinion."

Machiko cannot resist a faint smile.

Perhaps the most famous blades were made by the ancient
master Masamune in the fourteenth century, followed by
those of his son and grandson. These blades, some reputed to
thirst for blood, represent the best of the Koto period, produced prior to 1600. Later masters of the Shinto, or "new,"
period are generally considered to be not as good. However,

the best of the Shinto period masters produced blades better than many of the Koto period. The masters of the city of Osafune in Japan are considered to rank among the best. They produced many blades of the finest quality.

Machiko can well imagine the pleasure with which her "older brother" Sukayo would regard such a blade. "It is an honor to meet such ancient steel."

"It is yours," says Honjowara-*sama*.

The suggestion alone would be unsettling.

Machiko struggles to breathe, to remain calm. She bows, bows deeply. "Chairman-*sama*," she says. "Please forgive me, I am not worthy of such a gift. I am a crude barbarian kneeling before an instrument of god-inspired perfection. This sword deserves to be held by one who has sought the Buddha nature, who draws near enlightenment. I could never be worthy of such an honor."

Honjowara-*sama's* expression turns fierce. In a voice that is quiet yet filled with determined power, he says, "The warrior serves without thought of reward. Duty is duty. In former times, it was said that the foremost retainer thinks exclusively of the welfare of the lord, seeking neither honor nor wealth. Yet, all of man's work is a bloody business, and people are weak, and the loyal retainer must be encouraged. It is the obligation of a Chairman, from time to time, to express his satisfaction with those who loyally serve Nagato Combine. And it is my decision now to give this incontrovertible sign that I choose to accept your advice, Machiko-*san*, and draw the companion sword of the GSG."

And here Honjowara-*sama* takes the short sword from the hands of his aide and offers it resolutely to Machiko.

"I have drawn the companion sword. Now you, Machiko-*san*, must wield it."

She has no alternative. The Chairman's will is clear. Machiko bows. She accepts the sword and bows again. "How may I best serve Nagato Combine, Chairman-*sama*? Command me."

Honjowara-*sama* replies, "The deployment of the Guard, including that of the senior members, is for the acting senior to determine. Let duty be your guide."

Machiko breathes, breathes deeply, and bows.

16

The room is just one of many in the Critical Care Unit of the Kissena Park Hospital complex in Flushing, Queens. The ceiling is white, the walls beige, the floor a darker brown. There are no chairs or other conveniences such as might be provided for visitors. The shutters over the windows are shut, the lighting is subdued. Beside the only bed stands a sophisticated medical monitoring station, linked directly to the central station outside. The only patient seems lost among pillows, bed sheets, polished chrome side rails, and the array of wires and tubes coiling between bed and monitoring station.

There is much, however, that distinguishes Room 5 from the other rooms of the Critical Care Unit.

Two Nagato Security officers in civilian attire stand outside the door. Two members of the GSG stand watch just inside. A Buddhist priest chants a few prayers. Private duty medtechs give the patient a complete sponge bath, and when they are done a cosmetician attends the patient's hair and fingernails and all the other minor details essential to maintaining a meticulous appearance. And when all of that is done with, and the room is quiet and still, Machiko gently strokes the patient's cheek with the fragrant petals of a black rose, then takes the patient's left hand and encloses it in her own.

"Older Brother," she says softly. "The doctors say you are much improved. You must hasten your recovery. Your wisdom and strength are sorely needed."

The brain activity display on the med console shows subtle variations at nearly every word she speaks. Machiko wonders if that is good or bad. Is she helping in some small way? What else might she say or do to contribute to Sukayo's recovery?

Her eyes turn inevitably to the small black-draped table

beside the bed, to the lacquered stand bearing katana and wakizashi. Reverently, she lifts the katana and lowers it to the cranny between Sukayo's arm and chest. Gently, she curls his hand around the katana's grip. Is it her imagination or do the fingers of his powerful left hand briefly flicker with tension?

"Older Brother," she says at near a whisper, leaning down to his ear. "You killed that dog of an assassin. Your honor is unblemished. Now you must grow strong. Nagato Combine needs its warriors. The Chairman needs his foremost weapon. You must be focused on recovering. You must be resolved." More words come to mind, learned long ago in her youth. "You must chase down your enemy, Older Brother. Discern the enemy's rhythm and destroy it. Plunge recklessly into battle and defeat the thousand-handed threat."

The supine form in the bed does not answer, of course. Sukayo-*san* is unconscious, in stable but critical condition. The question now is not whether he will survive. The resources of Nagato Combine will ensure that he survives. Doctors and mage-physicians and a universe of advanced medical technology will ensure that Sukayo survives. The issue is whether he will survive as a warrior, one of the foremost warriors of the Guard, or face the rest of his life condemned as a crippled reflection of himself.

Sukayo must hold on. He must maintain vital signs above a certain threshold, avoid every touch of the surgeon's knife that can be avoided. He must hold his ground for the three to five weeks needed to prepare one hundred-percent compatible clonal duplicates for those of his organs damaged beyond hope of repair. Every surgical procedure and anything less than one hundred-percent compatible clonal transplants threaten to impair his ability to use mana, and therefore his mastery as a warrior.

The doctors have done the absolute minimum required to stabilize his condition. Now only waiting remains.

Machiko gazes briefly onto the astral, the plane of power, where all life reveals its truths, and mana ebbs and flows like the waters of a vast primordial sea. How easy it is to forget the mana, until now, a moment like this, when mana becomes all-important. That is because, like Sukayo, like all the elves of the Guard, she uses mana as she would use a sword, without thought, without design. They are all mages in this sense, wielding a brand of magic with unique application to the world of the physical. This is how she was able to thrust an old man toward the ground before a bomb could be detonated. How she could heal herself in one small part of a morning. How she could deflect the assault of a killer using only a slim strip of pliable steel.

Without the mana she would be just one more able warrior in a world of sly hunters and chrome killers. With it, all things become possible. With it, her sword, the primitive artifact of a feudal era, becomes a weapon the equal of any.

"You must fight, Older Brother," she says softly, urgently. "Fight as though you are already dead. Do not think of victory or defeat. Retaliate. Attack. Attack. And you will soon awaken from your dream."

Machiko bows her head and whispers entreaties to the kami of warriors and the kami of medicine and healing to promote Sukayo's recovery. She returns Sukayo's sword to its stand.

At the door, she pauses to tell the two GSG on watch, "Notify me at once if Sukayo-*san* awakes. Notify me of anything he says or seems to say, regardless of his condition."

"Understood," says the senior of the pair.

Just beyond the entrance to the Critical Care Unit, Machiko enters the unit lounge, a small pastel-shaded room rimmed in fauxplas chairs and cushioned benches. Here wait Sukayo's adoptive parents, two stepsisters, and spouses. All are Nagato employees. The parents are mid-level executives, the father in marketing, the mother in market research. Sukayo's sisters and their spouses are all employed by various Nagato subsidiaries.

They are watched over by a pair of Nagato security officers in plainclothes. Also present is a family counseling specialist from the Nagato Corp Office of Employee Services.

All present rise. They bow with great respect, to a degree greater than Machiko prefers, for it makes her uncomfortable. It appears that the wakizashi slung through her belt at the left of her waist has escaped no one's notice. Only the most senior GSG carry the sword, and only at the express invitation of the Chairman. The implication is that she now acts not merely in the Chairman's defense, but as his personal agent.

She bows. "I took hold of Sukayo-*san's* hand and felt his fingers tense, very faintly, as if he tried to respond to my grip. I believe Sukayo-*san* knows we are here and takes strength from our presence. I am encouraged."

Sukayo's stepfather, a norm, seems all but overwhelmed by emotion, unable to speak, his eyes rimmed in red, his cheeks and brow gleaming with moisture. Sukayo's stepmother, also a norm, grips her husband's elbow tightly with both hands, but bows and says, "Thank you, Machiko-*san*. Thank you for coming. Thank you for sending members of the Guard to watch over our son." It seems to require a considerable effort, but she offers a smile. "You are a loyal 'younger sister' to our son, Machinko-*san*. Thank you. Thank you for everything."

Machiko bows. It is difficult to maintain a settled spirit. It is difficult to see the pain on the face of Sukayo's father, and to endure the excessive thanks offered by his mother. She has been a not infrequent visitor to the home of Sukayo's parents. They are all aware of the measure of her friendship with Sukayo and have spoken to her in the past as if she were a member of their family. They have welcomed her to dinner and to any number of family gatherings. It is agonizingly clear how they are suffering. Every pain, every fear, seems highlighted in glaring neon.

"Machiko-*san* . . ." One of Sukayo's sisters shifts forward, bowing. "Are you able to tell us anything of what happened to Sukayo?"

Machiko tells what is she able to tell. She has only just taken hold of the sword Honjowara-*sama* gave her. She has determined how she will begin to wield that sword, and much will happen before this day is over, but first she had to come here, to visit her Older Brother.

Recalling the Chairman's words, she says, quietly, "The Chairman has mobilized Nagato Combine's resources. We have many indications as to what is happening. We seek clarity. In that regard, I must now turn to all of you."

"To us?"

As a group, they seem perplexed. "I have spoken with the doctors," Machiko explains. "They say that before he entered surgery, Sukayo-*san* was briefly conscious, or near-conscious. It is rumored that he may have spoken. I must ask if any of you heard anything that he may have said."

Many pairs of eyes glance back and forth. Finally, it is Sukayo's mother who says, "I am sorry, Machiko-*san*. Sukayo has said nothing. Nothing understandable."

"Yet he made an attempt to speak?"

"Like one who is asleep. Who dreams."

"Could you understand none of it?"

Sukayo's mother looks to the elder of the two sisters, who looks with uncertainty to Machiko, and says, "Once, he seemed to say something. A number, I thought."

"I thought he was just moaning," the younger sister says.

"What number?" Machiko asks.

"Two-six," says the elder sister.

"Four-two-six," says the younger.

The two exchange glances. "It was very hard to hear him," says the older sister. "I'm not sure about the four, but he definitely said two-six."

"I'm sure," the younger sister insists.

Machiko contains her surprise. Four-two-six—if Sukayo truly said this, it would imply much. It is a number with great significance within the Chinese hierarchy of beliefs. It is a number used to refer to the "Red Pole" in charge of enforcement for a Triad criminal organization.

Did Sukayo perceive some evidence that a Triad boss or group sent the assassin who attacked him? Or was this mere speculation? A guess? Machiko ponders this at some length and concludes that one thing is certainly clear. Older Brother could not have chosen a more succinct means of directing her attention to the possibility of Triad involvement, and that possibility, she decides, must be pursued.

Even Sukayo's "guesses" tend to prove out.

17

The street in Brooklyn is a river of flashing, flaring light squeezed between storefront shops and small plazas of stores, clogged by vehicle traffic and swarming with early evening shift-change crowds. From above comes the roaring of an express on an elevated subway line, from curbside the incessant babble of trideo and laserdis adstands. The crowds packing the sidewalks, surging across the roadway in sudden tides, include everything from suits and salarymen to chrome dogs and squatters: human, elf, ork, of every color, shape, and size. None pay lasting attention to the pair of silver-gray Infiniti E9 heavy sedans easing along the curb lane at walking speed. None give more than a glance at the pair of male norms in blue-trimmed black sports coats threading their way through the crowds on the sidewalk.

Then, abruptly, a man in brown cargo-utilities turns and breaks into a run.

Brake lights flare. *Kobun* of the Yoshida-*kai* pour from the Infiniti sedans. Lieutenant Enotori of Nagato Security Service starts out the passenger door of the second sedan, but then hesitates, looking into the rear of the car. Machiko gives no sign of noticing the lieutenant's hesitance. She switches off her handcomp, pushes out through her door, then mounts the sidewalk and follows the pursuit at a determined stride.

People who merely stepped aside to avoid the charging *kobun* draw back to form a wide swath around her.

It is not unexpected.

The pursuit ends just up the block in the confines of an alleyway lit by brilliant spotlights. The alley ends at a wall of macrolinked fencing topped by razor wire. Two vicious mongrels snarl and snap from the other side of the fence. The norm male with his back to the fence, hemmed in by a semicircle of *kobun* is known as Yakei, "Watchman." He brandishes a

butterfly knife and menaces the *kobun*, but as the datajack in **his** temple implies, his specialty is information.

The *kobun* draw back as Machiko advances. Yakei abruptly shifts his focus to her. He bares his teeth and, grunting, growling, slashes at the air between them with the knife. His desperation is clear.

"Enough," says Machiko.

The desperation lingers a moment more, then dismay blossoms full. The inevitability of what he must do is by then apparent. The knife drops to the ground. As Machiko advances nearer, Yakei withdraws to the corner formed of macrolink fencing and the rough concrete wall of the building on the left. Then there is no place else to go, nowhere to turn.

Machiko extends a hand to Yakei's shoulder. He winces. He feels something on the order of a gentle prickling of pin-points as she tickles the nerves at the crook of shoulder and neck. "It is a dangerous time to be an enemy of Nagato," she says softly, leaning close. "Swords have been drawn. Serpents walk the streets. Are you a friend or enemy? Tell me now."

Yakei licks his lips. "A friend. I—I'm a friend."

Machiko shifts nearer, near enough to feel the heat of the man's quick, deep breaths. "Enemies will be destroyed," she says softly as before. "Cut down ruthlessly and ground into dust. You understand this. You know the truth of what I say."

Abruptly, Yakei nods.

"You say you are a friend. Yet two months ago you issued threats against Nagato's Chairman. Is that not the Way of an enemy?"

Yakei swallows a huge breath. He seems to shudder. Seems to be struggling against a new rise of desperation, mingled with fear. "Hey, I was just jinked off. One of you, you Serpents jacked me around." Another large breath. "I didn't mean nothing."

"You have friends among the Triads."

"No—"

A pained expression suddenly grips his features as Machiko gives stronger stimulus to pressure points. "Do not lie," Machiko says. "Lies will not be tolerated."

"I didn't do . . . didn't do *nothing*!"

"Your friends. What do they tell you?"

"Nothing! They told me nothing!"

"What do you *hear*?"

Yakei begins shaking visibly. He wipes spittle from his lips with a trembling hand. "Somebody's buying heavy chrome. Freelance cutters. At bargain prices."

"Heavy chrome does not come cheaply."

"It does if a mage makes it that way."

"You suggest that a mage would use sorcery to influence chromed killers? You speak madness."

"It's what I heard. This slag. He heard it. He was at some trash bowl by Kennedy Airport. He said this chrome capper started jowling like he was blown on Talking Head BTL. The capper said he was running hits almost for free, for charity. Gonna make the world safe for crazies. Kill the fragging corps. Kill everybody. Till there's nobody but chrome-jobs left."

This could mean nothing. Yakei refers of course to the cybernetically enhanced. Those with the greatest amount of enhancements walk a fine line between sanity and madness. The use of mind-altering BTL has been known to push such metal maniacs over the edge, or deeper into psychosis. "This slag who heard this talk. He is a friend of yours?"

"It's a she. Just a chummer."

"She is Triad?"

"I don't know. Maybe one of their pillow biffs."

"What of the mage?"

"This capper said he had a mage for a Johnson. Called him the brain-buster."

The what? "Explain."

"I don't know any more!"

Machiko squeezes pressure points. A look of agony grips Yakei's features. He slips from his knees to sit in the filth gathered against the building wall and begins quaking violently. "What is the meaning of 'brain buster?' "

"I don't know I don't know!"

"What does it tell you?"

"Maybe he's a kick in the ass!"

Or perhaps this mage equips his chromed killers with cranial bombs. "The biff? What is her name?"

Yakei grunts harshly, panting rapidly.

Machiko rises, gestures to the headman of the Yoshida-*kai* kobun. "Escort Yakei-*san* to my car."

The headman bows. "At once, Machiko-*sama*."

18

Evening settles into night. The Infiniti E9 sedans criss-cross Brooklyn county, rolling through Flatbush to Canarsie and Starrett City, then across the line into Queens and Howard Beach, in sight of the airport, then back to Brownsville and finally Bedford-Stuy. It is like a brief excursion around the globe. The signs rising over the streets wink and gleam with the languages of eastern Europe, the Middle East, Asia, the Americas. They pass corporate enclaves and coffin hotels. They ride past blocks at least nominally controlled by Triad gangs and the Maf, and everyone's third-rater, Seoulpa rings. Crowds change color and clothes with the passing blocks. People in the cold dark places trail fiery halos of heat. Humans and metas under the brilliant lights of stores and the strobes of nightclubs and bars gleam faintly with warmth.

The night grows chill, and Yakei-*san*, seated between Machiko and Lieutenant Enotori in the rear of the second sedan, begins looking forlorn. It is good, in Machiko's view, if he feels that way. It is wise. It will encourage him to be mindful of his friends and to assume a cooperative spirit.

The hunt, of course, is for Yakei-*san's* biff friend, a woman politely described as *kayabasuke*, a "red light district woman." A particularly vile variety that has as much in common with the dreamqueens of simsense celebrity as the average pay-toilet. Yakei-*san* appears to believe that his hope for a long and prosperous life depends on finding this biff, finding her tonight. This, too, is wise.

While they drive, Machiko takes two calls via commlink. The first is from Ryokai, reporting that he has made many contacts and heard much talk about Triads, but nothing of a definite nature. The second call is from Gongoro.

"This is a waste of time!" Gongoro declares. "We should be questioning informants in the Yoshida-*kai*!"

Fortunately, Machiko uses the ear piece from her commlink. She replies, "You have your instructions," and breaks the link.

Tonight, Serpents walk. A number of senior GSG, Ryokai and Gongoro included, lead teams of *kobun* and selected Nagato Security officers on sorties throughout the plex. They are prepared to turn these sorties into armed assaults if necessary, but bloodshed is not the objective. Their true objective is twofold. First, they seek persons identified in the shared Nagato Security-GSG database, persons known to be hostile to Nagato Combine, or those who have committed hostile acts. Such persons are to be questioned and any relevant leads should be pursued. What will come of this remains to be seen. Their second objective, Machiko's objective, is more strategic in nature, and affects her with far more uncertainty. Tonight's operation will be noticed. One member of the Guard stopping people in Brooklyn and asking questions would likely be noticed. Numerous GSG moving throughout the megaplex, accompanied by plain-clothes Nagato Security officers and *kobun* of the three clans will almost certainly cause concern and perhaps stimulate a response. Machiko can only guess at what effect this will have on the enemy she seeks, but she hopes it will incite an impetuous response, anything that will prove revealing, and thus better enable her to prepare the Guard for war.

And war is the point. It is in expectation of war that Machiko utilizes the threat of violence to intimidate Yakei-*san*. It is with this same expectation that she will use whatever means necessary to make the unwilling talk and convey the information she needs. Those who refuse to willingly aid Nagato Combine prove themselves aligned deliberately or by default with the enemies of Nagato Combine. If such persons are not responsive to mere words, then they will be intimidated, even brutalized, till possessed of a more cooperative spirit. Gangsters may utilize such tactics, but that is coincidental and of no importance. The objective of gangsters is to eliminate competitors and improve market position. Gangsters want nuyen, profit. If they cannot have what they covet in a civilized manner, they resort to physical violence. This bears no relation whatsoever to the violence and brutality of war, or the need for warriors to commit acts of utter savagery.

The warrior's Way is death. The warrior's function is to serve as a weapon, to meet the enemy, to attack and to kill, to be prepared to wage war and to kill the enemy in all places, at all times, under any circumstances, whether facing a single enemy or an army of ten thousand. If, instead of killing, Machiko must intimidate, torture, or maim to defeat the enemies of Nagato Combine, she will utilize all her resources to do the deed and do it with success. The essence of all strategy is founded on the necessity of overcoming opponents and defeating enemies. The means is incidental, a question of spirit and technique. Machiko will do whatever she must to defeat Nagato Combine's enemies, defend the life of the Chairman and the people and property of Nagato Combine. How she does it is of little importance. Whether she lives to see the result of her efforts, the final defeat of Nagato Combine's enemies, is of no importance whatsoever.

They come to a twilit street beneath the rust-plated pillars of an elevated subway line. The buildings rise like soot-blackened sepulchers into the pall of night. The pavement is scattered with litter and anonymous bits of metal. The few people in sight lurk in dark doorways and on the fringes of the twisted wreckage and piles of debris clogging the ends of alleyways. The Infinitis slow to a halt before a gleaming red marquee of a bar advertising "Sliffs! Sips! Simsense!"

"Yeah," says Yakei-*san*. "This is it."

The *kobun* behind the Infiniti's wheel glances aside at his headman, and says, "Trouble coming."

The headman looks ahead, then to the rear.

A deep resonant rumbling rises suddenly to banshee screams. A pair of cycles, blurring with speed, flash past on the left. They are followed by three, then a pack numbering as many as eight, all moving at speed. The riders appear like go-gangers, brilliant reflective helmets, gleaming wet-look jackets and boots, vambraces and gauntlets, some perhaps studded and spiked. The cycles have the mercurial stream-lined forms of Rapiers, Auroras, and Scorpions, all of them high-powered street machines.

The pack slows and bunches up at the end of the block. The headman of *kobun* cranes his neck and then grunts. "Duelists," he says, glancing back at Machiko. "A thrill gang, Machiko-*sama*. Streetscag. They have been causing Brooklyn a lot of trouble."

"Trouble directed at Nagato Combine?"

"No, they make trouble for everyone."

Machiko nods, and looks aside to Lieutenant Enotori. "You may proceed."

Enotori directs a quick glance up the block. The Duelists fill the street, some circling through the intersection, others taking pause. "Perhaps, until the situation clarifies—"

"The situation will be handled," Machiko says, softening her tone to balance the brevity of her words. "Please proceed."

Enotori affects a polite bow and heads into the bar. He is an investigative officer with the Nagato Security Service and has much experience, not in warfare, but in undercover operations. Tonight, he wears an antiqued brown synth-leather duster and the twin cams of his eyes relay everything he sees to Machiko's handcomp. As he enters the bar, Machiko directs Yakei-*san's* attention to the changing images on the handcomp's screen.

The interior of the bar is stroboscopic. Everywhere trid screens flicker and flash with spectral images, most of them portraying hard-core sex. The tables of booths running down the left burn with the fast-paced action. The bar along the right winks and flashes with adverts for private dances and other services available on the second floor.

"Machiko-*sama*," says the headman of *kobun*.

Machiko looks up, looks to the end of the block. Beneath the gleaming red disks of traffic signals the go-gangers now circle like scavenging birds. The thudding and whining of their cycles carries across the night like the murmuring of a distant storm.

"Put one man outside," Machiko says. "Show steel."

The headman speaks into his commlink. The rear door of the lead Infiniti swings open, and a large, powerful-looking male stands up on the street-side of the sedan. An Ingram SuperMach SMG fitted with a high-density 60-round clip hangs casually from his hand.

This is a warning, a sign even gangers should understand. Do not involve yourselves in matters that do not concern you. Be wary of where you tread. You may step under the iron boot heel of a giant.

The view through Machiko's handcomp pans across the booths at the rear of the bar. Machiko catches glimpses of faces and bodies briefly lit by the stroboscopic flarings of the tridscreens; orks and norms and at least a few elves, wearing synthleather and chrome and studded neon-spandex, dreamchippers and slots and party packers. And then Yakei-*san* blurting, "That's her! That's the biff!"

Her name is Choca. For a dwarf she is not unattractive, voluptuous in form, covered with glinting, winking techno trinkets, crowned by masses of yellow-striped sable hair that cascade about her head and shoulders. Standing on spike-heeled boots that add much to her height, and now taking a seat, joining a husky ork on the cushions of a narrow booth.

"They're forming up," says the headman of *kobun*.

Engines roaring and whining, the go-gangers move their cycles into a battle line that crosses the end of the block. They have seen the warning of the *kobun* and they answer it with the threat of combat. They leave Machiko no choice. She cannot summon police, nor merely turn and leave. The threat of the gangers must be met. Nagato Combine must stand firm in the face of battle or it will be perceived as weak, and all manner of violent elements will be encouraged to strike.

"Prepare to fight."

The headman barks orders into the commlink on his arm. *Kobun* scramble from the sedans. Machiko strides up the sidewalk to the front of the lead Infiniti and the roaring of the cycles rises to a cyclone wail. Two of the gangers start forward, raising a churning cloud to their rear. Their intention is plain. Machiko unlimbers her SCK M-100 submachine gun, clears the safety, and opens fire.

The fusillade that erupts immediately around her is deafening, full of the stammering of Yoshida-*kai* SMGs and the rapid thumping of clan automags. The first of the gangers to start forward veers suddenly to the left and careens over the curb. The cycle flattens itself against a grim-faced wall of brick. The rider, going airborne, smashes against the metal slats of a security shutter at the front of a shop and falls out of sight behind the burnt-out husk of an automobile. The second of the gangers to start forward, front wheel rising high, topples over backward and sprawls skidding onto the pavement.

The rest lift weapons as if to fire, but thunder is already raging. A third bike falls over sideways. Its rider staggers around and drops. Two more gangers are clearly hit, swaying as if struck by bats, but manage to keep to their saddles. The man at Machiko's right stumbles to his knees on the curb. Then the cycles are roaring as never before and bunching into a phalanx of macroplas and metal and hurtling up the block.

Gunfire rises to a crescendo. Machiko draws her Beretta 200ST and empties both automag and SMG into the swiftly advancing pack. Two more of the howling cycles crash. Machiko draws her katana, chooses her opponent, and strides into the roadway to meet him. The ganger hunches low behind the windscreen of his machine and wrenches at the throttle, setting the engine to screaming.

In the final instant, Machiko steps sideways and cuts. She cuts with all the power of will and spirit. Her sword cleaves through macroplas cowling, through chromed steel and synthleather and flesh and bone and casts a foaming wave of gore and blood across the breadth of the street. A bisected corpse tumbles to the pavement, trailing a broad smear of red. A riderless Scorpion flips over its front fork and crashes tumbling down the asphalt.

A fuel tank explodes. Two bikes collide and crash to the pavement. Another smashes through a barricade of metal drums and trash and slides into an alleyway. The three surviving machines hurtle to the end of the block, and turning, skidding, shrieking, round the corner and vanish from sight.

Machiko sheaths her sword, retrieves her guns and reloads. A Nagato SDF combat medical team soon arrives to tend the wounded. Three *kobun* require assistance, one is serious. The fallen gangers are all dead. The headman of *kobun* calls for additional men and turns to Machiko like a victorious general, his spirit huge and full of pride. The sharp nod he gives Machiko erases any questions she may have entertained concerning the loyalty of the Yoshida-*kai*, or the views of the clan's rank and file on metas.

"Your instructions, Machiko-*sama*!"

Machiko motions at the bar. "Guard all exits."

The headman gestures. *Kobun* head down the alleyways flanking the bar. Machiko pushes through the door at the front of the bar and enters a cataclysm of noise, rant rock so loud it rises to the level of static. The air is humid with heat and sweat, but the glimmer of feverish bipedal bodies shows clearly against the dark, as though human and metahuman burn with an inner light, and skin and clothes, flush with heat, are merely the shades enclosing many lanterns.

She finds Lieutenant Enotori at the rear of the bar counter. He points to a dark passage leading to a door at the building's rear. "Women's lavatory!" he says loudly into Machiko's ear.

The door to this room is marked with a holographic image of a female lying spread-eagle. Walking into this room is like walking into a brightly lit open sewer. The air reeks. The only toilet has overflowed onto the floor. The walls, the mirror, sink, and floor are all covered with the evidence of former patrons' uncivilized habits. Yakei-*san's* dwarf female chummer kneels by the sink, giving service to a husky ork.

Kayabasuke. Joro. A whore.

Machiko takes hold of the ork's right wrist, applies pressure and twists, and sends him stumbling toward the door. Three *kobun* propel him forcibly through the doorway and out. The dwarf female, Choca, looks on incredulously, then curses, getting to her feet. She is little more than half Machiko's height, yet evokes an expression of impassioned outrage.

"What the frag? *What the frag!*"

And as these words are exclaimed, a knife appears. The attack is expected. Machiko allows it only to demonstrate that resistance is useless. She deflects the blade by driving the arm that wields it away to the left, striking, then snaring it by the wrist, and then drives the blade of her right hand against Choca's neck. Choca rasps. She staggers back against the sink and drops to the floor. Machiko takes the knife, tosses it aside, then goes to one knee and seizes Choca's left ear in a ruthless grip.

Choca shrieks, but the shriek immediately goes silent. She convulses, heaves herself out flat on the floor, and lies there jerking and twitching.

"You spoke of a chrome killer who works cheaply for a mage," Machiko says. "The mage was described as a brain-buster. The killer said he will make the world safe for crazies and destroy all corps. You will tell me more."

Choca screams out curses. She screams as one suffering agony when Machiko renews the pressure on her ear.

"Do not deceive yourself. You will talk. If you do not respond to pain, I will summon a mage and he will enter your mind. And when we are done you will desire only merciful death."

"Stop it! Stop!" Choca shrieks.

Machiko eases the pressure.

"You're asking me what I heard," Choca says hoarsely. "That's all I know. I heard this *gillette* in a *bar* talking all kinds of *drek*! I never seen him before. I swear!"

"Perhaps you gave him service."

"So what if I did."

"At his doss'?"

"I don't remember!"

More pressure. More shrieks and convulsive tremors.

"Okay! okay! okay! FRAG IT!"

"The killer's name."

"Jank! *Jank!*"

"His address."

Choca mumbles an address. Machiko stands and tells the *kobun* behind her, "This person will accompany us."

The *kobun* seize Choca. Machiko leads the group from the lavatory to the front door of the bar and onto the sidewalk. She sees at once that the scene outside has changed. Sirens whoop and wail. An emergency service van marked for the NYPD Inc. is just then turning onto the block, blue lights strobing. Several armored patrol vehicles are already parked up and down the block. Numerous uniformed officers are moving about, checking the bodies of the dead gangers, speaking into commlinks and shining flashlights around.

As she steps onto the sidewalk she nearly collides with a trio of officers.

All three turn to face her abruptly. All three look at her as if astonished. One commands her to halt. Another moves a hand to his gun. The third steps toward her, reaching out with both hands, but before he can close the distance, the headman of *kobun* steps in and shoves, and the officer staggers backward and falls.

All three officers draw guns. One shouts into a commlink, "Ten-thirteen! ten-thirteen!" The others shout, "We got a situation!" *"Get on the ground! Get on the ground!"*

Machiko crosses her arms and waits. Through it all, she hears the footsteps of the *kobun* exiting the bar, fanning across the sidewalk behind her. She sees the NYPD officers' surprise and uncertainty swelling rapidly toward panic. For every *kobun* that exits the bar, the NYPD officers shift back another step, then another. They move to take cover as the *kobun* from the side and rear exits of the bar join the group on the sidewalk. More excited calls over commlinks. More sirens arising from all around. Before long, Machiko and the others are staring into the guns of some twenty to twenty-five NYPD officers, some in heavy armor.

Machiko waits, arms crossed, spirit settled.

The men of Yoshida-*kai* follow suit.

"Oh, *drek!*" Choca mutters. *"Drek! drek! drek!"*

Inevitably, one man steps forward. His uniform is marked by gold braid and a captain's insignia. He comes to within about three meters and pauses. He pops something, candy or perhaps a nut, into his mouth, chews, then pops another. He conceals an anxious spirit behind a mask of nonchalance.

"My name's Burke," he says. "We got ourselves a little situation. Suppose we try to talk it out before somebody does something stupid and we all do a lot of shooting."

Machiko replies, "I have no objection."

The captain steps closer. Pops another small something into his mouth and chews. "Busy night for Nagato. For the Guard especially. You got the whole plex in an uproar. What gives?"

It is unfortunate that this captain and his officers wear the uniform of the NYPD Inc. Of the three major corps making a business of law enforcement in the plex, the NYPD Inc. ranks as the least corruptible, perhaps because the union that owns and controls the corp ruthlessly excises any members found to be corrupt. Machiko therefore expects that this Captain Burke will act in accordance with police regulations, and that he would be unlikely to accept a bribe as a solution to his "situation."

"We are engaged in proprietary operations involving a known corporate terrorist," Machiko says. "You need not involve yourself or the NYPD corporation in these activities."

"Not get involved?" The captain affects surprise. "You got this whole damn street littered with dead men."

"You have witnesses to this?"

"Take a look around. I can see three or four meatjobs from right where I'm standing."

"Corpses lying in the street are not my concern."

"You got nothing to do with this? Is that what you're telling me?"

"The corpses of gangers lying in the street is not a matter concerning Nagato Combine. Therefore, I will have nothing to do with it. That is what I am saying."

"You will if you say I you will."

"Do you wish to negotiate or to make threats you may come to regret?"

"You did notice this isn't Nagato property, right?"

"Indeed. It is part of the whole megaplex, which must be

defended from the violent criminal elements that threaten all our people. Our respective organizations share responsibility for meeting that threat, as do all corporate citizens."

The captain spends a moment gazing at Machiko steadily, perhaps considering what she has said. "Lemme explain something. I'm the police. That makes me the legal authority here. And the law says you and your people are civilians. That's my point."

"Like you," Machiko replies, "I am a corporate officer, and I am engaged in the business of my corporation. That is my point."

The captain chews another of his small treats. "Let's cut the hype. You're a yak. Nagato's a yak operation. Those boys behind you are yakuza muscle."

"I am GSG. You should know what that implies."

"I'm well aware. I've seen phys-adepts in action. That's why we're standing here having this talk. But what you better know is that I can't have civilians shoving my cops around. That doesn't wash. *Comprende?*"

"You mean that something must be done."

"Dead scoots are a problem. Cops come first."

A wise philosophy. "What do you propose?"

"It's your move. Make a suggestion."

Machiko considers, then turns her head slightly as if to look back. "Shoeo."

One of the *kobun* comes striding swiftly toward her. He pauses at her side and bows. Machiko extends a hand.

"Your weapons."

Shoeo hands her a heavy automatic, nunchaku, two knives, and a taser. Machiko passes these to the headman of *kobun*, then looks back to Shoeo.

"You should not have pushed the NYPD officer. This disreputable act has caused embarrassment not only to Nagato Combine, but also to the NYPD corporation. The captain will hear your confession."

Shoeo bows, then turns to the Captain and bows again. "I confess to the dishonorable shoving of the NYPD officer. Please arrest me at once."

The captain looks briefly to Machiko, then turns and motions two of his officers forward. They approach warily, but with guns in holsters. They put Shoeo in handcuffs, conduct a cursory search, then lead him away. The captain looks to Machiko. He watches her a moment, then says, "I don't want any more incidents tonight. Whatever you're doing, keep it discreet. And move it the hell outta my precinct."

Machiko bows politely.

Corporate honor is satisfied.

Machiko motions her group to the Infinitis. She moves to the leading sedan and puts Choca into the rear seat ahead of herself. They drive a total of nine blocks in the shadows of the elevated subway line, past shuttered stores and grime-smeared bars, and come to a halt in front of a blackened brick structure, five stories tall, bearing the sign, "Fulton Ave Hostel."

Lieutenant Enotori enters through the battered gray metal door at the front of the hostel. The headman of *kobun* sends several of his men to watch the decrepit-looking fire escape dangling over one alleyway and to check for a rear exit. Devil rats dart away from their feet, fleeing piles of rubbish in search of safer refuge.

Enotori returns looking a bit disheveled. "I had to get rough with the clerk."

"Jank is registered?"

"Room four-two-three."

Machiko wastes no time. She moves to the entrance, pursued by the headman and some number of *kobun*. The metal door opens on a lobby that is little more than a corridor, sided on the right by the service counter of the hostel clerk. The clerk meets Machiko's roving eyes with a look of shocked alarm, but holds himself motionless. This reaction is mimicked by the sundry dozen norms and orks camping on tattered cots and filthy blankets along the left wall of the entrance corridor.

Squatters' quarters. Sleeping space for the destitute, the SINless, the dispossessed, the victims of ever-advancing technology and intercorporate war. In them, Machiko sees the cost of defeat, the fate of all persons who lack the resources and determination to face their enemies and fight. The mere thought of the people of Nagato Combine ever suffering such a fate only strengthens her resolve.

She finds stairs just past the service counter, a stairway of steel mesh and rickety, rusting supports. The entire structure rattles and rings with her every step. She has no need for stealth.

On the third-floor landing, a trio of males, two orks, one

norm, see her coming and flatten their backs to the walls, hands uplifted, palms open.

One of the orks affects a bow.

Machiko seizes his nape, but gently. "You know a one named Jank?"

She speaks in English. The ork affects another bow, deeper this time, very respectful, and replies in accented Japanese, "Yes, honorable one! Yes, I do! Jank is one floor up!"

"Show me."

The ork leads hurriedly up the stairs. The fourth floor corridor is lined with more indigents, sitting, sleeping, sometimes two or more to a blanket or cot. The doors to rooms are barely three meters apart and only a rare few are marked by any numbers, and even these are scrawled like so much graffiti.

The ork indicates a door. Machiko gestures. The ork backs away and *kobun* move to either side of the door.

Machiko drives her fist against the door lock. The flimsy macroplas surrounding it shatters. The door bursts inward. Machiko reaches for the grip of her katana, moving forward, but then lowers her hand to her side.

The rank stink that meets her nose is almost overpowering. She must settle herself, focus, before moving forward.

The room is a squatdoss, an enlarged coffin: no window, no telecom, no accessories. The walls are brown with stains and the scrawlings of former tenants. The floor is ancient blackened tile that crackles underfoot. A small army of roaches darts across the floor and dives under the mattress lying along the right. Opposite on the left lie a backpack and duffel bag. Machiko signals the *kobun* to remain at the doorway and steps cautiously, quietly to the "bed."

Lying on the bed is a male norm, nude. Jank. He lies in a putrid pool of his own filth. His features are obviously Chinese. He does not look tall, but his physique is huge, his muscles like braided cables, bulging beneath the skin, his chest like a massive dynamo, even in repose. His skull is bare but for a wedge of hair arcing over the top and datajacks at his temples. A polymer armored sheath, bonded to his flesh, covers everything beneath the level of his jaw. Both lower arms scan like cybernetic replacements, bulging with compartments and accessories: a tactical comp, a gyrostabilizer for weapons fire.

Beside Jank's head lies the squat gray plas of a sensedeck, a deck obviously modified or repaired, held together by macroplas tape. The yellow cable descending from the data-jack in Jank's left temple connects to the deck. Beside the deck lie a number of simsense chip-carriers colored in bright reds and yellows and labeled as BTL, with names like "Bustout," and "Trogbash," and "Dirty Brown Scum."

The sensedeck is running, a chip is loaded.

Every few moments Jank twitches and murmurs, like an antique CD spinning around and around, outputting the same data endlessly.

The twitching turns convulsive. The murmurs rise into shouts. "Stinking trogs! Weed-eaters! *Take it take it take it! GONNA GET YOU ALL! EAT YOU ALIVE! BURY YOU! YOU AND ALL THE DREK-SUCKING SCUM-*"

Abruptly, his eyes snap open and gaze straight up at the ceiling like a man gone blind. He is nearly sitting up with the violence of the convulsions wracking his entire body.

"Machiko-*sama*!"

She finds the headman of *kobun* standing beside the foot of the bed, looking to her with an expression of startled amazement, amazement turning to revulsion, horror, and suddenly it all clicks.

She feels it in her belly.

"COVERRR!" she roars.

She turns and propels herself forward, away from the bed, into the headman of *kobun*, into him bodily, driving him back, away from the bed, toward the doorway, toward the corridor and safety. The headman's look turns to mindless astonishment. The *kobun* standing in the doorway seem to move as if encased in mud. She has time to see surprise registering on their faces, the sudden tension of alarm spreading through their bodies and limbs. Then the explosion erupts. She hears the dull rumbling of its beginning, rising into a deafening roar. She feels the shock wave batter her feet, sweeping up the length of her legs, catching her up like a fist, lifting her, hurling her forward.

The headman falls beneath her as if driven down by the breaking crest of a wave. The corridor wall comes at her. She prepares to fall against it, to break the impact, but then the impact is upon her and she feels the filth-smeared surface giving way beneath her chest.

Then nothing.

19

The rear compartment of the SDF medical van is lit brightly. Equipment beeps and hums. The air smells of disinfectant.

Machiko is a while persuading her eyes to open. The level of pain she felt in the wake of the explosion outside clan headquarters, little more than twenty-four hours ago, was nothing compared to what she feels now, like she has been pummeled by several shots from a rail gun. Her skull feels as fragile as the shell of an egg, her ribs like frail sticks. Sitting up takes an immense act of will. Medtechs speak of bruised bones, micro-fractures, concussion effects, but she ignores them. She pulls sensors from her temples, her chest, her wrist, and adjusts her clothes. Fortunately, the medtechs have made no attempts at treatment other than basic first aid. Any form of invasive treatment would likely do more harm than good.

She struggles to her feet, fighting the weakness and pain that make a haze of her vision and threaten to lay her out flat.

Outside the side door of the medvan she finds a scene of controlled chaos: a line of people laid out on blankets on the sidewalk, coughing, moaning, sobbing, armored SDF troopers and NYPD police, shouting, gesturing, security vans and fire-rescue vehicles, blue lights strobing, a chopper thumping by overhead.

Immediately to her right, she finds the headman of *kobun*, his head swathed in bandages, his cheek bruised almost black, his left arm in a sling. His black, blue-trimmed jacket lies over the arms of the *kobun* standing beside him. Machiko's swords lie over the jacket.

Both men bow deeply. Machiko accepts the swords and returns them to their places, katana behind her shoulder, wakizashi at her waist. "Tell me what has occurred," Machiko says. "Since the explosion."

The headman bows. "Please excuse my ignorance,

Machiko-*sama*. I was knocked unconscious by the blast.
When I awoke, I found that the Nagato lieutenant had summoned help."

"Where is Lieutenant Enotori?"

"Here, Machiko-*san*."

Machiko turns to find the man approaching from behind
her. His voice, so near, comes as enough of a surprise that
she momentarily forgets herself and turns without regard for
injury or pain. A new wave of feebleness sends her swaying
backward, off-balance, bumping into the side of the medvan.
Abruptly, she discovers herself sitting down, sitting on the
metal step beneath the side door of the medvan.

Enotori catches her shoulders. "Machiko-*san*," he says,
"you should be in the hospital."

This is out of the question. "Status."

Enotori rubs briefly at his brow. His face is smudged with
grime. "I notified the SDF teams on standby to respond to
our location. Fire and police services also responded. The
total damage done by the explosion was not so great, but
there was some smoke and the tenants on the fourth floor
panicked. Many were injured in the rush down the stairway.
The Yoshida-*kai* executive for this district has just arrived
with additional *kobun* to assist with the situation."

This is good. That uninvolved persons should have been
injured is very disturbing, but not the most pressing issue on
Machiko's mind. "What of the room? What of Jank?"

Enotori briefly explains that the precinct commander for
this area, a Winter Systems officer, has interceded on behalf
of Nagato Combine to forestall any unwanted interference.
"A Nagato forensics team has just begun examining the
room. It appears that Jank was fitted with a cranial bomb. He
is dead."

Machiko exerts herself to think. "What evidence has been
found?"

"Perhaps among the most significant comes from my
headware memory. I downloaded my recorded images of
Jank to the Nagato network. I ran a graphic comparison with
the partial images of the assassin who killed Mitsuharu-*san*
of the GSG."

Machiko puzzles over this. "We have images of this
assassin?"

"Yes, Machiko-*san*. A few partial images only. One of the
security cams at Mitsuharu-*san's* residence complex is a

dunce, a closed-circuit manually operated cam. It cannot be accessed through the Matrix. The Security Service discovered this only this morning, and there was some difficulty processing the images."

"What of your comparison?"

"According to the analyzer I ran, the chance is sixty-seven percent that Jank was the same killer captured on the cam at Mitsuharu-*san's* residence complex."

The implications are difficult to grasp. "You saw Jank?"

"Yes, I looked into the room just prior to the explosion."

Machiko struggles to clear her mind, subdue the pain. "Then we have a tentative connection. A connection between assassins and a mage. Perhaps the mage responsible for sending the bomb to the Open House is the same mage Jank spoke about. Have we found any clues about this mage in Jank's room?"

"We found these." Enotori shows her what appear to be three standard credsticks. "They are registered to a corporate account. The Red Pavilion, Inc. Located in the Bronx."

The name is well known. Its significance is such that Machiko feels a sudden surging of strength. For the first time since she woke, her mind seems to come clear. The Red Pavilion has for many years served as the gathering place for the most influential Triad bosses in the plex. It is the headquarters of the Large Circle League. "Then we are indeed at war, if not with the League, then with one of its affiliates."

Enotori's expression turns uncertain. "It is perhaps unlikely that Jank could have stolen Red Pavilion credsticks. However, his use of BTL disturbs me."

"Please explain."

"We have already found some dozens of BTL chips among the debris in Jank's room. The seals on these chips were all broken, indicating that they had been used. Jank's sensedeck appears to have been modified. We have the report on Jank's aberrant behavior, the boasts he made concerning the mage, destroying all corps, and we have the fact of the surroundings in which he lived."

"You suggest that Jank has abused BTL for some time."

"Particularly in light of the way he died. It would appear that Jank suffered some form of convulsive episode, a seizure, brought on by extreme sensory overload, similar in effect to the lethal feedback induced in deckers by killer IC.

This episode was sufficiently disruptive to the centers of the brain to trigger the bomb in Jank's head."

"Are you suggesting that this was deliberate? That Jank was situated here, jacked into a sensedeck, as a sort of booby trap?"

"I am aware of cases where this has been done, but I do not suspect that such could be the case here. The trail that led us to Jank was too tenuous, too reliant on coincidence, on the informants we happened to interview. A mage on the astral could have monitored our progress, but no one could have anticipated that we would be led to Jank."

"Enotori-*san*, what is your point?"

The lieutenant bows slightly, perhaps to apologize for being so verbose. "Merely this, Machiko-*san*. When BTL abuse leads to death, it is almost always a result of long-term abuse. I do not believe that the bosses of the Large Circle League would tolerate one of their soldiers abusing BTL."

Indeed.

Machiko considers this for some moments. Enotori's speculation leads her to a single conclusion. "Perhaps Jank was on the run from his own people."

"Yes, and the Security Service is already checking on this possibility. We have initiated a search of all relevant databases."

Unfortunately, broadband searches take time, especially when involving organizations such as Triads, with members numbering in the millions and activities spanning the globe. Machiko does not feel inclined to sit back and wait for search results. She could wait for many weeks to come and gain nothing by it, because nothing will ever come as clear and pure as crystal to her doorway. That is simply the Way of the world. She has been given the authority to act and that is what she must do.

When the sword will not cut, stab at the enemy's heart.

Machiko finds the strength to stand, then to walk to the Infiniti E9 sedans. The headman of *kobun* bows. "How may we serve, Machiko-*sama*?"

"We visit the Red Pavilion. Drive slowly."

The headman does not hesitate. He orders his men into the cars. They are on the verge of pulling out when another car comes to a screeching halt nearby. Ryokai emerges. Machiko lowers her window.

"I was told you were wounded!"

The expression on Ryokai's face is full of concern and wonder. It is unfortunate. Machiko has no wish to speak harshly to Ryokai, for he has always been loyal, but she can imagine no way around it. "If you were concerned for my injuries, you should have sent a protective detail. You have duties that require you to be elsewhere. Duties that take precedence."

"You are not wounded?"

Machiko summons the strength to take a tone of fellowship, of compassion. "Ryokai-*san*," she says, "if there is war, many will die. You must steel yourself for this."

"Just say if you are all right!"

It would cost nothing to give him the answer he wants, but Machiko finds she cannot say the words. Ryokai should not be here inquiring after her condition. He should be with his team on Staten Island pursuing their plan. A warrior cannot turn from battle merely because a comrade has been hurt. "Your heart is too great," she tells him. "Return to duty." Then, to the headman, "Drive."

The Infinitis move out. They take local streets to the Brooklyn Queens Expressway, leading to the Triborough Bridge. The sedans settle into the right lane and assume a sedate pace. Machiko closes her eyes and settles her spirit. She gains focus, strives to encourage flesh and bone to heal, to cast off the distractions of pain. She succeeds only to a degree. She has taken an excess of physical punishment in the last two days. Her resources are growing slim. She needs rest.

As the cars ride down onto the streets of the south Bronx, she hears the headman of *kobun* saying, "Machiko-*sama*, your action saved this old man his worthless life. I owe a great debt."

Machiko bows. "Please do not speak to me of debts. Duty determined my actions, as it determines yours. Duty must guide our every action if we are to defeat the enemies of Nagato Combine."

The headman bows.

Before long they are gliding to a halt before the broad red walkway leading to the Red Pavilion's main entrance. "Remain in the car."

"Yes, Machiko-*sama*."

The Pavilion is five stories of classic pagoda-style architecture rimmed in winking neon and accented by the flashing

laser displays in the upper windows. A large crowd, trailing
away from the entrance and halfway down the block, waits
behind velvet ropes along the right of the walkway. Portions
of the sidewalk flicker with images from inside the club:
people dancing, carousing, partaking of other amusements.
The men in red suits, keeping watch over the entrance, the
walk, the crowd and the street, begin backing rapidly to the
Pavilion's main entrance, some speaking into commlinks,
some looking frantically about, as Machiko advances.

She is met at the entrance by a wall of ten or more guards,
soldiers in red suits. Several conceal hands inside their suit
jackets as if holding weapons. More than a few appear very
nervous.

"What do you want?" asks one.

"Lau Tsang."

"He . . . he is not here!"

"Then I will wait."

She is not kept waiting long. She has unsettled her
enemy's spirit, upset their rhythm. Guards speak to headmen
who speak to bosses. A Serpent on our doorstep? It is perhaps unprecedented. It may be insanity. In the space of one
step, she has moved from Bronx County to a plot of land
controlled by some of the most ruthless criminal bosses to be
found in North America. They are the law here. There is no
other authority that might act to prevent them from killing
her where she stands.

However, the soldiers before her do not seem eager to
make the attempt. Their eyes keep moving to the grips of her
swords.

A short, slim man, a norm, with white razorslashed hair
and a dark blue suit, steps through the wall of soldiers. His
face like a wall of stone reveals nothing. His chrome eyes
dart up and down Machiko's front, then he says, "What is
your business with Lau Tsang?"

"I bring him a gift."

"What gift?"

"An item from a dead man."

The one with chrome eyes gives no immediate response.
Perhaps he makes use of headware communications. "I will
take you to Lau Tsang. This way."

The Pavilion's ground floor is half restaurant, half club. A
posh womb lined in velvet red. Music rampages like a fac-
tory raging out of control. Lasers flicker incessantly. Host-

esses in revealing electro-bodyware parade around with chrome-mirrored trays, necklaces of sensechips diving into incongruous depths of augmented cleavage.

Yet, in spite of all this static, Machiko notices many heads turning, people looking and gaping at her. The trappings of the Guard make her an outsider, a foreign enemy. Her genes make her *kawaruhito*, less than human. Machiko notices no other metas, nothing but norms, Asians, primarily Chinese. Even the tallest look no taller than her.

The man with chrome eyes leads her into one of a bank of escalators. At the second floor, they enter an elevator. This ascends to the fourth floor. A few steps along a corridor furnished all in red bring her to a private office paneled in red satin. She is left here alone for some minutes.

Then a side door opens and in steps a man, a norm, Chinese. Machiko knows him as Lau Tsang, the League's chief of enforcement. He looks rather like a corporate finance officer. His suit is gray and black and conservatively cut. He comes alone to show that he is not afraid. He moves to the side of a desk that appears hewn out of black marble and, affecting a casual manner, lights a cigarette. He hold Machiko's gaze for the space of two long drags on the cigarette, then says, "You're the chief Serpent now."

"For the moment."

"I hear it may be permanent. As permanent as these things ever get."

The sense in which his words might be construed as a threat seem incidental, but they give Machiko a thought. Just briefly, she considers taking the man's head. She could certainly do it. The man would be dead and growing cold before the guards in the corridor outside knew what had happened. She would probably be killed before she could fight her way out of the building, but Lau Tsang would still be dead.

The thought that keeps her sword in its scabbard is that killing Lau Tsang would not serve Nagato Combine. Wars are rarely won by killing the general, for there is always another general. It is the army that must be defeated. It is the ability to wage war that must be destroyed. It is the will of the ordinary soldier to fight that must be crushed.

She takes one of the credsticks from Jank's room, holds it up for Lau to see, then places it on his desk.

"Some gift," he says.

"Scan it."

Lau takes another drag of his cigarette. He moves around to the rear of the desk and slots the credstick into a port on the desktop telecom. His expression reveals only mild curiosity. "Where did you find this credstick?"

"On the person of a man called Jank."

"I do not know the name."

"Yet he had the credstick for a Red Pavilion account."

Lau shrugs. "Credsticks may be stolen. Account data can be forged. Why do you bring this to me?"

"To ask if you seek war."

Lau takes a drag of his cigarette. He appears very calm and cool. He opens a drawer of the desk and then lays a heavy automatic on the desktop and then quietly closes the drawer. He waves briefly at the automatic. "I have many guns," he says. "If the competition wants war, they will have it. The current troubles between your Toki-clan yakuza and my League will seem like minor disagreements compared to any war, if it comes."

Machiko watches the man. He does indeed seem prepared to make war. Machiko doubts he would fight it personally. "We have drawn a connection between this man Jank and the bombing attack on the clan headquarters in Newark. We have also identified Jank as one of the assassins who attacked members of the Guard."

"Is this to justify a threat of war?"

"Warriors do not make threats. They make war. If I had come here to make war, your head would be lying on the floor."

"And if I told you that the League has nothing to do with any of this, the attacks on your headquarters, on the Serpents, what then?"

"I would ask how this man Jank obtained a Red Pavilion credstick."

"Perhaps, at one time, I knew this man, under a different name. I have not heard of him for many months." Lau takes a deep drag of his cigarette and gazes briefly at Machiko, and says, "Men develop bad habits. They utilize excessive amounts of chrome. They grow unstable, and unreliable."

"And you let this man live?"

"We do not kill every person who fails us. It would be inhumane." Lau again pauses, gazing steadily at Machiko, then says, "Allow me to put this in perspective for you. My problem with the Nagato Combine involves only your Toki-clan. They tread on League territory. We have competing interests. I would not order these attacks you mentioned because I see no profit in going to war with the whole Nagato Combine. Small skirmishes can be useful in determining market position. A war would involve other interests that are currently content to leave us to our business. A war would have no true winner. Do you see?"

A gangster speaking of profit. Machiko can imagine nothing that would seem more natural. It is as natural as a gangster describing another's territory as his own. As natural as murdering one's competitors, assassinating entire families, in order to steal lucrative businesses, in order to amass power and wealth. The Large Circle League, like the other Triad organizations, has been many years rising out of the bloody gutters of the plex. Only in recent years have they managed to finally eclipse the Seoulpa Rings, formerly their closest competitors. Only now, as they finally become significant, as they reach a position where they may confront a potentially dangerous opponent such as the Toki-*gumi*, does Lau Tsang grow cautious, and in this he is indeed very wise.

Were the Yoshida-*kai* to extend the aid offered to the Toki-*gumi*, they would begin by sending enough *kobun* that Lau Tsang's "League" might well be smothered. Were the complete forces of Nagato Combine to be marshaled in the effort—including the military-grade units of the Security Defense Force—Lau Tsang would beg for peace, peace at any price.

But of course the need would have to be very extreme before Honjowara-*sama* would allow SDF units to roll on the Bronx. It would have to be morally just—a necessity to defend honorable working people from the violence of murderers and other vile felons. For any true military-style response would have inevitable consequences, not the least of which might be the loss of innocent lives.

"How did Jank fail you?"

Lau shrugs. "A small matter. He failed to complete an assignment. It does not concern yakuza."

Machiko struggles to maintain a settled spirit. Being referred to as "yakuza" by a gangster such as Lau Tsang is no compliment. It is very near to an insult that cannot be ignored. Indeed, the ancestors of the clans of Nagato Combine could only be described as yakuza, but in this context Lau's remark is a statement of pure arrogance. It shows only contempt for the fact that the days have long passed when the three clans worked like vicious gangsters. It shows only disdain for the fact that Honjowara-*sama* exerts himself relentlessly to see that such times do not return. Machiko lets this insult pass only with great difficulty. She tells herself that the type of "assignment" Jank is likely to have failed probably involved murder and therefore is absolutely antithetical to the ethics of the Chairman's New Way.

And thus the distinction between the Large Circle League and Nagato Combine becomes plain. And thus Lau Tsang is revealed as the arrogant, vile criminal that he is.

"What do you know of Jank's current associates?" Machiko asks.

"They attract Serpents to the Red Pavilion." Lau takes a quick drag of his cigarette. "This I do not like."

Neither does Machiko like it.

The man disgusts her.

20

When she wakes, the Infiniti E9 is parked on a dark street she does not immediately recognize. To the left, a row of low commercial structures like warehouses. To the right, a brick wall and an ornate iron gate. The characters beside the gate read, "Plum Festival Teahouse," and then the memory comes. A teahouse in Brooklyn, maintained by the Yoshida-*kai*.

"Machiko-*sama* . . . please."

She finds the headman of *kobun* leaning in through the open door at her right, inviting her with a gesture to emerge, to follow him to the gateway. She has no reserves of strength with which to argue. She remembers walking out of the Red Pavilion, getting into the car, struggling against the rise of fatigue. Apparently, the battle was lost.

Inside the entranceway of the teahouse wait the woman in charge and two of her geisha. They offer her tea, a bath, a massage. None of this is needed or desired. Flesh demands its due. Exhaustion is overwhelming. Pain returns. Machiko accepts the offer of a place to sleep and follows the geisha to a room, already prepared. The geisha help her undress. They provide a rack for her swords and a small chest for her other equipment. They take her clothes, presumably to see them laundered. She hardly hears them. She lies down on the bedding and closes her eyes, and, in just moments, it seems, goes under.

Sleep is deep and unrelenting, forcing her down, down, down, till even dreams are smothered.

When she wakes, the room is full of sunlight. Sliding panels off to her left stand open, looking into a small, domed garden. But it is neither the sunlight nor the garden that snare her attention. On the threshold of the room kneels a solitary figure, facing the light, the garden, his back to the room. His hair, black as the darkest heart of metahumanity, flows over his shoulders a halfway down his back. He wears the green *gi* of a master of the Guard. Machiko would know him regardless of such superficial traits as grooming and attire. Kuroda-*sensei* has the presence of a man whose body is made of rock, rooted in the earth, beyond doubt or uncertainty.

Machiko gets to her knees and bows deeply.

"Please dress," says Kuroda-*sensei*. "When you are ready, we will speak."

It is an overt invitation for Machiko to prepare herself properly. The warrior must be as meticulous in her appearance as she is in the condition of her weapons, for this demonstrates fanaticism in the Way. She calls for a bath. Two geisha move to assist, but she refuses all help. She washes, arranges her hair, trims fingernails and toenails and tends to all the other small details that demand her attention. She ignores the lingering aches from yesterday's injuries. Once she has donned her clothes and weapons, she moves to kneel at Kuroda-*sensei's* left, just slightly to his rear.

He says, "The ancient masters have written that it is an error to put forth effort, obtain a degree of understanding, then stop. The warrior's tenacity should be excessive. Something done with moderation may later be viewed as insufficient."

The point of this seems clear, Kuroda-*sensei* is familiar with the details of last night's operations. "You say that I should have killed Lau Tsang."

"Why did you let him live?"

"I did not think his death would serve Nagato Combine."

"You grow clever in your opinions. What has happened to the purity of your warrior spirit? Is it not your duty to strike down Nagato Combine's enemies wherever you may find them?"

Machiko bows deeply, shamed to think that she may have failed in this most essential manner. "Perhaps I turn from the Way. Sensei, it is hard to know what is right. The situation lacks clarity. The Chairman has charged me with seeking one enemy in particular, but I am not sure where this enemy will be found."

"Your spirit is unsettled."

"Yes."

"The warrior must distinguish between time of war and time of peace. You seek to enter battle before the war is truly begun, before the armies approach the field of battle. This is why you turn to clever opinions to explain why you allowed Lau Tsang to live. This is where you err."

"Yet we have been attacked. Blood has been spilled."

"The work of assassins. No war was ever won by such work. Perhaps it presages war and perhaps it does not. Perhaps the enemy you seek is incapable of waging war on Nagato Combine. Have you considered this?"

Machiko bows deeply. "No, *sensei*, I have not."

"Before battle comes, the warrior must spend every moment learning. She must ask questions. She must confer with others. She must discard all personal bias."

"Who should I consult?"

"Begin with me."

The idea nudges Machiko slightly off-balance. She had always assumed that the masters of the Guard spent most of their time at the GSG academy north of the city, along the banks of the Hudson, training neophytes and contemplating the writings of the ancients. What Kuroda-*sensei* says now suggests another possibility. "You know something of this situation, Kuroda-*sensei*?"

"The Nagato Directorate of Intelligence seeks mercenaries. They seek the White Octagon. They have information that the White Octagon is behind these recent attacks."

"I have not heard of this group before."

"That is because Adachi Dosan, director of intelligence, is a merchant, a son of Yoshida, a clan of merchants. How would it profit a merchant to speak to GSG? If Adachi and his directorate solve all our riddles and identify the threat, the Chairman must give praise and all of Yoshida will grow large in spirit."

"You speak harshly of Yoshida."

"We must avoid the appearance of impotence. The disloyal will use such an appearance to criticize the Chairman's New Way. They will use this to justify putting an end to the extravagance of the Guard and then to cleansing Nagato Combine of metas. You took a great risk walking into the headquarters of the Large Circle League. Extremists will view this as proof of a treasonous liaison."

Machiko finds this difficult to comprehend. "I have been wounded twice in as many days in the Chairman's cause. Who could possibly suspect me of treason?"

"Indeed," says Kuroda-*sensei*. "The timing of these events is fortunate. It is timing that makes all the difference. You must remain aware of that fact. Now tell me what passed between you and Lau Tsang."

This is swiftly done.

Kuroda-*sensei* sits motionless, facing the garden, eyes closed, for many moments. "Lau Tsang is a clever man, a player of Go. He will not wait for circumstances to escalate. He will act on the information you have provided him."

"Have I helped him in some way?"

"You have informed him that a person he once held as a valued asset has conducted offensive operations against Nagato Combine. This was done without his permission. And it threatens him with much more than a visit from one member of the Guard."

"What will he do?"

Before Kuroda-*sensei* gives any reply, Machiko's comm-link beeps. She finds Ryokai on the small screen on her left vambrace. "We have just received a very unusual delivery," he says.

"Please explain," Machiko replies.

Ryokai hesitates, then says, "This defies any simple explanation."

21

"What do you mean she's gone?"

"She's gone. Jacked out. Flipped off."

"Check with your people in Queens."

"Already did that. Poppy's buzzed—"

Abruptly, Gamma lifts his mage's wand, and the synth-leather-clad cutter before him staggers back, falls to the floor, and writhes, looking like a man in agony, an agony so intense he makes no sound. "I warn you as I warned her," Gamma says. "I do not appreciate disloyalty. Poppy allowed my pet decker to escape, so she was punished. Now she turns traitor and runs. You will send someone to find her. Before she can disrupt my plans. Do you understand?"

The cutter, still writhing, nods his head.

Gamma turns away.

Neona watches anxiously from her couch as Gamma turns, turns toward her. She clutches the platinum-hued case of her Fairlight Invader and wishes the cold steel manacles gripping her ankles would just disappear, like she wishes Gamma's anger would disappear. The manacles, she knows, are just for her protection, to deter anyone from trying to snatch her, but they make her anxious, like Gamma's anger makes her anxious. She knows Gamma's got every right to be angry, he's been so good to everyone in the group, but his anger, his moods, still make her anxious. Gamma's dangerous even when he's calm. Very sensitive about things. He could do a person serious harm.

Now he sits right beside her, lays his mage's wand across his lap, and slips an arm around Neona's back. The hand gripping his mage's wand is twisted and gnarly. The hand slipping up the back of Neona's neck feels like an invading army of creepy-crawling bugs, raising her hackles.

Gamma smiles. "It's time for you to meet your contacts in the Matrix."

Neona nods her head. "Yeah, wiz."

"I need more detailed information. I need specifics. I want to know what the defilers are planning. I want the names of their allies. I want details on the malefactors who lead them. Most of all, I want specifics on the great parasite himself, where he will be, whom he will meet. Do you understand?"

Neona nods her head. "Jewel."

"Remember. They are a cancer. A festering wound on the face of the planet. Once we have accumulated sufficient evidence, we will heal that wound forever. All is in alignment. The formula of our tomorrows is clear, bidding us onward."

Neona nods her head. "Got it."

Gently, Gamma kisses her brow, right near her datajack. It gives her shivers. "My electron Angel."

Yeah . . .

She jacks her Fairlight Invader into the telecom beside the couch, then snugs another fiber-optic lead into her head.

Then she's sliding down a quick blackness, flashing through the virtual workspace inside her deck, initialing progs, triggering utilities, and then diving down the dataline—swift as light, nimble as angels dancing on pins—into the burning neon nightscape of the local telecommunications grid.

Neona Jaxx no longer—she's a ramjamming electron Angel in pulsing gold armor, suited up with a halo and wings and her Invader iconic keyboard guitar.

She skates past a thousand nodes in the blink of one golden eye. She fires herself across the grid, a poseur fone call, a fantasy data transfer, slipping through node after node, disguising her signal, cloaking her backtrail. Not the easy way to play it, but for an Angel like herself it's the only trip to Paydata Heaven that doesn't include a free ride to Deadly Feedback Hell.

At exactly 11:03:01:47:14:29, a yellow dot appears on the dataline directly in front of her face and unfolds like a blossom of light into a twelve-sided polyhedron that shimmers like it's made of mirrors. In fact it's a teleporting SAN—system access node—that appears and disappears around the grid according to a time schedule defined by a very secret algorithm, one Neona's still trying to scope out.

She dives right into the node.

Then the weirdness happens.

It's like the much-fabled Ghost seizes her signal. She feels a tug. The whole LTG seems to flash blurring past her iconic eyes. She isn't sure what the frag's going on, and she's been trying to scan it for weeks, but, abruptly, she's in the node.

A sculptured node. Very weird.

She stands facing a narrow corridor of brilliant yellow light that extends on straight as a dataline to infinity. Something approaches out of the farthest reaches of the corridor. At first it looks like a simple rectangular icon. The rectangle swiftly evolves into a sort of booth, like from a carnival arcade. Two meters tall, trimmed in elaborate swirls of gold, with a transparent pane like a window. On the other side of the window sits something like a big life-sized puppet of a gypsy lady: eyes like pits; black hair wrapped in a bandanna; ears, neck, and arms loaded with gaudy jewelry; blood red talons adorning each finger.

As the booth draws near and halts, a thousand little glinting silvery motes swarm out from about the sides of the booth and surround Neona like a cloud.

Neona reaches out, and, with one golden electron finger, presses the button on the front of the booth.

"Press Here," it says.

Thunder rumbles and crashes. Something creaks. A cat yowls. The Gypsy Lady in the booth slowly lifts a blazing electron card to her brow, then says, "Your fortunes are on the rise. What do you desire?"

"Gamma wants more dirt on Nagato Corp," Neona says.

"The spirits give their answer."

Golden coins the size of soyburgers begin pouring from a chute in the front of the booth: datastores downloading. Neona snatches and scans each coin as it flies toward her belly: data on toxic waste, pollutants dumped raw into the environment, people paid off to look the other way. All kinds of squat like that. Just the kind of squat Gamma always wants, the kind he lives and breathes for. The kind that's kept him sending Neona into the Matrix over and over.

"What about the Great Defiler?" Neona asks, using Gamma's name for the slag. "Where's he gonna be?"

The Gypsy Lady lifts another card. "Spirits predict."

More coins sluice from the chute. Neona finds herself scanning plans for the Chrysanthemum Palace, an immense hotel and casino complex built someplace in Brooklyn, a place called "Coney Island." The datastores give every detail of the Palace's defenses, as well as the agenda for the Great Defiler's visit.

Absolutely jewel.

"Now spirits demand a service," the Gypsy Lady says.

"Null sheen, *omae*."

More coins, dozens and dozens of coins, every one of them winking with nuyen and the coordinates of distant LTGs. "Complete these data transfers," the Gypsy Lady says. "Take care that you are not traced. Dark forces watch the grid."

It's a steal of a deal, a little net running in exchange for proprietary data Neona would have to risk brain and body to get on her own. "What's the algorithm for our next meet?"

The Gypsy Lady downloads the data.

22

The man on the telecom is Adachi Dosan, Nagato Director of Intelligence, and his manner is modest and conciliatory. "My agents have heard only rumors concerning White Octagon, Machiko-*san*," he says. "We are investigating these rumors, but currently we know very little about this group. They are apparently a local bias group, virulently anti-meta. I have nothing as yet to tie White Octagon to the attacks on Nagato Combine. One source indicates that they may be a splinter faction of other, better-known bias groups, but this again is mere speculation."

"But potentially of significance," Machiko replies. "I would appreciate being kept apprised of such news, Adachi-*san*."

"I will certainly see that you are."

They end the call. Machiko turns from the telecom to the room's only other source of light, the broad pane of a two-way mirror providing a private view of the room immediately adjacent. In that room, otherwise bare, with walls of concrete, sits a young woman of Chinese blood. She sits slumped, handcuffed to her chair, head lolling forward. She wears black synthleather and boots and studded bands around neck and wrists. The evidence of a savage beating is quite clear. Her face and head are purple with bruises. Veins of dried blood descend from her nose and mouth. She is missing at least one tooth. Her arms and hands bear numerous abrasions. Her over-sized jacket, lying on the floor beside her, her sleeveless blouse and fitted slacks are dirty, stained and torn.

But what holds Machiko's attention are the octagonal tat-toos adorning both the woman's arms, and her hair. The hair about the sides of her head has been shaved in such a manner that, with her head slumped forward, the hair atop her head also takes the form of an octagon.

"You say she was dumped by the main entrance?"

"Correct," Gongora says tersely. "A car pulled up. She was thrown out. The *kobun* at the entrance said that a man in the car, a Chinese, said she is a gift from Lau Tsang."

The entrance Gongoro refers to is the entrance to the headquarters building of the Yoshida-*kai*, located in Bensonhurst, Brooklyn. The room where the "gift" now sits is in the basement of the headquarters building. Doubtless, Lau Tsang's people recognized that Machiko traveled with Yoshida-*kai* *kobun* and so chose the Yoshida-*kai* headquarters as the place to deliver his gift. The key point about all this, in Machiko's view, recalls Kuroda-*sensei's* words to mind: *Lau Tsang is a clever man . . . He will act on the information you have provided him . . . Someone conducts offense operations without his permission . . .*

Gongoro growls, "What has this to do with the attacks on Nagato?"

Machiko explains about her visit with Lau. "Apparently this woman is intended to demonstrate that the Large Circle League has no intention of inciting a war."

Ryokai appears astonished.

Gongoro seems unimpressed. "I could have told you this," he growls. "If for once you would just *listen to me!*"

"I seek intelligence," Machiko says. "Is that not what one does in expectation of war? You speak often and loudly, Gongoro-*san*, but you offer only words and more words to substantiate your claims."

"And what is this woman? She proves nothing! She is barely conscious!"

Machiko gives no reply.

A medtech arrives to treat the woman's wounds. Two techs from the Nagato Security Service arrive moments later to scan the woman for implanted cybernetics. The medtech reports that the woman is suffering no life-threatening injuries and requires rest. The senior security tech informs, "She has a number of basic street samurai augmentations, such as eye and ear replacements, an oral dart, not loaded, a fingertip compartment and hand razors, as well as muscle improvements and an adrenal pump."

"You found no evidence of cranial explosives?"

"None whatsoever."

Before the coming of war, the warrior must learn, ask questions, confer. Very well. Machiko turns again to the telecom and contacts Colonel Satomi, deputy chief of

Nagato security operations, and says, "I have not yet had the opportunity to review the latest findings concerning the killers who attacked Sukayo-*san*, Ryokai-*san*, and myself."

The colonel quickly arranges himself to give a quick briefing. The telecom screen divides into several windows. In one, Machiko sees the bodies of the dead killers laid out on metal tables.

"We have other sources yet to contact," the colonel says, "but it begins to appear as though these killers may be ciphers, their true identities erased from Matrix datastores. Genetically, one is Korean, one is Caucasian, and the last is Japanese."

"I see the Japanese bears tattoos."

"Yes, and we have examined these quite closely. They are not consistent with the type of tattoo used by any of the North American clans, or those native to Nippon. One of my officers with expertise in such matters indicates that although these tattoos cover much of the killer's body, they are many separate tattoos, rather than a traditional full-body tattoo."

Members of the clans wear full-body tattoos. This is the custom, as Machiko is well aware. The tattoo may include many distinct elements, such as the lotus and reed, as in the case of the Honjowara-*gumi*, but each element is incorporated into the overall design. The full-body tattoo is intended not merely as a work of art, or to demonstrate devotion to the clan, but also to signal the qualities of strength and patience. Such a tattoo applied in the traditional manner, by hand, using several dozens of different needles, may take as long as a year and a half to complete, and the process is not without discomfort.

Colonel Satomi continues. "The killers' cybernetics come from diverse sources, some of military grade, other of inferior commercial grade. This also applies to the devices used as cranial bombs."

"Have you discovered nothing of the killers' identities?"

"We have leads indicating that the Caucasian may at one time have been a hireling of the Maf, but possibly only for a single contract or series of contracts."

"Assassination contracts?"

"Certainly contracts of this general description."

"You have discovered no corporate connections to these killers?"

"Not at this time. However, I do have Security Service officers exploring a broad range of possibilities."

"What of the White Octagon?"

"That is a lead being developed by Adachi-*san*. The Security Service has nothing on that thus far."

Machiko thanks the colonel for his assistance, ends the call and looks back to the two-way mirror. So far the woman in the next room seems to have little or nothing in common with the assassins of two nights ago, or the bombing attack at Honjowara-*gumi* headquarters. Perhaps that will change. "What is her name?"

Ryokai says, "Poppy."

A plant that yields a gooey resin responsible for some of the Fifth World's most potent medicines, and lasting nightmares. Machiko wonders if this "Poppy" will provide cure or confusion.

She moves through the door to the room adjacent. Ryokai follows. Poppy is conscious now, slumped and exhausted, but conscious. She draws her head back as Machiko approaches. Her swollen, red-rimmed eyes widen as if with alarm.

"You have many enemies," Machiko says. "You have made a powerful enemy of the Large Circle League."

"You're not Triad," Poppy mutters.

"No. I am perhaps the reason you are still alive. You were given to me by Lau Tsang."

"Who?"

The indication of ignorance seems genuine. Machiko glances at Ryokai, who nods slightly, indicating that what he sees on the astral, Poppy's aura, gives no definite sign of a lie. "Lau Tsang is the chief enforcer for the League. He was most displeased to learn that a former soldier of the League makes war on Nagato Combine."

"What soldier?"

"Jank."

Faintly, Poppy smiles. "No one'll care once you're dead. You're the poison in the veins of humanity."

"I am that poison? Or corps like Nagato Corp?"

Poppy grunts. "Elves. Trogs. All the sub-races. We will exterminate you. Disintegrate you. Like poisonous isotopes. Bombarded by Gamma."

With one word, everything changes. The slurs and the anti-meta hate take on new substance. Machiko feels her own pulse grow strong, her spirit begin to churn, to rage. She exerts herself to give no sign, to remain calm. She focuses on details she has seen in security files. Gamma, a name she knows. Like many such terrorists, he is "alleged" to be a male norm. Reputed to have been a leading figure in the shadowy Alamos 20K anti-meta terrorist organization. Believed responsible for directing and executing innumerable incidents of anti-meta violence across North America. A campaign of violence that began in 2036, when Machiko was little more than a child, with the napalm fire-bombing of a small community in rural Ohio, announcing the arrival of the New Terrorism. Machiko still remembers seeing tridcast images, the sight of an elven girl running nude up a country lane, her face a mask of agony, her body blazing with a fire that would not die.

It brings stirrings of horror to her even now. Horror and outrage and a sorrow that bears down with all the weight of a mountain. "You look like a Sisters Sinister streetpunk," she says. "A nothing. You expect us to believe you are led by Gamma?"

Another faint smile. "He's my lover."

"Would you die for him?"

"Of course."

"Would you surrender your sanity?"

Poppy's eyes widen just slightly. The prospect of losing her mind perhaps disturbs her.

"You have undoubtedly heard," Machiko continues, "that we of the Guard are all physical adepts. Some of us are also mages. If you do not answer my questions willingly, I will summon a mage and he will enter your mind and extract the information I want. The process is not without danger. But this is to be expected. White Octagon makes war. There are always casualties in war."

The corner of Poppy's mouth begins twitching. "Stay out of my mind."

"Where is Gamma?"

"I don't know."

"He's your lover. You know."

"I don't—*don't remember*!"

Machiko glances at Ryokai. He gives a small sign with the fingers of his left hand. The sign indicates "confusion." A second sign suggests the influence of magic.

"Where do we find the members of White Octagon?" Machiko asks.

A torrent of words bursts from Poppy's swollen, blood-stained lips, rising into shouts, shrieks, incoherent ravings, seeming as if incited by a hysterical fear.

This continues unabated for some minutes.

Machiko turns to the door to the room adjacent and uses the telecom there to again contact Colonel Satomi.

23

"We're here, Doctor."

"Where?"

The place Kron names is of no particular interest. They have come here, wherever that is, because Yoi was asked to do so. It is not where he had been going when he first set out in his car, but that is of little import. Any time spent away from his library is so much wasted time, anyway. The time may be pleasant, diverting, or entertaining, occasionally informative, but ultimately it is a waste. Perhaps he will catch up with the fellows of the Logos Society later this afternoon, or sometime this evening. Whether that thought is realized or comes to nothing is only of very modest significance.

Yoi closes the covers of a privately published volume entitled, *Nandyavarta in the Sixth World*, an investigation of mystic labyrinths as guides to the inner mysteries. He looks to the massive ork leaning in through the limousine door.

"Taking your ritual kit, Doctor?" Kron asks.

Yoi replies, "It would seem indicated."

Kron takes the hard-shelled case of the ritual kit. Yoi takes up his bag, like a medical bag, and follows the ork to the sidewalk, through an entranceway guarded by a crowd of males with agitated auras, and into a small lobby area. Here he is met by three members of the Nagato Green Serpent Guard. Kron assists with introductions. The female among the three Guards appears to be in charge and greets Yoi with great formality and respect. She is an interesting specimen of female, elf female. Her aura burns like magma, full of hardened resolve. She is also tall and long of limb and possessed of an elf's natural elegance.

"What is your name?"

"Machiko," she replies.

It is occasionally useful to know such things.

"This way please, Doctor," says "Machiko."

They take an elevator down. They come to a room with a window looking into another room. The female, Machiko, explains that the female in the next, confined to a chair, is to be the subject of an examination. Machiko uses the term "interrogation," but this of course is inappropriate and misleading.

"What do you wish to learn?" Yoi asks.

Machiko says, "I must learn the whereabouts of an individual, a mage, known as Gamma."

"This is some form of sobriquet?"

"An assumed name, yes. So it would appear. I must also learn where to find the membership of Gamma's terrorist group, known as White Octagon."

"This is a racist group? opposed to metahumans?"

"You are familiar with the name."

"I conjecture, based on the use of the octagon. The octagon, or octagram, is a mystic figure, the subject of some speculation, as it has eight termini or points, yet is formed of a single, unbroken line. In various contexts it is often said to represent the concept of regeneration. Given terrorists with symbols of regeneration, or rebirth, and the color white, which may be said to represent death or purity, I conjecture that racists may be involved. And what are racists but those opposed to metahumans?"

Machiko appears to regard his comments with some degree of uncertainty, as though the chain of reasoning, admittedly tenuous, does not appear plain to her. Yet her aura shows only determination, resolve. A very interesting specimen of female indeed. "In any event," she says, "please begin your examination."

Yoi considers. "There is some slight possibility of my techniques causing damage to the subject. Is this of any concern?"

"I must have answers to my questions," Machiko says in a definite tone.

Yoi nods. "I will need tea."

A cup of tea is soon brought. A pleasant oolong variety, warming and mild. Yoi has a few sips and carries the cup into the room where his subject awaits. A norm female. Chinese. Poppy, she is called. She appears to have been beaten rather severely. Yoi sips his tea and looks to the woman's aura. This reveals that she is tired, nearly exhausted, clinging to consciousness in the wake of a fatiguing episode, full of stress and emotion, probably hysterical. Her aura also makes plain that she is mundane and that she is the subject of meta-magic, the spell or spells of an initiate, presumably Gamma, mentioned previously.

Kron opens the ritual kit and prepares a recording device so there will be a record of anything the subject may say. He turns on a Sony player and an enchanting Viennese melody, played with precision on a harpsichord, fills the room. Kron then begins lightning pots of incense. The incense has little significance, as Yoi expects he will have no need of con-juring elementals. The incense, like the pleasant-tasting oolong tea, like the music, merely aids him in becoming cen-tered. Focused.

Poppy lifts her head and looks at him with eyes that grow wide. "Stay outta my mind," she says. "Stay away."

Yoi lowers his hand over her eyes.

Poppy grunts. "Huh! I can't, *I can't see!*" she blurts. "Oh frag, *what . . . ? I'm blind! I'm blind!*"

A common misconception. In fact, Poppy's eyes are merely closed, cloaked so that no light reaches her eyes. The tendrils of glowing mana that surround her mind like a lat-tice, woven so precisely into the structure of her aura, guard her mind but do nothing to protect her eyes, or the major muscle groups of her body.

Poppy grunts plaintively. "Huh, huh . . . I can't move . . ." Her aura ripples with terror. She whispers, "Help me . . . oh, *god!*"

Yoi pours a fine stream of crystals, crystals so fine they seem like powder, over the woman's brow. "You are under the onus of a dark power," he intones. "A power which veils your mind. This power controls your actions, your thoughts. I will help you resist this power. I will show you the way. You must grow tranquil, serene. Fearful thoughts sub-side. Emotions wane. All fear ends with me. My voice, my touch, my presence. I am the way and the light. The alpha and the omega, beginning and ending. There is no other."

On the astral, a tide of pulsing mana rises around the lat-tice guarding Poppy's mind. Yoi's ally, clothed in the form of a surgeon, reflecting Yoi's own self-image, naturally, rises with the tide and adds mana to the gathering spell. Poppy's aura grows calm. It grows crimson with resolve, the resolve to do as Yoi instructs. Many of Yoi's colleagues would argue that the will of a mundane can by definition have no effect on mana, and perhaps they are right. Yoi has found, whoever, that beginning an examination by exerting mere "hypnotic" influence possesses value. It will make the demands on other skills less profound.

The spell weakens, Yoi's ally informs.

The lattice guarding Poppy's mind begins to fray. It unravels like a snake suddenly lunging toward prey. The mana lances upward and with a flash vanishes from sight.

On the material plane, Poppy breathes hard. Her lips struggle to smile. On some subconscious level, perhaps, she is aware that the first operation has been a success. Perhaps some sympathetic link between mage and subject provides her with shadings of intuition that suggest what is in fact occurring.

"I am the way and the light," Yoi intones.

"Yes . . ." Poppy whispers. "The way . . ."

On the astral, a new lattice of mana forms, interpenetrating the higher functions of mind. Yoi's ally provides the mana. Yoi guides it precisely into proper form and position. "Certain questions must be answered," Yoi intones. "You will answer truthfully."

"Yes . . ." Poppy whispers.

"Where is Gamma?"

"Cannot tell . . ."

"Where are the members of White Octagon?"

"Cannot . . . cannot tell . . ."

Another spell, Yoi's ally informs.

Yes, obviously. He gazes onto the astral and soon detects it, another spell woven cunningly into the woman's aura. Easily missed. A spell of influence. Perhaps this prevents the woman from telling what she knows. Yoi pauses to take more tea, to breathe the pleasant aroma of incense, then begins examining this spell, undermining it, dispelling it.

"Answer truthfully. Where is Gamma?"

"Don't . . . I don't . . . don't know . . ."

Is this possible?

Poppy's aura waxes blue with uncertainty and wavers with confusion. Yoi prepares his most invasive tool, a spell he must wield like a scalpel, his probe into the inner convolutions of mind. He extends his hand over Poppy's head. The mana coils around his fingers and descends from the tip of his index finger like the focused beam of a laser. The power of the spell is sufficiently great that Yoi feels the strain of

keeping it focused. Yet, the woman's surface thoughts come
to him clearly, a voice echoing across the etheric.

I don't know, I don't know, I don't ... Poppy thinks.
Where is Gamma ... *? Where IS he* ... *? Where* ... *?*
WHERE ... *?*

The question, Master, says Yoi's ally.

Of course. The question asks what the woman does not
know. Sloppy, very sloppy. "In what place did you last meet
with Gamma?"

"What place ... ?" Poppy murmurs.

More uncertainty, more confusion. Yoi probes deeper. He
glimpses bits of mind-pictures, dark images, dark buildings
with weathered faces, gloomy interiors. Poppy gives up
these images without resistance. She knows the place where
she last met with Gamma, but does not know where this
place may be found.

She rode there in a vehicle, a van. She spent much time
talking and little paying heed to landmarks.

Unfamiliar territory.

Tracing the route through her mind will be difficult and
very costly in time and energy.

"Where might the members of White Octagon be found?"

"Queens ..." Poppy murmurs. "Most in Queens ...
dosses in Queens ... a loft in the Bronx ... some bars ...
restaurants ..."

She yields names and addresses.

24

The sweep begins at three p.m. Teams of Honjowara-*gumi* and Yoshida-*kai kobun,* led by Machiko, Ryokai, Gongoro, and several others fan out across Brooklyn and Queens. They hunt the membership of White Octagon.

By seven p.m. they have rendezvoused at a Honjowara-*gumi* warehouse in Jamaica, Queens. Only Gongoro's team returns without prisoners. Several members of his team are wounded. Gongoro himself appears smeared with soot. "The punk was chromed!" he growls. "He gave fire, then took a hit and his skullbomb detonated!"

"Where is the body?" Machiko asks.

Gongoro waves a hand and walks off.

Kobun drive a Toyota Tornado into the loading bay at the end of the warehouse and open the trunk. Machiko surveys the corpse lying there on a dark stained tarp. It is the body of a male norm, a Caucasian, outfitted with as much apparent cybernetics as Jank and the other assassins. This one, though, bears the tattoo of an octagon at his left temple, the words "Alamos 20K" in bold letters across his chest, and, on his right upper arm, the catch-phrase, *"Reach out and snuff somebody . . ."*

Machiko wonders if this is the last of the five assassins who attacked Sukayo-*san* and her and the other GSG. If so, then they are avenged. The killers are all dead. The thought brings her a tender tickling of grief over the madness of purpose that has shed so much blood, but she cannot let this weaken her resolve. The threat against Nagato Combine remains to be neutralized.

She begins the interrogations at once. The members of White Octagon appear to be enemies of Nagato Combine, so she does not hesitate to speak crudely, in tones of menace, or to threaten the use of physical methods. Where threats alone do not suffice, she manipulates pressure points and applies varying degrees of pain. Where mere pain is not enough, she allows Gongoro to temporarily take her place and inflict actual wounds.

The members of White Octagon are diverse: Caucasians, several Asians, two blacks, one Hispanic. Nine males and three females. Their similarities begin with the fact that all are norms and most bear symbols of anti-meta hatred, designs on jewelry or clothing or shorn into slash-cut hair, if not actual tattoos. Several possess only minor bits of chrome. Several have none at all. Only two are equipped with cranial explosives.

They appear less an army than a small militant group with the capability of waging armed conflict.

"You make war on Nagato Combine," Machiko says. "Why? What is your ultimate objective? Who is your leader? Who is Gamma? Where may he be found? How many others belong to White Octagon? Where do you get your weapons and supplies?"

Some spit. All of them curse. All of them speak as though elves and other metas are the greatest abominations ever to walk the planet, a twisted malignancy afflicting humanity, a malevolent aberration inspired by some diabolical conspiracy, fiends that must be eradicated, slaughtered, massacred.

Machiko has heard talk like this before—what meta hasn't?— but rarely with such conviction, such fanatical fervor. She finds it unsettling. She is at pains to understand how anyone could regard her, or others like her, as the enemy of all that is human.

Even were she not born of a human womb, or raised by a man and woman as norm as norm can be, she could not view all norms as her enemy. As Kuroda-*sensei* himself reminded her, there is no room in the warrior spirit for any such bias.

Enemies are enemies. They must be evaluated for their strengths and weaknesses. Whether they are norm or meta is irrelevant, except as this may influence the conduct of their aggression.

"Yeah, we geeked the GSG," the members of White Octagon say. "We're gonna lay Nagato Combine to waste."

Why do they single out Nagato Combine? Many corps and other organizations include metas within their ranks. Machiko is answered only with hate, more venom, more terrorist babble, nothing that indicates a definite, rational motivation.

The few who appear to have knowledge regarding Gamma's whereabouts are not responsive to questioning. Machiko calls in Yoi-*san*, the mage sent by Colonel Satomi.

"These persons are under the compulsions of an initiate," Yoi-*san* says. "Once I have rested, I will remove the compulsions."

"How long must you rest?"

"Till morning."

This does not help.

Machiko comes at length to the most unassuming member of the group, a dark little man, a norm, with many cybernetic enhancements, nearly all of them beneath the skin. Nagato security techs do not succeed in disabling every possible weapon built into the man's body when his turn for questioning comes, so Machiko begins the interrogation with a *kobun* holding the muzzle of an Ares Alpha Combatgun to the man's head.

As Machiko formulates her first question, the man says, simply, "I'm S.A."

"Explain."

"You know Fuchi. You know S.A."

This is a highly unexpected development. Ryokai does not seem to recognize what the man is talking about. Machiko herself only knows of this because her "Older Brother" made a point of seeing that she was fully briefed.

Fuchi Industrial Electronics maintains at least two distinct security organizations: IntSec, responsible for facilities and personnel, and the Special Administration, which deals with every manner of covert operation. Machiko has never before encountered a self-confessed agent of the S.A. Indeed, few people are even aware of its existence. She glances at Ryokai, who signals that the man speaks in a truthful manner. Then she says, "I am familiar with the Special Administration of Fuchi Industrial Electronics. You claim to be an agent of this agency?"

The man nods. "You don't wanna screw with me."

"We are already doing that," Machiko says. "How we proceed depends on your spirit. If you cooperate."

"I transmitted a burst signal by headware when your people busted in. My control knows exactly who you are and who you work for. There could be an assault party coming in here any sec."

"Quite true," Machiko says. "However, whether such a party would find you alive is an open issue."

The man glances toward the Ares gun pressed against the side of his head. "I'll grant you that."

"You are generous," Machiko says. "Now demonstrate that you are also wise. Identify yourself and your control."

"My operational handle is Scudder. That's all you get."

Machiko says, "If we are to accept your claim regarding the Special Administration, we must confirm it."

"Operational protocols are proprietary. You should remember who you're dealing with. Last I heard, Nagato Corp is not on the top ten list of megacorps."

"The status of Nagato Corp is not your concern. Why does the Fuchi Special Administration have an agent inside the White Octagon?"

"To monitor extremist activity in the plex."

"Does the Special Administration consider this group a major threat?"

"That's a policy issue. I wouldn't know."

"What is so significant about White Octagon that the Special Administration would take an interest?"

"Reputed ties to the Alamos 20K."

"What form of ties?"

"Weapons. Cyber. Maybe you noticed that some of the group have cranial bombs. They got that from the K."

"Who is White Octagon's leader?"

"A slag called Gamma. A very bad dude."

"He is a mage?"

"I've heard it said. I haven't gotten close enough to tell."

"Where may he be found?"

"I been working on that. So far to no effect. Gamma's got a core cadre of razorfreaks that he keeps with him twenty-four hours. The shag-artists they sent against your GSG were part of that cadre. The rest, what you got here, are all second-tier stringers. They know what Gamma wants 'em to know."

"We have information indicating that certain members of White Octagon were formerly with Triad organizations."

"Wouldn't surprise me. Gamma collects his people from all over."

Machiko's commlink beeps. She takes the call in the corridor outside the room being used for interrogations. Arinori, the Chairman's personal aide, informs her, "The Chairman will be convening a meeting within the hour. He asks that you attend."

The notification is welcome. This so-called agent of the Fuchi Special Administration has provided much information, but Machiko is uncertain whether to believe his claims, and, if she believes, what to make of Fuchi involvement with White Octagon. She feels an urge to consult with a higher authority and the Chairman's meeting will provide the perfect opportunity. She leaves Ryokai and Gongoro to continue the questioning. A headman of Honjowara-*gumi kobun* volunteers a car, and before long she is striding into the main lobby of Nagato Tower and riding the elevator to the Chairman's suite. She finds the meeting about to begin. Already present are Adachi-*san* of Nagato Intelligence, chief of security Bessho Chikayo and his deputy Colonel Satomi, and two of the Chairman's counselors, Zoge-*san* and Ohana Toyonari. They sit on cushions arranged in a semi-circle before the low dais that crosses the head of the room. Machiko goes to one knee on the only unoccupied cushion. Moments later, a side door opens and the Honjowara-*sama* enters, without escort.

All bow.

Honjowara-*sama* does not sit. He steps to the center of the dais, clad in a dark suit, and there pauses, hands behind his back. "Zoge," he says.

Zoge-*san* bows, then turns toward Machiko, and says, "We have received inquiries from certain of the corporations responsible for police services in the New York-New Jersey megaplex regarding recent activities by members of Nagato Combine, led by members of the Green Serpent Guard. I have also received personal inquiries from the office of the Mayor and various members of the city Corporate Advisory Board regarding recent raids conducted by members of Nagato Combine. These persons making inquiries expressed concern about certain incidents of violence. Certain of these incidents have been given broad treatment by the media."

The meaning of this is apparent. Machiko may possess the authority to deploy the Guard as she wishes, and the power to draw on other resources of Nagato Combine, but her actions are not without consequences. Her actions have sent ripples throughout the plex. Her actions have perhaps caused embarrassment both to the leadership of Nagato Combine and Nagato Combine itself.

She bows deeply. But before she can ask forgiveness, Honjowara-*sama* is saying, "Is it true that you entered the Red Pavilion and met with Lau Tsang?"

Again, Machiko bows deeply. "Yes, Chairman-*sama*. That is true."

"And you consulted with no one before undertaking this brash adventure?"

Machiko bows more deeply. "Yes, Chairman-*sama*. That is true."

For an instant, one corner of Honjowara-*sama's* mouth seems almost to flick upward in the manner of a smile. His expression immediately turns as hard and unyielding as granite. He taps a fan bearing the *mon* of Nagato Combine against his hand, and says, impatiently, "What could have motivated such an adventure? What was your intention?"

"To stab at the enemy's heart, Chairman-*sama*."

Some moments of quiet pass. But they are not tranquil moments. Honjowara-*sama* does not seem pleased by Machiko's reply. He gazes at her sternly, as if seeking the truth in her spirit. Machiko fears what he might find, that she might in some way fail to meet the measure of his vision. Then Zoge-*san* coughs politely. He and Honjowara-*sama* exchange looks, and Honjowara-*sama* nods. Zoge-*san* looks to Machiko, and says, "Do you mean that you intended to attack the leadership of the Large Circle League?"

Machiko bows, and says, "At the time, it seemed possible that the League was the enemy I sought, responsible for the bombing attack and the attacks on GSG. I went to the Red Pavilion with the idea of upsetting the leaders' timing, with the hope of confusing Lau Tsang into making some revealing admission."

"And what occurred?"

Machiko tells the tale, beginning with the discovery of Jank, a former Triad soldier, and ending with the interrogation of the White Octagon membership, and the man claiming to be an operative of the Fuchi Special Administration.

Ohara-*san* says, "A racially integrated corp like Fuchi has much to fear from fanatics associated with the Alamos 20K."

"Nagato Combine has much to lose," says Adachi-*san*, "if the Fuchi Special Administration is using White Octagon to further its covert objectives."

The idea is somewhat chilling. Nagato Combine is a large and powerful organization with influence that extends beyond the corporate world, yet Machiko can only wonder if Nagato Combine would survive any form of direct conflict with a giant on the scale of Fuchi Industrial Electronics. Several of the men before her seem at least briefly possessed of a similar concern.

Then Zoge-*san* politely coughs, and looks to Machiko. "What assurance have we that this man, Scudder, is in fact a Fuchi agent?"

Machiko bows, and says, "Ryokai-*san* monitored the man's aura throughout the interrogation and discerned no indication that he was lying. Beyond this, the matter has not been confirmed."

Zoge-*san* says, "Ryokai-*san* is skilled at reading auras."

"It is one of his foremost abilities," Machiko replies.

"Yet he is not a mage."

"No, he is not."

"And we have some indication that certain members of White Octagon have been mentally controlled by the group's leader, Gamma, who is a mage—perhaps an initiate mage. It may therefore be the case that this man Scudder has also been controlled, persuaded of the belief that he is a Fuchi agent."

"Toward what end?" Ohara-*san* asks.

"Perhaps to mislead us into regarding Fuchi as our enemy."

"What would this accomplish? We would not launch a direct reprisal at Fuchi. This would be suicide. Would not the most natural reaction be to simply eliminate this group, regardless of who may be giving them orders?"

"Fuchi is not the impregnable leviathan they desire to appear," says Adachi-*san*. "It would certainly be expected that we would eliminate White Octagon, once their plans are revealed. However, we do have other means of striking back at Fuchi. At any corp, regardless of size or influence."

Adachi-*san* does not elaborate. The entire group falls silent as Honjowara-*sama* begins tapping his fan against his open palm. His discontent shows clearly through the granite of his expression.

In a voice full of power, he says, "A group relying on the resources of an organization like the Alamos 20K must be considered allied with this pernicious evil that threatens the whole fabric of Sixth World society. Surely, we have all seen their heinous crimes. We know too well of what they are capable. It was their violence that incited the worldwide riots we know as the Night of Rage. Their violence killed hundreds here in New York alone, and left many thousands maimed and wounded. The destruction of Nagato Combine can be only their first objective. A symbolic first assault. We are a natural target because we judge all people by the quality of their character, rather than the character of their genes. It is the Way of Nagato Combine. It is integral to our existence. The existence of a group such as White Octagon is a direct challenge to our guiding principles. Therefore, we must do everything in our power to see that this campaign of iniquity is defeated. These racist fanatics must be eliminated. That is the only path to peace. The only manner in which we can guarantee the safety of our people."

Machiko bows. She is heartened to see that Honjowara-*sama's* will is unshaken, that he holds resolutely to the tenets of this New Way. His bold words impart in her a spirit so settled, so resolved, that even the prospect of war with a giant like Fuchi no longer has any power over her.

Politely, Zoge-*san* coughs. "We must of course ensure that our people and property are safe from terrorist attack. However, we are subject to UCAS law and may be held accountable. The wholesale elimination of any group may have repercussions."

"We could invite retaliation by other fanatics," says Bessho-*san*. "A direct assault by the Alamos 20K, for example."

Honjowara-*sama* slaps his fan against his open palm. "The possibility of retaliation by terrorists and other fanatics is of no significance!" he declares. "We will not be coerced like sheep into any action that violates our principles!"

Bessho-*san* bows deeply.

Politely, Zoge-*san* says, "Nevertheless, we are subject to UCAS law. It is known that our forces have conducted raids and it may be known that we have taken certain persons into custody. We are being accorded a degree of latitude because the Chairman's benevolent principles are well-known and Nagato Combine's forces have always acted with great discipline in the past. There are, however, limits to what the legal authorities will tolerate. If we are seen as using gangster tactics, we will be forcefully condemned."

Adachi-*san* says, "It would be no great difficulty to

convey our captives onto Nagato Corporation property and thus avoid any additional legal entanglements."

"This would be viewed as a mere evasion."

"But would be no less effective."

"The point is certainly open to debate."

"And if Fuchi supports the White Octagon?" says Ohana-*san.* "What then?"

Honjowara-*sama* looks to Machiko.

She bows. "When the sword will not cut, Chairman-*sama,* stab at the enemy's heart."

Honjowara-*sama* is not long in giving his reply.

25

The diamond-faceted exterior of their delta icon noses up against a system icon that has the trademarked look of a Fat Man's Face. Negative alert, says Rad238. Camo on, says SmoKe. Initializing entry prog, says NodeBoy.

May we take your virtual order? flash the Fat Man's eyes.

The Fat Man's iconic mouth yawns open wide and they slide into the node beyond with hardly a moment's delay. Their icon assumes the swept-wing form of *Musca domestica*, the common house fly, with diamond-faceted eyes. The blue-hued node before them takes the form of a Koppa Kaf food bar: animated service window shaped like the trademarked Fat Man face, service counter winking and flashing with iconic dispensers, walls lined with vending machine icons from StufferSnacks, TacoRama, SoyBran, and PizzaMia. Hostile incoming, says Rad238. A brilliant blue counter clerk icon in the Koppa Kaf soy bean uniform comes leaping over the service counter waving a fly swatter. Evasive, says SmoKe. They spiral toward the ceiling of the node. Initializing combat progs, says NodeBoy. Dumbframes launch. A dozen buzzing house fly icons encircle the counter clerk's head and the clerk begins looping, spinning circles, swatting at its own face.

Easy as decking the UCAS regional grid, NodeBoy concludes. More to come, SmoKe warns.

Access point detected, says Rad238. Winking red arrows lead toward the Koppa Kaf service counter. Manuevering, says SmoKe. They spiral over the service counter, past the iconic slaves of bean-grinders, hash-friers, and soy-grillers to the pulsing blue soybean icon all the way in the rear. The soybean with its pulsing blue roots and gleaming touch-sensitive bean keys represents the host controlling the entire Koppa Kaf node.

Initializing entry prog, says NodeBoy.

The soybean spreads wide like stretchable blue goo into a dataline portal they slide through with hardly a pause.

Next stop: Splendiferous Food Distribution, Inc.

The run is already mapped. Splendiferous is easy Code Green and they ride a secured line into the central cortex of the host. They pause at the center of a gigantic virtual warehouse where a thousand Chinese cook icons hurl blurring streams of databytes in the form of knives, cleavers, animal parts, bottles and cans and boxes across the length of the warehouse floor.

At 02:13:51:20:17:46, a green uniformed Rent-A-Cop icon steps onto the warehouse floor. "I am not recognizing your program icon," the Rent-A-Cop says. "Please to be identifying yourself with great alacrity."

Negative alert, says Rad238.

Sleazing, NodeBoy says.

Their icon resembles just another aproned Chinese cook. They lift one iconic hand to the Rent-A-Cop. They gesture. "We're not the cook you're looking for."

"You are not the cook for which I am presently looking," the Rent-A-Cop says.

"No need for a system alert."

"I am perceiving no require for an alert."

"Go about your business."

"You will be going about your business, please. As I also will be doing."

At 02:13:51:20:18:14, a port in the warehouse floor slides open and out steps a green-suited comptroller icon who begins interrogating the Chinese cooks for accounting data.

Maneuvering, says SmoKe.

They dive through the port. They join the river of data plunging through the dataline to the Code Orange host operated by Paragon Provisions International. They break through the Paragon virtual shell in the native Orange-5 host supporting the virtual machine and ride a datarush of transfers through TRW CredCorp's Red-7 mainframe to the black depths of their primary target.

Freese detected online, says Rad238. Are we ready?

Never readier, says SmoKe. Cloaking. Armor on.

Initializing combat progs, says NodeBoy.

The danger ahead is great, but freedom is worth the risk. And nuyen will buy it.

26

It's just past 2 a.m. when the optical workstation console in the touch-sensitive top of the gleaming onyx desk begins beeping. Gordon Ito turns in his high-backed chair from the broad window overlooking the Hudson to face the multi-screen display risen out of the desktop. He sips his Brazilian coffee and takes a drag from his Platinum Select. The display screens give him a view direct into the Fuchi telecommunications grid.

View number one shows a vast cavern formed by the gleaming black cliffs of a pair of immense datastores, soaring up infinitely high into the electron night. Between the two cliffs burn the cobalt blue beams of a trio of datastreams, each looking as hot as the interior of a sun. Bucky Freese and his team of deckers are already onscreen in flashing blue hard hats and blue-striped vests. They construct a temporary node around one of the datastreams using program icons like opaque black panels. They then step through the walls of the node and onto the verge of a virtual highway a thousand lanes wide and streaming in both direction with iconic sedans that blur with impossible speed, representing transfers between financial accounts.

View number two shows much the same scenes, but comes via Gordon's special programming group, lead by Alonzo Ukita.

Ukita and his group are all employees of Fuchi Americas. Freese and his team are not. They are employed by a Fuchi subsidiary. In the event that they are discovered or jumped by Fuchi Internal Security, Gordon will disavow knowledge of their activities. Ukita's people will provide covering documentation indicating that they and Gordon have only just discovered Freese's treasonous activities and were preparing to take Freese down. Any evidence to the contrary has of course been destroyed. Any indication that such evidence might ever have existed has also been eliminated.

Freese and his team do not themselves have a bright future, all things considered.

Freese and his deckers, now resembling traffic cops, begin directing iconic sedans down a newly constructed exit ramp. The ramp briefly winks, *Dataline To Secret Pacific Rim Accounts*. The counter in the exit ramp's pavement keeps a running tally of the nuyen being diverted. The total swiftly climbs.

And, abruptly, things start happening.

The horizon grows dark. A cloud of blackness comes rushing up the near-infinite length of the virtual highway. The cloud resolves into a teeming swarm of iconic birds, a blurring river of bats hurtling around Freese and his traffic cop deckers and a horde of flashing pterodactyls, which seize iconic sedans on the exit ramp with tremendous claws and vanish into the distance.

Freese and his deckers seem immobilized.

Ukita's team steps onto the verge of the exit ramp looking like heavily armored metrocops. One fires a grappling hook winking *Trace or Die!* at a flashing pterodactyl and soars into the air as the cord between them snaps tight. The cord is instantly severed and the decker enveloped in a cloud of bats.

The other deckers fire Ripper, Tar Pit, black IC. A rivulet of bats crashes into the pavement. A trio of pterodactyls drop their loot and spiral to the ground. Meanwhile, a few million nuyen in financial transactions flies toward the horizon.

In another moment, it's over. If the battle had taken place in any other node on the Fuchi grid, every last host would be on full alert by now and Freese and his group would be blown.

Gordon snuffs his Platinum Select and sits back in his chair and ponders. Someone's fucking with his organization, and it has to be more than just one decker acting alone, because one decker acting alone doesn't frag Fuchi mainframes twice in a row, even with help from inside. So it's either a corp or a gov with a drek-hot programming group and a building full of computer power.

And either way they're going down.

Down, down to the ground.

27

"Proceed directly ahead," says the uniformed guard. "Follow
the directions of officers to the next checkpoint."

The Toyota Elite rolls ahead, through the checkpoint,
down the ramp, into the depths of the cavernous parking
facility located beneath Fuchi Plaza. Rows of parked vehicles extend away to left and right, gleaming beneath stark
white light. Uniformed security officers stand watch at every
intersection of aisles. Each one motions the Elite onward,
like the green arrows winking from panels set into the garage
floor.

The Elite rolls onto an elevator. Two guards guide the car
to a halt. Heavy doors to the rear shunt closed and the elevator briefly rises, then the doors directly ahead slide open
and the Elite rolls briefly ahead.

A formal entranceway comes up on the right, a small area
brightly lit, carpeted in red, adorned with plants and an artificial waterfall and more uniformed guards.

Machiko pushes her door and stands up beside the Elite.
Ryokai emerges beside her. They are faced by three male
norms, all in suits. Two have the air of fighters, perhaps
physical adepts. The third politely bows, and says, "Please
come with me."

They proceed through the glittery transparex doors of the
entranceway to the elevators at the rear of a lobby area composed of polished marble. But for several uniformed guards,
the lobby is deserted. The elevator ride to the fiftieth floor is
swift. They soon come to a room like a small private lounge.
Sectional sofas line three walls; a semi-circular bar bulges
out from the fourth. Tables between the sofa sections are all
fitted with deluxe telecoms. A tridscreen two meters broad
fills the wall over the bar. The atmosphere is informal, but
not without significance. The large floor-to-ceiling window
at one end of the room provides a view of Manhattan's

Lower East Side, often described as "The Pit." Perhaps the most violent, uncontrolled district anywhere on the island. Machiko wonders if the choice of views is deliberate. If this is intended as a message to her.

The Fuchi escorts exit. Three minutes pass. Then a lone elf enters, looking like the perfect corporate jack. His head is shorn almost completely bald. A silver datajack gleams from his left temple. His suit is black and cut to make the body beneath it sleek and anonymous. His face seems incapable of expression, like the face of a computer terminal.

"My name is Donelson," he says. "I'm Mr. Ito's deputy. A prior engagement prevents Mr. Ito from meeting with you now. I'm cleared for anything you wish to discuss."

Machiko considers whether Ito's absence is intended as a deliberate insult, or merely another reflection of the Fuchi perspective on the relative status of Nagato Combine. Could Gordon Ito regard Nagato Combine as nothing more than an unusually disciplined gang, such as might arise from The Pit? Could he be sitting somewhere in the Fuchi towers, observing all on security monitors, putting words in Donelson's mouth via implanted headware?

"I would like to discuss one of your agents," Machiko says.

"That's do-able," Donelson replies. "What agent?"

Machiko hands Donelson a small digipic of the man. "His operational name is 'Scudder.' We discovered him among a terrorist group called White Octagon. He identified himself as an agent of the S.A."

"That would be a violation of operations protocols."

"Indeed, he was reluctant to speak of such matters. Doubtless, he recognized my primary interest and confined the majority of his remarks to what he knew of White Octagon."

"What's your interest?"

"That is my question for you," Machiko says. "What is the Special Administration's interest in White Octagon?"

"Nobody's saying we have an interest."

"Then why is your agent in this group?"

"Nobody's saying he's our agent."

"You deny it?"

"Why do you care? Why ask about it? Are you proposing to create a relationship between Fuchi and Nagato Corp that would be founded on the free exchange of intelligence information?"

A very interesting question. Machiko is immediately torn

by thoughts of how such a relationship might benefit Nagato Combine, and how dangerous it might eventually prove to be. "For the moment," Machiko says, "I am merely proposing to release this man, called Scudder, unharmed. This I will do in exchange for certain information."

"You're holding captive a man you believe to be an agent of the Special Administration?"

"Until such time as I have confirmed his story, I can imagine no reason why I should release him. Why I should not subject him to the most rigorous interrogation."

"Have you subjected him to such an interrogation?"

"I have questioned him, certainly."

"What information do you want in exchange for his release?"

"I want to know why the Special Administration is interested in White Octagon. I want to know why you have planted an agent in this group. I want to know what you hope to achieve."

"Again, I'll ask if you're proposing to create a proprietary relationship for the exchange of intelligence."

"I would require clear and compelling evidence that any such exchange relationship would be mutual."

"How mutual?"

"Explain your interest in White Octagon and I will give you your agent. I would consider that mutual."

Donelson seems to consider the point for some moments; then, he says, "We're interested in the work being conducted by your Neurocomp advanced technology subsidiary."

That is rather puzzling. However, Machiko's response is preordained. "Any work being conducted by a Nagato Corp division or subsidiary is of a proprietary nature and therefore cannot be the subject of an exchange of intelligence."

"We work in a dynamic environment," Donelson says. "Friends have to be flexible."

"I have not yet subjected your agent to interrogation by a mage. I have come here offering to return him to you. Am I not being flexible?"

"A friend might offer this as a demonstration of good will."

"Indeed, you are correct," Machiko says. "But we are not yet friends nor allies. I come here seeking some indication that we are not in fact enemies."

Donelson smiles. "The Special Administration has no

need for another enemy. We have enough enemies. We would prefer to regard Nagato Combine as a possible new friend or ally. We can be very helpful to those who are helpful to us."

Clever talk. "In ancient writings," Machiko says, "there is a story about a man who admired dragons. So deep was his admiration that his clothes and the furnishings of his home were all adorned with dragon designs. One day a dragon appeared at this man's window and he died of fright. It is said that here was a man who talked great talk of large and powerful creatures, yet when such a creature actually appeared the man was revealed as a coward and his great words as meaning nothing."

Donelson's smile disappears. "That scans like a challenge," he says. "You should keep in mind where you are and who you're talking to. I don't indulge in idle buzz."

"Then show how helpful you may be to a potential ally."

Donelson appears to consider. Perhaps he merely listens to instructions relayed over an implanted commlink. "The Special Administration," he says, "has been investigating rumors of an impending action against Fuchi corporate holdings here in New York. We believe that the Alamos 20K may be planning such action. We are therefore investigating a number of groups related to the Alamos 20K."

"Such as the White Octagon."

"Yes."

"Why do you believe that Alamos 20K is involved?"

Donelson says nothing for several moments. He merely waits, watching Machiko, his expression blank and unreadable. Finally, he says, "We have indications that one or more leading members of Alamos 20K may have recently come to the New York megaplex."

"Such as a member known as Gamma."

Again, Donelson pauses. "The Special Administration would be interested in any information you may have about this individual called Gamma."

Machiko crosses her arms. She spends several moments merely waiting, gazing at Donelson, striving to keep her expression blank and unreadable. Finally, she says, "I would be interested in any information a potential ally might obtain about Gamma, terrorist groups operating in the plex, and the possible intentions of such groups. In exchange, I would be willing to divulge such information as might come to my attention, in this venue."

Donelson asks, "You have info about Gamma?"

"It is conceivable that I may at some point take this person into custody."

"We would be very interested in questioning Gamma ourselves."

Perhaps this can be arranged. For the moment, Donelson has provided little but words, words indicating that Gamma is indeed somewhere in the megaplex, and more words indicating that the Special Administration would rather deal as allies than as enemies. Has Donelson spoken only lies? Once back at their Toyota Elite limo, Machiko looks to Ryokai, who says, "Donelson was cyber-equipped. I'm guessing headware."

"Did he speak truthfully?"

"As he knows the truth? I think so." Ryokai frowns, and adds, "The idea of an alliance with Fuchi makes me uneasy."

"As it should."

"The Special Administration is known for loyalty only to itself."

Machiko nods agreement. "Yet, there is a thought that came to my mind, something Sukayo-*san* said."

"There is safety in the shadows of giants?"

Machiko hesitates, surprised that Ryokai would recall this. Surprised that he would recall this particular remark of all that Sukayo has said. She allows herself the faint smile that rises impulsively to her lips. "Fuchi's power is such that it could overwhelm us in any market Nagato Combine might choose to enter. The giant need have no fear of us. He may safely ignore us. And if we are helpful he may offer us rewards at no risk to his own interests."

"Still, it seems a dangerous course, merely attracting the giant's attention."

How like Ryokai to deliberate, to brood. The reminder is irksome. It incites Machiko to action. She seizes his hand, grips it, squeezes till both their arms are shaking and the pressure of hand against hand brings a fierce look to Ryokai's face. "Decide your course in seven breaths," Machiko says. "Be resolved to dying in battle. Then there is no risk."

Abruptly, Ryokai nods.

For the moment, at least, his spirit seems strong.

28

Machiko stops her Tachi Monarch behind a line of glistening limousines, leaves the car to a valet, and crosses the broad sloping drive to the marble-faced main entrance of the Miller Ridge Inn.

The guards in civilian clothes by the entranceway merely nod in passing her inside. She has been here before and the guards are well aware of her official legal status as a Nagato Corporation security officer. She finds her parents waiting beneath the glittering chandelier of the small lobby: her father in a smartly tailored dark gray suit, her mother in a particularly elegant Vashon Island skirt-suit of gray tweed. They are guarded by a trio of Security Service officers in dark suits.

Machiko questions her mother's skirt-suit with her eyes and is answered with a brilliant smile and a kiss on the cheek. "We're very proud," her mother says at her ear. "Very proud indeed."

Proud? Machiko puzzles. But only for a moment.

The maître'd escorts the three of them to a table in a dining room like a great open-air atrium, surrounded on three sides by walls of windows that rise three stories to the single skylight of the ceiling, adorned with plants and dangling vines and hanging bits of golden abstract sculpture.

Machiko hesitates at the table, but then sits, though the Guard is still on alert and technically she is still on duty. As a practical matter, she has little choice and must make this one exception to usual protocols.

Of course, both Machiko's step-parents have noticed the new sword at her waist, the wakizashi given to her by the Chairman. And they have heard how she came to have it. Her father does not ask but is obviously eager to examine this artifact of favor. He swells visibly with pleasure, perhaps also with pride, as he accepts the sheathed weapon into his hands with a small but formal bow. He seems nearly breathless, his eyes growing huge, as he looks from sword to Machiko, and says, "Could it be . . . ? Machiko, this is a true antique, is it not?"

Machiko nods. "The blade was forged in Osafune, Father."

Her mother hesitates. "In Nippon?"

"Yes, of course," her father explains, seeming awed. "Osafune was a famous center for swordsmiths. Where worked the finest smiths of the new period."

Her mother's eyebrows rise to considerable heights.

"Machiko . . ."

"Please examine the blade, Father."

Machiko struggles to maintain her composure, but cannot help smiling. Her father draws just a portion of the blade from its scabbard, exposing barely five centimeters of the polished steel, then just a bit more, regarding the blade as reverently as the image of a Buddhist god; then, turning, seeming enthralled, showing the blade to Machiko's mother. Then they are both enthralled, seeming pleased beyond measure, and in this moment the two of them seem as one, a single mind, a single spirit, looking from the sword to Machiko in harmony and with love.

Seeing the pleasure on her parents' faces, feeling their affection, their love, is an honor almost too great to bear. It moves Machiko very deeply. It warms her beyond measure. She has pleased them, her parents, brought them honor and feelings of pride. This recognition suddenly makes everything she has ever striven for seem to acquire new meaning, makes her life's path seem perfect and whole and as valuable as diamond.

With a bow, her father returns the sword, and once Machiko has returned sword to belt, he says, "When this current situation has been resolved, and the alert has ended, we will celebrate this great honor that is yours."

"This great good fortune," her mother adds, smiling broadly. "And the honor of your new status among the Guard."

Machiko bows. She also recalls how she came by this great good fortune, and her new status, and that her Older Brother, Sukayo, still clings to life in intensive care. She keeps this to herself, however. It would ruin the moment and spoil her parents' pleasure. It would defeat the entire point of his luncheon.

Four days have passed and much has happened since the night of the assassins' attacks. Machiko's mother made contact via commlink to ask her to lunch. Machiko could not find any reasonable justification for refusing. One hour lost, just now, would make little difference to Nagato Combine, and it is her duty as both a warrior and a daughter to honor these her parents, a duty no less important than any other. That her parents' delight brings her an intimate warmth is merely a pleasant effect of circumstance. She would honor these two regardless of her own personal emotional responses, for they are the only parents she has ever known. They risked much in accepting her for a child. They have devoted many years and much effort to her upbringing. They have shown her much love and care.

Her father orders French wine, but once the wine is poured he seems to deliberate, considering the wine, growing sober of mien. He takes hold of her mother's hand and then says, looking to Machiko, "We are greatly honored to have a daughter such as you. So too, I believe, are our ancestors honored."

Machiko bows deeply. "Words cannot express how greatly I am honored to have such parents."

Her mother smiles, wipes briefly at one eye.

Lunch soon arrives, first appetizers of fruit, then fish and rice and a select assemblage of vegetables, all in delicious and rather artful combinations.

"Machiko," her mother says, "what is really going on? These attacks. We have heard so many conflicting stories. Nagato Corporate Affairs says these are random acts of terrorists, but some people say it's bias, the pure human fascists."

Before Machiko can say a word, her father says, quietly, "You should not ask our daughter questions like this. She knows we are always concerned about bias. If she is able to tell us anything, she would simply tell us."

"A mother is not always able to maintain such an objective perspective."

"Then a mother should recall that the Chairman relies upon our daughter's discretion. Recall her obligations as a member of the Guard. She stands at the Chairman's side

during many confidential meetings. She is privy to the words
of the Chairman's closest advisors."

"You are right, of course." Still, her mother's eyes yearn
for an answer. With a glance at Machiko, she asks her question again, but immediately looks to her food.

"Besides," Father says, "this is 2058. People do not fear
metas like they once did. The Night of Rage occurred nearly
twenty years ago. Even if these recent attacks are the result
of bias, it is undoubtedly the work of a small group of
deranged fanatics, perhaps a single demented sociopath, who
will soon be apprehended."

And it is only natural that Father would hold such views.
He spends his days surrounded by the enlightened personnel
of a Nagato Corp subsidiary. His executive aide is an elf.
Many of his managing directors are metas. More than a
quarter of Nagato Corp's complete personnel roster are
metas: elves, dwarfs, orks, even trolls. It is as fully integrated a corp as one is likely to find.

"I am very foolish," Mother says. "Please forgive me."

But she is not foolish, in no need of forgiveness. She
speaks politely, but Machiko cannot regard her words with a
settled spirit. It is a mother's duty to care for her child, and
but for the single act of conception, a moment in time, they
are truly mother and child. Machiko knows this for a fact.
She was adopted not as a child or infant. Her original biological parents, both elves, were killed in a terrorist bombing, but the egg from which she evolved had been previously
stored in a vault at a fertility clinic. When her true parents
decided, out of loyalty to the Chairman's New Way, to adopt
a metahuman child, they selected her egg, and this was medi-
cally implanted in the womb of the woman beside her now,
her true mother in both flesh and spirit.

It was not an easy path to walk. Her mother's health has
always been delicate and she suffers from many allergies. She
and Father tried many times to have children in the natural way, but always mother miscarried, usually in the first
few weeks. Only the most extreme forms of medical intervention allowed her to carry Machiko to term and she spent
the last five months of her pregnancy confined to bed, the
last two months in the bed of a hospital.

The actual delivery was difficult and full of pain. Machiko
has seen the trideo record. She has heard her mother's cries,
her desperate pleas to the doctors.

"Oh, *help me! Help my baby live!*"

She reaches out, lays a hand over her mother's hand, and gently squeezes. "Do not worry," Machiko says softly. "We will find our enemies soon. Even the Guard aids in the hunt."

Mother nods, seeming somewhat reassured. Or perhaps she tries to seem reassured. "Yes," Father says, "we saw this on the news. Gongoro-*san* met with some violence."

Machiko nods. "The Chairman has authorized me to deploy the Guard, to divide our responsibilities. We are working with the forces of Nagato Corp and the clans."

"You could have been killed at clan headquarters," Mother says.

Father scowls, but says softly, "You must not speak like this."

"I cannot help it."

"Machiko fulfilled her duty. She saved the Chairman and earned great honor."

"I am just so afraid." And now Mother smiles embarassedly. She looks to Machiko and says, "Afraid for you."

"I understand," Machiko replies.

"Do you?" She takes Machiko's hand in both of her own and says, "Your warrior's ways are sometimes so foreign to me. I am so proud of everything you have accomplished, and yet I sometimes wonder what happened to the little girl I used to take shopping. You giggled so sweetly. Now it's rare to see you even smile."

Machiko considers, then says, "I have my mother's heart and my father's resolve. Both these gifts vie within me constantly. My thoughts are preoccupied by duty, but sitting here with you I am filled with feelings of love and devotion."

"Are you happy with how your life has gone?"

"Very happy." And, discreetly, Machiko smiles.

Mother briefly rises and comes to embrace her.

Dessert soon arrives, and then tea, and then lunch is over. Machiko walks her parents to their car. They have come in one car, a Toyota Elite driven by a Security Service officer and further escorted by an unmarked sedan. As they pause beside the limo, Machiko looks to her father, and says, "Is there anything going on at Neurocomp that might give rise to special interest on the part of another corp?"

Father seems puzzled by the question, puzzled and yet wary of it. He is the chief executive officer of the Nagato subsidiary named "Neurocomp." "Why do you ask?" he says.

"Interest was expressed to me by a security officer of another corp," Machiko says. "I'm wondering if anything special is going on. Anything that might attract attention."

Father does not want to speak of this in the open, so they all get into the rear of the limo and close the doors. "The research division has been engaged in a special project for some time," he says. "Have we suffered a breach in security?"

"I do not know," Machiko says. "It may be that nothing definite is known, that only word of a special project has slipped out, but its nature remains unknown."

Father looks to Mother, and says, "We will have to initiate an immediate check on our facility and people."

"Yes, of course," Mother agrees.

"What does the special project involve?" Machiko asks.

Father looks at her, hesitates. "Am I permitted to tell you?"

The question is surprising enough that Machiko herself hesitates. Ordinarily, it would never come up.

Machiko's salary and other benefits flow through the Security Directorate of Nagato Corporation, and for purely legal purposes she is registered as a security officer of the corp, but she is not truly a corporate employee. The Green Serpent Guard is the elite force belonging exclusively to the Chairman. They obey only those orders that come from Honjowara-*sama* himself. They accompany Honjowara-*sama* wherever he goes and everyone knows this and so no one would ever question their right of access to any clan or corporate property.

Information regarding a highly secret research project is a different matter. Ordinarily, Machiko would have no reason to request such information. That her request should be allowed immediately becomes apparent. "Father, I am acting senior of the Guard. In effect, I ask as the Chairman's personal agent."

"Yes, of course." Father lifts a hand to his brow and briefly shakes his head, as if now imagining he had temporarily lost his senses. "Access to this project has been very tightly controlled. Forgive me. The suggestion that our security may have been compromised in some degree is very unsettling."

Mother says, in a worried tone, "Only the highest-rated personnel have any access to the project at all."

Father nods agreement. "It began as matter of curiosity," he says. "A few of our senior researchers began considering the processing power of linked processors. They performed some tests in their spare time and eventually these tests led to promising models and their after-hours experiments became an official project."

"How is this different from other projects?"

"Because here the processors are human specialists," Mother says. "Deckers, Machiko. Very highly skilled deckers." A frustrated look abruptly comes over her features. "It is difficult to explain in lay terminology."

"There is the issue of translation," father says.

"Yes." Mother nods abruptly. "The ordinary interface between mind and machine is a sort of filter. Computer code must be translated into a form that can be understood by the human brain. And the language of the brain must be translated for the computer. And as with all transactions something is always lost. In time, if not also accuracy of command transfer. As a practical matter, the loss is infinitesimal and of no real significance. The human mind is hardly any less powerful for venturing into the Matrix. By this, I mean that the effect on processing power is negligible. But as we strive toward higher orders of processing operations, the loss becomes more pronounced. When we have several deckers working in combination through the Matrix, with all their sharing of data and commands being translated and retranslated, we find the machines must wait and wait while the human command processors are making decisions about system operations."

"This begins to sound," Machiko says, "as though it leads to people utilizing the Matrix without cyberdecks."

"Otaku?" Father smiles as if pained. "As your mother will tell you, we are dealing here in science, not in urban myths."

"I meant no insult, of course."

And no apology is needed. What Machiko knows of modern science has come primarily from trid documentaries and mealtime conversation. Her parents understand this. Her parents themselves owe their own acquaintance with the technical sciences to their positions at Neurocomp and frequent exchanges with working scientists. Her mother, like father, is primarily an administrator, an executive, Vice-President for Research, with a pair of Masters degrees and a doctorate in management.

"The project, as it has developed," Mother says, "has really become an investigation into the structure of mind, expanding the awareness of mind, its capabilities."

"Our senior mage-technologist," Father says, "describes it as a change in theoretical approach."

"Yes," Mother immediately agrees, nodding her head. "Rather than merely add cyberware to our people, we are in a sense trying to add our people together, achieve a fusion of minds, a cerebral network processor."

"Hence, the gamo-cerebroprocessor project, as we call it. Or simply, GCP."

Precisely what this means, or how it will work, Machiko can only imagine. And for her purposes, a precise understanding is probably not necessary. The special project is pushing the frontiers of magic and technology and therefore might be of interest to many other corps. That is the main point.

"Will this GCP project profit Neurocomp in some way, eventually?" Machiko asks.

"For the moment, any practical application of data developed by GCP is not an issue," Mother explains. "When the first cyberterminals were unveiled, no one could be sure where the technology would lead. Command speed and efficiency was enhanced. This was the short-term objective in 2029 and it is our short-term objective now. We expect to expand the envelope of the GCP project as it progresses. We may well develop data on areas of knowledge that today are all but unknown."

"I was not aware that Neurocomp performs research that is so theoretical in nature," Machiko says.

Father says, "The resources available for such research are of course rather limited as compared to our overall operating budget. But the opportunity to perform such research has brought us many of our top people, in some cases without reference to such benefits as salary. These are people of a caliber that allows them, even in their spare time, to develop many practical technologies that have generated substantial profits."

Machiko considers that, and says, "So one could say that this GCP project has value even if it leads nowhere."

"Most certainly."

"Is it likely that other corps would be aware of the quality of people Neurocomp is attracting?"

Father says, "Specialist positions in such fields as magic and science are very limited. Perhaps only a handful of mages may possess a particular expertise, and the top people are naturally under constant scrutiny. They cannot change corporation affiliations without being noticed. It's impossible. Regardless of the corps involved."

"The science-oriented telezines always find out," Mother adds, with a faint smile.

"Then other corps might presume Neurocomp is doing something special because otherwise you would not be attracting such valuable people."

"It is certainly a question other corps might ask."

"So we might have no breach in security," Mother says.

Father replies, "We must still check."

"Have there been any threats against the GCP project personnel?" Machiko asks. "Any attempts at theft of project data?"

Father says no. "Most of our mainframes are on the Nagato proprietary network, but no attempts at penetration have been made for several months, and the only attempt ever made against the GCP project mainframe was a documented failure."

Machiko considers briefly, then says, "I have one other question. Please consider it purely hypothetical. If the two of you were both removed, if you were compelled to leave your positions with Neurocomp, would the GCP project suffer?"

Mother seems disturbed by the question, but Father says plainly, "We merely administrate the GCP project, Machiko. We do not direct the experiments. And the project began with the agreement of all the senior officers. Unless the whole board was removed, the GCP project would almost certainly continue for the foreseeable future."

"You mean if the assassin had meant to kill your father and I," Mother says.

Machiko nods. "The thought occurred that perhaps the attacks against GSG were mere deception, that the assassin who attacked me did not want me at his back while he sought you, his primary targets. If your GCP project is so valuable, perhaps it is worth the price of assassins. But given what Father has said, I do not think it very likely that you were the targets."

"Yet the Security Service is guarding us day and night."

"That is the protocol," Machiko says. "Merely a precaution." Any time a person is menaced or assaulted, the family is provided with extra security until such time as any threat appears to have passed. That is as integral to the Way of Nagato combine as the Green Serpent Guard, as the Chairman himself. Machiko reminds her mother of several instances where one friend or another was also guarded day and night, and the reminder seems to ease her concerns. Especially when she recalls herself saying that a certain friend really did not need any guards, that the Security Service was being needlessly sensitive.

Machiko then takes her leave, for her duty here is done and others await her.

One she does not cherish.

29

The ceremonies begin early in the afternoon at the Amida Buddhist Temple, located on the grounds of the Nagato Commercial Park in a region of western Suffolk County known as Melville.

The temple is ringed by a wall of polished marble. Statues of the Myo-o, vanquishers of evil, guard the main gateway. The inner sanctuary is tiled in marble and full of platinum, brass, and gold, crowded with statues of the Buddhas, such as the Bosatsu known as Kwannon and Jizo, who have both attained enlightenment, but refrain from entering nirvana in order that they might aid others in finding the Way. And of course dominating the inner sanctuary is the image of Amida, Lord of the Western Paradise, and merciful lord of the dead.

Honjowara-*sama* himself is present to clap hands and ring the bells at the outset of the ceremony. The first row of attendees is composed of the families and friends of the fallen GSG—Mitsuharu and Jiksumi. Behind these are representatives of the three clans, the Honjowara-*gumi*, Yoshida-*kai*, and Toki-*gumi*, as well as leaders of the several small clans allied with the major three. Filling out the assembly crowded into the sanctuary are members of the board of Nagato Corporation and officers and executives of numerous Nagato subsidiaries. Machiko's parents are present as well.

These many dignitaries are here because Honjowara-*sama* is here, and Honjowara-*sama* is here to honor the dead and to honor the Guard, to refute by his presence any suggestion that Mitsuharu and Jiksumi were dishonored when they allowed themselves to be killed.

GSG line the walls. Machiko, Gongoro, and ten others flank the altar. The rituals go on long.

Mitsuhara-*san* was a Buddhist and Catholic-Christian. Jiksumi-*san* practiced no religion, but his family is com-

posed of Buddhists, Methodist-Christians, and members of
the Church of Gaia, a naturalist religion. And so five distinct
sects drawn from three distinct religions are represented in
the inner sanctuary. All play their part in the ceremony.
There is no contradiction in this, no hypocrisy, at least not in
Machiko's view. For all peoples are basically the same. They
share a common essence. They may give their gods different
names, but these too are all basically the same, concerned
with life and the living, spirits, eternity. Spiritual matters,
enlightenment. Whatever the names, whatever the particular
concerns, it is all basically the same, all with similar intentions. That people should live in peace, respect their neighbors, honor their parents, revere their ancestors, worship the
divine. Gods, *kami,* enlightened spirits—all understand this.
As long as the tenets of their own particular faith are observed, the divine take no insult, no affront, if other faiths
are also observed. Enlightened beings possess the wisdom to
respect all forms of pious living and sacred ritual.

Priests lead the assembly outside, onto the temple
grounds, into a broad grassy meadow ringed by trees and
lush, flowering gardens.

Once all have taken their places, Honjowara-*sama* strides
through the middle of the assembly and pauses before the
funeral pyre, surmounted by a platform veiled in silk bearing
the *mon* of the Honjowara-*gumi.* Upon this platform, clothed
in their uniforms, lie the bodies of the dead.

Honjowara-*sama* joins his hands in prayer. He bows.
Briefly, he kneels. As he moves to the dais beyond the pyre,
as he climbs the steps to the priests and the alter, Machiko is
one-half step behind him, and nearer still when he pauses,
facing the gathering from the center of the dais.

Honjowara-*sama* addresses the gathering in a calm clear
voice that resonates with power. "Seasons change," he
declares. "Blossoms wither. Petals blanket the ground. The
sky turns gray with cold and winter comes, inexorable. Each
woman and man must reach an accommodation with destiny.
For life's tenuous hold on this plane is but a fleeting illusion,
and all must inevitably slip away. From dust to dust and ash
to ash. We honor the departed. We honor their selfless devotion to duty, their courage and their strength. We pray that
their bold spirits find peace and salvation, secure in the
knowledge that one day they will return as glorious beings to
show us the path to enlightenment."

Many bow or murmur amens. Machiko watches the crowd, the gardens and trees, the sky. She briefly reflects that Mitsuharu-*san's* difficulties with teeth and gums have been forever cured, and the troubles Jiksumi sought to evade by indulging in alcohol have been permanently washed away. She struggles against whispers rising from her undisciplined heart, but finds the battle difficult.

The lifestyle of the Guard is full of difficulties. The stark white pall of their faces and the violence of which they are capable chills most casual relationships before any can begin. Many of the more traditional Japanese see the white faces of the Guard as symbolic of death. Besides Sukayo and his family, Machiko can think of few she would account as friends, and that is their secret sorrow. They enjoy much respect and privilege, they are greatly honored. Their material rewards far exceed what any of them really need and can only be regarded with satisfaction and delight. Yet, they pass much of their time alone, sealed within the iron fist of duty and martial discipline.

Not until they retire from active duty and join the masters of the Guard at the GSG academy have any of them taken partners or borne children. Machiko has considered this often, pondered it, worried about it, but now is not the time.

One day . . . perhaps . . . if fate will allow it.

Burners beneath the pyre are ignited. The flames swiftly rise into a roaring pillar of fire. Several persons of the Honjowara-*gumi* and the Nagato Office of Corporate Affairs move about with portacams, recording everything.

The Security Service is more discreet, utilizing officers with implanted headware to make a visual record.

As the ceremonies end, the Chairman's close advisor Zoge-*san* moves to the families of the dead to invite them all to the Chairman's estate. There, they will be met by counselors of the Nagato Office of Employee Services. They will be advised about legal matters and encouraged to accept various counseling services. They will of course be accorded paid leave from their jobs. Leaves of absence will be arranged for those younger persons attending school. The Chairman will meet with all of them personally in the days to come to ensure that their needs have been accommodated. He will likely also see that any special wants such as might require a special favor are also satisfied.

Honjowara-*sama* descends the dais and begins the brief

trip to Nagato Communications Corp complex located here in Nagato Commercial Park. He and several other clan leaders and officers of Nagato Corp will meet with the board of NCC and attend an assembly of NCC employees.

Machiko leaves Gongoro to supervise the body detail and other activities of the Guard and proceeds directly to the Nagato Commercial Park aerodrome.

An unmarked Federated-Boeing Commander tilt-wing aircraft waits in the flight line, turbines whining, back-draft from the spinning rotors making the plane and pavement around it seeming to waver with heat.

Machiko climbs onboard. Twenty GSG follow, a hurriedly assembled advance team. The last two into the cabin turn and yank the hatch shut.

The interior of the main cabin has only fifteen seats. Those without seats kneel in the center aisle and prepare to steady themselves as best they can. The gun ports along both sides, a custom modification, are of course closed, weapons secured. In the event of a tactical emergency, the plane can be swiftly converted to unleash a devastating barrage against hostile ground forces.

Machiko turns to the flight cabin. The two-person flight crew wears the uniform of the Air Services Division of the Security Defense Force. Most such personnel are former UCAS military. These two are both orks, plainly of Japanese blood.

The pilot-captain turns in her seat to look back. She affects a quick bow. "Our orders are to make best possible time," she says. "We'll have to stay low to clear the traffic pattern at JFK. That'll probably mean shaking some windows."

Machiko replies, "We lack time to be polite."

"Check roger," the pilot says, turning back to her controls. "Let's ram it. Full power."

The engines howl. The cabin vibrates. The ship rises so suddenly that Machiko feels the floor thrust up against her legs. The plane is already tilting nose-downward, the ground sliding past and falling away. In another moment they are climbing past 50 meters and the landscape below is rushing by, the aerodrome left somewhere behind.

The flight is swift. They are across the county line and winging over Nassau County in just moments. Central Nassau's congested sprawl soon gathers into the dense conglomeration of stone and steel that is Queens. Machiko

catches sight through the flight cabin windows of the
strobing lights of the runways at JFK airport, off to the right.
Then they are over the islets and channels of Jamaica Bay,
veering past the UCAS military installations at Floyd Ben-
nett Field, and swooping down over the eastern extent of the
peninsula known as Coney Island.

Extending out nearly 400 meters beyond the southern
shoreline, creating a shoreline of its own, complete with
boardwalk and slips for pleasure cruisers, is the expansive
complex of the Chrysanthemum Palace Hotel and Casino.
Perhaps the most ambitious project Nagato Combine has
ever attempted. Already, in just its first few months of operation, it has brought in millions of nuyen. And as even
Machiko is aware, it must bring in many millions more if it
is to pay off its debt.

"Palace Control, this is Workhorse Five," says the pilot
into her commlink. "We are priority five, inbound."

A voice replies, "Check roger, Workhorse. Call the ball."

"ILS lock-on. Coming down hot and heavy."

"Check roger. On glidepath."

"Transition to vertical flight in three, two, one, mark."

It seems to come an instant too late. The massive ten-sided
pyramid of the Chrysanthemum Palace Hotel, rising more
than forty stories into the cloudy haze of the afternoon,
swiftly swells large, then immense. They seem like a missile
diving directly for the roof of the pyramid. The landing pads
atop the roof seem about to swallow the nose of the aircraft.
Then, suddenly, the nose of the ship kicks upward and the
cabin floor is shoving against Machiko's legs so hard she
must wedge herself into the doorway at the flight cabin's
rear to keep upright.

"Stand by," the pilot comments.

Engines scream. A piercing electronic tone begins pulsing and the plane shudders and the impact nearly hurls
Machiko to the floor. Even as she straightens, the pilot is
saying, "Hope that was fast enough. Any faster, we'd be in
the penthouse."

"My thanks to the SDF," Machiko replies.

The pilot grins around diminutive fangs. "Always glad to
be of help."

Two GSG thrust the main cabin hatchway open. Machiko
is first down the steps. The deputy director for hotel security
and the director for security of the entire complex are

waiting at the doors to the aeropad miniterm. They escort Machiko directly to the hotel's security command center: an expansive room walled with display screens, lined with security consoles, filled with the murmur of commlinks and the beeps of sense-touch console keys.

The hotel deputy briefs Machiko on the situation. On various of the display screens, she sees members of her advance team taking up their positions, many already guarded by Security Service officers and troopers of the SDF.

In expectation of the Chairman's arrival, security has been greatly heightened. Access to the hotel complex has been limited to the hotel's two main entrances. Everyone entering is scanned for weapons not merely by the discreetly disguised weapons detectors built into the entrances, but also by plainclothes officers of the Security Service, watched over by uniformed officers. These are further supported by heavily armed and armored troopers of the SDF, waiting in certain selected locations just out of sight. All persons who are not registered or expected as guests of the hotel or arriving for some legitimate, documented purpose are denied entrance.

Here there is no question of clan Honjowara bearing the burden of security. The complex is an official venture of Nagato Corporation, and the official security forces of the Corporation are directly responsible for the entire facility. The GSG is advised and consulted on all matters pertaining to the Chairman's impending visit, but Machiko need concern herself only with the Chairman's person and his immediate surroundings.

Rowdy gangers and other troublemakers who may approach the hotel will only become her responsibility if they come near Honjowara-*sama,* and that prospect seems very unlikely.

Machiko chooses the elevator Honjowara-*sama* will ride in. This is placed under the direct control of the GSG elevator detail. They will have complete command-override control.

A brief code beeps over Machiko's commlink.

No need to answer.

Momentarily, an aide reports to the deputy director of security, "Orchid Garden has initiated, sir."

The Chairman's flight to Brooklyn has begun.

Machiko is on the roof when the aircraft arrive: a pair of

Federated-Boeing Commanders descending simultaneously
to the rooftop aeropads. A trio of helicopter gunships,
Q-modified Hughes Airstars, take up positions around the
roof as the tilt-wing Commanders descend. A third F-B
Commander stands off, slowly circling the pyramid of the
hotel. Machiko's discerning eye observes that although this
third plane displays no obvious weapons, its gunports are
open. Doubtless, a full complement of combat-ready SDF
aircrew man the firing stations.

As the paired Commanders touch down, a twin-engine
Mistral whisks by overhead. The plane is outfitted with a
complement of sensors that far exceed the cost of the air-
frame—and keeps many watchful eyes on surrounding air-
space, as well as the ground, Lower New York Bay, Coney
Island Channel, and the nearby expanse of the Atlantic
Ocean.

One F-B Commander is crowded with GSG, immediately
moving to form a phalanx around the passengers waiting to
debark from the other plane.

"Machiko," says Honjowara-*sama* as he emerges.

He motions her to his side.

They ride an elevator down three levels to the hotel
director's suite. The suite has been checked and cleared.
Inside the main bedroom waits Honjowara-*sama's* personal
valet with several changes of clothing as well as a suitcase
full of toilet articles. Honjowara-*sama* strips to his shorts
and makes brief use of the adjoining lavatory. There is only
one means of access to this lavatory. Therefore, Machiko,
the only member of the Guard now present inside the suite,
waits just outside the lavatory doorway, rather than in it.

When the valet enters, she enters.

Honjowara-*sama* stands at the vanity counter running
water into the sink. He begins washing his neck and shoulders. "Machiko," he says, "how have you progressed?"

The valet's family has belonged to the Honjowara-*gumi*
for five generations and has always served with meticulous
loyalty, so there is no need for guarded talk.

Machiko tells her encounter with Gordon Ito's deputy,
including the deputy's expression of interest in the Nagato
subsidiary Neurocomp.

"Gordon Ito is an executive and a subordinate to merchants," Honjowara-*sama* says once Machiko has finished.
"He will do nothing that does not advance his own ends,

which ultimately will relate to the economic objectives of his corporation. If he inquiries about Nagato activities, there is a reason. It remains to be determined, based on what you have said, whether that reason bears any relationship to the immediate objective of your investigation."

Honjowara-*sama* pauses to choose from several deodorants offered by the valet. "It may be that your visit to Fuchi merely presented Ito with a convenient means of expressing an interest he has held for some time. I want you to confer with Bessho-*san* in the near future. The Security Service maintains varying degrees of relationships with the security organs of a number of major corporations. You should be informed as to the state of these relations. The trade in intelligence can be a delicate business."

"Chairman-*sama*," Machiko says, bowing, "I am no merchant. I have no training in any form of trading or negotiating. Perhaps such delicate business as the trade in intelligence should be left to others."

Honjowara-*sama* finishes brushing his teeth, and says, "Nagato Combine has no need of another merchant. Your loyalty is beyond question. Your blade is keenly honed. Consider the lessons of your *sensei* Kuroda-*san* and look forward to the day when you will join the masters of the Guard."

This is so startling, Machiko blurts, "Join them, Chairman-*sama*? At the academy?"

Honjowara-*sama* turns fully to look at her, and says, "Do you suppose that such capable individuals as Kuroda-*san* spend the whole of their time instructing the neophytes of the Guard?"

Machiko hesitates. Her thoughts travel back to Kuroda-*sensei's* unexpected appearance at the Yoshida-*kai* teahouse in Brooklyn, then further, to her years of training at the GSG academy. In fact, such masters as Kuroda-*sensei* spent many hours training her and others in the sword and other martial disciplines. Various of the masters from time to time were said to go into "seclusion," presumably for purposes of meditation. Machiko had occasionally supposed that perhaps certain masters had gone away from the academy to perform certain special duties—perhaps familial duties—especially when their terms of "seclusion" ran on long, but she has never really inquired as to the nature of the duties performed.

Honjowara-*sama's* words give abrupt rise to a new vista of possibilities. Could it be that there is an elite corp within a corp? That the masters of the Guard are in fact far more active in the affairs of Nagato Combine than she has previously supposed?

Would it not be wise of the Chairman to apply a weapon as keen as Kuroda-*sensei* wherever he might have effect?

Honjowara-*sama* says nothing more on the subject. He returns to the bedroom, selects a fresh suit and begins to dress. In just a few moments more, he strides boldly into a nearby room arranged like a boardroom. Eight men and three women, mostly norms, mostly Caucasians, wait around the mahogany table at the center of the room. All eleven rise and applaud as Honjowara-*sama* enters. The leader of the group, Joseph Durkin, president of the powerful New York Transport Mechanics and Load Handlers' Free Trade Union, greets Honjowara-*sama* with a bow, then smiles broadly as Honjowara-*sama* extends a hand to complete the greeting in the western style.

"My good friend," Honjowara-*sama* remarks.

"My special father!" says Durkin-*san*.

There is some laughter over this.

A general discussion of union business soon begins. Toward the end, one man says, "We've heard some concern from our members about these attacks against your people, the bombing in Newark. I guess some of our people are nervous."

"I know I am," says one of the women.

"Stuff like this gets around and I don't want nobody blasting or bombing my members."

"Your concerns are understandable," Honjowara-*sama* replies. "Our people must always come first. However, you may be certain that the forces of Nagato Combine are actively seeking the criminals behind the violence. Machiko-*san*, the acting senior of the Guard, is herself participating in the investigation."

Every eye turns to Machiko. She says nothing. She gives no sign of noticing that she has become the center of attention. Inwardly, she feels a twinge of uncertainty, wondering where the moment is leading. She is not the only GSG in the room, but she feels as though she is suddenly very alone.

"What can you tell us of the investigation?" Honjowara-*sama* asks.

Machiko looks to the Chairman, but hesitates to say anything. Honjowara-*sama* has thrust her into a position with which she has little experience.

The union leaders do not belong to Nagato Combine. The Chairman addresses them as friends and allies, but the strength of their friendship and the certainty of any alliance is far less, in Machiko's view, than the bonds that join the three clans. In past meetings, Honjowara-*sama* has always been careful to maintain the attitude of an ally, but to Machiko it seems that he has kept a certain distance, telling the union leaders only those portions of the truth that they are in need of knowing.

"Details of an ongoing investigation must of course be protected," Honjowara-*sama* adds. "Generally, what have you determined? Speak freely."

To Machiko, it seems significant that the Chairman tells her to "speak freely." When told to speak, she would not ordinarily even consider speaking in any other manner. She cannot imagine that Honjowara-*sama* would doubt this for even an instant, or that he would ever consider it necessary to tell her to speak without restraint, unless he intended his words differently than they might otherwise appear.

Machiko considers what she knows, what she suspects. She considers Gordon Ito and his Special Administration. She considers the interest expressed by Ito's deputy regarding Neurocomp and what that might imply. She considers the many uncertainties that remain, but she says, "The violence against Nagato Combine appears to be the work of terrorists."

"You have definite indications."

This does not seem to be a question. It seems to be a statement that Honjowara-*sama* wants confirmed. The gaze he directs toward her seems particularly strong.

"Yes, Chairman-*sama*," Machiko says. "That is correct."

"How would you characterize the progress you are making?"

It has been little more than three days since the bombing at clan headquarters, a few hours more than that since the assassins' attacks. In that time, Machiko has followed leads and taken captives and conducted interrogations. She has pursued her enemy across the plex and gained much valuable information. She cannot say where or when she will find her enemy, but this is not what the Chairman asked. "We are making swift progress, Chairman-*sama*," she says. "Very swift."

Honjowara-*sama* looks to the union leaders. They appear
much impressed. Several appear to grow uneasy beneath
Machiko's roving gaze and direct their attention elsewhere.

"Our Serpents are swift, and very determined,"
Honjowara-*sama* says, making a rare use of the slang term
for the Guard. "Do not be concerned about the violence
directed against us. These criminals do not know the danger
they face. They will soon be brought to justice!"

The union leaders do not seem to doubt it.

The meeting soon ends. Honjowara-*sama* moves to
another room like a western-style sitting room with sofas and
armchairs around a large marble hearth. The GSG detail at
the door pass through a number of persons in twos and
threes, minor union officials and union members and members of their families, all here to spend a few minutes with
the Chairman of Nagato Combine. Honjowara-*sama* speaks
casually and shows several of the children great favor,
inquiring about their schools and relations with their parents.

Each guest receives a small gift. A union photog and persons from the Nagato Office of Corporate Affairs take
digipics and trideo to commemorate the occasion. A Security
Service officer with cybercams for eyes watches from
nearby.

Then comes the main event.

They ride an elevator to the hotel's main floor. They take
a passage guarded by every form of security personnel to the
very edge of the satin-draped stage facing the hotel's Grand
Ballroom. Then comes the duty that cannot be avoided.

Machiko is commanded by Honjowara-*sama* to stop and
wait at the edge of the stage, to remain with the entire body
detail as Honjowara-*sama* walks alone toward Durkin-*san*
and the podium at the front-center of the stage.

Each passing moment is a nightmare of expectation. From
the moment that Honjowara-*sama* first steps onto the stage,
pandemonium erupts. The entire assemblage of people
crowded among the rows and rows of tables filling the ballroom comes to its feet, applauding, exclaiming, filling the
hall with the uproar of their voices. A barrage of machine-
gun fire could erupt and Machiko would not hear it until
too late.

GSG stand in a line before the stage, and also wait behind
the lush hangings crossing the rear of the stage, but none
accompany Honjowara-*sama* to where he is most exposed.

Machiko breathes deeply. She battles to settle her spirit, but knows this battle will not be won till Honjowara-*sama* retires from the stage. She is little assured by the thought that the gathering reacts with immense favor to the Chairman's appearance.

It is no surprise that the people filling the ballroom react as they do. It is no coincidence that the Transport Mechanics and Load Handlers' Free Trade Union chooses the Chrysanthemum Palace for its annual meeting, or that the Chairman honors the gathering by appearing on the dais. The Chairman's own personal funds assisted Durkin-*san's* hard-fought climb to the presidency. *Kobun* of the Honjowara-*gumi* stood guard at union meetings and defended local election committees when ruthless criminal elements allied with the Maf sought to maintain the oppressive iron grip of their control over the union membership.

These people have elected a president of their own choosing, but they know well who is primarily responsible for the influence and power they now possess.

"*Hon-go! Hon-go! Hon-go!*" they chant. What they mean is "the main word." He who speaks the words of truth, words that matter.

And now Honjowara-*sama* arrives at the center of the stage. He lifts one hand high, index finger extended and roars into the mikes on the podium, "*Number one!*"

The assembly goes wild. Shouting, screaming. Pounding fists on tables and feet against floor till the ballroom resounds with thunder.

"*Number one! Number one!*"

The outcry goes on for five minutes or more. When some measure of order finally seems about to descend, Honjowara-*sama* says into the mikes, "We have only now begun."

Another thunderous outburst arises.

But when Honjowara-*sama* thrusts both his hands palm-out to the assembly, the uproar quickly settles into quiet.

"Under the leadership of your president!" Honjowara-*sama* says in a powerful voice, "you have taken many steps toward securing a prosperous future for yourselves and for your families! Know that the bond between Nagato Combine and your leadership remains strong! That your president works tirelessly to guarantee you the benefits you profoundly deserve!"

The tumultuous ovation that arises now drowns out

Honjowara-*sama's* voice. It becomes deafening as Honjowara-*sama* draws Durkin-*san* to his side, both men thrusting fisted hands toward the soaring ceiling of the ballroom, index fingers erect.

"NUMBER ONE!" the pair bellow into the mikes.

"Spellcasting!" shouts into Machiko's ears.

It is her worst nightmare come true.

She does not look into the astral to determine what is happening. To gaze into the astral is to open oneself to attack from the astral. Rather, Machiko accepts the word of those of the Guard who are responsible for watching the astral, and she blurts, into her commlink, *"Green wave green wave green wave. . . !"*

She propels herself across the stage. The details waiting in the wings of the stage are already in motion. Those nearest her are barely a step behind her.

As she moves toward Honjowara-*sama* at center-stage, a trio of naga, Ujitaro's Awakened serpents, sluice across the stage in front of her feet.

And then she sees it, far above the ballroom floor, out over the center of the floor, something forming, coalescing out of the empty air, an enormous globe of brimstone red, now flaring with sparks and tendrils of the fire and expanding by the moment as if to incinerate the entire ballroom.

Honjowara-*sama* hesitates, lifting his gaze to the globe. As the tumultuous acclamation of the crowd begins filling with cries of horror, Honjowara-*sama's* expression grows adamant with defiance.

Machiko bruises past Durkin-*san* and drives herself bodily into Honjowara-*sama's* flank. Others strike her, thrust against her. For a moment, Honjowara-*sama* seems like the immovable boulder half immersed in a churning sea; then they are moving around him like an inexorable wave, forcing him toward the side of the stage, lifting him right from the floor and forming a bullet-shaped barricade that batters past anyone in their path.

The crackling, flaming globe seems only to grow larger. A shrill wind arises. Lightning tears at the stage, the podium. Peals of horror and fear peak into screams of agony.

A deafening discharge erupts, like detonating artillery.

Machiko feels the blast vibrating through the floor. She feels the shock wave shoving at her shoulders. She feels its heat and smells its acrid smoke and hears the shrieks of its victims. But she can do nothing about that. Duty keeps her driving ahead, carrying Honjowara-*sama* along, through the wings of the stage, down corridors and stairways, finally to the sub-levels of the hotel, the expansive parking complex. Here waits a convoy: GSG and SDF troopers, weapons ready; armored sedans and security vans and armored limousines, engines running. Once Honjowara-*sama* has been installed in a swift and highly maneuverable Toyota Elite, Machiko orders an abrupt halt so that she may access the situation.

She will not rush the Chairman into the streets and into a potential ambush. The magical attack could be pure subterfuge.

Even the priority channel on her commlink is overwhelmed with traffic. Many long moments pass before she can contact the hotel command center. A first report suggests that the hotel's Grand Ballroom is burning, that the main level of the hotel is filling with smoke. Another indicates that the fury of the magic attack has incited a panic, that security personnel at the hotel exits are being overwhelmed, in one case trampled, by hundreds of terrified fleeing people.

"Find the mage!" Machiko shouts into her commlink. "The mage! *Find the mage!*"

Like hunting a minnow in a flood.

She orders the convoy to roll.

30

Honjowara-*sama* is brought safely to the Brooklyn headquarters of the Yoshida-*kai*. From there, Machiko arranges
for him to be conveyed by limo and helicopter to his estate in
the eastern reaches of Suffolk County. The attack at the
Chrysanthemum Palace Hotel must be considered an attack
against the Chairman, and Machiko will take no chances.
She assigns both Ryokai and Gongoro to Honjowara-*sama's*
body detail and to take command of the GSG at the estate.

Then, she commandeers a car and returns to the Chrysanthemum Palace Hotel.

The streets leading to the complex are clogged with emergency vehicles and blocked by Winter Systems police.
Machiko abandons the car and jogs the final blocks to the
hotel and casino complex. The scene she encounters there is
apocalyptic.

The fire is already extinguished. Damage to the Grand
Ballroom is merely superficial. The main level of the hotel is
hazy with smoke, but the true damage may only be measured
in terms of persons killed or injured.

They lie everywhere, the dead, the wounded moaning for
help, crying for loved ones, screaming with the anguish of
broken bones and shattered joints, along every corridor con-
necting with the Grand Ballroom, across the main lobby,
heaped atop one another about the two main entrances.
Medics and paramedics move frantically from one victim to
the next, all but overwhelmed by the sheer numbers of the
fallen.

Machiko comes upon a man recording all with a portacam.
So great is her frustration, so intense her horror over what
has happened, that she seizes the camera, smashes it on the
floor, and then, sword drawn, sends the man running for the
nearest exit.

In a lounge on the mezzanine, she finds Ujitaro lying

slumped on a sofa, surrounded by his coiling naga, and watched over by a small crowd of GSG. "We found him unconscious after the attack," informs the senior one of the group, one of the Guard's few other woman members. "He says he is merely exhausted. I thought to move him away from the smoke and confusion. I also summoned the thaumaturgic medical unit. They will be arriving shortly."

Mages are no less likely than physical adepts to suffer irreparable harm at the hands of doctors, and so the Kissena Park Medical Center, a subsidiary of People's Health Centers of New York, which is itself a subsidiary of Nagato Corp, maintains a special team specifically for the treatment of persons who are magically active.

Likely, the same personnel who first attended Sukayo will attend Ujitaro—attend him with the utmost care.

Machiko crouches beside the mage. He appears disheveled and battered, as if recently subjected to a beating. A purplish welt dives from the right side of his forehead into the wild disarray of his hair. A smear that could be dried blood stains his chin. His voice is like a raspy grunt. "What do you want?"

Quietly, Machiko says, "When we spoke of the mage who sent the old man with the bomb to Honjowara-*gumi* headquarters, you said you would know this mage by his work."

Ujitaro nods. "It was the same one today."

"You did not detect his presence before he attacked?"

Ujitaro's look turns acid. "Initiates mask their auras."

"Why did you not attack?"

"I battled his magic. Or you would all be cinders!"

Compassion yearns to make some statement, Machiko's heart feels moved to sympathy, but duty must take precedence now. There is only duty and death. They must all be prepared to hurl themselves selflessly at an irrational death.

Machiko rides an elevator to the security command center. She finds the deputy director for hotel security in the middle of a ferocious tirade, a tirade that abruptly halts as the man's eyes meet her own.

The man invites her into his private office and there bows deeply. So very deeply he appears shamed. "As soon as this current emergency is past, I will submit my resignation to the hotel director."

"What? Please explain."

"We believe we have captured the intruder, presumably a

magician, on security cams. It appears that he gained access to the hotel via a sublevel door that should have been secured. The door has been physically checked and found to be unlocked, though our systems continue to show the door as secure. We can discover no physical or operating malfunction in the security systems themselves. It therefore appears likely that the mainframe responsible for supervising hotel security systems has been successfully penetrated."

Machiko shakes her head as if to clear it. But the attempt does not help. What the deputy is telling her is just one more incredible event in a series of such events.

"Show me this magician," she says tersely.

The deputy turns to the telecom on his desk and makes swift use of the keyboard. One of the images that appears on the telecom's screen shows the hotel's Grand Ballroom. At the middle of a crowd of cheering people, many waving arms over their heads, one man holds out not merely his arms but also some form of intricately crafted black wand above his head.

"Have you any images of his face?"

The deputy bows, embarrassed.

"Please enhance the wand."

The image zooms in till the wand fills the screen. The images carved into its length appear to be grotesque, misshapen faces, the faces of demons perhaps, or the tormented in one of the many Buddhist hells. Machiko uses the telecom to contact Nagato Corp Operations Center and thereby connects with Colonel Satomi, deputy chief of security operations, apparently riding in a car.

She transmits the images provided by hotel security, and says, "I am curious about this mage's wand, if it is such a wand. I would like a thaumaturgic evaluation."

"I was just on-line with the director of thaumaturgic investigations." A moment passes, then the screen divides into two windows. Machiko recognizes the woman who appears in the second window as Oki-*san*. She is a norm and very aged, her hair white and sparse, her face thin and frail. Her voice, though, is full and resonant, almost sultry. "It appears that this wand is intended as a mage's device," she says. "However, it is impossible to determine from a superficial visual examination the exact form of magic practiced. I would theorize that it is not a form likely to be beneficial to people."

And, with that, the second window winks out.

Machiko struggles to restrain a sudden surge of anger. *Why must all magicians be so difficult to deal with?*

They are not even tokenly polite!

She thanks Satomi-*san* for his assistance and breaks the link. The deputy for hotel security proceeds to display other images of the mage, the trail he followed in entering the hotel. In each new frame that appears, the mage's face is hidden from view, either by the brim of his hat or because he has turned his face away from the cam. "It would appear that this individual knows the locations of your cams," Machiko says.

The deputy agrees.

The trail ends, or rather begins in the sublevel parking complex. A wide-angled cam panning across a broad area filled with parked cars briefly displays a white van, the mage emerging from it. The van is plainly marked with the five-pointed star of Fuchi Industrial Electronics.

"Have you checked the vehicle registration?"

"Yes. We have a direct line to the state department of licensing. It is a Fuchi van."

"Could it be stolen?"

"It has not been reported stolen to any police."

Machiko breathes deeply, but not even her most determined effort can suppress the fears that snatch ravenously at her spirit. If Fuchi is indeed behind this campaign of terrorist violence, if Gordon Ito truly desires the destruction of Nagato Combine, if . . .

But surely this is absurd! Not even Gordon Ito would be so bold as to send an agent, a mage, in a Fuchi van!

What is happening?

Even as Machiko struggles with the confusion of her own thoughts, the telecom beeps with an incoming call. The deputy answers. And bows. "Chairman-*sama*."

Machiko looks to the screen and sees the harshly determined features of Honjowara-*sama* gazing back at her. "Machiko," he says. "I am at Yoshida-*kai* headquarters. Come now."

"Yes, Chairman-*sama*," Machiko replies.

At once.

31

The scene on the plaza before the hotel's main lobby is no less horrific for seeming somewhat more orderly than earlier in the evening. The dazzling strobes on emergency vehicles flicker and flare. Emergency workers arrange the trampled corpses of victims in neat lines along walkways and fountains. Trauma teams rush the living toward the waiting lines of ambulances, medics treat others under the open sky. Priests give blessings. Winter Systems police confer with Security Service officers. Media snoops infest the plaza like insects. Several rush toward Machiko's flanks.

"Who's responsible for the attack . . . ?"

"How many dead . . . ?"

"Where's the Chairman . . . ?"

"Kill anybody . . . ?"

Certain snoops habitually offer insult in the form of questions in hopes of provoking a reaction. They fail. GSG do not address the media, do not acknowledge snoops as extant. The requirements of duty are normally far too critical for members of the Guard to allow anyone to interfere with them in any way. Thus, there are occasional incidents wherein members of the Guard are compelled to use force, such as to get a particularly intrusive scooper out of the way.

Tonight, these representatives of news and entertainment corps keep out of Machiko's path. They remain at a "polite" distance. Machiko breaks into a trot and leaves them behind.

Roads made impassable by cordons of Winter Systems police and emergency vehicles are now further burdened by media vans and commissary wagons and cars and motorcycles of onlookers. Machiko does not bother looking for the car sent to meet her. She lengthens her stride. It is not far to the headquarters of the Yoshida-*kai,* a mere few blocks. She soon covers the distance.

The street before the headquarters of the Yoshida-*kai* is

blocked at both ends by armored vans marked for the Security Defense Force. The headquarters building itself is dark red brick, low and long and filling the middle third of the block. SDF troopers line the front of the building and hold positions on the roof. Helicopters buzz by overhead. Ryokai stands with a detail of GSG at the main entrance.

He smiles as if relieved. "You're all right."

Machiko almost gapes. *How can he think of such things . . . ?* Of her personal well-being. They are facing a major calamity and only Buddha and his angels know how this night will end. As warriors, they must be resolved to death. "Where is the Chairman?"

"In the second-floor conference room," Ryokai says. "The heavies are all in."

Machiko soon sees this for herself.

The room is large, paneled in black with a lacquered wood floor. A low black table easily six or seven meters long runs from near the door to the far end of the room, gleaming with the light of translucent ceiling panels.

At the far end sits Honjowara-*sama*. To his rear kneel only two GSG, Gongoro and one other.

Seated on low cushions nearest Honjowara-*sama* are Yoshida Mabuchi, head of Yoshida-*kai*, and, opposite him, Toki Bentaro, head of Toki-*gumi*. Yoshida Mabuchi is often referred to as "oyabun," father or parent, or simply "boss." With his antique vested suit and glasses, he looks like a shopkeeper, or a banker, and his fear of personal injury is well-known, but his mind is clever and his words can be very sharp. Toki Bentaro, the more progressive of the pair, prefers a title more in keeping with Honjowara-*sama's* New Way, that of "chief executive." He styles himself like a modern corporate executive, a team player, and he is careful to avoid any suggestion of impropriety, yet where the private ventures of the Toki-*gumi* are concerned he can be very self-minded, and ruthless.

Down both sides of the table sit the senior advisers and counselors, such as Zoge-*san* and Ohana Toyonari, and others Machiko recognizes as owing their primary allegiance to either Yoshida Mabuchi or Toki Bentaro. Here also are the senior executives of Nagato Corporation, such as Adachi Dosan of the Intelligence Directorate, and Bessho Chikayo of the Security Directorate.

Lining the walls are the deputies, advisors to the advisors,

aides, and bodyguards. The one troll in the room, head near
the lofty carved wood ceiling, serves as Toki Bentaro's personal bodyguard.

As Machiko enters, moving to kneel beside the door, all
eyes are focused on the table's many small display screens,
those set into the paneled walls, or the one large screen occu-
pying the entire wall at the end of the room to Honjowara-
sama's rear.

Channel 113 BizZene News tridcast.

". . . the body count is still rising. More than thirty
confirmed dead at this moment and the number is certain to
rise . . .

"Sources close to Winter Systems investigators indicate
that the bomber arrived at the Chrysanthemum Palace Hotel
complex in a van tentatively linked to Fuchi Industrial Electronics. With more on that aspect of the story we now go to
Yoyo Chang in Fuchi-Town . . ."

". . . Here in the shadows of the Fuchi monoliths, the
alleged link of Fuchi IE to the Chrysanthemum Palace
attack, an attack that might otherwise be labeled just another
terrorist event, is raising quite a few eyebrows. Market
traders and investors remember all too well the recent Fuchi
fiasco in Detroit wherein certain expendable assets were
hurled pell mell against the Morgan-Mellon joint venture
that held controlling interests in numerous advanced technology corps. The question now on everyone's mind is
whether Fuchi is once again preparing to go to the wall in its
apparent campaign against Nagato Corp. Is this the beginning of yet another corporate war? Plainly, secret negotiations between Nagato Corp and Fuchi have been going on
for some time, as this next sequence of video will show."

The screens show a Toyota Elite limousine rolling down
the ramp into the garage complex beneath Fuchi Plaza. A
second window briefly appears, displaying the Elite's registration tags, identified as belonging to Nagato Corporation.

The limo reminds Machiko of the Security Service car that
conveyed her to the Fuchi towers for her meeting with
Gordon Ito's deputy.

"As to the nature and purpose of the negotiations we can
only speculate. However, this latest development gives
strong indications that the negotiations are not going well
and Nagato Tower now finds itself under direct assault."

To Machiko, it seems impossible that she could be seeing

and hearing such things on a tridcast. How could anyone even know of the Fuchi van beneath the Chrysanthemum Palace Hotel? Certainly, there were many news snoops prowling the complex in the wake of the attack, but how could anyone have divined the van's possible significance? How could they have learned that the mage responsible for the attack emerged from that van? How could they speak of a war between Nagato Corp and Fuchi as if it is already a proven fact?

She is distracted from her thoughts when another GSG enters through the door at her immediate left. He kneels to the left of the doorway, glances at her, briefly bows. The settled strength of his posture seems familiar, and marks him clearly as a warrior, yet his face is unknown, and young. Machiko concludes that he must have come only very recently from the GSG academy. Otherwise, she would have met him before now. Had there been any doubt as to his identity, he would not have passed the twenty GSG standing watch outside this room.

But now Honjowara-*sama* looks sternly to the leaders flanking the table. "There will be no war," he says in a low tone, "because, if something is not done swiftly, if this situation is not rectified, *there will be no Nagato Corp!*"

Several of the leaders look to Honjowara-*sama* with widened eyes. Honjowara-*sama* looks to Zoge-*san*, who politely coughs, and says, "Word of this alleged war has spread throughout all financial markets. It is having a severely detrimental effect on the financial ratings of Nagato Corp and its subsidiaries and our various bonds and commercial paper. If this trend is not soon reversed, the banks will begin demanding repayment of outstanding loans. Various other creditors will attempt to have Nagato assets frozen and held as collateral for outstanding debt. Given the degree of investment in Chrysanthemum Palace Ventures, we may be left with no choice but to divest ourselves of assets in order to satisfy the recall of debts, or to declare Nagato Corp bankrupt."

Yoshida Mabuchi looks to Zoge-*san*, and says, "What is Fuchi's objective in creating this appearance of war?"

Possible objectives are discussed. Zoge-*san* expresses the belief that the objective may be to force Nagato Corp to divest certain assets, which Fuchi would then swallow whole. The discussion continues along these lines until

Adachi-*san* says, "Of course, we have only the use of this
van to indicate Fuchi involvement."

"Machiko-*san* has recently been to the Fuchi towers."
Zoge-*san* looks down the length of the table to Machiko, and
says, "I am curious as to your perspective. Do you believe
that Fuchi is responsible for the Chrysanthemum Palace
attack or the other recent attacks against Nagato Combine?"

The inquiry seems made with great ease. Formulating an
answer is difficult. The difficulty is compounded by the fact
that the leaders of Nagato Combine have just spent much
time considering Fuchi's objective in creating the appearance of war. To say that Fuchi would be unlikely to do this is
tantamount to saying that the leaders have been wasting
time; worse, that their basic assumption is wrong. Who is
Machiko to say something like that?

She bows, and says, "The Fuchi security apparatus is very
highly regarded. I have difficulty understanding why they
would allow a Fuchi vehicle to be used in an attack by Fuchi
agents."

"Perhaps they wish the world to accept the premise that
Fuchi makes war on Nagato Combine."

Machiko hesitates. Zoge-*san* speaks of corporate strate-
gies. He is the expert on corps, the legal and financial specialist. Who is she to offer comments? Yet the man's remark
was directed to her and he waits, watching her, obviously
expecting a reply. She must say something, something relevant, something meaningful, if only to avoid dishonoring the
Guard. If she is to serve Nagato Combine as a warrior must
serve, she must say what she thinks.

She bows, and says, "Please excuse me, but I do not think
that Fuchi would adopt such a strategy."

Zoge-*san* questions her with his eyes, and says, "I would
be interested to hear your reasoning."

Machiko struggles to order her thoughts. The many
leaders looking to her, awaiting her words, adding the weight
of their presence to the already considerable weight of Zoge-
san's eyes, do not aid in the effort. And of course the unyielding gaze of Honjowara-*sama* only makes her more
keenly aware of her inexperience in matters of corporate
strategy.

Her first words emerge abruptly. "Plans go awry," she
says. "A general planning campaign must account for this in
some manner. Any plan to send covert agents against an

enemy must be prepared for the possibility that these agents will be discovered. If Fuchi were planning a campaign against Nagato Combine, and wishing to create the appearance of war, I do not believe they would call attention to themselves. That would be to invite disaster, to announce the ambush before it is sprung. I believe they would use some other corps to create the desired effect. There are other megacorps, sufficiently powerful as to seem like giants compared to Nagato Combine. Creating the appearance that another corp goes to war with Nagato Combine would seem to reduce the chance that the deception is discovered and traced to Fuchi."

Zoge-*san* appears to consider all this, then says, "You suggest, then, that perhaps some other corp or organization utilizes this strategy, using Fuchi as their dupe."

Machiko had not thought of that, had not carried her thoughts far enough to reach that conclusion, but the idea, now presented to her, seems like the only logical conclusion. She bows. "This seems plausible to me."

Yoshida Mabuchi says, "What corp would dare to use Fuchi as its dupe?"

A discussion of this point begins, but before a conclusion can be reached Machiko finds the young GSG kneeling near her by the door signaling for a withdrawal. She questions this with her eyes, but when he repeats the signal vehemently she complies and follows him through the door, across the hallway and into an unoccupied office.

Here, he turns to face her. As he turns, he lifts a hand to the rear of his jaw and pulls at his skin and removes a mask every bit as supple and lifelike as real skin.

Machiko blinks, astonished. She lowers the sword that came so swiftly to hand. "*Sensei* . . ."

Kuroda-*sensei* gazes at her with steel-gray eyes, and says, softly, "Even in the Void, there is timing. Is this not so?"

"It is," Machiko replies. "But *sensei,* why—?"

Kuroda-*sensei* cuts her off with a brief movement of his chin, like the flourish of a sword seeking its scabbard. "The river we travel is full of swirling currents. Now you must focus on the currents around you. This hotel attack has unsettled the spirit of the corporate over-world. What advice did you give Honjowara-*sama* when you first spoke of Fuchi?"

Machiko thinks back. "When the sword will not cut, stab at the enemy's heart."

Kuroda-*sensei* says, "Now you must consider timing. You must capitalize on the moment. Call Gordon Ito. Demand a meeting. Insist upon it. Ito will recognize how your visit to the Fuchi towers is being used to substantiate this talk of war. He is not a man who exposes his face or his hand without cause. Perhaps now he has cause. Perhaps now he will speak to you."

Machiko can barely contain her puzzlement. "*Sensei,* you have had dealings with Gordon Ito? You speak as though you know his sword."

Kuroda-*sensei* says, quietly, "We will talk again."

32

The diamond-faceted exterior of their delta icon noses up against a system icon in the form of a generic white cube. Negative alert, says Rad238. Camo on, says SmoKe. Initializing entry prog, says NodeBoy.

They slide through a reed and cloud insignia and invade the node. Multiple sub-nodes detected, says Rad238. Cloaking, says SmoKe. Launching progs, says NodeBoy.

There are dozens of sec cams and sensors. The assembled data-feeds paint a picture as true and complete as direct sensory experience. Watch devices 25B004 through 12, Rad238 informs. Recording, SmoKe says.

The room is large and paneled in black. A long low table runs down the center of the lacquered floor. All the leaders are present. News tridcasts report on the hotel attack. There is much talk. They don't ken, says SmoKe. They think someone's out to bankrupt their corp. Limited viewpoints, says Rad238.

The way we want 'em, NodeBoy says.

"The Fuchi security apparatus is very highly regarded. I have difficulty understanding why they would allow a Fuchi vehicle to be used in an attack by Fuchi agents."

"Perhaps they wish the world to accept the premise that Fuchi makes war on Nagato Combine."

"Please excuse me, but I do not thing that Fuchi would adopt such a strategy."

Dangerous, says Rad238. Watch this one.

The one he means is female. Onboard database IDs her as Machiko 29-077346GSG. She goes to speak with another, a male. Kurada 11-422059GSG. The room is small and private. "When the sword will not cut," says Machiko 29-077346GSG, "stab at the enemy's heart."

Kuroda 11-422059GSG replies, "Now you must consider

timing. You must capitalize on the moment. Call Gordon
Ito."

Reference database.

Ito. We've heard this name before.

Another one to watch.

Watch closely.

Yes.

33

The drive to the Brooklyn Bridge takes only a few minutes. However, they must stop at the checkpoint before the bridge. The checkpoint, like the bridge, is grim and grimy, lit by weak floodlights, and looks like something from the last century.

The City of New York maintains checkpoints at all access points to Manhattan island. Machiko is unsure why. Much of the region has always seemed as rampant with crime as the rest of the New York-New Jersey megaplex. The necessity of stopping to show "passes" at every bridge and tunnel appears to accomplish little but the wasting of valuable time.

A uniformed officer for the Port Authority comes to the driver's side window. The SDF officer at the wheel lifts a gray corporate card for the officer to see. "The car in back is with us."

"You're in, chummer."

The Port Authority officer waves them on. He also waves at the second car, the car containing the Fuchi agent, Scudder.

The surface of the bridge is pocked with ruts and holes and comes down in the face of City Center. The SDF driver turns them up Park Row and drives past Bowery Avenue onto East Broadway. That takes them into the Pit and to a narrow street not far from Chinatown, except in terms of general aspect.

Debris lines the sidewalks. Fires burn in alleyways and inside the blackened wounds of windows. The rusted, burnt-out wrecks of automobiles sit along both curbs. A pair of gangers on Harley Scorpions circle the middle of the block, then tear off for the distant corner, rearing up on their back wheels, only to turn and come racing back.

Along the right, between brick-faced ruins, stands a narrow parking garage, apparently abandoned, but far from deserted. A garbage dumpster stands before the entrance. Beside the dumpster waits a small group of figures in grim synthleather, studs and spikes and chains, and an assortment of ferocious weapons. Two norms, an elf and a troll, all of them female. With slashcut hair and menacing face tats and the vicious grinning logo of the Sisters Sinister. Machiko signals a halt and lowers her window. One of the "Sisters" looks in, then signals, and the female troll shoves the dumpster aside

The SDF driver eases the sedan ahead.

The main floor of the parking garage is lit by fires flickering from rusty metal cans. Perhaps as many as forty motorcycles, most of them gleaming with aerodynamic NeoKevlar armor, sit parked in small scattered groups. The bikes' riders are similarly scattered, some dancing to roaring dredrock, some drinking, others off in the shadows as if standing watch. Most are female and most are attired like the four at the entrance. One of the few males Machiko spots sits with his back to a concrete column, the chain ringing the column attached to the manacle ringing his neck.

The current leader of the gang waits just inside the entrance. She is called "Stitch." She has Japanese features and a slight build, but carries herself like one experienced in combat.

"No *omae-Sukayo*?" she says, at Machiko's window.

"Sukayo-*san* is engaged elsewhere," Machiko replies. She lifts a credstick to window-level. "The garage is clear?"

"This is Hotel Sinister, lady snake. It's clear as shick."

"Your cooperation is appreciated."

The credstick is accepted. The "Sister" claps one fist into the palm of her other hand and affects a bow. "Cheks to the oyabun."

An acknowledgment of favor shown by agents of Nagato Combine and hence the Chairman, here called "oyabun." It is intended as a respectful acknowledgment. Machiko affects a very slight bow, despite her true inclinations. She sees little difference between gangers like the Sisters Sinister and murderers like Lau Tsang of the Large Circle League. She does not like dealing with such persons. She does not like allowing such persons to roam freely. They are criminals and belong in prisons. However, there is no denying that such tasks as Nagato Combine may periodically assign them takes up time that might be spent in far more nefarious ways.

The SDF driver rolls the sedan ahead. The second car follows closely. They ride up the ramp to the second level and there turn around and park, facing the ramp. They do not wait long.

Two heavy Nissan sedans come up the ramp and park side by side. Momentarily, headlights wink out and a male norm emerges and walks forward. He is slim and tall and wears a long black duster over an executive style of suit. His short white hair seems almost luminous in the wavering aura of his heat signature. There are no cool points of contrast in his heat signature to suggest the possible presence of either body armor or weapons.

Machiko steps out to meet him.

They spend several moments gazing at each other, surveying, scrutinizing. "You know who I am?"

Machiko nods. He is Gordon Ito. "Nagato Security Service is very limited compared to your own organization, but in some regards it is very well-informed."

Ito light a cigarette. The smell no less disagreeable for being relatively mild. "This is some site for a meet."

"You expressed a desire for privacy."

"Those your razors downstairs? The Sisters Sinister?"

"Tonight, a certain relationship exists, paid for in nuyen. They will not disturb us."

"I believe you owe me something."

Machiko lifts a hand and signals.

To her rear, a car door opens. Three sets of feet echo against the floor, two in heavy boots, one in soft-soled shoes. A pair of SDF troopers in combat fatigues appear on Machiko's left. Between them is the Fuchi agent, Scudder. Ito motions with his chin, and Scudder walks ahead to the Nissan sedans. Machiko gestures and the two SDF troopers return to her rear.

Ito takes a drag on his cigarette. "That concludes old business," he says. "You've got new business?"

"I believe you are being used."

"That's an interesting assertion. If I am being used, it's my problem and I'll handle it."

"I believe your problem is related to my problem."

"Meaning the alleged Fuchi-Nagato war." Ito shrugs. "I wouldn't say that's much of a problem. The potential for damage to the Fuchi image is minimal. Some of our publicly traded ventures might take a hit at the exchange. In the long run it's meaningless."

Machiko is a bit puzzled by this reaction. She finds it difficult to accept. For she knows how she would feel were she in Gordon Ito's position, and that is not very different from how she feels being in her own position. "I wonder if this is how you truly feel, Ito-*san*."

"Feeling's got nothing to do with it."

This Machiko can well believe. Here, in all likelihood, she faces a man who is never guided by emotion, only intellect, the checks and balances of a merchant's records, the account sheets of an executive. What words would affect such a man? "Certain files I have read say that you rarely come down from Fuchi's tall towers. You do not generally micromanage operations. This leads me to wonder, Ito-*san*, why you are standing here now. What could your motivation be to speak with me? Why did you agree to this meeting? Why did you answer the telecom?"

Ito takes a drag on his cigarette. His features reveal nothing of his thoughts. "I'm here to collect Scudder."

"You trusted no one else for this task?"

"I'm also evaluating a potential new source of intelligence. You."

"Is there anything about me you do not already know? which you have not already previously evaluated?"

Ito seems to consider that, then says, "I know you're an expert in the serpent-style of aikido developed by your *sensei* Kuroda. I know you can hit moving targets with shuriken at twenty meters five times out of five. You're qualified with just about every man-portable weapon in the inventory. You're a phys-adept. You see heat. You're very quick. You can probably see the astral, but you use it selectively because the ability makes you vulnerable. You entered the GSG academy at age fourteen. You started training in kendo at age five. You had a pet snake as a kid and you wear a size six shoe, six-narrow. You honor your adoptive parents and you're fanatically loyal to Nagato's Chairman." Ito paused to take a drag on his cigarette. "Yeah, I've got all the basics. What I don't know is how far I can trust you."

"Then I will tell you," Machiko says. "You can trust me to consider all that I do with regard to the wishes of Chairman Honjowara Akido, and the interests of Nagato Combine."

"Nothing's ever that simple."

"It is duty," Machiko says. "Duty may be easy or hard, as easily fulfilled as a child's game, or a true challenge to loyalty and honor. But it is almost always very simple. If the search for my enemy and yours were this simple, the danger would already be past."

Ito seems to consider that, but then says, "How deep did you go interrogating Scudder?"

"Deeply enough to confirm that his words are accurate."

Briefly, Ito nods. He does not appear surprised. "I've got real problems with people who don't make good on their agreements. You said you'd bring Scudder and you performed. That's the kind of currency I trade in. It's worth a gesture of my goodwill."

The last word is almost alarming, coming from a man like Gordon Ito. But Machiko maintains a settled spirit. She asks, "What form of goodwill, Ito-*san*?"

"Information." Ito takes a drag his cigarette. "I've been tracking attempts at penetrating Fuchi subsidiary mainframes. That's brought out some interesting discoveries. You may not be familiar with the financial details, so I'll tell you that your Nagato Corporation is mortgaged to the fragging hilt. And somebody's buying your debt. They've swallowed a few of your most major creditors whole. A few more big buys and they'll own you."

Machiko wonders if this is even feasible. She knows little of finance and corporate law, but the one thing she does know is that the leaders of the three clans own the entire body of Nagato Corp stock. So what Gordon Ito says cannot be true in precisely the way that he says it. "Nagato Corp stock is not publicly traded."

"Own your debt, I own you," Ito says. "I call in your loans. You can't pay everything at once. So I make you a deal. Sell me blocks of stock to satisfy the debt or sell me certain selected assets. Either way, I take the best parts of Nagato in hand."

"You mean that an attempt is being made to take over Nagato Corp?"

"I've been watching funds transfer in and out of Zurich. You don't move the kind of coin that's being moved just to make a couple of nuyen factoring people's debt. Someone's staging to carve you up. That's what this so-called corp war is about. Making Nagato look two steps short of the grave. By this time tomorrow your creditors will be selling your debt at a discount, just to get out. Then the process snow-balls. You don't have much time."

The prospect, the theory, is more than a little unsettling. Even if only half of what Ito says is true, disaster looms. Machiko wants so much to face an enemy she may defeat with sword and fist she could scream with outrage. She had never known anything so frustrating as this elusive enemy who attacks from the north and from the south, down from the mountains and up from the sea. How can she fight such an enemy?

She struggles to keep calm, to breathe. She says, "Ito-*san*, you began by saying that you have been tracking attempts at penetrating Fuchi computers. How did this lead to discoveries about Nagato debt and transfers of funds to and from Zurich?"

Ito takes a drag on his cigarette, and says, "Do you know who designed the operating systems for the local tele-communications grid?"

In fact, Machiko has no idea. But, based on what Ito is saying, his manner in saying it, the answer seems apparent.

Ito says, "There's quirks in the software that the freaks decking out of Vaux Hall and Shadowland never hear about. There's layers of code that Telco security doesn't know exists. How did I make my discoveries? I put a genii into the grid. We'll leave it at that. Except for one other thing.

"The orders to the Zurich banks buying your debt are coming out of the Nagato private grid, the system access node assigned to your Chairman's estate. So tell me again how simple a thing duty is.

"You've got a loyalty problem."

Ito blows one final stream of cigarette smoke toward the blackened concrete floor, then turns and walks back to the Nissan sedans awaiting him.

Machiko breathes a slow, deep breath.

34

The ride to Downtown is short—up Bowery Street to Park and Twenty-ninth and Nagato Tower—but it seems to last hours.

A loyalty problem, Ito said. A strategy to make Nagato Combine appear to be on the verge of destruction so that banks and other creditors will sell Nagato debt cheaply, all into a single pair of hands, hands striving to seize control. That's what it's all about, Ito said. But is he right? And if he is right, who orchestrates the offensive? Is this truly the work of Gamma and the White Octagon? Or is there another greater enemy, perhaps an enemy with knowledge of business, and thus the vision to conceive of such a campaign?

That the orders to the Zurich banks should be routed through the access node for Honjowara-*sama's* estate seems almost a joke. Honjowara-*sama* is no traitor. Of this, Machiko has no doubt. The man would not betray Nagato Combine for the simple reason that he would be dishonored, and without honor he would be nothing, a ruined man. He would rather die, he would welcome it with open arms. By strength of character and force of principle he has all but single-handedly guided Nagato Combine back to the honorable path of their ancient ancestors. For Honjowara-*sama* to turn from this now would be impossible, a betrayal not merely of Nagato Combine, but of everything he believes, his values, his whole life.

If the node for his estate has been used by traitors, that is mere coincidence, or perhaps an attempt to deflect suspicion, or possibly to cast doubt where no doubt should ever arise and so cast Nagato Combine into confusion.

Confusion to the enemy. An ancient martial strategy. Machiko must see it defeated.

When her car arrives in the parking complex beneath Nagato Tower, she waits for the SDF troopers to get out, then uses the sedan's telecom to contact Colonel Satomi. "Do you have any reason to doubt the loyalty of any Nagato Corp personnel with expertise in computers?"

"None at all," Satomi-*san* replies. But then he frowns and adds, "We of course conduct periodic reviews of all corporate personnel. Have you some new data that I should be aware of?"

Machiko relates what Gordon Ito has said.

Satomi-*san* replies, "I will make inquiries with my people. Possibly there are some borderline individuals who should be investigated."

The time is just past one a.m. when Maeda Komachi steps briskly into her walnut-paneled office on the fifteenth floor of Nagato Tower. She comes abruptly to a halt, eyes widening. Machiko sits in the tall synthleather chair located behind Maeda-*san's* desk. Maeda-*san* stares at her as if astonished. Machiko understands. It is unlikely that Maeda-*san* has ever seen a member of the Guard sit behind anyone's desk, much less her own.

A small soft sound of startlement or dismay slips from her lips. She hesitates. She bows more deeply than is necessary to show proper respect, and says, in a voice that briefly wavers, "Machiko-*san* . . . I . . . I . . . that is . . ."

An awkward moment, intended to be so. Machiko has seen this woman many times before, at various meetings, but does not know her very well at all, does not know what to expect of her, or whether she is as loyal as Machiko might ordinarily suppose. Were Maeda-*san* in fact a traitor, she would have unparalleled opportunities to utilize the Nagato private computer grid. She is in fact in charge of that grid, Director of Network Administration.

"Please excuse me if I seem rude or presumptuous," Machiko says. "I have had little rest since before dawn. This chair seemed available."

Maeda-*san* slowly rises from her bow, looking very anxious and uncertain. "P—please," she says. "My office is yours. I am merely, merely confused . . . your telecom call . . ."

"I have been authorized by Honjowara-*sama* to make certain inquiries," Machiko says.

Maeda-*san*'s expression turns to fear. She swallows. "Have I committed some offense? Is that why . . . why you are here?"

To Machiko, it does not now seem very likely that Maeda-

san has committed any crimes, small or large. She does not speak clever words. She responds as would a loyal executive of Nagato Corp, who is also a woman of delicate stature and apparently of a sensitive nature—with surprise and fear and perhaps now even a touch of horror. She shows these things openly, like one genuinely afflicted by emotion, like one who has nothing to hide.

"In the Chairman's name," Machiko says, "I must request your assistance."

"I will do anything, of course," says Maeda-*san,* abruptly bowing.

"There is possibly a traitor in Nagato Corp," Machiko explains. "This traitor, if extant, may be using the system access node of the Chairman's estate to send certain messages to Zurich banks. These messages may include instructions directing the banks to purchase Nagato debt. How may we determine if this is so?"

Maeda-*san* seems troubled by all of this. "It would be a tremendous task, Machiko-*san,*" she says. "Perhaps impossible. Computer activity is routinely monitored and the records compressed and archived. We might find some indication of these messages you speak of within the archives, but these archives contain immense quantities of data. And certain records are kept for only a short period. If these messages are very old, the records may no longer exist."

Machiko considers, and says, "If the messages have been sent at all, they are most likely very recent. Perhaps only days old."

Maeda-*san* nods. "Then the relevant records should exist."

"Then they must be examined."

"I will summon a team of analysts at once. My most capable people." Maeda-*san* moves to the side of her desk and swivels the telecom to face her. "We have little direct traffic with Zurich. That should aid in our search."

Machiko says, "I do not know if the messages went directly to Zurich."

"We will do whatever we must to find what you want."

Machiko opens her mouth to praise this display of dedication and loyalty, but the woman is already speaking to the telecom. She makes several calls. Each time, she says, "I must ask you to come in at once to assist with a matter of vital importance to the Chairman."

It is not long before Maeda-*san's* experts have assembled

in her office. They are an eclectic group of both metas and norms and both genders, some in suits, others dressed like vagabonds. Machiko tells them what little she knows. Maeda-*san* then gives her own instructions, using language of such a technical nature that Machiko grasps very little of what is said.

Semi-autonomous knowbots?

Did she even hear this correctly?

Maeda-*san* concludes, "Advise me the moment you find anything you believe may be significant. I will be here until we reach some result."

The experts bow and file out.

Machiko considers what she might do while the experts work at their computers. "It may be some time until we do obtain some results," says Maeda-*san*. "At least several hours. Perhaps not until morning."

"Is there no way to hasten the process?"

"Even with unlimited resources, it would still take time, Machiko-*san*. We have many terapulses of datastores to search, and only a few clues to guide us."

Machiko grows conscious of the fatigue in her shoulder and the gnawing in her stomach. "You may contact me via the command center," she tells Maeda-*san*. "I will be in the building."

"I will call the moment we find anything."

Machiko rides the elevator to the ninth-floor dining room. The hour is late, but Nagato Tower operates twenty-four hours and that includes the dining room. Machiko eats a brief "supper" and then rides to the suite reserved for GSG and lies down to rest. But her spirit will not cooperate. So much has happened in so little time. She has visited the heights of the corporate overworld and the lowest depths of the street. Four nights ago she rose from sleep to meet the onslaught of an assassin. Everything since then swirls through her mind like a vision of kaleidoscopic confusion, evolving into utter chaos.

She turns to a telecom, but the Urban Blitz Nightly News immediately reports, ". . . at least fifty-seven people tragically lost their lives earlier tonight as the result of a terrorist-style attack at the Chrysanthemum Palace Hotel in Coney Island, Brooklyn . . ."

She checks in with Ryokai via commlink, then rides down to ground level and steps outside.

The night is cool, Park Avenue South is busy with traffic. Machiko walks. Few people move along the broad sidewalks at this hour, for although the district is well-patrolled by NYPD Inc. and others, and no part of Manhattan ever truly seems to sleep, the district is not without problems. Those few who are out and about stay in groups and move briskly. They keep to the brilliant lights of the avenues, shunning the darker confines of cross-streets.

The wisdom in this becomes apparent as Machiko reaches Thirty-sixth Street. Before the renaissance stonework of the Pierpont Morgan Library rages a brawl attended by at least ten or twelve uniformed police. The strobing turret lights of their patrol wagons and sedans glance off the mirrored windows of high-rises and the chrome-faces of skyscrapers, illuminating the night like incandescent blue fire. Who they fight does not become clear until Machiko draws near.

Something has climbed from its grease pit to spread its stain along Thirty-sixth Street.

He wears tight synthleather slacks and tall boots, and both bear the lime and azure slashes of the Ancients. Above the waist he is nude, displaying the wall of thorns tattooed onto his gleaming, sweat-soaked flesh. The datajack set into his shaven skull and the wild maniacal gaze of one riding a persona-chip psychosis high tell all that need be told, in so far as Machiko is concerned. That and his aura, rippling with violence, a repugnant living presence clearly visible on the astral.

Three police lie sprawled on the sidewalk. Five others are down, injured but not yet disabled, looking to Machiko as she pauses just three meters from the center of the conflict.

"Now a serpent," says the Ancients ganger, grinning at her. "What fun."

As he says these last words, he attacks. Like a sudden barrage of bullets, quick and full of devastating power, punching, kicking, smashing. One blow smashes the window of a police sedan, another seems almost to explode, driving a path through the air. Machiko evades each point of impact, turning, bending, side-stepping. Her hands and arms, like coiling serpents, mislead and deflect the blows that follow up. And always there is another blow, another strike, snapping, flashing toward her.

They remain engaged for several minutes. The ganger fills the air with a heat signature that blazes with heat. He grunts and growls like a ferocious animal. And then he sends a fist at her face that misses by a significant margin, and, for one moment, tips him slightly off-balance.

Machiko clasps his forearms and urges him further off-balance. Like a man falling feet-first onto a steeply pitched incline, the ganger runs staggering into the armored flank of a patrol wagon.

He stumbles back, blood pouring from his nose and mouth, and then crumbles.

Five NYPD officers seize him, put him in cuffs.

Onlookers hoot and applaud. One panting officer haltingly expresses gratitude. Machiko bows and continues down the block to Madison, then south toward Twenty-ninth and Nagato Tower. A satisfying exercise, an exercise her spirit yearned for, an affirmation of the Chairman's New Way. To some small degree, it will likely aid relations between Nagato Combine and NYPD, Inc. Yet, Machiko rebukes herself. She is a fool for wasting time. For walking the streets when her enemy awaits her, somewhere, perhaps somewhere very near, within the very ranks of Nagato Combine.

It is difficult to imagine such a despicable traitor existing. Few real traitors have ever come to light. People are not always perfectly satisfied with their positions in Nagato Combine, but generally, in Machiko's experience, differences can be worked out.

It is nearly dawn when Machiko wakes, slumped on a sofa in the GSG suite of Nagato Tower. Her left vambrace vibrates, her commlink beeps.

"We have made a disturbing discovery," says Maeda Komachi.

Machiko takes the elevator down. She finds Maeda-*san* amid the gray-paneled cubicles belonging to the programmers and analysts of Network Administration. Maeda-*san* gives quick instructions to an eccentric-looking group of ten, then turns to Machiko as the ten hasten to various cubies.

"It appears we have a phantom host," Maeda-*san* explains. "I am in the process of summoning my entire department to deal with this, Machiko-*san*."

Machiko asks, "How is this related to my inquiry?"

"It must be related."

"Please explain."

"Well, whether it is evidence of treason is not for me to

say, but it is certainly indicative of illicit and illegitimate use of network resources."

"What is this 'phantom host?' "

Maeda-*san* frowns, and says, "In a sense, it is a virtual computer. A simulation. To discourage illegal intrusions, many computer systems have installed software systems that put up a false front or a mask that simulate all the functions of the native host, or actual computer operating systems. Like the native host, the simulation has access nodes and datastores, but nothing done to the simulation can affect the native host. And usually all the data in the stores of the simulation are watered down or filtered in certain critical respects so as to be of no use to illegal intruders."

"And such a simulation has been found in the node for the Chairman's estate?"

Maeda-*san* hesitates, glancing at Machiko, then bows and says, "Excuse me, Machiko-*san*. I would say yes, but there is no single 'node' for the Chairman's estate. Network resources at that site include such things as the Chairman's personal mininet, terminal nodes for the Senior Executive Information System, access nodes into the local telecommunications grid and various portions of the Nagato private grid. This phantom we have found is running on the Chairman's personal mininet, and at this early stage I can only guess at what it is intended to do."

"How could this phantom have been installed without your knowledge?"

"It is partly a result of the network design, Machiko-*san*. You must bear in mind that Intrusion Countermeasures utilize system and network resources. If we use the most powerful IC available to us in every node and in such quantities as to yield us an impregnable fortress, our systems will never be comprised, but we will get no work done because no resources will be available. The Chairman's mininet is not itself heavily defended or routinely monitored by Network Administration. It is, however, defended by the mainframe responsible for the Senior Executive Information System. A decker of sufficient expertise to slip through this mainframe undetected could, once into the Chairman's mininet, do practically anything he or she might want. That at least is my guess. To make sure we are not compromised any worse than we already have, I have initiated measures to enhance our total network security posture."

Indeed, even as the two of them converse, more people are coming in, conferring with others and moving to various cubicles. The urgency on their faces is plain. Those passing near Machiko walk briskly and keep their eyes averted.

Machiko asks, "Would it be correct to say that the purpose of this phantom host would be to deceive anyone who might be watching as to how the Chairman's mininet is being utilized?"

Maeda-*san* frowns, looking very grave. "I can imagine no other purpose, Machiko-*san*. Certainly, if there had been any legitimate purpose for creating the phantom I would have been informed long before now. This should not have been done without my personal authorization."

"Could it have been done by someone from outside Nagato Corporation?"

"It is certainly within the realm of possibility. It would require expert knowledge and support, but it could be done."

"Could it have been done by one or more of our own people?"

Maeda-*san* appears to consider this for several long moments. Finally, she says, "I have great confidence in my managers, Machiko-*san*. They know my people. I believe I would have had some indication before now if someone in my department is responsible for this."

Machiko has little on which to evaluate Maeda-*san's* opinion, but that is of no immediate concern.

Duty commands her next move.

35

The room in Brooklyn is small, enclosed by pastel-shaded panels and adorned with a pair of black-framed paintings. The lacquered floor resembles sandalwood. Honjowara-*sama* sits cross-legged in a kimono-style robe at a small black table bearing the remains of breakfast. He faces a pair of open panels, which, like double doors thrown open, provide a view of the small but spectacular garden. Machiko is well aware that this room, the Summer Garden room, is Honjowara-*sama's* favorite part of the Yoshida-*kai* headquarters building. He has breakfasted here many times. It is not unexpected to find him here.

What is unexpected, in Machiko's experience, is that she would find Kuroda-*sensei* seated across the table from Honjowara-*sama*. But this of course is becoming the surprise that no longer surprises. She has encountered *sensei* more frequently in the last four days than in the four weeks immediately preceding. She has seen more of him now than in the last several months.

"Machiko."

Honjowara-*sama* invites her with a gesture to sit beside Kuroda-*sensei*. She bows and moves to the table and goes to one knee. She gives the report that duty demands, telling all that Gordon Ito has told her, and what she has learned from Maeda Komachi. "Thus, we are under attack from both within and without. White Octagon may be only a pawn, their activities a tactic of deceit, in the campaign to seize Nagato debts. It therefore seems all the more crucial that we find Gamma, determine his true objectives, and ascertain whether he is his own master."

Honjowara-*sama* pays close attention until her last word is spoken, then looks to the open door-panels providing a view of the garden. He gives no clue as to what he is thinking, and his silence soon becomes oppressive, weighing heavily on

Machiko's spirit. Perhaps Honjowara-*sama* has some secret information that proves she is wrong, all wrong, that she is a fool, her efforts vain. The idea brings her a sickening sense of dismay.

A few birds whistle from the garden, the first birds Machiko can recall having heard since before last winter. How lucky are the birds—free of the troubles of metahumanity!

"This riddle will never be solved," says Kuroda-*sensei*, "unless the flower is laid bare."

Machiko puzzles over this. She supposes that *sensei* refers to Gamma, or possible traitors, or more generally to the repugnant "flower" of racism, anti-meta hatred, that rises like so many poisonous weeds from many innocuous-looking gardens. Perhaps he wishes to interrogate the members of White Octagon personally, to lay bare their deepest secrets. Yet, Machiko is forced to reconsider her thoughts when Honjowara-*sama* glances at Kuroda-*sensei*, and says, "Do not speak in riddles, old friend."

"I speak of Gamma," *sensei* replies. "And all that has gone unsaid."

Honjowara-*sama's* expression abruptly turns incandescent, his voice fierce with rage. "You were told *never to refer to this!*"

Machiko tenses, surprised, but Kuroda-*sensei* merely bows politely, and says, calmly, "In ancient days, a lord went hunting at Nishime. He grew angry and drew his sword, scabbard and all, and used it to beat one of his servants, a warrior. But his hand slipped and the sword fell into a ravine. The warrior, seeing this, leapt into the ravine after the sword, retrieved it, and returned it to his lord. It is said that this demonstrates loyalty and honor."

Honjowara-*sama* gazes fixedly at Kuroda-*sensei*. He appears to spend many moments gaining control of his anger. Finally, with settled spirit, he says, "You know the danger. If this matter were to become generally known."

What matter? Machiko wonders. What are they talking about?

"The greater danger lies now in silence," says Kuroda-*sensei*. "From outside the forest of your daily concerns. This is clear."

"And the opportunity presents itself."

"Indeed. It lingers very near."

To Machiko, it seems then as if some unseen signal passes

between the two men. Honjowara-*sama* looks from Kuroda-*sensei* to the door at his right, an interior door resembling a rice-paper panel. "Sashi," he says.

The door slides open and Sashi-*san*, Lady of the Tir, lady of mystery and long-time associate of Honjowara-*sama*, enters the room. She wears a delicate high-waisted jacket over an elegant long dress that glimmers like waves of liquid gold. She moves with fluid grace. She gives her hand into the hand that Honjowara-*sama* offers and, like a petal settling to the earth, descends gracefully to her knees, and bows, to Honjowara-*sama*, then to Kuroda-*sensei* and Machiko.

Why does Honjowara-*sama* call this lady into the room, into a meeting concerning terrorists and possible traitors? Machiko looks closely at Sashi-*san* and notices something she has never observed before, a discordant element in the Lady's manner. Sashi-*san's* expression seems clouded, troubled. She lifts her eyes from the floor only to glance at Honjowara-*sama* and present him with a fleeting phantom of a smile. She does not look up at all in bowing to Kuroda-*sensei* and Machiko. Neither does she smile.

Once she is settled at Honjowara-*sama's* side, Kuroda-*sensei* bows, rises, and walks from the room.

Into the quiet that follows Sashi-*san* says something to Honjowara-*sama*. Her voice is soft and as melodic as a song and the words she speaks are all but unknown. Is this Sperethiell, the elven tongue of Tir Tairngire? Machiko is unsure. She has always intended to learn something of the elven language, but time and opportunity have always been lacking.

And now Honjowara-*sama* again takes Sashi-*san's* hand in his own and gently squeezes; and, looking at the lady gravely, he nods. Obviously, he means to reassure the lady, to support her, but why? What is the need?

Honjowara-*sama* looks to Machiko, and says, "This lady has certain information to convey to you. This information may be troubling, a challenge to the spirit, but you must not doubt its veracity. I tell you that Sashi-*san* is a lady of great and noble spirit. She will speak only the truth to you. Only the truth."

Machiko accepts this with a bow. She merely wonders why Honjowara-*sama* would choose to assure her that this lady, a close associate of many years, considered by some to be his mistress, would speak only the truth. Machiko would expect such a person, no less than Zoge-*san* and Honjowara-*sama's* other close associates, to speak only the truth. The assurance seems unnecessary, and yet she knows that Honjowara-*sama* rarely does things that are unnecessary.

Then, to Machiko's surprise, Honjowara-*sama* rises and walks from the room.

What is going on here?

Moments pass. Sashi-*san* briefly lifts her eyes as if glancing toward the open doors at Machiko's back. In a soft voice, she says, "Spring is upon us. Even here in the plex the air tastes of new, fresh scents. Perhaps we could sit in the garden?"

Machiko hesitates, then says, "If that is your wish."

"Yes. Please."

They move into the sunny warmth of the garden. It is a garden surrounded on all four sides by buildings of the Yoshida-*kai*, the headquarters building and others. The transparex roof two stories overhead admits the sun, but gives shelter to an atmosphere of serene quiet. Sashi-*san*, with her long dress and graceful movements, seems almost to glide over the curving stone walkway that leads to the garden's heart.

She alights on a low wooden dais just large enough for the round cushion lying upon it, situated beside a bed of pebbles that resembles a vast ocean, marked by rocky outcrops that seem like mountainous isles amid an infinite sea, surmounted by moss like broad meadows and a few scattered bonzai like huge primeval trees.

Machiko deliberates, decides to remain standing.

"It is difficult," Sashi-*san* say, "facing you now. We have rarely spoken, and only briefly. Politely. Even here, in this lovely place, I am uncertain of how to choose my words or how to use them."

To Machiko, it seems that the lady is being excessively polite. "Please do not worry unduly about your choice of words. I am primarily concerned with the information the Chairman said you have to convey."

"You are a hardy warrior. A proven member of the Green Serpent Guard."

Machiko hesitates. "Have you some question about my status?"

"I merely remind myself," Sashi-*san* says with a brief

smile. "You wear the colors of the Guard well, but you are also a woman and very attractive. Forgive me, but I have little experience in the company of women warriors. I do not wish to offend you."

It is all very curious, this lady, her words, her manner, but Machiko thrusts such thoughts from mind and focuses on the point of her and Sashi-*san* being together. "Please do not worry about offending me," Machiko says. "Recent events compel us to move ahead as efficiently as possible."

Sashi-*san* seems to grasp the veiled suggestion in this. She appears to consider her thoughts very briefly. "I should perhaps begin by speaking of Tir Tairngire. You are aware, I'm certain, that the Tir rose from within the lands formerly occupied by the Salish-Shidhe tribal peoples. And that independence did not come until 2035."

Machiko nods. "I am familiar with the Tir's historical background."

"What elf is not?" And here Sashi-*san* smiles, but the smile seems tentative, perhaps tender. To Machiko, it seems as if the lady is unsure, yet wishes to convey some discreet meaning, woman to woman. Machiko wonders what is intended. Obviously, they are both elves. They are both just as obviously of Asian lineage, despite the statement of Sashi-*san's* golden hair.

"In the early days," Sashi-*san* says, "it was never certain that we would succeed in founding the Land of Promise. At first, there were only a very few involved. We faced much determined opposition. Many worked actively against us. Certain of our number struggled constantly to find what allies we could. We knew of course that a country could not be woven wholly out of dreams and pleasant desires. There must be concrete resources to match the vision. Did you know that Honjowara Okido helped to supply these resources?"

"No, I did not know," Machiko replies. Yet, it has always been clear that some connection exists between Nagato Combine and the Tir. It has often been said that Sashi-*san*, in some capacity, represents the interests of the Tir to Honjowara-*sama*.

Sashi-*san* smiles, and says, "Okido-*san* helped us in many ways. He served as our factor in a world dominated by norms, and as our friend in a world controlled by many enemies. Most importantly, in the beginning, he helped us to secure credit, and to obtain the materials and expertise we so desperately needed."

In an effort to move the talk along, Machiko asks, "Why does Honjowara-*sama* believe it is important for me to know this?"

"Because this is where it all begins, everything I must tell you. It is bound together by relations between Tir Tairngire and Nagato Combine, between Okido-*san* and I. It is where your beginning may be found, as well."

"My beginning? I have never been to the Tir."

"You have," Sashi-*san* says. And placing a hand at her waist, over the stomach, she adds, "When you were here. With me."

Machiko is a moment grasping the implication. A moment more ascertaining that Sashi-*san* does not appear to be joking. "Excuse me, but this is not possible, what you are saying."

The tender look returns to Sashi-*san's* features. Her smile grows almost excruciatingly vulnerable. "We met in Seattle, Okido-*san* and I. It was the year that the Native American Nations opened their lands to metas. There had been no riots for some time. The terror that was to come was many years away. It seemed, to some of us, that the world was finally becoming accustomed to the Awakening. We were hearing much in those days of Okido-*san* and his New Way. I remember so clearly his words, how we must move with the tide of the Sixth World, or be swallowed by hatred. We who believed in the Land of Promise, who sought to create it, were very impressed with the man. When he traveled to Seattle, it was in the spring. I was sent to meet him, to determine if his words could be believed, if he was prepared to back his ideals. I had only the Promise to offer, future consideration, yet Okido-*san* not only met me but talked with me through the night. There was a chemistry between us. We both felt it. We had so much in common, beginning with the most basic ideals. We soon fell in love. Later that year, I discovered that love had borne fruit. There could be no doubt as to the father, as I have never been with any man but one."

Machiko struggles to maintain a settled spirit, but this is very difficult. She feels as though she is listening to a fantasy that goes beyond impossible. "Excuse me if I seem rude," she says, "but you clearly have me confused with someone else. Of course, I accept what you say concerning your relations with Honjowara-*sama*. I feel greatly privileged to be entrusted with such intimate information. But there is no question about my lineage. I have seen the records. My biological parents were both elves and they were killed in a terrorist bombing."

Sashi-*san's* expression grows very clouded. "I am sure that you must be aware that no records are inviolate. That they may be changed. Created out of whole cloth."

"Not without reason."

"There were compelling reasons. There still are. Consider the world around us. It is nearly five decades since the Awakening and still bigotry simmers. Hatred foments. Why must Okido-*san* be constantly surrounded by loyal warriors? Why must he work constantly to keep Nagato Combine bound together? Because the divisive elements will use any excuse to tear apart what he has brought together. And we of Tir Tairngire are confronted daily by many of these same enemies."

This would be intolerable, an outrage, coming from anyone less than Honjowara-*sama's* own mistress. "If Honjowara-*sama* were indeed my biological father, a concept I regard as incredible, and do not accept, he would not leave it to you to inform me of the fact. He would face me and say what must be said and then he would explain it."

Sashi-*san* looks briefly down at her lap, then meets Machiko's gaze directly and says, quietly, "A son he would face. A daughter he gives to my hands. Should not a mother be the one to speak of such things with a daughter? If you wish, I will ask Okido-*san* to come here in my place."

It is not as simple as that. Honjowara-*sama* has already said that Sashi-*san* would speak only the truth. What she says may be unbelievable—as much a challenge to the spirit as to simple comprehension—but to seek confirmation from Honjowara-*sama*, that would be an intolerable affront. An insult directed at him personally. "I still have heard no compelling reasons why the records of my background should be falsified."

Sashi-*san* brushes briefly at her eyes. "When I returned from Seattle," she says, softly, "I reported that Okido-*san* was very eager to help us found the Land of Promise. He was willing to work with us, though we had little to offer but the future. There were those among us who entertained doubts, who suspected that Okido-*san* offered help only as a means to gain power over us, and all that we were to create. When they learned that Okido-*san* and I were lovers, they presented me with a plan. A plan designed to test my loyalty and Okido-*san's* ideals."

"What plan?" Machiko asks.

"A very difficult plan," Sashi-*san* says. "I only hope that you will understand because you have sworn to surrender your life in defense of Okido-*san*. That is the depth of your commitment. I have made a similar commitment, a comparable sacrifice. I have given up part of my life."

The meaning of this is clear. Sashi-*san* has done what she has done because of duty. Is no sacrifice too great if duty demands it? Machiko hesitates to ask what must be asked, the question that her heart compels her to ask. "What have you given up?"

"The plan I speak of required me to surrender my unborn child, the small embryo that had taken root inside me during my time in Seattle. It was exchanged for the embryo of a norm taken from among Okido-*san's* people. From Chizu-*san*. Sumatsu Chizu."

This name, the name of Machiko's adoptive mother, her "birth" mother, brings a gnawing feeling of dread. It brings Machiko a sense of horror that grows and grows. "This is not possible," she says, but the lack of conviction in her voice reveals her inner fears. "My mother, she could never . . . You do not know her. You do not know how desperately she wanted a child, her own child."

"Chizu-*san* is a loyal executive. As is her husband. Both your surrogate parents have fully embraced the Chairman's New Way."

Machiko cannot deny this. Cannot imagine anything to say, but, "You do not know them."

Sashi-*san* looks to her with eyes that gleam with pain, and, in an anguished tone, says, "Consider your name. Who but Honjowara Okido could have given you such a name?"

It is like a small sword, slipping into Machiko's midsection.

The question has always been there, throughout her whole life. Never really considered in a serious way, but never entirely dismissed or forgotten. It is impossible not to see the similarity between "Machiko" and the name, "machi-yakko," for the ancient warriors, ancestor of the Honjowara-*gumi,* who defended the common peoples against unruly bands of ronin samurai. It is just as impossible not to see the

implied connection between the name and Honjowara-*sama's* New Way, the condemnation of gangster methods and hatred against metahumans, the campaign to return the clans to the honorable path of their ancestors.

Machiko has always been proud to have such a name. She has always felt that Machiko Combine is her own in as close and personal a way as her parents are her own. Yet, she has often wondered why her parents, her step-parents, would choose such a name for her. They are very loyal and honorable people and approve whole-heartedly of the New Way. However, their first loyalty is not to Nagato Combine, but to Nagato Corp, and that is perfectly natural, for they are both executives, but it does present a certain puzzle.

Why would they honor her with a name remembering so much of the ancient clans? Machiko has asked this a number of times. Always, the answers she received suggested that any reasons for giving her the name were considered only casually.

Now Machiko wonders if the answer kneels before her, with eyes bleeding drops of gold.

"You are a child of exchange," Sashi-*san* says softly. "My child. The adopted child of Nagato Combine. The first of many."

Machiko struggles to find some response. "You mean there are others . . . ?"

"Have you never marveled that so many elves, so many with capabilities like your own, should emerge from the ranks of Nagato Combine?"

For this, Machiko has no answer. The ranks of Nagato Combine include many thousands of people and many of them are elves. Machiko has never concerned herself with the precise figures or percentages because she is no statistician. She is a warrior, member of the Guard. That the GSG should be composed primarily of elves who are also physical adepts has never been anything but a source of pride in herself, in the Guard, and in Nagato Combine.

"You see yourselves as symbolic of the Chairman's New Way, and indeed you are this, but this is not all you are. To those of Tir Tairngire, you represent Okido-*san's* commitment to his own principles. Wherever he goes, he walks with elves, he relies on elves for his safety, in plain view of the whole world. Few people know such commitment."

Machiko struggles to settle her spirit. She is not

succeeding at this task. "What you are describing to me is not a plan, or a test. It is a program. A covert program of exchange."

Sashi-*san* bows in acknowledgment. "It was presented to me as a test. Later, it became apparent that more was involved."

"Why?" Machiko struggles to breathe, to breath freely. The dread and horror filling her belly rise into her chest, aching unbearably. "What savage mind could conceive of—?"

For a moment, she can say no more.

Sashi-*san* fills the void, using a voice grown as frail and tender as a reed. "The princes of Tir Tairngire take a long view. A dispassionate view. They gaze upon the world through the lens of the Promise and consider what must be done to preserve our land. They foresaw a time when our small land would be surrounded by many powerful enemies. They foresaw the inevitable, inescapable fact that we must know what our enemies intend. We must have information. They knew we must develop strong allies, and indeed our allies tell us much, but there is much that even allies such as Okido-*san* cannot tell us. We must have resources of our own, and some of our greatest resources are not elves, but norms. Adopted children. Norms raised and educated among elves. Norms loyal to the Promise. Norms as ardently loyal to Tir Tairngire as you of the Guard are loyal to Nagato Combine."

"And why would Honjowara-*sama* cooperate with such a program?"

"For all these same reasons. For the sake of allies and what allies may provide. For promises made and promises fulfilled. For the future. For all that he has ever hoped to accomplish and all that he dreams of one day making real." Sashi pauses to smile a pained smile, then adds, "The princes of Tir Tairngire may have once been in need of financial resources, but they are not without power. Arcane power. Power one might equate with the Great Ghost Dance."

The rationales do little to soothe Machiko's heart. The underlying cruelty of the exchange program hacks at her ruthlessly. Can there be anything more savage than to separate mother and child? What monster could conceive of such a program? It is heinous. Insidious. And yet the rational part of her mind whispers the words, Sashi's words, that seem so loathsome. What would she not sacrifice to defend the Chairman of Nagato Combine? Could the commands of duty ever be too great?

She does not know. Has no answer. She has lived all her life with duty at her shoulder, always at the forefront of her daily concerns. Is there anything she would not do? Can any person really know until they are put to the test?

The warrior's Way is death. The warrior must live as though she is already dead, her life already given up.

Wise words. Small comfort.

"Perhaps the norms are right," Machiko says, battling through the churning sea of her own emotion. "Perhaps we are heartless monsters. Nefarious schemers. We elves."

The suggestion seems to afflict Sashi-*san* more than anything thus far said or hinted at. She looks to Machiko with an expression like agony. She rises. She draws near a step at a time, reaching out, lifting her hands to Machiko's cheeks. For a moment, she gazes steadily into Machiko's eyes, and the air is full of the fragrant garden of her perfume, and the suffering inside her sloping almond eyes is like a gray pall of pain spreading to the horizon.

Then, she leans her head to Machiko's shoulder, standing perfectly still, all but her fingers. Her long slender fingers quiver like autumn leaves against Machiko's cheeks. "You feel betrayed," Sashi-*san* says at a whisper. "You feel only your own pain and it is right that you should. But, for one moment, imagine mine. Imagine all that I have missed, all that will never be again. Things too precious, forever lost. I beg you, please, to find something for me in your heart, something more than hatred and scorn."

It is difficult to decide how to react, to know what is right or wrong or merely humane. There is so much pain, so much unknown, uncertain. Machiko is not sure what she feels, except that it hurts. It hurts very deeply. "I do not know you," she says. "I do not know the first thing about you. I do not even know where you live, in the Tir or anywhere."

"For many years," Sashi-*san* whispers, "I have lived in dreams. Immersed in dreams. Surrounded by dreams. But to you I have always been near. I have watched over you from the beginning. Often, in the night, I have thought, perhaps only hoped, that you could feel my hand, sense my presence. Perhaps I am a fool."

The words strive for an intimacy Machiko is not ready to face. She gropes for some reply, uselessly.

"So many things I could tell you," Sashi-*san* murmurs. "So many things come to my mind. When you were just a child, three norms attacked you in the street. And you were ashamed. For although you fought them off, you went home bleeding from the nose. You cried that night to Chizu-*san*, she you called mother, you cried that Kuroda-*san* would not have allowed the bullies to hurt him. You wanted so desperately to be like him. How can I make you understand what this meant for me? Did you not think it remarkable when, a few weeks later, a dojo run by an elf, a master in the katana, opened just a block from where you lived? Did you not imagine that perhaps some unseen hand was at work?"

The incident was forgotten till this moment. The attack in the street. The surprise of the new dojo. All lost in time.

It is enough of a shock to force the words from Machiko's lips. "This is all very hard. I am very confused. My spirit is in turmoil. There is so much I do not know." And then, her heart compels her to add, "I do not mean to make you suffer."

"You are very strong," Sashi-*san* replies. "I am trying to act worthy of your respect. I do not have your warrior's discipline."

"I do not understand how you could wait so long," Machiko says. "Why do you come to me only now? How could Honjowara-*sama*—?"

Sashi-*san* gently takes her hands. "Please . . . sit with me."

It is not much to ask. They move to the small dais beside the bed of stones and kneel. There is just enough room for the two of them on the round cushion. Sashi-*san* spends some moments brushing at her eyes, perhaps strengthening her composure.

"We could not tell you," Sashi-*san* says. "A child could not bear such news. The foundations of your world would have been crushed. You would have been torn with resentment, filled with bile."

"It is some years since I was a child."

"We have kept the truth too long. I see that now. Forgive me. Forgive both of us. Try to understand."

"What is there to understand?"

Again, Sashi-*san's* features grow pained. "Your father can never truly be your father," she says. "In rare moments of privacy, perhaps. The world will not otherwise allow it. Okido-*san* dreams of a world in which racial hatred will finally glimmer and die, like the fading of a flame. But it is all he can do to hold his part of the world together. He has managed to bring together the clans of Nagato Combine because he is respected, because he leads the clans to honor, to the path of their ancestors. The traditional peoples of the clans accept his ideals and program regarding metahumans because of the great respect he has earned. Because in many ways he seems a traditionalist himself. He honors traditional ways. He has a traditional wife and children, all of them norms. His leading advisors are norms. Yes, he meets with a lady believed to come from the Tir, and perhaps she is somewhat more than a secret business contact, but this lady's influence, if any, is negligible and easily dismissed."

"Is it so easily dismissed?" Machiko asks.

Sashi-*san* lowers her face, brushes at her eyes. "It is as it must be. I cannot be his wife just as you cannot be his daughter. It would destroy all that he has built."

"Because we are elves."

"It is one thing to take an elf for a lover, another to have an elf for a wife, and another to engender an elf child. He would prove himself not merely a lover of elves but perhaps even an elf himself."

Honjowara-*sama* an elf? "That is not possible. Any mage—"

Gently, Sashi-*san* shakes her head. "Okido-*san* was born in the last year of the last century. Even to a mage, there is little difference between a true norm and one who carries the elf genes, one who is an elf but was born too soon for the elven qualities to find expression. Yes, the right mage might detect a difference, might see that Okido-*san* is purely a norm, but the point could never be prove absolutely. And a mere shadow of suspicion would bring everything to ruin. Surely you can see this."

Machiko, at this point, is unsure what she can and cannot see. Her thoughts are in as much turmoil as her heart. "And what of Kuroda-*sensei*? Why did he leave when Honjowara-*sama* called for you? Does he know the truth?"

"Kuroda-*san* is my brother. He came to Okido-*san* first as an emissary. For a time, he served as a spy. In time, he came to accept Okido-*san's* ideals as his own."

It is merely another shock atop other shocking revelations. "And are you here as a spy?"

Faintly, Sashi-*san* shakes her head. "I am here because my love and my daughter are in need, and you are in need of information I possess."

"What information?"

Sashi-*san* looks to Machiko with an expression of compassion and concern, and says, "It begins with your surrogate mother, Chizu-*san*."

"Yes?"

"As a young woman, she scored a five-plus on the Wachs-Chandler test. You know this, do you not?"

"Yes?" In fact, Machiko has known this for years. It was no secret. The Wachs-Chandler "test," really a series of examinations, was an early attempt by certain corps to evaluate the magical potential of employees and family members. It is a subject her adoptive mother has occasionally addressed with amusement. Her score of five-plus supposedly indicated that she has little magical potential herself, but could perhaps pass the ability to any children she might have. "What significance does this have?"

"Consider your own abilities," Sashi-*san* says softly. "Consider what would be required for any exchange of unborn to be equitable."

Machiko hesitates. What Sashi-*san* suggests is clear, but it does not seem possible. "My parents were desperate to have children. They would not have given up a natural child."

"After Chizu-*san*'s third miscarriage, both your surrogate parents were keenly aware of the extraordinary measures Nagato Corporation, through its medical plan, was taking on their behalf, in the effort to give them children. When they were offered the chance to participate in the program of exchange, they felt an obligation, a duty. They felt they could not refuse."

Machiko shakes her head. "I do not understand. With all the difficulties my mother has had with pregnancy, why would anyone choose her?"

"Because of Chizu-*san*'s latent talent. Because advances in the medical arts made it seem likely that Chizu-*san*'s next pregnancy could be aided to term successfully. And because of obligation. Others were approached, but they declined."

"So you are telling me that my parents did not choose to have me for a child? That they felt obliged?"

"Is there anyone whose motives for having a child are not complex? Please listen, try to understand. Your surrogate parents felt honored as well as obliged. They were perhaps horrified at the prospect of giving up their natural child. They were also proud of the honor offered to them. And when you were born, born of Chizu-*san's* own body, they felt love and joy. Do not ever underestimate how very much this means, that you emerged from Chizu-*san's* womb. That you lived within her, developed from a small seed within her. Whatever her motives for consenting to the exchange, in her mind you became her natural child long before you were born."

All this talk of Chizu-*san* reaches deeply into Machiko's spirit, reaches her heart. It smoothes over anger and stirs other thoughts, other feelings. "How could you know all this?" she asks. "How could you know so much of what my parents felt?"

"I have always been near," Sashi-*san* says. "And I have walked a similar path. Chizu-*san's* path."

"How . . . ? How is that possible?"

Sashi-*san* says, "The embryo Chizu-*san* surrendered became my child. My adopted child, you might say. And yet my natural child. A child I nurtured, a child to whom I gave life. It is this child that you seek."

Machiko shakes her head. "I seek no child."

"Like you, he is no longer a child." Sashi-*san* smiles sadly. "I named him Liam. The name is said by some to come from the French, meaning to tie or bind. I feel a very strong connection to Chizu-*san,* though we have never met. That is why I chose the name. I also saw him as a bridge between norm and meta, all that Okido-*san* would like to bind together. That is another reason I chose the name."

This minor revelation speaks subtly, not about Liam or programs of exchange, but about the woman speaking the words, her nature, her beliefs. Machiko cannot help feeling affected, yet she says, softly, "Why do you say that I seek Liam?"

"Because he is the one." Pain rises clearly in Sashi-*san's* eyes. She brushes at the tears, but seems unable to quiet the pain. "You must please try to understand, Machiko. Life can be very hard for a norm in Tir Tairngire. We are mostly elves and many hold prejudice against any who are not elves. Liam has suffered much, perhaps in ways you could understand only with great difficulty. You have always drawn strength from your warrior Ways and the vast extended family of Nagato Combine. Liam had only me and his hermetic texts. His thaumaturgical studies seemed only to add to his feelings of isolation. He found answers in these studies for the prejudices of others. He came to believe that the root cause for his suffering was not mere racism, but the harm that norms for so many years have been doing to the earth. That he was seen not simply as a norm, but as a representative of the race that has ravaged the environment. As one of the great defilers. By the time he reached the age of majority he became quite fanatical in this belief. It has guided him ever since."

"How has it guided him? Toward what goal?"

"The white octagram is his symbol, Machiko. To him, it represents death and rebirth. Liam believes that in order for the earth to be reborn, the great defilers must die. All norms, all metas who serve norms or have relationships with norms."

"Would this not include most of the earth's population?"

Faintly, Sashi-*san* nods. "He uses the name Gamma."

Machiko draws a deep breath. The garden now seems very silent and still. "Are you aware that Gamma is believed to be the name of a former member of Alamos 20K? That Gamma is reputed to be an anti-meta terrorist?"

Faintly, Sashi-*san* nods her head, and once more the pain in her eyes swells like agony. "Yes," she whispers. "Yes, I know. Liam resents elves for what he suffered as a child. But he blames everyone."

"Does he also blame Nagato Combine?"

"Of course," Sashi-*san* says. "Liam knows the truth of his origin. And he knows of my relations with Nagato Combine. And he is not so great a fool as to imagine that a coincidence." Sashi-*san* pauses, brushing at her eyes, then seems to exert herself to say, "The persons you detained, members of White Octagon, they may be Liam's pawns. Mere tools of his mystic formulae. I say this because they do not seem to understand as small a thing as the significance of the name he uses."

"The name Gamma has some special significance?"

"It is not drawn from physics. It derives, I believe, from the gammadion, an ancient mystic symbol resembling a swastika. It represents the solstices and equinoxes, the four cardinal directions, the four basic elements, and the four divine guardians of the world."

Machiko is unsure whether she herself understands the importance of this. "Do you mean that Gamma, Liam, views himself as a divine guardian?"

"A guardian, certainly. An avenger."

"Where might we find him?"

"Wherever the earth is most grievously wounded. That is where he will be."

36

By noon, Machiko stands in the transparex-paneled office beside the Nagato Operations Center on Sub-level B of Nagato Tower. She and Colonel Satomi and a handful of Security Service executives watch as a digital records analyst conducts a computer-augmented evaluation.

The first set of digipics comes from a chip-carrier provided by Sashi-*san;* the second set from video records of the mage conducting the attack at the Chrysanthemum Palace Hotel.

"It is highly likely," the analyst concludes, "that the individual from Machiko-*san's* digipics, identified as Gamma, is the mage who launched the attack."

"Numerically, how certain is this?" asks Colonel Satomi.

"The evaluation software assigns an eighty-seven likelihood. I prefer a more generalized rating of between eighty and ninety percent certainly."

Machiko asks, "You are able to make this determination even though the security cam record from the hotel does not show the mage's face?"

The analyst bows, and says, "We use very sophisticated algorithms to conduct comparative evaluations, Machiko-*san.* These algorithms take into account a variety of biodynamic factors such as anatomical structure and its influence on physical motion. A person's face may be easily modified, or, as in this case, largely concealed. How a person walks, however, is not so easily disguised. An analysis of this type is not as precise as one might obtain from genetics, or even fingerprints, but it is generally able to provide a reliable indication. It would perhaps be more precise to say that the mage from the hotel record moves in a manner highly consistent with the individual, called Gamma, in the digipics you have provided."

"It appears then that we have confirmation that Gamma

did indeed execute the hotel attack," says Colonel Satomi, turning to Machiko. "Where did you obtain these digipics of Gamma?"

"Unfortunately," Machiko replies, "I am prevented from divulging that information."

Colonel Satomi appears briefly surprised, but does not pursue the point. He would naturally assume that since Machiko reports only to the Chairman of Nagato Combine she must have been instructed by the Chairman to keep her source private. In this particular case, Machiko encourages that assumption because she cannot imagine Honjowara-*sama* ever desiring the truth be made plain.

The shocks of her morning with Sashi-*san* reverberate still through her insides. She feels emotionally traumatized, as though the fabric of her world has been rent, her most basic assumptions torn away.

Is Sashi-*san* truly her genetic mother? Could her true genetic father be not an elf, but a norm, the Chairman of Nagato Combine? Is it even conceivable that her own surrogate parents, her true parents, could be the genetic parents of Gamma? And the program of exchange—she can barely formulate a question—how could such a thing exist? It boggles the mind. It challenges not merely her spirit but her very capacity for understanding.

Intellectually, she knows she must accept all this as true, that she has Honjowara-*sama's* assurance that Sashi would speak only truth, but emotionally the adjustment has not even begun. The truths Sashi has spoken go so far beyond anything previously known that Machiko feels only awe and amazement and an acute sense of incredulity. She must have time to sort it all out, to consider the implications for her life, her relations with her parents, and with Sashi-*san*, and with Honjowara-*sama* himself.

But now there is no time.

Before the noon hour is done, an armed SDF courier arrives with the data-storage modules from the SDF's pair of twin-engine Mistral sensor aircraft. At Machiko's request, these aircraft have completed over-flights of the two regions in the New York-New Jersey megaplex, where, as Sashi-*san* said, "the earth is most grievously wounded." The first region is a portion of the Newark sprawl known as Sector 13, said to be the result of some massive metaphysical catastrophe. The second region is located along Long Island's

northern shoreline, a portion known as the Slag Heap, a toxic
waste dump further poisoned shortly after the Awakening by
the crash of a military transport carrying an eclectic mixture
of toxic materials.

Security Service analysts upload data from the Mistral
modules to the Security Service security mainframe. They
soon project a detailed map on a wall-sized display screen.
Color-coded indicators appear on the screen to identify the
presence and location of sources of heat and light radiation.

"These are from artificial sources?" Colonel Satomi asks.

The analysts confirm it.

Both of the toxic regions appear to be sparsely inhabited.
That is not especially surprising because the numbers of poor
inhabiting the plex are legion. Rarely does a week pass
without a story in the media about some SINless indigent
found dead among the waste containers, or in the tunnels or
passage of some abandoned property. Stories that would
rouse even the most granite of hearts to compassionate
feelings.

"How long might an unprotected individual survive in
such places?" Machiko asks.

The chief of the Nagato Corp medical division is consulted. He states, via telecom, "I have seen nothing to indicate that an unprotected human or metahuman could not
survive a short-term exposure to the toxins reputed to be
present in these two regions. However, to date, there have
been no comprehensive studies of the hazards to biological
organisms present in these areas, and I am under the impres-
sion that such hazards are not limited to strictly mundane
chemical and/or radiological hazards."

"Do you suggest that there may be hazards of a metaphysical nature?" asks Colonel Satomi.

"That is precisely what I suggest."

But the point is irrelevant. It is clear to Machiko what
must be done. The swords at her back and waist make it
clear. A lifetime of duty and loyalty make it clear. She may
come in time to question the principles of those she serves,
she may come to make inquiries and to weigh all answers
with care, but that time is not now.

Now she must remain focused, if only out of loyalty to
herself, to the Way, and to the spirit of the ancient warriors
who have guided her throughout her life.

"We must seek Gamma regardless of the risk."

Colonel Satomi concurs.

By five p.m., a pair of task forces are prepared, briefed, and ready. Ground units are ordered to staging zones. Machiko dispatches Gongoro and a team of GSG to monitor and support the SDF force that will sweep through the wastes of Newark's Sector 13. Machiko herself will join a team waiting to link with the forces already converging on the Slag Heap.

At twenty minutes past five, Colonel Satomi turns to a telecom and contacts his opposite numbers at the various corps responsible for police services in the plex.

"We are launching proprietary anti-terrorist operations," he tells them. "Please advise your forces to remain clear of these areas."

It is more a warning than a request. Satomi does not ask permission for the sweeps and his opposites merely acknowledge that the message is understood. This is the protocol.

Corporations in the New York region do not generally interfere with the mass movements of other corps' forces to neutral territory. That would be a prescription for intercorporate warfare. It could lead too easily to the unfortunate consequences of misconceptions. Told that Nagato SDF is on the move, Lone Star and the other police service corps will almost certainly stand back and merely monitor events. Any legal issues that may arise can be handled later, negotiated by lawyers, once the guns have been put away and relative calm is restored.

On the aeropad atop Nagato Tower, Machiko mounts a waiting Hughes Stallion helo marked for the SDF. The helo immediately lifts off. Machiko distributes digipics of Gamma to her team of five GSG and reaffirms the central message of the mission briefing. "He must absolutely be taken alive."

Gamma is a mage. He did not himself penetrate the Nagato computer network. He did not himself send messages to Zurich banks. If he is the force behind the attempt to acquire Nagato debt and bring the corp to ruin, he commands others with expertise in business and computers and these persons must absolutely be apprehended. They must be stopped, and Gamma may be the only means of finding them. He must be captured and compelled to reveal the totality of his plans, everything he knows.

The SDF helo slices across northern Queens, skirting

LaGuardia Airport, then cleaves a path down the center of Long Island, over Nassau and then Suffolk County airspaces, then swings north toward the shoreline.

The SDF pilot shouts over the commlink, *"Command signals ready! Initiate Black Typhoon!"*

Machiko nods in acknowledgment. She signals her team to prepare for combat. The helo's lone ork crewman yanks open the side door to the main cabin and swings an M107 Stoner-Ares heavy machine gun into position.

A moment more and aircraft appear from the east, a flight of SDF helos accompanied by a twin-engine Commander VTOL gunship and a pair of attack choppers.

Then, the region of the Slag Heap comes into visual range.

According to Machiko's maps, it is centered around an abandoned village once known as Kings Park. The terrain at dusk grows vague with curling mists, obscured in places by swirling clouds like miniature whirlwinds, but the larger details are plain. Whole blocks of houses lie in ruins. Debris clogs the ruptured pavement of the streets. Festering pools of noxious liquids boil and simmer and steam beneath carpets of twisted vines and gnarled trees and the rotting sentinels of ancient wooden utility poles.

The primary target zone lies on the fringe of the old village center, a sprawling expanse of poisoned woodlands and wasted, withered meadows and abandoned brick buildings, some of them five and six stories tall, as grim and foreboding as any medieval prison, or perhaps something worse, an asylum for the insane.

Machiko has only to glance onto the astral to see the twisted energies here, to grasp the malevolent nature of the power afflicting the land, to recognize that here, if anywhere, is where evil dwells. She feels it in the quick shiver that slips up her back. She feels it in her soul.

On the ground, a trio of MVN-17 armored personnel carriers with turret-mounted hardpoints move rapidly up the warped and shattered concrete of a road, led by a six-wheeled Appaloosa armed and armored scout vehicle and an Ares Citymaster armored command vehicle. Helos descend. SDF troopers deploy. Machiko directs her pilot to swing around to the rear of the massive building that gave the most definite indications of habitation to the Mistral over-flight. Two other helos swoop in to follow.

And here the enemy first appears. Backed up to the

building rear are a pair of vehicles: the streamlined form of a Leyland-Rover van and a heavy Roadmaster cargo vehicle marked for Nagato Corporation.

"What the frag!" shouts the SDF pilot.

Machiko ignores this. She looks to the men standing around the rear of the Roadmaster. They wear synthleather and camo and the other hallmarks of gangers, much like the captive members of White Octagon. They appear to be loading the Roadmaster with cargo containers, squat metallic cylinders with bright orange labels. Machiko cannot make out what the labels say. However, all questions regarding the lotus and reed insignia on the Roadmaster's side are answered as one man at the vehicle's rear looks up at the approaching helos and immediately lifts an SMG.

The SMG's muzzle flares red. Machiko hears a voice from her commlink shouting, "Taking fire! taking fire!" The ork crewman two steps behind her immediately opens up. The chattering rhythm of the Ares-Stoner MG rises above the beating of the helo's rotors. Tracer fire streams through the twilight. Other men by the Roadmaster brandish weapons. The tracers dance among them, clawing at the ground, pounding the flank of the Roadmaster, tearing at unarmored clothing and sending bodies tumbling to the ground.

The ground comes up swiftly, then.

Machiko goes through the open door, hits the ground, rolls and comes to her feet loping toward the Roadmaster and van, past the bodies of the fallen and the dead, then to the rear of the building. A blackened door stands open. As Machiko reaches the side of the door, another man in camo emerges, swinging an M22 assault rifle toward the lingering helos.

As the assault rifle rises, Machiko catches the back of the man's elbow, squeezes and pulls. The man staggers around her in a half-circle. The GSG immediately to her rear catches the man's neck, and the man crumbles.

More shooting erupts, the staccato reports of automatic fire. Helos thump and whine, tracked vehicles squeal and rumble. Every roar, every report, every detonation seems to vibrate through the earth beneath Machiko's feet. This is the nearest she has ever been to a live shooting war, and yet she feels no fear. Only resolve. A calm resolve that allows no fear, no hesitancy, no uncertainty. A calm like that of the dead.

Rarely has she felt such calm.

The open doorway provides entrance to a long dark corridor. There is light at the end of the corridor, but the space in-between is very dark. She does not see the doorway along the right-hand wall till she is just one step away. She does not detect the female norm coming through the doorway until that woman is stepping into the corridor. Her heat signature then makes her like a lantern amid the dark. She is dressed like the others. She gasps and lifts a Crusader machine-pistol. Machiko reaches out, paralyzes the arm holding the gun, then propels the woman into the corridor wall opposite the doorway.

Another GSG brushes Machiko's side. A sword flashes. The enemy sprawls.

Outside, the battle grows deafening.

In here, death is swift and silent.

Without warning, a new figure appears, a norm male. He comes into view at the distant end of the corridor. He is slim and short, very compact. He wears a full-length black duster and broad-brimmed hat. The hand he thrusts out before him holds a black rod that appears intricately carved.

A mage's rod.

Gamma.

In the same instant Gamma thrusts with the rod, the entire length of the corridor erupts with fire, an inferno—floor, ceiling, walls, and the spaces in between—all raging, roaring. Machiko feels the flames licking at her cheeks, her eyes. She shouts and hurls herself bodily at the doorway in the right-hand wall of the corridor. The cool empty air of the room beyond hits her like a pool of water. For an instant, she cannot breathe. Then she is shouting to her brothers of the Guard. "To *ME!*"

The first to enter emerges from the portal of fire swirling with smoke. The last emerges like a torch. They smother the flames with their own bodies. They assess their injuries and gather their resolve. That is when Machiko notices the squat metallic cylinders standing against one wall.

They are just like the cylinders she saw being loaded onto the vehicle outside, the Roadmaster marked for Nagato Corporation. Each of the cylinders here before her also bears a bright orange label. The labels are marked with the symbol for biohazards and the legend, *Sero-Ebola-D*. On the astral, the cylinders seem almost alive, glimmering with the power of the arcane.

Was this to be the next stage? No more assassins, no mere
magical assaults. Rather, an attack utilizing a biological warfare agent enhanced by magic.

How many would have died if the forces of Black
Typhoon had been delayed by a minute or two?

But there is no time for questions like this. Her brothers of
the Guard give quick signals of the hand: "Prepared for
combat," "Advance," *"Advance!"* The corridor from which
they came remains a blazing inferno. Machiko steps up onto
one of the squat cylinders and splits a rough wooden panel
covering an opening in the wall like a window opening. This
provides access to another room. This new room has two
doors. Machiko and her team move from there into a new
corridor, dark but hardly deserted.

As they move up this new corridor, they pass a room
where two men fire auto-weapons through shattered windows at SDF forces outside the building.

Machiko signals. The GSG second in line fires two rounds
with a silenced weapon. Both men fall.

The corridor ends at the side of a large open area like a
lobby, two stories tall and lit by portable lights. Three sets of
double doors and a pair of tall windows cross the front of the
space. Eight members of the enemy stand, kneel, and crouch
at the windows and doors, firing an assortment of rifles,
SMGs, and pistols through holes, slits, and gashes at the
forces outside.

Machiko signals. A silent assault is not viable. Two of her
team throw stun grenades. She and the remaining three open
up with SCK M-100 submachine guns. The lobby area
echoes with the relentless stammering of autofire. Three seconds later the enemy combatants lay sprawled on the floor,
dead or unconscious. Machiko feels a dull ache where a stray
round struck the armored fabric covering her right shoulder,
but such pain is easily dismissed.

A solitary figure waits by the doorway at the rear of the
lobby area. It is Gamma again. Machiko advances into the
open, moving toward him. "Surrender and you will not be
harmed."

Gamma's features seem contorted with rage. "Manipu-
lator!" he exclaims. *"Defiler!"*

An enormous hound with the red-glaring eyes of a
paranatural emerges from the doorway at Gamma's right and
charges. Machiko slips the blade of her katana between the

beast's flashing jaws. The creature impales itself on her steel. The carcass falls to her side. She flicks the blade clean and returns it to its sheath. "Do not force me to hurt you."

Gamma sneers. "Be damned."

He lifts a hand and the air around Machiko thickens. It becomes difficult to breathe, even more difficult to move forward, more and more difficult when the floor beneath Machiko's feet suddenly becomes as slippery as ice.

She hears one of her team grunt as with surprise, glimpses another slipping, sliding, almost falling.

"Now you will die," Gamma says in a voice hideous with menace and hate. "Die like the dogs that you are! Tools of the corporate defilers! *Traitors of the earth!*"

But it is not so simple. The mage's power is great, but Machiko's spirit is resolute. Smash one's boots to the earth and pass through a wall of iron. Machiko thrusts her feet to the floor, drives them to the shattered tiles and blackened concrete as if to smash two holes direct to the core of the planet. Forcing herself forward. Forcing body ahead and feet securely to the floor with a spirit that does not admit to even the possibility of failure.

Gamma looks to her sharply. "What—?"

One word slips from Gamma's mouth and then Machiko reaches out. By force of will alone, she bridges the distance between them—a measure in meters far beyond the reach of mere flesh and blood limbs. She seizes Gamma's right wrist. She pressures certain nerves and twists. She watches as Gamma's arm suddenly swings out to his side, and his body arches backward, and his feet, stumbling, desperately seek for balance.

"NO!" Gamma shouts.

The left arm gestures and abruptly a barrier arises, like a gleaming wall of water. The right wrist slips from Machiko's control. Gamma regains his balance. He raises both arms in the manner of spellcasting. Machiko, struggling forward—straining forward with every last scintilla of will—draws three star shuriken from her left vambrace and gives them flight.

It is a last desperate attempt. The mages with the SDF force will not arrive in time to counter Gamma's spells. Machiko must hope that Gamma is not so powerful a mage that he can know every conceivable spell, that there is some limit to the sheer number of spells he can sustain at any one time. She must hope that the barrier he uses to guard himself against her attempt at manipulation is a creation of the purest mana, useful against spells, against all forms of magic, but not against purely mundane physical objects.

She watches her flight of three shuriken. Gamma seems to anticipate the attack and begins moving a step aside while again lifting both arms. He is an instant too slow. He sways as two of the whirling stars strike him across the chest. He staggers back against the rear lobby wall and seems about to succumb to the soporific drug coating the shuriken when the unexpected occurs.

Evanescent flashes of red like fleeting tongues of fire appear and disappear, circling Gamma's head, arms, and body. As moment passes into moment the flashes grow stronger and brighter and circle faster. Gamma shouts. He begins screaming. And Machiko realizes she is watching magic go wrong, a spell misfiring, backfiring. Turning back on the mage himself.

In another moment the flashes evolve into a whirlwind of fire. Gamma's screams rise into a peal of agony and terror. And Machiko can imagine only one course of action.

The warrior must not consider victory or defeat or even her own personal survival. She plunges recklessly toward an irrational death.

She hurls herself forward, intent on smothering the flames.

As the first flash of heat strokes across her chest, she feels an impact like the fist of a leviathan, and then hears a crash like a deafening blast of thunder, and then her feet leave the floor.

She seems to glide through empty space—without body or form—a ghost buoyed aloft on the winds of the etheric.

Everything grows silent and still.

37

The world assumes shades of gray, then shape and texture, blurry at first, and then sound, voices, footsteps, clattering equipment, and then scents, a scent like smoke, like burnt fabric. Machiko realizes she must be alive when she feels the stinging in the vicinity of her eyebrows and the dull ache working throughout her chest and back. It seems good that she is alive. She marvels at the number of times she has come near to death in just the last several days, five days, since the assassin's initial attacks. Now here she is again.

She opens her eyes and finds the five GSG of her team crouching around her. An SDF medic kneeling beside her holds some form of scanner just beneath her chin. She presses the medic back, out of the way. "Where is Gamma?"

A brother of the Guard shows the way with a glance. Machiko lifts her head to look down beyond her feet. A small crowd of SDF troopers and a team of medics are formed into a crouching, kneeling group just a few meters away. "Gamma's down," says one GSG. "Unconscious. Badly burned. Unknown whether he'll make it."

Machiko suffers a wave of dismay. After all this, all the death and bloodshed, has she failed? The medic at her side waves his scanner right in front of Machiko's face. She pushes him back. She spends a moment finding her center, settling her spirit, gathering resolve, then climbs first to her knees and then to her feet. "Machiko-san, *please*!" the medic exclaims. "You're injured!"

Tired. Very tired. Full of minor aches and pains. But now is not a time for fatigue or for pain. Machiko glances around. The doors at the front of the lobby area have all been smashed inward. The SDF Citymaster command vehicle sits just beyond the empty door frames. Nearby stands the major in command of the SDF force, along with the troopers of his headquarters echelon.

As Machiko steps up, the major lowers his commlink, snaps off a brisk salute, and commences to give a succinct status report. The sweep of the region continues. There are many buildings in the vicinity and every one will be searched. The nearest buildings appear abandoned. Friendly casualties are light.

"What prisoners have you taken?"

"Only three thus far, Machiko-*san*. Two combatants and one decker."

The major's adjutant shows Machiko to the room where the decker waits. A trooper stands guard at the room's only door. Machiko pauses on the threshold. What she sees inside the room strikes her as very curious.

The decker is a norm female. Her skin is quite dark, but her facial features otherwise suggest a Caucasian. She has the usual datajack at her temple and slashcut hair and synthleather and studs and everything else, including a cyberdeck, couched in a gray-platinum case and clutched to her chest. The detail that catches Machiko's eyes, and that which seems so curious, has nothing to do with any of this. It is unrelated to the torn plastic-upholstered couch the decker sits on or the drab green telecom positioned nearby. Rather, it has to do with the decker's ankles. Steel manacles ring both her ankles. The chain that joins them is secured to a large metal bolt that appears to have been recently driven into the filthy tile and concrete of the floor.

There is one other thing Machiko notes. The decker does not sit. She cowers, cringing, in the corner of the couch most distant from the door. She is wide-eyed, apparently with terror.

"Frag, oh frag . . ." she quavers.

Machiko moves one step further into the room and swings the door shut. The decker seems only to grow more afraid. Machiko can well imagine why. She can see herself as this decker must see her: clothes singed and smeared with soot, heavily armed, and calm, very calm, like an executioner.

The decker snivels. "Don't—!"

"What is your name?"

The reply appears to prove difficult, as though it does not wish to emerge from the decker's mouth. "Nnn-nee . . . Nnn-neee-yoooo . . ." She gasps. "Nnn-nee-yooo-naaa . . ."

"Neona."

The decker nods her head.

"You are an associate of Gamma?"

Neona-*san* appears to struggle to answer. She grunts and snivels and gasps. No recognizable words actually emerge. Momentarily, Neona-*san* shakes her head. She shakes it vehemently, looks to Machiko and then shakes it again.

"You are under some compulsion of the mage?"

"Wha . . . Wha-what?"

"A spell that Gamma cast on you."

This appears to give Neona-*san* even more difficulty than the previous question. She grunts and snivels and makes other noises, straining forward as if to thrust an answer forcibly through her lips. She moves her head about, up and down and around, as if giving a nod and a shake of the head all in one gesture.

Still, it is an answer of sorts, and the manacles and chain make a strong statement. Neona-*san* does not appear to have been a willing servant of the enemy.

She begins making more noises, struggling to speak. Some moments pass before Machiko realizes what she intends. She motions with her chin directly at Machiko, but, with her eyes, gestures toward the reams of hardcopy lying in heaps along the left wall of the room. Machiko turns to have a look. The very first page she examines gives a mild shock.

On the page is a diagram of the Nagato Commercial Park in Melville, where the ceremonies for the dead were so recently conducted. Machiko looks about and finds other pages with other diagrams, portions of the grounds and various buildings at the Commercial Park. Certain diagrams are highly detailed. Aside from entrances and exits and security checkpoints, they show such items as water conduits and ventilation ducts, and these bring to mind a collection of squat metallic cylinders partly loaded onto a Roadmaster cargo vehicle marked for Nagato Corporation.

"What is Sero-Ebola-D?"

Neona-*san* grunts and stammers. She seems to grow almost frantic to force language through her lips, but manages only to blurt, "Smogger . . . Flatline . . ."

Poison gas? Machiko supposes that the specific details do not matter. Gamma's intent is apparent. To kill. To destroy. Perhaps to poison every living being at the Nagato Commercial Park. Perhaps even more. Amid the heaps of paper, Machiko finds diagrams of the Chairman's personal estate and Nagato Tower as well.

"Where does this data come from?"

Neona-*san* stammers a response. "Ma-matrix. . . . gypsy, gypsy la la-la-lady . . . Snagged me . . . . Trrrrryyiing . . . Trying to crack . . . Crack Nnn-naa, Nnnn-naa-gaa-too nnn-nnn-network . . . G-gave me p-pay-data . . . Ev-everything . . . Everything about everyyy thinggg . . . Ssss-scheds. . . . Sss-sched-ules . . . P-plans . . . Floor floor plans . . ."

"Who is this gypsy lady?"

"D-decker . . . i-icon . . ."

A decker using the icon of a gypsy lady caught Neona-*san* breaking into the Nagato network. This same individual passed Neona-*san* whole reams of proprietary info regarding Nagato Corp. Could this be anyone but a traitor, the very traitor who has apparently manipulated the Nagato computer network?

Machiko keys her commlink. She will need expert assistance to further question Neona-*san* and to scrutinize the decker's cyberdeck. But before her call connects, she receives a priority signal from Nagato operations.

Maeda Komachi, Director of Network Administration.

"Machiko-*san,* a violation of network protocol has just occurred. I thought you should be informed."

"What sort of violation?" Machiko asks.

"We have detected a penetration of a database belonging to the Nagato Corp transport division. Our initial analysis indicates that an attempt has been made to add a new vehicle to the transport division registry."

Does this have some significance? "What vehicle?" Machiko asks.

"A Roadmaster cargo vehicle."

One of the most common forms of cargo vehicles to be found anywhere in North America. However, Machiko recalls the Roadmaster she passed on her way into the building around her, a Roadmaster partly loaded with cylinders containing some toxic substance. Mere coincidence? Machiko strides to the rear of the building and steps outside. She reads off the numbers painted on the sides of the Roadmaster and imprinted on the vehicle's registration tags. Maeda-*san* confirms that these very numbers are the numbers used in the false entries introduced to the transport division database.

In a moment, perhaps two, the point of this becomes apparent. A vehicle falsely identified as a Nagato vehicle,

perhaps driven by an individual falsely identified as a
Nagato Corp employee, might easily gain entrance to Nagato
facilities. Perhaps false entries were made to Nagato personnel rosters, security personnel rosters, to expedite the
entry of a van marked for Fuchi IE onto the property of the
Chrysanthemum Palace Hotel.

All such registries must be checked and verified. Machiko
informs Maeda-*san* of the need, and then says, "Can you tell
me who attempted to add this Roadmaster vehicle to the
transport division registry?"

"I believe that I can, Machiko-*san*. Fortunately, I have had
the entire network on alert since you came to my office. I
have now initiated a Level Chi alert. In effect, Machiko-*san*,
I have shut down the network, prohibiting traffic in and out
of the network, as well as between the various systems of the
network."

Maeda-*san* goes on to explain that the violation originated
from within the Nagato network, and that the violation was
detected and traced because every node on the network, in
effect the entire network, was being monitored in ways both
subtle and overt for any illicit activity.

The source Maeda-*san* identifies as responsible for the
violation is as unsettling as it is chilling.

"Are you certain of this?"

"The chance that we are wrong is very, very slight,"
Maeda-*san* says. "Given the extent of the network alert, the
resources we committed to monitoring network activity, I
would say that the chance of an error is negligible."

Machiko sees no point in continuing the discussion.

She places a priority call via commlink to Chairman Honjowara. Before the connection is made, she gives instructions
as to the disposition of the detainees, including Gamma, and
the decker Neona-*san*, and summons an SDF helo to the rear
of the building. The helo is carrying her swiftly up through
the ground-haze and into the night when Honjowara-*sama's*
image appears on the small screen on her left vambrace.

"I believe that I have identified the traitors," Machiko
says. "I am moving now to place them . . . place them under
restraint."

Honjowara-*sama* listens to the entirety of her explanation.
She cannot yet say whether or not Gamma was the power
behind all that has happened. For the moment, it is enough

that the mage has been stopped and the traitors to Nagato Corp identified.

"Your discussion with Sashi—"

For the first and only time in her life, Machiko interrupts the Chairman of Nagato Combine, shaking her head, and saying, saying sharply, *"Please! Please excuse me . . ."*

She can say nothing more. The affront she commits with just four words twists as savagely at her insides as all that Honjowara-*sama* recalls to her mind. She has interrupted, she feels too chagrined to continue speaking. She has learned too much from Sashi-*san*, too much of an intensely personal and intimate nature, too much that conflicts with her most basic assumptions, to consider such things now, now in the face of this man who is said to be her genetic father.

"Machiko," says Honjowara-*sama*, in a tone that seems unusually subdued, "you have my full authority to proceed. The senior executives will be advised to expect you."

She nods. "Understood, Chairman-*sama*."

And he, not she, breaks the link.

For this, here and now, Machiko feels only gratitude and relief.

38

The Neurocomp building is low and broad, just three stories tall, located in the nearby Nagato Commercial Park, just a few hundred meters from the Amida Buddhist Temple where the funeral rites for Mitsuharu and Jiksumi were performed. That the investigation into the cause for those two deaths should bring her so near the temple affects Machiko with a cruel sense of irony.

There is much about the last five days that affect her in this way. It is not a sense she finds pleasing.

The SDF helo settles onto the aeropad near the rear entrance to the Neurocomp building. Machiko disembarks and strides up the concrete walk to the entrance. There she meets just two executives, the deputy VP for research and the director for the special GCP project. They are accompanied by two guards, uniformed members of the Nagato Security Service.

All four bow as Machiko approaches. The depth of their bows indicates clearly that the Chairman's words have preceded her here. "I must speak with the computer specialists of the GCP special project," Machiko says.

The deputy VP bows, but the director for the GCP project looks uncertainly at Machiko, and says, "Do you mean the specialists who are themselves the subjects of the project?"

"I will begin with them, yes."

No further questions are asked. The deputy VP shows Machiko the way to the GCP project center. The trip takes several minutes, for they must pass through a pair of security checkpoints requiring retina scans, voice print, and palm print verification. Also, Machiko is issued a temporary identity card. Any person moving beyond the entranceway without such a card would instigate an immediate security alert.

Machiko's weapons add to the delay at the checkpoints,

instigating a pair of automated alerts, which are then canceled by the onsite Security Service guards. Weapon pods in the ceiling and along certain stretches of hallway snap open and immediately snap shut.

They come to a room with several rows of computer consoles. Beside the consoles is a wall of windows that look down onto the floor of the GCP project laboratory. The lab itself, to Machiko's eyes, appears like a tangled mass of electronic equipment, tended by several individuals swathed in white clothing that leaves only their eyes uncovered. All that really stands out are the three vats or "tanks" located at the center of the lab floor. Each tank is filled with a hazy blue fluid. Within each sea of blue hangs a vague form like a human, possibly norms, motionless.

"Those are the three subjects of the experiment," the deputy VP informs, with a brief gesture toward the tanks.

"Voluntary subjects?" Machiko asks.

The deputy VP reacts as if startled. "Most definitely," he says at once. "There were more than a dozen volunteers, Machiko-*san*. Each underwent a lengthy evaluation process."

Machiko nods understanding. "How may I communicate with them?"

The deputy VP directs her attention to the large display screen that nearly fills the wall at the head of the room. At the touch of a console key, the screen divides into three virtual windows. Momentarily, an image appears in each window, images of three faces, norm faces, two males and one female. All are depicted in pulsing neochromatic colors.

Beneath each window appears a word, names apparently: Rad238, NodeBoy, SmoKe. Machiko supposes that these must be the informal appellations commonly adopted by eccentric deckers.

"Conference link on," says Rad238. "GSG member present."

"Quite an honor," says SmoKe.

"What's the occasion?" asks NodeBoy. "Excuse us if we don't bow."

Apparently, the communication link provides the deckers with a visual as well as audio feed. Machiko takes a moment to consider her words, then says, "I am here to ask why you have violated your oath to Nagato Corporation."

"Odd question," says SmoKe.

"Who says we're in violation?" asks NodeBoy.

Machiko says, "An attempt was just made to insert false information into the Nagato transport division vehicle registry. This attempt was traced to you."

Rad238 says, "Voice stress analysis indicates you think you're telling the truth. Is your truth founded on verifiable facts?"

Machiko is surprised by the suggestion that the deckers are able to analyze her voice, but she considers Rad238's question, and says, "Your manner is presumptuous and rude. I would not ask the question I have asked unless I possessed compelling reasons. Please provide me with the courtesy of an answer."

"Don't freak on us," says SmoKe.

"We won't deny it," says NodeBoy. "Sure, we violated network protocol. Do you know why we did that?"

Machiko can hardly believe what she is hearing, that such an admission would be made so casually. It makes the reason for the violation of network protocol seem all the more incredible. "You were attempting to expedite the entry onto Nagato Corp property of a Roadmaster cargo vehicle carrying a supply of toxic materials."

"You're a wiz banger," says SmoKe.

"What else have you figured out?" asks NodeBoy.

"That you have provided Gamma, a known terrorist, and his White Octagon, a terrorist group, with plans and specifications for a number of Nagato facilities, including the Chrysanthemum Palace Hotel. That you have promoted a plan with the goal of acquiring Nagato Corp debt."

Rad238 says, "Voice stress analysis indicates you're speculating."

"Good guesses, though," says NodeBoy. "You're right on. We're the ones. And in fact we've just achieved our goals. We acquired the last major Nagato Corp creditor as of nine thirty-five local time. You're about an hour too late."

A strangled grunt emerges from the mouth of the deputy VP. Machiko glances aside and sees the man gazing wide-eyed and white-faced at the display screen. The GPC project director appears no less incredulous. Machiko can well understand their reactions. Though she struggles to retain a settled spirit, she begins to feel a bit like the two uniformed Security Service guards, who look nothing if not impotent and also rather confused.

One point about all this puzzles her. Money. Nuyen. Credit. Honjowara-*sama* himself remarked that no corporation can function without credit. And even she is aware of that one basic reality of the Sixth World, that it is a world ruled by corporate behemoths, a world where even modest corps such as Nagato possess resources measured in the billions, if not the trillions of nuyen. Not even Honjowara-*sama*, in so far as Machiko is aware, possesses wealth on the scale that would be necessary to purchase all of Nagato Corp's outstanding debt.

And so . . .

"Tell me," Machiko says. "Where do persons such as yourselves, computer specialists, confined for many months inside isolation tanks, acquire the resources to purchase a corporation's entire debt?"

"We've got our methods," says SmoKe.

"Would such methods include theft?"

"That's a possibility," NodeBoy says. "Fortunately, your little telezine war with Fuchi kicked down the prices a little, so we didn't need as much juice as we originally expected."

Machiko considers that briefly, then shakes her head. She is straying from the point. She must keep focused. "Then you admit to having committed acts of treason against Nagato Corporation."

SmoKe says, "Treason? That's your law."

"Look out those windows," says NodeBoy. "Look at those vats on the lab floor. That's all that's left of us. All that's left of our meat bodies. We're never coming out. Maybe no one told you. The magic that made us a gamo-cerebroprocessor also induced advanced hyper-atrophy. Applied metabiology is all that's keeping us alive. Pull us out of those tanks and we're so much dust."

Could this be so? Machiko looks to the deputy VP. The man tugs at the collar of his shirt and licks at his lips, looking like one on the verge of fainting.

In answer to Machiko's questioning eyes, he nods once, and also bows. But it is the project director who says, "An unfortunate and wholly unforeseen consequence of the metaphysics involved, Machiko-*san*. We are making every attempt to identify the specific causal factor of the hyper-atrophy. In fact, it has been the primary objective of the project for the last several months. Once the cause is identified, we will endeavor to reverse the process."

SmoKe says, "We're not waiting for some Nagato suit to decide to scrag the project and shuffle our tanks and the rest of our lives into a corner somewhere. Nagato is squat. We're loyal to the corporation of us. We're making our own laws. We're taking control from our side of the jack, the land of Matrix."

"Now the fun really begins," says NodeBoy.

And suddenly understanding dawns. Things have not gone well for the deckers of the GCP project. Machiko experiences a rush of pity like she has rarely known, pity settling into a sea of outrage and disgust. "Do you admit to assisting Gamma in staging the attack on the Chrysanthemum Palace hotel?"

"Sure," says NodeBoy. "That's where we gave Fuchi a new van. You think they'd at least thank us."

Machiko struggles to keep her voice calm, saying, "More than one hundred people died in the panic following that attack."

"A little blood must fall into every revolution."

"The blood of innocent persons?"

"Wrong place, wrong time. It happens."

"Time to open negotiations," says SmoKe. "Here's how it works. You can carry this to your Chairman. We've got enough Nagato debt to make chop suey out of your corp, but we just want Neurocomp and a few other choice bits. In exchange for complete stringless control, we give you back your debt."

"Get it?" says NodeBoy. "Neurocomp owns our employment contracts, *omae,* but now we own Neurocomp. So, in effect, we end up owning ourselves. We own ourselves free and clear."

"Thus we are free to control our own destiny," says Rad238.

Machiko grapples with what they are saying, struggles for understanding. It is nearly beyond comprehension. To kill and wound hundreds of people merely to achieve their own selfish aims? To slaughter innocent persons, persons not even aware of these deckers' existence, merely as a means of escaping their corporate contracts? of effecting a change in their personal status? It goes beyond heinous, beyond abomination. It is evil. As pure and terrible an evil as Machiko has ever encountered.

"You are murderers," she says. "And you are traitors. And

your savage plans end here." She turns to the deputy VP. "You will immediately sever all connections between these traitors and the Nagato computer network. You will take every step necessary to ensure that they are in effect placed under security detention and thus can commit no more acts of malefaction."

The deputy VP bows, saying, "At once, Machiko-*san*."

"I don't think so," says SmoKe.

STEEL RAIN

39

The digital face of Gordon Ito's platinum Patek Nautilus watch reads 10:11 p.m. when he hears the multi-screen display of his broad onyx desktop quietly beep. He doesn't think much of it until he looks at the primary screen. Then he knows something's wrong.

"How did you like our demonstration?" a voice asks.

It's not a human voice, human or metahuman. Some kind of computer simulation: a composite of several voices, maybe. Full of clashing harmonics. On the screen is a Janus-like icon: a head with three distinct faces. Faces like game-simulation deckers, formed of flaming, pulsating colors, with slashcut hair and mirrorshades and the inevitable data-jacks. Gordon takes a drag of his Platinum Select and considers the hardwired telltales beneath the vidscreen's lower edge. The telltales indicate that the display's audio/visual pickups are on, so whoever's on his screen can both see him and hear him. The display isn't supposed to work like this. The pickups should not be on unless he physically taps the keys on the optical workstation console displayed on the touch-sensitive top of his desk.

Gordon draws one hand back to his hip, cocks his fist on his hip, and presses the onyx head of a ring into his hip. Two seconds later the door beyond the front of his desk snaps open and three members of his exec protect detail look in, weapons drawn.

They see Gordon taking another drag from the cigarette, then leaning an elbow on the arm of his chair and lifting one hand, one finger, to his upper lip. A contemplative pose as well as a prearranged signal meaning "intruder." Gordon keeps his eyes fixed on the display screen. The chief of the detail follows his gaze.

"Who am I talking to?" Gordon says. "You're not coming through like a standard telecom call."

The chief of the detail signals, *Understood.* He steps back outside, presumably to get someone working on a trace. "This isn't a standard call, *omae,*" says the voice, the voice of the Janus-like face. "We're the ghost in your grid. The ghost with sticky fingers."

That gets Gordon's attention. "You're coming to me through the Matrix?"

"It's not the first time."

Gordon extends a hand to the optical keyboard on the touch-sensitive top of his desk. No comment from the Janus-head on the vidscreen. He taps a key to launch a sequence of trace and killer IC, particularly vicious progs that don't appear in the Fuchi catalogs. They should show results in just seconds. Several seconds pass and nothing appears to change.

"We've disabled your keyboard," the Janus-face says.

Gordon sits back in his chair, takes another drag. "You're very hot deckers," he says. "You've arrogated my desktop. I'm waiting for the explanation."

"Glad to oblige," says the Janus-face.

A second window appears on the display. In it, a member of Nagato Combine's Green Serpent Guard stands facing Gordon from in front of a room full of high-tech consoles. Gordon recognizes the Serpent at once. It's Machiko-*san.*

She says, "I am here to ask why you have violated your oath to Nagato Corporation. Why you have made the attempt to insert false information into the Nagato transport division vehicle registry. Why you have provided a known terrorist group with plans and specifications for a number of Nagato facilities, including the Chrysanthemum Palace Hotel. Why you have promoted a plan with the goal of acquiring Nagato Corp debt."

Interesting. This is either a replay or a simulation based on recorded speech and images of the woman. Does it accurately reflect an actual event? Good question. Gordon wants more data before making a decision. "Why show me this?"

"To give a clue where we're coming from," says the Janus-face. "Or aren't you interested in what we've been doing with your cred?"

Gordon resists the urge to snap off a sharp retort. This game, whatever game is being played, isn't going to be won by alluding to Fuchi's power. It's going to require a degree of care and caution. "Let's say I'm interested. What then?"

"We deal you in."

"In on what?"

"The tech that busted the Fuchi grid."

Gordon takes another drag of his Platinum Select. He keeps very calm. He didn't come to the command of Special Administration covert operations by racing his pulse every time somebody held out a carrot. In fact, the moment people start offering him things he might want, he asks himself who's trying to scag him and why? The problem, in this case, is that the Fuchi grid was actually penetrated and no one is supposed to know about it, no one but the people he knows he can control. "Who's got this tech?"

"We do."

"And who would you be?"

Machiko-*san's* image briefly re-animates, saying, "Where do persons such as yourselves, computer specialists, confined for many months in isolation, acquire the resources to purchase a corporation's entire debt?"

That adds more or less mass to Gordon's suspicions. "So you're on Neurocomp's special project."

"We *are* the project," Janus-face replies.

And that adds more or less mass to another of Gordon's suspicions. "And you're willing to give away this hot new tech."

"We keep Neurocomp. We'll give you the project data and the rest of Nagato's outstanding debt."

"You'll give me Nagato debt. You hijacked Nagato debt." Using funds hijacked from Fuchi. Transactions like that would stand up for about ten minutes in a session of the Corporate Court. Stolen funds buy nada. The court would issue a mandate authorizing Fuchi to take any necessary steps to recoup its losses. Nagato debt would revert to its previous owners.

"Are you planning to sue, Mr. Ito?"

Gordon says nothing. He is mildly reassured, though, to learn that Janus-face actually knows his name. It's some slight evidence that his desktop wasn't picked completely at random from the Fuchi grid. Another indication he isn't dealing with gutterpunks.

"Remember, you're vulnerable, too."

"Tai No Sen."

"Wiz. What's it mean?"

"Literally, to wait for the initiative. One of Miyamoto

Musashi's three methods of forestalling an enemy attack. Feign weakness." Gordon takes a drag of his cigarette, and adds, "Ask Machiko-*sun* about it. She'll explain."

Janus-face says, "We are much more interested in what you have to say about our proposal."

Naturally.

Obviously, what they want is for Fuchi to validate their hijacking of Fuchi funds. If Fuchi says no theft occurred, then the decker's transactions acquiring Nagato debt are valid to the nth degree. When the dust finally clears, they come out owning Neurocomp legally. The real question is *why do they want Neurocomp*? What is Neurocomp worth if they give up the data on the special project? Neurocomp's collected a lot of first-rate people over the last few years. What else have they got going on?

"Let's see if I understand this. I give you license to take Neurocomp and whatever the corp's got going, and I get the debt on a corporate infrastructure that's equivalent in Fuchi terms to small change."

"You also get the tech that busted the Fuchi grid."

The point is like a match applied to the nape of Gordon's neck. It pains and there's no minimizing the pain. The Neurocomp special project has apparently developed a technology sufficiently advanced to allow a cadre of deckers to challenge the best on the Fuchi private grid. A tech that's just possibly an order of magnitude beyond anything else on the planet. With tech like that, Fuchi could go anywhere. The Special Administration could conceivably invade any host and carry off the secrets of any corp. It is without a doubt a dream come true. And there is just one problem with it. The fatal flaw.

The truth might come out. Gordon's own manipulations of Fuchi funds might be discovered if anything about these deckers' so-called "demonstration" is made known to anyone. Fuchi Internal Security would certainly launch an investigation given only half an excuse. They would inevitably uncover enough to bury Gordon, if not also the entire Special Administration, as it presently exists, because that is how the Sixth World works. Once one thread is discovered, the entire cord unravels, and Gordon is unwilling to give up that single thread.

The people on top would gladly accept any deal to get this

new tech. If certain revelations forced them to dispense with Gordon it would be viewed as a necessary expense.

What should he do? How does he answer the deckers' proposal? Say yes? Then everything goes to shit. Say no? If he turns the deckers away, if they know how vulnerable he really is, they go to somebody else, someone without Gordon's reservations, and they'll make a deal in about two minutes. They'll provide detailed data on their runs against Fuchi mainframes to prove their worth. And then nothing on the Fuchi grid or in the Special Administration datastores will ever be secure again.

He has to decide what the *fuck* is really going on here, and how to salvage this situation and come out of it alive and intact. Think, dammit. Think.

One point comes to mind.

"Why are you talking to a Serpent?" Gordon asks.

The image of Machiko-*san* re-animates. She says, "I am here to expedite the re-acquisition of Nagato Corp debt."

"Is that supposed to mean something?"

"We are conducting an auction," Janus-face says. "Between you and Nagato Corp. Whoever bids first wins."

That doesn't sound right.

Senior GSG do covert action for Chairman Honjowara, Gordon knows that very well, but not a job like this. Not for stakes like this. Machiko-*san* was raised a warrior. If Honjowara knew the stakes, if there really was an auction going on, Honjowara would be there himself, or be represented by one of his senior advisors, probably a committee of senior advisors.

And that means the deckers are lying. There's no auction. Gordon looks to the screen, the image of the Serpent, Machiko. She is the key. The warrior. The selfless defender of Chairman Honjowara and Nagato Combine. She's talking to the deckers, probably inside the Neurocomp facility, but why? Has she followed the clues Gordon offered her to their final destination? Has she deduced the identity of the parties behind the buy-out of Nagato debt? Could she be even now confronting the deckers? accusing them of corporate treason? preparing to, what? cut them off from the Matrix?

What in Christ is she thinking? What will she do when faced with the imminent destruction of the very foundation of her whole world?

It means taking a gamble.

Gambling that the deckers will play Machiko-*san* the same way they're playing him. "I need authorization from my director," Gordon says. "Two minutes."

"Two minutes may be too long," Janus-face says.

Gordon rises and walks through the door to his outer office. His entire exec protect detail is waiting on the far side of the doorway. His deputy and his deputy's deputy and the chief of his special operations staff and the rest of his senior staff are all standing there, obviously tense and alert, and they all seem about to start talking at once except Gordon immediately slashes a hand across the front of his throat.

No one says a word.

Gordon looks to his watch. He waits for one minute and fifteen seconds to tick past, then returns to his private office and sits at his desk. Janus-face is still on-screen.

"You've got a deal," Gordon says. "I'm authorized by the chief of Fuchi America to negotiate an immediate transfer of every property involved. Money's no object."

"You're got a quick mind, *omae*."

"I know a sweet deal when I see it."

40

"I don't think so," says SmoKe.

Machiko looks back to the wall-sized display screen. "What you think is of no significance. You will be detained. Your access to the Matrix will be eliminated. In due course, you will be questioned by the Security Service. You would be wise to consider the likelihood that ultimately your fate will be determined by Chairman Honjowara."

The decker's neochromatic icons on the display darken and fade into blackness. They give no reply. Machiko puzzles over this, but then the deputy VP turns to the GCP project director, saying, "See that Machiko-*san's* instructions are carried out at once."

The project director bows, looking pale, and turns to the door. Only the door does not open. The man, hastening to exit the room, impacts the door with surprising force and staggers back, wobbling. Machiko takes three steps and catches his arm. The others, the deputy VP, the two Security Service guards, help to maneuver the man into a nearby chair. He is bruised and unsettled, but not seriously hurt. In another few moments he and the others are all wondering about the door.

The guards make a cursory inspection. A small red bulb beside the door indicates that it is locked. The deputy VP himself works the lock's keypad, but the door remains locked. One of the guards keys a telecom, but that is not working either. Machiko opens the commlink on her left vambrace, keys the code for Nagato Corp operations center, but is answered only by static.

The deputy VP checks several of the consoles lining the room. His expression rises from puzzlement to disbelief to apparent amazement. "It would appear that nothing in this room is working."

"How is that possible?" Machiko asks.

The project director, frowning intently, looks from the consoles to Machiko, then to the wall-sized display screen at the head of the room. "The entire facility is computer-controlled."

"Are you saying that the GCP deckers—"

"Good guess, *omae*."

Machiko looks to the display at the head of the room. The deckers' neochromatic icons are back. "You will surrender control of this facility's systems at once."

"I don't think so," says SmoKe.

"Do not compel me to take extreme measures."

"You don't want to do that," says NodeBoy. "You wouldn't like the results. We've got all the hole cards. We own the game. Here, check it out."

A secondary window opens on the display screen, presenting an image of Gordon Ito. He sits in a tall-backed chair, a wall of windows behind him, the lights of Manhattan and the Jersey shore clearly visible. "I'm authorized by the chief of Fuchi America to negotiate an immediate transfer of Neurocomp," Ito-*san* says. "Money's no object."

The image freezes. Machiko holds herself motionless. Why do the deckers show this sequence involving Gordon Ito? Does it mean that Ito-*san* has been manipulating events, the true force behind the deckers' revolt, since the beginning? "Please explain yourselves at once," Machiko says lowly.

"Null sheen," says SmoKe.

"We're negotiating a change in ownership," says Node-Boy. "If you try to interfere, we'll throw the whole load of Nagato debt into the deal. And you can flush your precious Nagato Combine down the nearest squathole."

Machiko stands immobile, feeling as if rooted to the floor. She finds NodeBoy's explanation difficult to understand and all but impossible to accept. Only a few minutes ago the GCP deckers were claiming to be engaged in a bloody revolution to escape corporate control. Now they are negotiating the transfer of Neurocomp to Fuchi ownership? To *Fuchi Industrial Electronics*? She cannot believe that, cannot believe they would even suggest it, for it makes no sense. The only way that it would make any sense at all is if they are using the device of a traitor or enemy, a tactic of delay, a maneuver intended to deceive, a lie designed to forestall any action that might unhinge the deckers' plan.

Why use such a tactic? Because they need time. There is timing in everything. The timing here is especially crucial. How much time do they need? Minutes? Perhaps only seconds?

What is their true plan? What could they be doing to accomplish their stated objective of "taking control"? Could they be negotiating with Gordon Ito, with Fuchi, not for ownership of Neurocomp but for the entire body of Nagato Corporation?

Could it be anything but that, given their depraved disregard for the many lives they have spent, the blood shed, and the malice they bear Nagato Combine?

"You would destroy Nagato Combine?" Machiko asks.

"In a nanoflash," SmoKe replies.

The path then is clear. The deckers have the power and the motivation to destroy, and the blood they have shed more than proves their willingness to commit any crime, any treason, any evil, no matter how diabolic. What they are actually doing is no longer of any importance. Machiko must act. She must do as she has been trained to do. She must remember the Way, and the Way is death. Inexorable death. Stamp both feet to the earth and pass through a wall of iron. Do not consider victory or defeat. Consider only that the enemy must be destroyed.

"I will give you one chance to surrender."

SmoKe begins howling with laughter.

Machiko turns to the broad wall of windows overlooking the floor of the GCP lab. She lifts her SCK M-100 SMG from her side, tabs the safety, and squeezes the trigger.

The savage clattering of the weapon gives rise to a deafening tumult: the crashing of shattered transparex panes, shouts and screams, the sudden blaring of alarms. Machiko does not pause to look back, for she knows what she will see, knows it intuitively. She will see the two executives looking at her in astonishment. She will see the two Security Service guards watching in alarm, perhaps seizing the grips of their sidearms, but hesitating to draw, unsure of what to do. She did not take the time to explain her intentions, could not reveal her intent to the enemy, and now she must live with that and the likely consequences.

"*COVER!*" she shouts.

As she thrusts herself at the shattered pane before her, she hears the rapid stammering of an autofire weapon, the ruthless noise of an Ares single-barrel machine gun. She does not have to look. The sound comes from directly behind her. The door to the room has opened and the weapon pod mounted in the ceiling of the corridor outside has unlimbered and opened fire.

As she dives through the shattered pane, toward the floor of the lab, bullets pound at the armored fabric of her overvest. An electrostatic screen that a moment ago did not exist snaps on, clawing past her waist and hips. The bullets batter her flesh even as electrostatic energy stabs through her nerves like ten thousand electrified razors.

The pain can be muted, injuries suppressed, yet the screams rising from the room at her back close around her heart like a savage crushing fist.

Forgive me . . .

She cannot let herself hear it.

The floor of the GCP lab is now two, three meters beneath her, coming up fast. She has only instants. She holds the SCK out before her, gripped in both hands. She points the weapon at the center of the three tanks filled with their murky blue fluids and dark humanoid shapes. She sees the figures in white coats scattered about the floor of the lab, some turning, looking toward her, looking terrified or filled with horror or paralyzed by shock and astonishment. The first one is just opening her mouth to shriek or shout as Machiko again squeezes the trigger.

The bullets smash at the center tank. The walls of the tank seem almost to bulge outward, before exploding.

"Nnnnnnnooooooohhhhhh!" rises one voice.

Machiko sees the humanoid shape still hanging suspended in the ruptured tank—amid arrays of tubes and wires— twitching and shaking under the assault from her SCK.

She has just enough time to see the murky fluids that gush from the sides of the ruptured tank flickering with spectral blue flames.

Then, she lands.

She lands badly, amid crashing console screens and cables that fill the air around her with blazing showers of sparks. She tumbles to the floor and seeks shelter beneath the front ledge of a console. The facility's computer-automated weapons systems pursue her even here, to the white-tiled floor of the lab.

Off to her far right another door stands open and another

ceiling-mounted weapon tracks her, and now she feels the pounding against her feet, her legs, her hips. She rolls backwards onto her feet and flips herself bodily over a console that appears lined with nothing but row after row of touch-sensitive keys. Shards of metal and shattered plastic shower the top of her head as she lands on toes and fingertips behind the console.

Two meters to her rear a man in a white coat slowly spins and spins, wounds erupting like red puckered sores in a line from his right shoulder down to his groin.

Machiko rams a fresh clip into the SCK. The pain is getting more insistent. She is aware of at least half a dozen minor wounds that will eventually require medical attention. The impact of her fall, the electrostatic barrier, the bullets—it is all adding up. How much more she can take is not a calculation that matters. She will go on till either the enemy is crushes or she is dead.

Without warning, a new enemy attacks. Machiko feels their paranatural power filling her belly with the frigid chill of fear even as their sudden, shocking howls seize at her limbs and body, trying to slow her down.

Then the hounds are upon her. Barghests. Like Neapolitan mastiffs, but larger, heavier. Barghests are used by the Security Service in many Nagato facilities. Why they come into this lab and attack her, Machiko does not even attempt to guess.

The beasts impact her side. Mass and momentum combine to drive her sideways against a console burning with graphic displays. Machiko's katana sword flashes downward, cleaving the neck of the beast that rips at her right thigh. She twists and heaves and flips the beast gnawing at her left arm over the ridge at the rear of a console, snapping its spine.

Blood streams from her wounds like veins of death.

She breathes deeply, harshly.

Spirit settled, she skirts a line of consoles and drops to a crouch at one corner of a large boxy unit disgorging thick white smoke. She unleashes another clattering barrage of autofire. The second tank ruptures. The norm male within bucks and jerks beneath her barrage. The murky fluids that shower the floor and surrounding consoles rage with bluish fire. Wherever the fluids fall, plastic evaporates like steam and metal runs like water. Floor tiles bubble and sag.

The entire installation supporting the first ruptured tank

abruptly crashes, dropping a meter beneath the level of the lab floor.

As Machiko moves to the third and final tank, she becomes aware of the console displays flashing around her. "Stop shooting," the display reads. "I don't want to fight any more."

Machiko understands. Tai No Sen, it is called. A tactic of the ancient masters. Feign weakness, then attack.

She rises fully to her feet, discarding the empty SCK and extending the Beretta 200ST out before her. She pulls the trigger rapid-fire, unleashing three-round bursts till all twenty-six rounds have shattered the panes of the tank and pummeled the norm female twitching within.

And now a whirlwind arises, a glimmer in the air that evolves into a mass of churning black and affects the lab like a cyclone. A handcomp is snatched from the floor and driven into the metal wall of the lab like a nail into wood. A woman is hurled five or six meters through the air. Machiko risks a glance into the astral and sees a firestorm of raging mana, some elemental force, some creature of the arcane, swelling to fill the space around her as if to overwhelm her.

She lets the Beretta fall. Guns are useless against astral beings. She takes two swords in hand, sword and companion sword, katana and wakizashi. With these two extensions of her force of will, her settled spirit, she will defeat even this creation of the astral. She does not know how this creation came to be, but she assumes it is a product of the arcane blend of magic and science used on the GCP project.

The whirlwind grows stronger. The mass of churning black draws near, then fades. It vanishes from sight. The whirlwind dies away.

On the astral, nothing remains.

The installation supporting the third ruptured tank crashes beneath floor level. Machiko watches the body inside it wither, shrinking into a blackened lump not even vaguely resembling a human or metahuman. The other two are the same. They are dead. Her enemy is defeated. Nagato Combine may yet be crushed or divided, but she has done all that a warrior may ever do.

She finds a chair beside a dead man, a dead man in a white coat, and sits, and breathes. Her commlink works now. Works perfectly. She puts through a priority call to Honjowara-*sama* and explains all that she knows briefly and succinctly, and concludes, "The GCP project has been terminated. The traitors are dead."

Honjowara-*sama* says he understands.

Machiko doubts this is possible, but breaks the link and closes her eyes, wanting only rest.

Epilogue

The sound brushes her ears like the soft rustle of leaves on a cool night in the spring: the flutter of silk, the whisper of a footstep against varnished wood flooring.

Machiko wakes, but does not open her eyes. She listens to the night, the quiet. Soon, the sliding wood door at the rear of the house softly grumbles, slipping open, and the subtle footsteps go on, moving to the back porch, then finally into the garden at the rear of the house.

Machiko waits a little while, then rises, draws on a short jade green robe, and ties the belt tight. She dismisses the twinges and aches of injuries still healing. She reaches for her katana, not because she may need it, but because it is as much a part of her as the green serpent tattoos twining around her body.

She finds the night outside pleasantly cool and still. She finds her mother at the rear of the garden, as expected. Mother sits on a small stone bench beside a small artificial pond, ringed by fragrant flowers and flowering forsythia. Her long robe is so pale a pastel pink it seems white, a luminous white, lit by the crescent moon just visible through the trees at the rear of the property. That same light makes mother's jet black hair seem lush and glossy. She once had hair as long as Machiko's own. Now she wears it close by the shoulders, softly styled.

As Machiko sits beside her, she stiffens and catches her breath. "Oh!" she gasps. "Machiko . . ."

A response so familiar it is poignant. The pained smile that curves Mother's lips speaks the words Machiko has heard a thousand times before. *Daughter, you move too quietly. Like a ghost. I did not hear you approaching.*

"Please excuse me," Machiko murmurs.

But there is no need for apologies. Mother shifts near and

embraces her about the shoulders, then joins their hands. "Couldn't you sleep?" Mother asks.

"I heard you pass by."

Mother's smile turns warm. "I'm sorry. You must be used to it by now. I could never walk quietly enough, even when you were a child. You always woke up."

Machiko nods, and says, "Why aren't you sleeping?"

"I don't know. I'm so tired. Tired but yet awake. Your father is so upset with all this business, all that's happened."

"You should take a sedative."

"I take so many pills already."

For allergies, primarily. "Mother, the Security Service investigation will go on for days, perhaps weeks. You must rest. You and father must both be rested or you will not be able to think clearly."

"I wish I could stop thinking long enough to sleep."

"You must try."

"I try every night."

But it is very difficult. Machiko knows this too well. In the weeks since the carnage at Neurocomp, Father has had two episodes of angina, brief episodes, but of concern because they came so close together. His doctors have ordered him to take a long weekend, to rest, and have pre-scribed tranquilizers and sleeping pills.

Nagato Corp debt still lies in the hands of Zurich bankers. For several days, Nagato Corporation has seemed to teeter on the brink of the abyss. However, Honjowara-*sama* has lodged an appeal with the Corporate Court, claiming the debt was procured illegally, and, curiously, a number of corps have come forward with evidence that their financial accounts have been penetrated, funds stolen.

Of course, none of these corps has any connection with Nagato Combine or with Fuchi. The traitors were careful to be very discreet.

Mother, as Neurocomp's VP for Research, has had to face the brunt of the Security Service investigation regarding the GCP project. Like father, she feels personally responsible for all that has happened. She feels that tighter controls should have been placed on the GCP deckers. How much worse she would feel if she knew the whole story, the truth of Gamma's origin, but this she will never know. The story will never be told.

"If my own daughter had not revealed the traitors," Mother says, softly, "I could not bear to go on living."

The words move Machiko deeply. She knows the depths of her mother's pain, the shame she feels. Machiko can only answer, "If not for my mother's many lessons, I would not have succeeded in revealing anything."

Her mother's eyes meet hers. The moment grows intensely personal. Everything they have ever meant to each other is right there between them. Neither has any doubt as to the reality of their relationship, a bond never to be broken. Again, they embrace. Mother whispers, "I go to meet Sashi-*san* tomorrow morning. You still have not said whether you will join me."

"I have not yet decided."

"A child should honor her genetic mother."

"I do not know if this is possible."

"I do." Mother touches Machiko's cheek, says simply, "There is nothing you could not do, if you wish to do it."

"If you want me to go with you, I will go."

Mother joins their hands again. She spends a time gazing toward the pond. She speaks in an earnest tone, saying, "Machiko, I believe that this lady cares about you very deeply. I feel it would be wrong to hold the past against her. We must at least give her the chance to show us her true feelings."

"If that is your feeling, I will go with you."

"Do you not agree?"

"I do not trust myself to agree or disagree. I know what duty demands of me. It is my heart that feels betrayed."

Mother seems dismayed, even anguished. Expressively, she says, "Daughter, the heart is easily betrayed. It comprehends only the now. It does not easily make allowances. Understanding comes only with time. Acceptance comes only with time."

"There has been little time."

"When you first began at the academy, you recited a certain aphorism over and over. Something you heard from your *sensei*. I have never forgotten. It was your answer for everything. Do you remember? Who is the greater servant? you would ask. She who is talented and wise and indulges in selfish thinking? Or she who is stupid and dull, but thinks only of her lord?"

Tears as hard as steel rain rise into Machiko's eyes. She

brushes the tears away, but more follow. Yes, she remembers. She could not possibly forget.

How loudly that lesson of the ancients resounds now. Selfish thinking—is that not the key to everything? It led the GCP deckers to murder and treason. It gave racism the power to scar Gamma for life. And now it brings Machiko to take umbrage with Sashi-*san,* and with the man said to be her genetic father, the man who has made possible everything she values: Nagato Combine, the Guard, the entire course of her life.

She should look at all she has been given. Consider the parents who raised her. Could any life have been more fortunate? more auspicious? She has been deprived of nothing. Nothing but a few scraps of truth that now seem like mere illusions.

"You are very wise," she murmurs. "You know me so well."

"I know your heart," mother says with a small smile. "The rest is sometimes very puzzling."

"My heart knows only love for you."

"And mine for you."

Again, they embrace; then, Mother rises, saying she will try once more to sleep.

With only her ears, Machiko follows her mother's steps back through the garden to the porch, then through the door and into the house. Quiet descends. She closes her eyes and draws her legs up to sit lotus-style and consider, contemplate. It is a while before she becomes aware of another presence, a new presence. She does not have to open her eyes to confirm who is there. She feels it in his presence, the sense that, once he is settled, kneeling, facing her from across the pond, he is as stable as the earth, rooted in the ground.

"You said nothing of the Tir," Kuroda-*sensei* quietly intones.

Faintly, Machiko shakes her head. She has said nothing to either her mother or father about alliances with Tir Tairngire, of programs of exchange, or of the man said to be her genetic father. For the sake of Nagato Combine, its Chairman, his New Way, and all hope for the future, such things must never be told. Sashi-*san* has already made this very clear.

"You have questions. Doubts."

Machiko considers, and says, "I have parents who love me. For this, I am very grateful."

"And what of Okido-*san*?"

"The Chairman?" Machiko is unsure what to say. "Once, I believed that I understood him. Now I wonder if I know anything of him but the face he chooses to show."

Kuroda-*sensei* says, "If you know the Way broadly, you will see it in all things. You will understand the duty of a man bearing a mountain of obligation. You will perceive the sacrifices that have been made. You will discover a devotion even greater than your own. Beyond even the fanaticism of a warrior."

Perhaps this is so. If Honjowara-*sama* is indeed the man she has always believed him to be, it must be so. "Would not such a man desire to honor his every obligation, regardless of how large or small?"

Slightly, Kuroda-*sensei* bows. "It is so."

Machiko breathes deeply, and says, "Such a man should fulfill his obligation to his genetic daughter. He should face her and tell her of the past, of the many things a daughter has the right to know and understand."

Again, Kuroda-*sensei* bows. "And now a man awaits only your request or summons, humbly, with regret for what has happened, and hope for what may be. He desires to speak of all these things."

"He asked you here to say this?"

"He did indeed."

Machiko, then, can only bow and say, "Then I will go and meet with him. And I will listen to all he has to say."

A generic daughter's obligation.

One she will honor most willingly.

ABOUT THE AUTHOR

Nathan Yale Xavier ("Nyx") Smith began his writing career by revising the Twenty-third Psalm to excoriate Richard Nixon about Watergate, only to be called down to the principal's office, and has been getting into trouble ever since. His early experiences as an altar boy (passing out from the summer heat) perhaps inspired his late-adolescent abhorrence of anything resembling a suit and tie, as well as a lingering aversion to ever becoming a "suit" himself. He has not seen a barber (or other tonsorial artist) in ten years. He has worked as a dishwasher, custodian, landscaper, shipping manager, bookkeeper, and computer operator while making no money for lots of writing. He drives an old car that's very nondescript. He originally thought a cyber-esque world with magic and elves a pretty strange idea, but then Striper came along and asserted that it all makes perfect sense.

The author strives always to avoid arguing with characters of as menacing a stripe as Striper, and recommends this practice to all those with a hankering toward longevity.

Nyx Smith continues to live in a basement on Long Island (New York's most notable sandbar) along with a salmagundi of doloris nocturnum, but has traded his Selectrics for a 486/33 that occasionally shows signs of paranatural infestation. He invites readers of his Shadowrun® novels *Striper Assassin, Fade To Black, Who Hunts The Hunter,* and this book, *Steel Rain,* to send him comments, critiques, or complaints about his writing, characters, plots, and so on, in care of FASA Corporation, 1100 W. Cermack, B305, Chicago, IL, 60608.

**2058, 0250 EST, Miami, Florida, Caribbean
League, near the FEZ.**

A trembling hand broke through the full moon, sending
ripples of dancing silver across the water's oily surface.
Steadily, the human hand rose from the polluted Biscayne
Bay to grasp hold of a rusty iron cleat attached to the old
weathered wood of the oceanside dock.

Painfully levering himself onto the splintery planks, Alan
Terhune barely managed to roll over away from the ragged
oak edge. Hands red from the toxic chemicals in the sea, he
peeled the scuba mask off his sweating face, the muscles in
his jaw rigid to stop a groan from escaping. Alive. He was
still alive!

Unlike everybody else on the hellish run. Fragging drek, it
had been like walking naked into a meat grinder. Worse. If
reduced to sausage, at least there would be the satisfaction
that some hungry chummer in the sprawl might eat his flesh
and live for another miserable day. But this . . . this was
pointless! Useless!

Casting the mask aside, Terhune faintly heard it splash
back into the stinking brine as his fingers performed a
combat ritual over his combatsuit. Boot knife gone, Belgium
9 Derringer gone, Ares Predator gone—when had THAT
happened?—ammo clips long emptied, night goggles burned

out by that fragging hermetic mage, and the narcoject pistol
had been used to jimmy open an elevator shaft door.

There was nothing remaining of all the equipment so carefully gathered over his years on the streets. Even Laura Red-
Feather's Fuchi desk had been sacrificed into a simple
bludgeon over that troll guard's head. The poor fragger had
probably never expected that desperate a ploy from any
decker. Who would? Even Laura had seemed surprised when
she did the deed. Wham! Chips and blood went everywhere,
the merc went down for the count, and thus Terhune and the
deckless decker made it alive out of the hellhole and safely
into the sea.

Safely? Choking on a bitter laugh, Terhune lay prone on
the ancient wood, drinking in lungfuls of night air, the cold
water pooling about him, running rivulets off his bodysuit,
his muscular form appearing inhuman from the badly dented
armor plating covering his vital kill zones.

Safe. Ha. They'd been anything but freaking safe. Pure
pluperfect hell—who knew the corp had packs of chipped
sharks running as guard dogs in the water? Terhune hadn't
even known a fish/microchip interface was possible! Laura
had gone under with a blood-curling scream.

Chipped sharks. One of the many things wrong with this
run. One of the thousands. The glint of the searchlights off
the chromed jack in her temple was the last he saw of her.
Blind rage had almost made him strike back at the sharks,
but with only bare hands remaining, and troll and human
guards on the way in paramilitary hovercraft covered with
automatic weapons, Terhune knew he had to use her flesh to
buy him time to escape with the tide.

Used the flesh of a lover one last time. He felt filthy inside
as if he'd been drinking chem slime in the sea. What he
wouldn't give for a DocWagon team to come and fly him
away to a warm clean hospital full of people struggling to
make him stop hurting. Yeah, and if wishes were drek the
sewers would be heaven.

Stop ya whining, chummer. Still work to do. This run
wasn't over yet. No, not quite yet. One more thing to do.

When some of his strength returned, Alan forced open the
velcro of the swimsuit and peeled it off. The ballistic material stuck to him in several places and had to be painfully
pulled free. His body was a mass of bruises, and bleeding
cuts were already starting to swell in spots. No chance of

infection after the sea water got in, but poisoning was a fair bet. The throbbing bullet hole in his shoulder already had a slap patch on it, but the polluted Atlantic had weakened the adhesive and it was starting to come away. Diluted, the metaphanimes were wearing off fast.

Only pure raw adrenaline was keeping him awake. "And hate, let's not forget hate," he told himself bitterly.

Wearing only briefs, Terhune struggled to his sore feet and staggered toward the small blue light that had been his goal for the past four hours. Faintly illuminated by the tiny indigo bulb set in the wall above it, the riveted steel door to the warehouse was stained and marred from the constant acid rains this year. But the maglock responded to his palm on the plate, and the massive portal swung open silently. Incredible. Maybe the sewers were heaven after all.

Stumbling more and stepping into the darkness, he pushed the huge door shut behind him, and the internal lights came on automatically with blinding force. Momentarily stunned, he stood there blinking against the harsh intrusion. If there was going to be a double-cross, this was the perfect spot. A pimple-faced ganger with a two-nuyen zip gun could take him now. Not that there'd be much they could do with him. Even the organleggers wouldn't want him as a decoy in some bait-and-switch scam. Tense ticks passed in dripping silence. As his vision slowly returned, Terhune saw that the shoreline warehouse was stuffed to the ceiling with marine equipment; bales of nets, bundles of oars, canvas net, sleeved props and similar equipment. Tools designed a thousand years ago, but still as viable today as ever. Equipment so basic that it could not be improved. No matter what the techies said, ya can't improve a nail with a microchip. End of discussion.

A slim path wound through the towering jumbles of oceanic equipment, and the exhausted man lurched from crate to crate, keeping a hand on the dank plastic boxes for support. There was an open area in the center of the warehouse with a huge pile of synthleather bags pooled in the harsh light of a slightly dim EverBright. Proof that even the independent powerpacks of those supposedly eternal light bulbs would weaken with age.

Clumsily, Terhune dug into the packs, tossing aside unneeded civilian clothes for dead friends until he found the medical supplies. Awkwardly using his left hand to rig a sling for the right, he then bit off strips of adhesive to tape his busted ribs. Try as they might, those hellhounds inside the building couldn't use their flame breath to hurt his team through the protection song of their shaman, Iron Jimmy. And as the metabeasts charged closer, his own red-hot Ares Predator had made short work of them. But each dead animal had continued on through sheer inertia and slammed into him and his team like sledgehammers. Terhune had heard Jimmy's neck snap before he went down under the onslaught of the hound corpses.

Now with his chest bound tight, the agony of breathing lessened to mere discomfort, and he began to paw through a pile of plastic envelopes and forbidden aerosol cans, looking for more bandaging. Finding a fresh trauma patch, he slapped it over the bullet hold in his shoulder, and added a few stim patches to undamaged areas on his arms.

Terhune inhaled sharply as the organic plastic sterilized and sealed the 5.57mm hole, the taste of olives filling his mouth as the DMSO rushed healants through his body. Looking around, he found what he was looking for—a small black box prominently marked with a red cross. Clumsily he activated the pocket-doc and held it to his side. The robotic device hummed in consultation as it ascertained his condition and then began a long series of hisses, pumping god-knows-what into his system. Finally, the doc went quiet and Terhune tossed the precious machine away, too tired to care. It crashed in the shadows, breaking apart and spilling out its electronic guts.

Soon, a tingling wave of relief washed over him and he felt his head miraculously clear. Back on line. Looking for a spare gun in the equipment bags, Terhune was surprised to find a couple of amber bottles. But then, Big George had loved his booze. No drugs or chips for that elf. Here's to you, George!

Pulling one of the bottles into view, Terhune was startled to find that it wasn't cheap synathol, but honesttofrag scotch. Something called Irish Mist, with a dated label, import seal, and everything! He worked off the twist cap with his teeth, and poured the single malt generously down his throat.

The chill left his stomach, and he was just beginning to feel almost human once more when a dark figure stepped from the shadows and partially into the circle of light. Only small shoes and a hand-held case of some sort were visible.

"*Konnichiwa*, Terhune," said the newcomer, bowing slightly from the waist as she set down the expensive leather briefcase. "I have the rest of your payment here, as requested." There was a brief flash of white teeth edged with crimson lipstick in the dimness beyond. A bit old fashioned, but everyone on the street had their quirks. "Where is my merchandise, please?"

"F-frag you, Mr. Johnson," coughed Terhune. He took another swig off the bottle and slumped onto a barrel of engine lubricant. He'd been feeling better only minutes before. Why was he so tired all of a sudden?

The Mr. Johnson stepped closer, her body in the light, but not her face. "What do you mean? Didn't you get the prototype?"

"Drek no."

An icy pause. "And why not?" she demanded.

"Because your fragging nerve gas didn't kill the guards! That's why!"

"And?" asked the woman calmly.

"And?" Terhune roared, casting the bottle of whiskey aside. He was having trouble marshaling his thoughts for some reason, and there was a new strange taste on his lips. "And? Ya muck-sucking null. And they had more mercs than we were informed! They had different weapons, too, and fragging hellhounds—not just dogs. There was even UCAS military support, for drek's sake! Plus, some unkillable troll goomba with a mustache showed from nowhere and shot the living bloody drek out of my whole fragging team!"

"Most unfortunate," acknowledged Mr. Johnson solemnly.

"Unfortunate, yeah," growled Terhune, cradling his aching ribcage. "I lost my best decker to the sharks, and if the damn tide hadn't been coming in, I wouldn't be here either."

The woman rested one foot on a small crate of engine parts. Her skirt parted as she did, exposing a lot of well-tanned, smooth thigh and more. "Yes, I had counted on the evening tide. But only in an emergency. I gather this was."

His mind fogging, Terhune tore his sight away from her. Hawking to clear his throat, he spit whiskey-flavored blood on the floor. "Damn straight it was! I lost all three of my partners before we reached the main building, and the goddamn helo was blown out from under me by a missile! I barely jumped in time."

A manicured hand barely managed to cover a yawn. "Indeed. Sounds like the Gunderson corp security did a most thorough job."

Sky blue eyes meet those of space-black. "A thorough job?" snarled Terhune, feeling the blood throb in his neck. "Listen, Johnson, those mercs did us up a royal treat!"

"Yes," she demurred softly. "Dunkelzahn must have trained them well."

Alan Terhune felt his heart stop. "The dragon? We went up against dragon-trained guards?" Before the Johnson could answer, the awful truth hit him like a wild punch. "Holy drek, this was one of his companies, then? Motherfragger!"

"Such language. Now, really, Terhune . . ."

Furious, he grabbed at a boarding pike lying against a nearby plastic crate and pulled himself erect. His limbs felt like they had lead weights attached. Why was he so sleepy? Mounting anger alone gave him the strength to speak. "This assignment was a dry hump from the word go! We sure as drek didn't have proper intelligence! In fact, almost everything you told us was just wrong enough that once we got started, there was nowhere to go but forward, and that direction got us promptly blown to hell! It was almost as if we weren't supposed to make it!"

Terhune bent over double with a coughing spell, not seeing the woman known as Mr. Johnson when she smiled for the first time, her white teeth feral in the darkness.

"No, you most definitely were not supposed to succeed," she said softly. "Nor were you supposed to return, moron."

As comprehension dawned, Terhune balled a fist, and razor-sharp titanium blades slid from his forearm to gleam like new sin as he lunged for her. But a series of soft chugs stopped him, the pencil-thin flames from the silenced H&K automatic tracking his riddled body to the floor.

"And my name actually is Johnson," stated Erika Johnson as she continued to empty all eighteen of the pistol's caseless rounds into the still form. "Isn't that amusing? *Hai?*"

There was no reply, but a low, moist gargling noise almost too soft to hear. Holstering her weapon, she went calmly to the dock outside and found the remains of the wet suit. The mask was nowhere to be found. An inconvenience at most.

She folded the suit neatly into a square and put it in her empty attaché case. Returning inside, she stripped the wet shorts off the corpse and dressed the bloody body in a grease-stained worksuit taken from a wall locker. The pockets already contained a wallet and a deluxe, three-ring, executive credstick with over 10,000 nuyen registered.

She smiled at that. Her expense account for this test of the Gunderson Corporation's Miami security had been carte blanche, as befitting an executive of her rank. Only Rashamor Hotosama himself and the *gaijin* Brian Varley were above her in the corp hierarchy. And soon, that would change also. Oh yes, very soon.

Erika Johnson whistled a tune while donning a pair of medical gloves from her belt pouch, then skillfully used a surgical probe to remove all of the bullets from the dead man, depositing the bloody lumps of metal into a small plastic container, which she sealed and placed inside her coat. Next, she opened another container and re-inserted a different spent round into the still warm wound. There, one left for Lone Star to find. If the incompetent fools could, that is.

She dragged the corpse over to the small machine shop in the corner of the warehouse and carefully positioned it under a shelf deliberately overloaded with tools. A gentle tap from a broom handle made the previously weakened support collapse, and with a mighty crash the heavy shelf smashed the once handsome features into an unrecognizable mess. Perfect. Erika stayed for a moment to look at the disfigured corpse, feeling oddly excited, then turned and walked away, dropping the telltale broom alongside the mess.

After checking her own expensive clothes for splatters, she left the warehouse and went into the front office. There, she used a pair of tweezers to remove a business card from a glassine envelope. It bore the name of a rival warehouse firm presently at street war with the owners of this one. As if these small-timers even understood what the word meant. All business was war.

Gingerly she placed the card in the middle of a small puddle of water directly under a leaking water cooler. Judging the drip factor to be adequate, she refrained from enlarging the hole made by the ice pick in her skirt pocket. No sense overdoing it.

Moving swiftly, in the hallway she opened a panel in the wall, and a simple yank tore loose a wire, deactivating the old-style thermal fire alarm. Thank goodness the owners had yet to spend nuyen on updating the system. Chipped sensors were a lot more difficult to beat than this prehistoric piece of street drek.

Striding for the front door, Erika Johnson took a cigar from the pocket of the pale security guard sitting limply in a chair behind an armor-plated desk. A swollen tongue protruded out of the dead woman's mouth, her neck dark purple from where the garrote had bitten deep into the flesh. Her machine pistol was still tucked uselessly in her belt holster.

Puffing the cigar into life, Erika set the smoking leaves halfway into a puddle of paint thinner on the linoleum floor. A trail of the clear liquid reached across the room and under the door of a utility closet jammed full of rusty paint cans and oily rags. All lovingly stacked in a nice pyramid just for tonight.

As the glowing tip inched downward toward the fire trail, Erika patiently reviewed her actions. When satisfied, she departed, locking the front door behind her and sliding the access card back inside through a crack in the plastic window pane.

A nondescript Chrysler/Nissan Caravaner was waiting by the curb. Thumbing the lock, she climbed in. Immediately, the windows mirrored for privacy. Not a standard feature for this make and model, should anybody have been watching from the refuse-filled alleys or windowless buildings in the area. The green paint job was badly scratched, the simwood panels peeling with rust spots showing in the standard pattern of a car near saltwater and not washed regularly. Nobody in their right mind would bother to steal the molding tires off the wretched piece of Detroit drek.

As she disarmed the ICE, the multiple cybersecurity systems went into passive mode. Then Erika touched the ignition, the onboard computer accepting her fingerprint. In a microsecond the CDP ascertained she was alone, with no other being pointing anything metallic at her. With a gentle purr, the oversized 400 hp motor was activated. Soft halogen headlights flared on and the powerful car effortlessly pulled away from the curb and tooled off silently into the darkness. Only its bullet-proof tires sighing on the old macadam street.

Strictly maintaining the speed limit, in spite of the many blast craters and pot holes, Erika drove along the canal toward downtown. A barricade of overturned cars momentarily slowed her, the hungry gang in the darkness awakening to the possibility of fresh meat tonight. Calmly, almost amused, Erika radically shifted gears and wheeled into an unlit alley.

Garbage, both human and food, lined the passageway. A single shot hit the rear of the Caravaner and musically ricocheted off the military armor plating under the artistically bad paint job. No further rounds came her way. The locals accepted merely shouting their displeasure at the unseen driver's rank callousness.

The van now heading west, other vehicles of various descriptions moved along with her; limos, sports coupes, rusted wrecks looking like her own, and lots of cybertrucks, some with, but most without, their lights on.

This was an industrial section of town supposedly, although smuggling was actually the prime activity here, according to her reconnaissance reports. Several go-gangs of humans and trolls roared by on their gleaming bikes, talismans and human scalps flailing in the wind. Street lights lined the road, the twenty-meter posts topped with wire-reinforced quartz lenses offering feeble illumination over the sheer distance so necessary to retard the locals shooting out the lights. The weak glare was tinted gray by the inner city smog and general miasma of the decaying streets. Standing forgotten on debris-piled corners was the occasional Lone Star post with their panic buttons showing only as dangling wires from the call boxes.

Nobody here wanted the law, it only got in the way of making a few creds. And justice, like everything else in the Awakened world these days, was something you made yourself or did without.

ENTER THE SHADOWS SHADOWRUN ®

☐ *WORLDS WITHOUT END* by Caroline Spector. Aina remembers the world of centuries ago, but now she's in the Awakened era of shadowrunners and simulations, magic and metas. And she may have brought an ancient nemesis along with her. . . . (453719—$4.99)

☐ *JUST COMPENSATION* by Robert N. Charette. Andy is happy as a shadowrunner wannabe, but when he accidentally gets involved with real runners, the game of Let's Pretend is over. So is his safe, corporate life. (453727—$4.99)

☐ *BLACK MADONNA* by Carl Sargent and Marc Gascoigne. Michael Sutherland is a hardened decker who's been around. But when a panicked Renraku Corp enlists his services, he quickly realizes this is no ordinary crisis—he's up against an immortal elf, who's engineered the most stylish and sophisticated electronic virus ever to destroy a computer system. (453735—$5.50)

☐ *PREYING FOR KEEPS* by Mel Odom. When ace shadowrunner Jack Skater leads his team of commandos in a raid on an elven ocean freighter, things get a little sticky. Yakuza hit men crash the party, and a Japanese shaman whips up a titanic sea creature just to make sure nobody gets out alive. And as a ghastly virus hits Seattle, unleashing hordes of homicidal cannibals onto the streets, Skater and company have to bring in some artillery just to stay alive. (453753—$5.50)

☐ *DEAD AIR* by Jak Koke. It's fast and furious inside the Combat Biker maze, where armor-plated hogs and juiced-up rice grinders blast, pound, and pummel each other for points. But it's barely up to speed for Jonathon and Tamara, two elven bikers at the head of the Los Angeles Sabers. (453751—$5.50)

☐ *SHADOWRUN® THE LUCIFER DECK* by Lisa Smedman. Life on the streets of 21st-century Seattle can be tough, especially for a young ork like Pita. And it gets a lot tougher when she witnesses a corporate mage murdered by the violent spirit he just conjured from another dimension. (453788—$5.99)

Prices slightly higher in Canada
